Anthony Trollope

The Complete Short Stories

VOLUME III

Tourists and Colonials

Edited, with introduction, by
Betty Jane Slemp Breyer

Texas Christian University Press
Fort Worth, Texas 76129

Published by Texas Christian University Press

Manufactured in the United States of America

LIBRARY OF CONGRESS CATALOG CARD NO.: 80-54162

ISBN 0-912646-62-4

Contents

Introduction

"MAD DOGS AND ENGLISHMEN," so Noel Coward's song tells us, "go out in the midday sun"; and wherever the midday sun shone on Englishmen, there, like as not, would be Anthony Trollope. At the foot of a pyramid, in the midst of a jungle, in Tasmania or the Transvaal, in Ceylon, New Zealand, the West Indies, on a mail packet, a camel, a dog cart, a donkey, there would be Anthony Trollope, England's "tireless traveller."

Trollope was not the first, but the last of his immediate family to travel abroad. His mother, Mrs. Frances Trollope, became the first of the family to be known for her travels. On November 4, 1827, she sailed from England for America with three of her five children and a hopelessly impractical scheme to repair the failing family fortune by establishing an emporium to sell "fancy goods" in Cincinnati. With a curious combination of enthusiasm, stamina, naiveté, and determination and with some incredibly foolish advice from two idealistic friends, Mrs. Trollope and her three children established themselves in Cincinnati. Unfortunately, Mrs. Trollope knew nothing about the business of selling, and Cincinnati knew nothing about "fancy goods." At the end of three years Mrs. Trollope had lost almost everything and had hardly enough to keep her and her children from starving. Mr. Trollope and Tom, the eldest son, came to America in 1830 to bring Mrs. Trollope home. Anthony was left behind in England at Winchester College without friends, without family, and, by his own account, without money while the rest of the family was in America.

Mrs. Trollope may not have known anything about the business of selling, but she was an acute observer of the new world around her, and she had a taste for the ironic tinged with comic malice. After she returned to England in 1831 she published a

book entitled *Domestic Manners of the Americans.* Her observations were written with freshness, flair, and a certain natural bias
calculated to please her readers. She knew very well how to pro-
voke the indignation and arouse the amusement of her countrymen — by exploiting issues about which Englishmen and Americans violently disagreed and about which both knew they were
right:

> The immense superiority of the American to the British
> navy was a constant theme, and to this I always listened, as
> nearly as possible, in silence. I repeatedly heard it stated,
> (so often, indeed, and from such various quarters, that I
> think there must be some truth in it), that the American
> sailors fire with a certainty of slaughter, whereas our shots
> are sent very nearly at random. "This," said a naval officer
> of high reputation, "is the blessed effect of your game laws;
> your sailors never fire at a mark; whilst our free tars, from
> their practice in pursuit of game, can any of them split a
> hair."

The book established Mrs. Trollope as a popular writer and
brought much needed revenues into the family coffer. But the
Trollopes were not a family given to domestic economies; and,
despite Mrs. Trollope's success, by 1834 the bailiffs were literally
at the door. The family fled to Belgium, and Anthony, this time,
went with them. What he thought of his first taste of travel he
does not tell us. He has left only this faint picture in *An Autobiography:* "As well as I can remember I was fairly happy, for there
were pretty girls at Bruges with whom I could fancy that I was in
love . . . ." He was then what he describes as "that most hopeless
of human beings, a hobbledehoy of nineteen."

Indeed, he tells us very little about his early trips to the con-
tinent. But by 1857 the miseries of childhood and adolescence
were long over, if not forgotten. Trollope was now married, well
established as a Surveyor for the General Post Office in Ireland
and known as the author of *Barchester Towers.* In that year he
travelled to Florence to visit his mother, who had made her home
with her son Tom. Trollope had become a close observer of his
fellow travellers, and nothing of the humour and misfortunes of
the experience escaped him. Even at the distance of almost
twenty years as he was writing *An Autobiography* he could recall

with astonishing clarity some of the adventures he had on his trip, and as he says: "On these foreign tours I always encountered adventures."

Early in 1858 he was sent by the GPO to negotiate a postal treaty in Egypt. While there he toured Palestine, and after the treaty was completed he returned home by Malta, Gibraltar, and Spain. The same year he was sent to the West Indies on a postal inspection and returned to England in 1859 by way of New York with a travel book, *The West Indies and the Spanish Main,* and the idea to write a series of short stories set in the countries he had visited. In 1860 he was back in Florence to visit his mother, now in her eightieth year. In August of 1861 he left for Washington on a postal mission and while in the United States travelled extensively in New England and parts of the Midwest, but was unable to travel farther south than Virginia. When he returned to England in 1862, he had written another travel book, *North America.* In 1868 he was again sent to the United States on a postal mission, and in 1871 he sailed to Australia with his wife to visit their son. They returned to England on December 20, 1872, by way of San Francisco and New York, and Trollope had completed yet another travel book, *Australia and New Zealand,* on the voyage home.

Trollope was now fifty-seven years old. He had retired from the GPO after thirty-three years as a civil servant (1834-1867), had stood for a Parliamentary election and been defeated (1868), had published twenty-seven novels, more than a score of short stories, two travel books, and had travelled around the world. But he never seemed to tire of travelling or writing. Early in 1875 he left again for Australia by way of Ceylon. As he travelled he wrote a series of letters about his trip for the *Liverpool Mercury.* From Australia he went to Hawaii and then San Francisco and New York. With his return to England in the fall of '75 he had completed his second circumnavigation of the globe. (He had completed a new novel as well — *The American Senator;* and this was by no means the only one he had written during the long sea passages to and from England.) In 1877 he left for South Africa and returned with another travel book, *South Africa.* In 1878 he joined friends on the yacht "Mastiff" and sailed to Iceland on holiday. In 1882 he made two trips to Ireland to collect material for *The Landleaguers,* the novel he was writing at the time of his fatal stroke in December of 1882. In a long life filled with more of the work of this world than most men know, Trollope never lost a taste for the adventure of travelling among his fellowmen.

Perhaps that is what makes these tales unique. They are, indeed, adventures. Some of these stories are adventures, slightly altered and embroidered, that he himself had. The John Bull of that story's title is admittedly Trollope without, of course, the romance. Some stories are based on events that occurred during his travels. That is true of "Returning Home" and "Aaron Trow." Some stories such as "An Unprotected Female at the Pyramids" and "The Man Who Kept His Money in a Box" are his keen observations on the actions and accidents of his fellow travellers.

The traveller (and here it is the English traveller) had a special appeal for Trollope as a writer because he saw the traveller as prey to the most comic of ironies. For one thing, the traveller is the most vulnerable of all characters. By seeking the far away, the exotic, the foreign and by surrounding himself with people of different customs and language, he finds himself without the protection of the familiar. Nothing he sees or hears reassures him of what or who he is, and it takes very little to make him wish he were at home. As one of Trollope's characters says: "I was not happy at Cairo, for I knew nobody there, and the people at the hotel were, as I thought, uncivil. It seemed to me as though I were allowed to go in and out merely by sufferance; and yet I paid my bill regularly every week." Even Trollope himself, though a seasoned traveller, was sometimes a prey to such feelings. In a letter to George Eliot and George Lewes from Melbourne in 1872 he comments: ". . . mentally I cannot be at ease with all the new people and new things."

Then, the traveller must suffer before he can enjoy. Man is never so forlorn as when he is enduring the discomforts of travel in the expectation of future pleasure. The irony of the traveller's lot is only too obvious in this little bit of conversation from "The Man Who Kept His Money in a Box: "'We don't mean to enjoy ourselves till we get down to the Lake of Como,' said Mr. Green. As I looked at him cowering over the stove, and saw how oppressed he was with greatcoats and warm wrappings for his throat, I quite agreed with him that he had not begun to enjoy himself yet."

And finally, Trollope realized that the traveller is the unwitting victim of the curious irony of proximity. Here is how he explains it in "An Unprotected Female at the Pyramids":

> It is astonishing how much things lose their great interest
> as men find themselves in their close neighborhood. To one
> living in New York or London, how ecstatic is the interest
> inspired by these huge structures. One feels that no price
> would be too high to pay for seeing them, as long as time
> and distance, and the world's inexorable taskwork, forbid
> such a visit. . . .
>
> But all these feelings become strangely dim, their acute
> edges wonderfully worn, as the subjects which inspired
> them are brought near to us. "Ah! so those are the Pyra-
> mids, are they?" says the traveller, when the first glimpse of
> them is shown to him from the window of a railway car-
> riage. "Dear Heaven's sake put the blind down, or we shall
> be destroyed by the sand." And then the ecstacy and keen
> delight of the Pyramids has vanished, and for ever.

Such is the traveller's fate—a fate Trollope knew well as he tells us in *The West Indies and the Spanish Main:* "The Pacific! I was absolutely there, on the ocean in which lie the Sandwich Islands, Queen Pomare, and the Cannibals! But no; I had no such feeling. My only solicitude was whether my clean shirts would last me on to the capital of Costa Rica."

As we might expect, there is very little of the picturesque in his stories. He had neither the knack nor the patience to fill his stories with vivid descriptions of vivid sunsets. Even in the novels, scenery gives way to *mise en scène.* He is always more interested in recording how the individual copes with the daily routine of "getting on with it" than where it is done. His characters tend to define the landscape rather than the other way around. Yet he could convey a sense of place with a few bold strokes and the help of his characters as in this brief passage from "George Walker at Suez":

> I stood for a while in the verandah, looking down at the few
> small vessels which were moored at the quay, but there was
> no life in them; not a sail was set, not a boatman or sailor
> was to be seen, and the very water looked as though it were

hot. I could fancy that the glare of the sun was cracking the paint on the gunwales of the boats. I was the only visitor in the house, and during the long hours of the morning it seemed as though the servants had deserted it.

Trollopean characters, with the possible exception of Septimus Harding in *The Warden*, are always thoroughly human characters with a mixture of faults and virtues, wisdom and folly, self-deception and self-knowledge. Nowhere is this fact more obvious than here among the pilgrims of the world. They are drawn with the sympathy and humour that come from skill and experienced observation and must surely represent a sampling of all whom Trollope had seen and known. From the very English Mr. Horne, a well nurtured clergyman of the Barchester type who loses his breeches in Antwerp, to the irritatingly ingratiating Miss Dawkins who, as an "unprotected" female traveller, is constantly demanding protection, each bears the mark of a creator with an understanding of the human comedy. A sure sense of the comic never deserts Trollope, and with it he could make the ludicrous laughable, the pretentious delightfully absurd, and the faraway and strange strangely familiar.

Of all the character portraits he created, his colonials are among the most sympathetic perhaps because his connections with the British colonies were many and frequent. His younger son, Frederick, had emigrated to New South Wales and had married there and established himself at Mortray Station, which became the setting for *Harry Heathcote of Gangoil*. Fred typified for him the essential qualities that were required of the men and women in these rough new worlds. He writes to an Australian friend from Mortray Station: ". . . I find my son all I could wish — steady, hardworking, skillful and determined." These qualities Trollope saw as essential to the survival of any colonist. Even with these qualities success was a precarious thing. Creating new nations, new economies, new traditions and cultures was an Herculean task even when the colonist was aware only of his own struggle to create a place for himself. Trollope saw all this as he travelled among England's far-flung sons, and his characters reflect what he saw. With astonishing prescience he sensed in both the colonists he saw and the characters he created the strengths and weaknesses of colonialism.

He has presented his colonials as a hardy, resourceful lot willing to endure privation and toil in the most extraordinary circumstances and surroundings. By their own energies (he says in *Australia and New Zealand*) they have made their country fit for the occupation of "our multiplying race." It is, he says, the people who have made the colonies.

There was, however, a curious ambiguity about these colonists — one that Trollope records in his travel books as well as the stories. They were willing to give their energies and intellects to building a new country. They were fiercely proud of what they had done and expected others to be proud of them as well. No personal sacrifice was too great for them to accept if they could establish themselves and their way of life on a secure footing. And even in a colony such as Jamaica, whose moment of glory and richness had passed when Trollope wrote of it, the colonists who remained clung tenaciously to the hope of bringing the colony once again to its former state. Of one such colonial he created he says: ". . . it is hardly too much to say that misfortune had nearly crushed him. But, nevertheless, it had not crushed him. He, and some others like him had still hoped against hope, had still persisted in looking forward to a future for the island which once was so generous in its gifts."

But, though the colonist would give his whole mind, talent, and energy to his new land, he would not give quite his whole heart. Part of his heart always belonged to his "home," and "home" was always England:

> In some distant parts of the world it may be that an Englishman acknowledges his permanent resting-place, but there are many others in which he will not call his daily house his home. He would, in his own idea, desecrate the word by doing so. His home is across the blue waters, in the little northern island, which, perhaps, he may visit no more; which he has left at any rate for half his life; from which circumstances, and the necessity of living, have banished him. His home is still in England; and when he speaks of home his thoughts are there.

Wherever the colonist went his spiritual center was England, and he carried with him what little bits and pieces of "home" he could. He ate roast beef and Yorkshire pudding in the middle of the jungle or insisted on having Worcester sauce even if it had to be carried for miles up mountains on pack mules. And though he might go out in the mid-day sun, he was sure to have tea at the proper hour. Whatever of home he could, he transplanted even in the most inhospitable of soils.

Proud as he was of what he had created, he was also loyal to England. Trollope defines this colonial ambiguity at the beginning of *Australia and New Zealand*:

> He is proud of England, though very generally angry with England because England will not do exactly what he wants. He reconciles this to his mind by telling himself that it is the England of the past of which he is proud, and the England of the present with which he is angry. But his hopes are as bright as his memories . . . and he still clings to the prospects of England in the future . . . He is in truth loyal. He remembers the Queen's birthday, and knows the names of the Queen's grandchildren. He is jealous of the fame of Nelson and Wellington; and tells you in praise of this or that favorite colonial orator, that — he would be listened to in the House of Commons. All this is true loyalty, — which I take to be an adherence to certain persons or things from sentiment rather than from reason.

From their strengths and struggles, their sentiment and loyalties Trollope created his colonial characters. What he saw of them he saw with a sympathetic eye, and when he wrote of them, he wrote with understanding.

Some part of Trollope's success as a writer lies in his talent for observing his fellowman and some in never seeing himself as exempted from the humanity he watched. He was also the perfect Victorian traveller — energetic, curious, adaptable, interested, and ever ready for another adventure. To these qualities he added a self-effacing modesty which allowed him always to see the comedy of life in himself. "Dearest Love," he wrote to his wife from Aden on his way to Australia in 1875, "I have got so far, and have not as yet lost my luggage." Wherever he went he carried with him his pen and paper, his humour and humanism.

Miss Sarah Jack, of Spanish Town, Jamaica

THERE IS NOTHING SO MELANCHOLY as a country in its decadence, unless it be a people in their decadence. I am not aware that the latter misfortune can be attributed to the Anglo-Saxon race in any part of the world; but there is reason to fear that it has fallen on an English colony in the island of Jamaica.

Jamaica was one of those spots on which Fortune shone with the full warmth of all her noon-day splendour. That sun has set; whether for ever or no, none but a prophet can tell; but, as far as a plain man may see, there are at present but few signs of a coming morrow or of another summer.

It is not just or proper that one should grieve over the misfortunes of Jamaica with a stronger grief because her savannahs are so lovely, her forests so rich, her mountains so green, and her rivers so rapid; but yet it is so. It is so piteous that a land so beautiful should be one which Fate has marked for misfortune. Had Guiana, with its flat, level, unlovely soil, become poverty-stricken, one would hardly sorrow over it as one does sorrow for Jamaica.

As regards scenery, she is the gem of the western tropics. It is impossible to conceive spots on the earth's surface more gracious to the eye than those steep green valleys which stretch down to the southwest, from the blue mountain peak towards the sea; and but little behind them in beauty are the rich wooded hills, which in the western part of the island divide the counties of Hanover and Westmoreland. The hero of the tale which I am going to tell was a sugar-grower in this latter district, and the heroine was a girl who lived under that mountain peak.

The very name of a sugar-grower, as connected with Jamaica, savours of fruitless struggle, failure, and desolation; and, from his earliest days, fruitless struggle, failure, and desolation had been the lot of Maurice Cumming. At eighteen years of age he had been left by his father sole possessor of the Mount Pleasant Estate, than which, in her palmy days, Jamaica had little to boast of that was more pleasant or more palmy; but those days had passed by before Roger Cumming, the father of our friend, had died.

Three misfortunes, coming one on the head of another at intervals of a few years, had first stunned and then killed him. His slaves rose against him, as they did against other proprietors around him, and burned down his house and mills, his homestead and offices. Those who know the amount of capital which a sugar-grower must invest in such buildings will understand the extent of this misfortune. Then the slaves were emancipated. It is not, perhaps, possible that we, now-a-days, should regard this as a calamity; but it was quite impossible that a Jamaica proprietor of those days should not have done so. Men will do much for philanthropy — they will work hard, they will give the coat from their back, nay, the very shirt from their body; but few men will endure to look on with satisfaction while their commerce is destroyed.

But even this Mr. Cumming did bear after a while, and kept his shoulder to the wheel. He kept his shoulder to the wheel till that third misfortune came upon him — till the protective duty on Jamaica sugar was abolished. Then he turned his face to the wall and died.

His son, at this time, was not of age, and the large but lessening property which Mr. Cumming left behind him was for three years in the hands of trustees. But, nevertheless, Maurice, young as he was, managed the estate. It was he who grew the canes, and made the sugar, or else failed to make it. He was the "massa," to whom the free negroes looked as the source from whence their wants should be supplied; notwithstanding that,

2

being free, they were ill inclined to work for him, let his want of work be ever so sore.

Mount Pleasant had been a very large property. In addition to his sugar canes, Mr. Cumming had grown coffee, for his land ran up into the hills of Trelawney to that altitude which, in the tropics, seems necessary for the perfect growth of the coffee berry. But it soon became evident that labour for the double product could not be had, and the coffee plantation was abandoned. Wild bush and the thick undergrowth of forest reappeared on the hill sides, which had been rich with produce. And then the evil re-created and exaggerated itself. Negroes squatted on the abandoned property, and being able to live with abundance from their stolen garden, were less willing than ever to work in the cane pieces.

And thus things went from bad to worse. In the good old times, Mr. Cumming's sugar produce had spread itself annually over some three hundred acres; but by degrees this dwindled down to half that extent of land. And then, in those old golden days, they had always taken a full hogshead from the acre — very often more. The estate had sometimes given four hundred hogsheads in the year. But in the days of which we now speak the crop had fallen below fifty.

At this time Maurice Cumming was eight-and-twenty, and it is hardly too much to say that misfortune had nearly crushed him. But, nevertheless, it had not crushed him. He, and some few like him, had still hoped against hope, and still persisted in looking forward to a future for the island which once was so generous in its gifts. When his father died, he might still have had enough for all the wants of life, had he sold his property for what it would fetch. There was money in England, and the remains of large wealth; but he would not sacrifice Mount Pleasant, and the mill was still going; but all other property had departed from his hands.

By nature, Maurice Cumming would have been gay and lively — a man with a happy spirit and easy temper; but struggling had made him silent, if not morose, and had saddened, if not soured his temper. He had lived alone at Mount Pleasant, or generally alone. Work, and want of money, and the constant difficulty of getting labour for his estate, had left him but little time for a young man's ordinary amusements. Of the charm of ladies' society he had known but little. Very many of the estates around him had been absolutely abandoned, as was the case with his own coffee plantation, and from others men had sent away their wives and daughters; nay, most of the proprietors had gone themselves, leaving an overseer to extract what little might yet be extracted out of the property. It too often happened that that little was not sufficient to meet the demands of the overseer himself.

The house at Mount Pleasant had been an irregular, low-roofed, picturesque residence, built with only one floor, and surrounded on all sides by large shady verandahs. In the old days, it had always been kept in perfect order; but now this was far from being the case. Few young bachelors can keep a house in order; but no bachelor, young or old, can do so under such a doom as that of Maurice Cumming. Every shilling that Maurice Cumming could collect was spent in bribing negroes to work for him. But bribe as he would, the negroes would not work. "No, massa; me pain here; me no workie to-day," and Sambo would lay his fat hand on his fat stomach.

I have said that he lived generally alone. Occasionally his house at Mount Pleasant was enlivened by the visits of an aunt, a maiden sister of his mother's, whose usual residence was at Spanish Town. It is or should be known to all men, that Spanish Town was and is the seat of the Jamaican Legislature.

But Maurice was not over fond of his relative. In this he was both wrong and foolish, for Miss Sarah Jack — such was her name — was in many respects a good woman, and was certainly a rich woman. It is true that she was not a handsome woman, nor a fashionable woman, nor perhaps altogether an agreeable woman. She was tall, thin, ungainly, and yellow. Her voice, which she used freely, was harsh. She was a politician and a patriot. She regarded England as the greatest of countries, and Jamaica as the greatest of colonies. But, much as she loved England, she was very loud in denouncing what she called the perfidy of the mother to the brightest of her children; and, much as she loved Jamaica, she was equally severe in her taunts against those of her brother islanders who would not believe that the island might yet flourish as it had flourished in her father's days.

"It is because you, and men like you, will not do your duty by your country," she had said some score of times to Maurice — not with much justice, considering the laboriousness of his life.

But Maurice knew well what she meant. "What could I do up there at Spanish Town," he would answer, "among such a pack as there are there? Here, I may do something."

And then she would reply with the full swing of her eloquence, "It is because you, and such as you, think only of yourself, and not of Jamaica, that Jamaica has come to such a pass as this. Why is there 'a pack' there, as you call them, in the Honourable House of Assembly? Why are not the best men in the island to be found there, as the best men in England are to be found in the British House of Commons? A pack, indeed! My father was proud of a seat in that House; and I remember the day, Maurice Cumming, when your father also thought it no shame to represent his own parish. If men like you, who have a stake in the country, will not go there, of course the House is filled with men who have no stake. If they are 'a pack,' it is you who send them there — you, and others like you."

All this had its effect, though, at the moment, Maurice would shrug his shoulders, and turn away his head from the torrent of the lady's discourse. But Miss Jack, though she was not greatly liked, was greatly respected. Maurice would not own that she convinced him; but, at last, he did allow his name to be put up as candidate for his own parish, and in due time he became a member of the Honourable House of Assembly in Jamaica.

This honour entails on the holder of it the necessity of living at or within reach of Spanish Town for some ten weeks towards the close of every year. Now, on the whole face of the inhabited globe, there is, perhaps, no spot more dull to look at, more Lethean in its aspect, more corpse-like or more cadaverous, than Spanish Town. It is the headquarters of the Government, the seat of the Legislature, the residence of the Governor; but nevertheless it is, as it were, a city of the very dead.

Here, as we have said before, lived Miss Jack, in a large, forlorn, ghostlike house, in which her father and all his family had lived before her. And, as a matter of course, Maurice Cumming, when he came up to attend to his duties as a member of the Legislature, took up his abode with her.

Now, at the time of which we are specially speaking, he had completed the first of these annual visits. He had already benefited his country by sitting out one session of the colonial Parliament, and had satisfied himself that he did no other good than that of keeping away some person more objectionable than himself. He was, however, prepared to repeat this self-sacrifice, in a spirit of patriotism, for which he received a very meagre meed of eulogy from Miss Jack, and an amount of self-applause which was not much more extensive.

"Down at Mount Pleasant I can do something," he would say, over and over again; "but what good can any man do up here?"

"You can do your duty," Miss Jack would answer, "as others did before you, when the colony was made to prosper." And then they would run off into a long discussion about free labour and protective duties. But, at the present moment, Maurice Cumming had another vexation on his mind, over and above those arising from his wasted hours at Spanish Town, and his fruitless labours at Mount Pleasant. He was in love, and was not altogether satisfied with the conduct of his lady love.

Miss Jack had other nephews besides Maurice Cumming, and nieces also, of whom Marian Leslie was one. The family of the Leslies lived up near Newcastle, in the mountains which stand over Kingston—at a distance of some eighteen miles from Kingston, but in a climate as different from that of the town as the climate of Naples is from that of Berlin. In Kingston the heat is all but intolerable throughout the year, by day and by night, in the house and out of it. In the mountains round Newcastle, some four thousand feet above the sea, it is merely warm during the day, and cool enough at night to make a blanket desirable.

It is pleasant enough living up among these green mountains. There are no roads there for wheeled carriages; nor are there carriages with or without wheels. All journeys are made on horseback. Every visit paid from house to house is performed in this manner. Ladies, old and young, live before dinner in their riding habits. The hospitality is free, easy, and unembarrassed; the scenery is magnificent; the tropical foliage is wild and luxuriant beyond measure. There may be enjoyed all that a southern climate has to offer of enjoyment, without the penalties which such enjoyments so usually entail.

Mrs. Leslie was a half sister of Miss Jack's, and Miss Jack had been a half sister also of Mrs. Cumming; but Mrs. Leslie and Mrs.

Cumming had been in no way related. And it had so happened that up to the period of his legislative efforts Maurice Cumming had seen nothing of the Leslies. Soon after his arrival at Spanish Town he had been taken by Miss Jack to Shandy Hall, for so the residence of the Leslies was called, and, having remained there for three days, had fallen in love with Marian Leslie. Now, in the West Indies, all young ladies flirt; it is the first habit of their nature; and few young ladies in the West Indies were more given to flirting, or understood the science better, than Marian Leslie.

Maurice Cumming fell violently in love; and during his first visit at Shandy Hall found that Marian was perfection — for during this first visit her propensities were exerted altogether in his favour. That little circumstance does make such a difference in a young man's judgment of a girl! He came back full of admiration — not altogether to Miss Jack's dissatisfaction; for Miss Jack was willing enough that both her nephew and her niece should settle down into married life.

But, after that, Maurice met the fair Marian at a governor's ball — at a ball where red coats abounded, and *aides-de-camp* dancing in spurs, and narrow-waisted lieutenants with sashes and epaulets! The *aides-de-camp* and narrow-waisted lieutenants waltzed better than he did; and as one after the other whisked round the ball-room with Marian firmly clasped in his arm, Maurice's feelings were not of the sweetest. Nor was this the worst of it. Had the whisking been divided equally among ten, he might have forgiven it; but there was one specially narrow-waisted lieutenant, who, towards the end of the evening, kept Marian nearly wholly to himself. Now, to a man in love, who had had but little experience of either balls or young ladies, this is intolerable.

He only met her twice after that before his return to Mount Pleasant, and, on the first occasion, that odious soldier was not there; but a specially devout young clergyman was present — an unmarried, evangelical, handsome young curate, fresh from England; and Marian's piety had been so excited that she had ears for no one else. It appeared, moreover, that the curate's gifts for conversion were confined, as regarded that opportunity, to Marian's advantage. "I will have nothing more to say to her," said Maurice, as he sat by himself, scowling. But, just as he went

7

away, Marian had given him her hand and called him Maurice
— for she pretended that they were cousins — and had looked
into his eyes and declared that she did hope that the Assembly
at Spanish Town would soon be sitting again. Hitherto, she said,
she had not cared one straw about it. Then poor Maurice pressed
the little fingers which lay within his own, and swore that he
would be at Shandy Hall on the day before his return to Mount
Pleasant. So he was; and there he found the narrow-waisted lieutenant, not now bedecked with sash and epaulets, but lolling, at
his ease, on Mrs. Leslie's sofa, in a white jacket, while Marian
sat at his feet telling his fortune with a book about flowers.

"Oh, a musk rose, Mr. Ewing! You know what a musk rose
means?" Then she got up and shook hands with Mr. Cumming;
but her eyes still went away to the white jacket and the sofa. Poor
Maurice had often been nearly broken-hearted in his endeavours
to manage his free black labourers; but even that was easier than
managing such as Marian Leslie.

Marian Leslie was a Creole—as also were Miss Jack and Maurice Cumming — a child of the tropics; but by no means such a
child as tropical children are in general thought to be by us in
more northern latitudes. She was black-haired and black-eyed;
but her lips were as red and her cheeks as rosy as though she had
been born and bred in regions where the snow lies in winter. She
was a small, pretty, beautifully-made little creature, somewhat
idle as regards the work of the world, but active and strong
enough when dancing or riding were required from her. Her
father was a banker, and was fairly prosperous in spite of the pov-
erty of his country. His house of business was at Kingston, and
he usually slept there twice a-week; but he always resided at
Shandy Hall, and Mrs. Leslie and her children knew but very little of the miseries of Kingston. For be it known to all men, that
of all towns Kingston, Jamaica, is the most miserable.

I fear that I shall have set my readers very much against Marian
Leslie — much more so than I would wish to do. As a rule, they
will not know how thoroughly flirting is an institution in the
West Indies — practised by all young ladies, and laid aside by
them when they marry exactly as their young lady names and
young lady habits of various kinds are laid aside. All I would say
of Marian Leslie is this—that she understood the working of the

institution more thoroughly than others did; and I must add also in her favour, that she did not keep her flirting for sly corners, nor bid her admirers keep their distance till mamma was out of the way. It mattered not to her who was present. Had she been called on to make one at a synod of the clergy of the island, she would have flirted with the bishop before all his clergy; and there have been bishops in the colony who would not have gainsayed her.

But Maurice Cumming did not rightly calculate all this; nor, indeed, did Miss Jack do so as thoroughly as she should have done; for Miss Jack knew more about such matters than did poor Maurice. "If you like Marian why don't you marry her?" Miss Jack had once said to him; and this, coming from Miss Jack, who was made of money, was a great deal.

"She wouldn't have me," Maurice had answered.

"That's more than you know, or I either," was Miss Jack's reply. "But, if you like to try, I'll help you."

With reference to this, Maurice, as he left Miss Jack's residence on his return to Mount Pleasant, had declared that Marian Leslie was not worth an honest man's love.

"Pshaw!" Miss Jack replied. "Marian will do like other girls. When you marry a wife I suppose you mean to be the master?"

"At any rate, I shall not marry her," said Maurice. And so he went his way back to Hanover with a soured heart; and no wonder, for that was the very day on which Lieutenant Ewing had asked the question about the musk rose.

But there was a dogged constancy of feeling about Maurice which would not allow him to disburden himself of his love. When he was again at Mount Pleasant, among his sugar-canes and hogsheads, he could not help thinking of Marian. It is true he always thought of her as flying round that hall in Ewing's arms, or looking up with rapt admiration into that young parson's face; and so he got but little pleasure from his thoughts. But not the less was he in love with her—not the less, though he would swear to himself three times in the day that for no earthly consideration would he marry Marian Leslie.

The early months of the year—from January to May—are the busiest with a Jamaica sugar-grower, and in this year they were very busy months with Maurice Cumming. It seemed as though there were actually some truth in Miss Jack's prediction, that prosperity would return to him if he attended to his country; for the prices of sugar had risen higher than they had ever been since the duty had been withdrawn, and there was more promise of a crop at Mount Pleasant than he had seen since his reign commenced. But then the question of labour? How he slaved in trying to get work from those free negroes; and, alas! how often he slaved in vain! But it was not all in vain; for, as things went on, it became clear to him that in this year he would, for the first time since he commenced, obtain something like a return from his land. What if the turning-point had come, and things were now about to run the other way?

But then, any happiness which might have accrued to him from this source was dashed by his thoughts of Marian Leslie. Why had he thrown himself in the way of that syren? Why had he left Mount Pleasant at all? He knew that on his return to Spanish Town his first work would be to visit Shandy Hall; and yet he felt that, of all places in the island, Shandy Hall was the last which he ought to visit.

And then, about the beginning of May, when he was hard at work, turning the last of his canes into sugar and rum, he received his annual visit from Miss Jack. And whom should Miss Jack bring with her but Mr. Leslie?

"I'll tell you what it is," said Miss Jack; "I have spoken to Mr. Leslie about you and Marian."

"Then you had no business to do anything of the kind," said Maurice, blushing up to his ears.

"Nonsense!" replied Miss Jack. "I understand what I am about. Of course Mr. Leslie will want to know something about the estate."

"Then he may go back as wise as he came, for he'll learn nothing from me; not that I have anything to hide."

"So I told him. Now, there are a large family of them, you see; and of course he can't give Marian much."

"I don't care a straw if he doesn't give her a shilling. If she cared for me and I for her, I shouldn't look after her for her money."

"But a little money is not a bad thing, Maurice," said Miss Jack, who, in her time, had had a good deal and had managed to take care of it.

"It is all one to me."

"But what I was going to say is this. Hum!—ha!—I don't like to pledge myself for fear I should raise hopes which mayn't be fulfilled."

"Don't pledge yourself to anything, aunt, in which Marian Leslie and I are concerned together."

"But what I was going to say is this. My money—what little I have, you know—must go, some day, either to you or to the Leslies."

"You may give it all to them, if you please."

"Of course I may, and I dare say I shall," said Miss Jack, who was beginning to be irritated. "But, at any rate, you might have the civility to listen to me, when I am endeavouring to put you on your legs. I am sure I think about nothing else, morning, noon, and night; and yet I never get a decent word from you. Marian is too good for you—that's the truth!"

But at length Miss Jack was allowed to open her budget, and to make her proposition, which amounted to this—that she had already told Mr. Leslie that she would settle the bulk of her property conjointly on Maurice and Marian, if they would make a match of it. Now, as Mr. Leslie had long been casting a hankering eye after Miss Jack's money, with a strong conviction, however, that Maurice Cumming was her favourite nephew and probable heir, this proposition was not unpalatable. So he agreed to go down to Mount Pleasant and look about him.

"But you may live for the next thirty years, my dear Miss Jack," Mr. Leslie had said.

"Yes, I may," Miss Jack replied, looking very dry.

"And I am sure I hope you will," continued Mr. Leslie. And then the subject was allowed to drop; for Mr. Leslie knew that it was not always easy to talk to Miss Jack on such matters.

Miss Jack was a person in whom, I think, we may say, that the good predominated over the bad. She was often morose, crabbed, and self-opinionated; but then she knew her own imperfections, and forgave those she loved for evincing their dislike of them. Maurice Cumming was often inattentive to her, plainly showing that he was worried by her importunities, and ill at ease in her company. But she loved her nephew with all her heart, and

though she dearly liked to tyrannise over him, never allowed herself to be really angry with him, though he so frequently refused
to bow to her dictation. And she loved Marian Leslie also,
though Marian was so sweet and lovely, and she herself so harsh
and ill-favoured. She loved Marian, though Marian would often
be impertinent. She forgave the flirting, the light-heartedness,
the love of amusement. Marian, she said to herself, was young
and pretty. She, Miss Jack, had never known Marian's tempta-
tions. And so she resolved, in her own mind, that Marian should
be made a good and happy woman; but always as the wife of
Maurice Cumming.

But Maurice turned a deaf ear to all these good tidings; or,
rather, he turned to them an ear that seemed to be deaf. He
dearly, ardently loved that little flirt; but seeing that she was a
flirt, that had flirted so grossly when he was by, he would not
confess his love to a human being. He would not have it known
that he was wasting his heart for a worthless little chit, to whom
every man was the same, except that those were most eligible
whose toes were the lightest, and their outside trappings the
brightest. That he did love her, he could not deny, but he would
not disgrace himself by acknowledging it.

He was very civil to Mr. Leslie, but he would not speak a word
that could be taken as a proposal for Marian. It had been part of
Miss Jack's plan that the engagement should absolutely be made
down there at Mount Pleasant, without any reference to the
young lady; but Maurice could not be induced to break the ice.
So he took Mr. Leslie through his mills and over his cane-pieces;
talked to him about the laziness of the niggers, while the niggers
themselves stood by tittering; and rode with him away to the high
grounds, where the coffee plantation had been in the good old
days; — but not a word was said between them about Marian.
And yet Marian was never out of his heart.

And then came the day on which Mr. Leslie was to go back to
Kingston. "And you won't have her, then?" said Miss Jack to her
nephew early that morning. "You won't be ruled by me?"

"Not in this matter, aunt."

"Then you will live and die a poor man? You mean that, I
suppose?"

"It's likely enough that I shall. There's this comfort, at any rate, I'm used to it."

And then Miss Jack was again silent for a while.

"Very well, sir; that's enough," she said, angrily. And then she began again: "But, Maurice, you wouldn't have to wait for my death, you know." And she put out her hand, and touched his arm, entreating him, as it were, to yield to her. "Oh, Maurice," she said, "I do so want to make you comfortable. Let me speak to Mr. Leslie."

But Maurice would not. He took her hand and thanked her, but said that in this matter he must be his own master. "Very well, sir," she exclaimed; "I have done. In future, you may manage for yourself. As for me, I shall go back with Mr. Leslie to Kingston." And so she did. Mr. Leslie returned that day, taking her with him. When he took his leave, his invitation to Maurice to come to Shandy Hall was not very pressing. "Mrs. Leslie and the children will always be glad to see you," said he.

"Remember me very kindly to Mrs. Leslie—and the children," said Maurice. And so they parted.

"You have brought me down here on a regular fool's errand," said Mr. Leslie, on their journey up to town.

"It will all come right yet," replied Miss Jack. "Take my word for it, he loves her."

"Fudge!" said Mr. Leslie. But he could not afford to quarrel with his rich connection.

In spite of all that he had said and thought to the contrary, Maurice did look forward, during the remainder of the summer, to his return to Spanish Town with something like impatience. It was very dull work, being there alone at Mount Pleasant; and, let him do what he would to prevent it, his very dreams took him to Shandy Hall. But at last the slow time passed away, and he found himself once more in his aunt's house.

A couple of days went by, and no word was said about the Leslies. On the morning of the third day, he determined to go to Shandy Hall. Hitherto he had never been there without staying for the night, but on this occasion he made up his mind to return the same day. "It would not be civil of me not to go there," he said to his aunt.

"Certainly not," she replied, forbearing to press the matter further. "But why make such a terrible hard day's work of it?"

13

"Oh, I shall go down in the cool, before breakfast; and then I need not have the bother of taking a bag."

And in this way he started. Miss Jack said nothing further, but she longed, in her heart, that she might be at Marian's elbow, unseen, during the visit.

He found them all at breakfast, and the first to welcome him at the hall door was Marian. "Oh, Mr. Cumming, we are so glad to see you;" and she looked up into his eyes with a way she had, that was enough to make a man's heart wild. But she did not call him Maurice now.

Miss Jack had spoken to her sister, Mrs. Leslie, as well as to Mr. Leslie, about the marriage scheme. "Just let them alone," was Mrs. Leslie's advice. "You can't alter Marian by lecturing her. If they really love each other, they'll come together; and if they don't, why then they'd better not."

"And you really mean that you're going back to Spanish Town to-day?" said Mrs. Leslie to her visitor.

"I'm afraid I must. Indeed, I haven't brought my things with me." And then he again caught Marian's eye, and began to wish that his resolution had not been so sternly made.

"I suppose you're so fond of that House of Assembly," said Marian, "that you cannot tear yourself away for more than one day. You'll not be able, I suppose, to find time to come to our picnic next week?"

Maurice said that he feared that he should not have time to go to a picnic.

"Oh, nonsense!" said Fanny, one of the younger girls. "You must come, we can't do without him; can we?"

"Marian has got your name down first on the list of the gentlemen," said another.

"Yes; and Captain Ewing's second," said Bell, the youngest.

"I'm afraid I must induce your sister to alter her list," said Maurice, in his sternest manner. "I cannot manage to go, and I am sure she will not miss me."

Marian looked at the little girl who had so unfortunately mentioned the warrior's name, and the little girl knew that she had sinned.

"Oh, we cannot possibly do without you; can we, Marian?" said Fanny. "It's to be at Bingley's Dell, and we've got a bed for you at Newcastle, quite near, you know."

"And another for — ," began Bell, but she stopped herself.

"Go away to your lessons, Bell," said Marian. "You know how angry mamma will be at your staying here all the morning." And poor Bell, with a sorrowful look, left the room.

"We are all certainly very anxious that you should come — very anxious, for a great many reasons," said Marian, in a voice that was rather solemn, and as though the matter were one of considerable import. "But if you really cannot, why, of course, there is no more to be said."

"There will be plenty without me, I am sure."

"As regards numbers, I dare say there will; for we shall have pretty nearly the whole of the two regiments" — and Marian, as she alluded to the officers, spoke in a tone which might lead one to think that she would much rather be without them — "but we counted on you, as being one of ourselves; and, as you had been away so long, we thought — we thought — " and then she turned away her face, and did not finish her speech. Before he could make up his mind as to his answer, she had risen from her chair, and walked out of the room. Maurice almost thought that he saw a tear in her eye as she went.

He did ride back to Spanish Town that afternoon, after an early dinner; but, before he went, Marian spoke to him alone for one minute.

"I hope you are not offended with me?" she said.

"Offended! Oh, no; how could I be offended with you?"

"Because you seem so stern. I'm sure I would do anything I could to oblige you — if I knew how. It would be so shocking not to be good friends with a cousin like you."

"But there are so many different sorts of friends," said Maurice.

"Of course there are. There are a great many friends that one does not care a bit for — people that one meets at balls, and places like that —"

"And at picnics," said Maurice.

"Well; some of them there, too. But we are not like that; are we?"

What could Maurice do but say, "No;" and declare that their friendship was of a warmer description? And how could he resist promising to go to the picnic, though, as he made the promise he

15

knew that misery would be in store for him? He did promise, and then she gave him her hand, and called him "Maurice."

"Oh, I am so glad," she said. "It seemed so shocking that you should refuse to join us. And mind and be early, Maurice; for I shall want to explain it all. We are to meet, you know, at Clifton Gate at one o'clock; but do you be a little before that, and we shall be there."

Maurice Cumming resolved within his own breast, as he rode back to Spanish Town, that if Marian behaved to him all that day at the picnic as she had done this day at Shandy Hall, he would ask her to be his wife before he left her.

And Miss Jack also was to be at the picnic. "There is no need of going so early," said she, when her nephew made a fuss about the starting; "people are never very punctual at such affairs as that; and then they are always quite long enough." But Maurice explained that he was anxious to be early, and on this occasion he carried his point.

When they reached Clifton Gate the Leslies were already there — not in carriages, as people go to picnics in other and tamer countries, but each on his own horse, or her own pony. But they were not alone. Beside Miss Leslie was a gentleman whom Maurice knew as Lieutenant Graham, of the flagship at Port Royal; and at a little distance — a distance which quite enabled him to join in the conversation — was Captain Ewing, the lieutenant with the narrow waist of the previous year.

"We shall have a delightful day, Miss Leslie," said the lieutenant.

"Oh, charming, isn't it?" said Marian. "But now, to choose a place for dinner. Captain Ewing, what do you say?"

"Will you commission me to select? You know I'm very well up in geometry, and all that."

"But that won't teach you to know what sort of place does for a picnic dinner, will it, Mr. Cumming?" And then she shook hands with Maurice, but did not take any further special notice of him. "We'll all go together, if you please. The commission is too important to be left to one." And then Marian rode off, and the lieutenant and the captain rode with her.

It was open for Maurice to join them if he chose, but he did not choose. He had come there ever so much earlier than he need have done, dragging his aunt with him, because Marian had told him that his services would be specially required by her; and now, as soon as she saw him, she went away with those two officers! — went away without vouchsafing him a word! He made up his mind, there on the spot, that he would never think of her again; never speak to her otherwise than he might speak to the most indifferent of mortals.

And yet he was a man that could struggle right manfully with the world's troubles — one who had struggled with them from his boyhood and had never been overcome. Now he was unable to conceal the bitterness of his wrath because a little girl had ridden off to look for a green spot for her tablecloth, without asking his assistance! What apes men are!

Picnics are, I think, in general, rather tedious for the elderly people who go to them. When the joints become a little stiff, dinners are eaten most comfortably with the accompaniment of chairs and tables, and a roof overhead is an *agrément de plus*. But, nevertheless, picnics cannot exist without a certain allowance of elderly people. The Miss Marians and Captain Ewings cannot go out to dine on the grass without some one to look after them. So the elderly people go to picnics, in a dull, tame way, doing their duty, and wishing the day over. Now, on the morning in question, when Marian rode off with Captain Ewing and Lieutenant Graham, Maurice Cumming remained among the elderly people.

A certain Mr. Pomken, a great Jamaica agriculturist, one of the Council, a man who had known the good old times, got him by the button and held him fast, discoursing wisely of sugar and rum, of Gadsden pans and recreant negroes, on all which subjects Maurice Cumming was known to have an opinion of his own. But as Mr. Pomken's words sounded into one ear, into the other fell notes, listened to from afar — the shrill, laughing voice of Marian Leslie, as she gave her happy orders to her satellites around her, and ever and anon the base "haw-haw!" of Captain Ewing, who was made welcome as the chief of her attendants. That evening, in a whisper to a brother councillor, Mr. Pomken communicated his opinion that, after all, there was not so much in that young Cumming as some people said. But Mr. Pomken had no idea that young Cumming was in love.

And then the dinner came, spread over half an acre. Maurice

17

was one of the last who seated himself; and, when he did so, it was in an awkward, comfortless corner, behind Mr. Pomken's back, and far away from the laughter and mirth of the day. But yet from his comfortless corner he could see Marian as she sat in her pride of power, with her friend Julia Davis near her, a flirt as bad as herself, and her satellites around her, obedient to her nod, and happy in her smiles.

"Now, I won't allow any more champagne," said Marian, "or who will there be steady enough to help me over the rocks to the grotto?"

"Oh, you have promised me!" cried the captain.

"Indeed I have not; have I, Julia?"

"Miss Davis has certainly promised me," said the lieutenant.

"I have made no promises, and don't think I shall go at all," said Julia, who was sometimes inclined to imagine that Captain Ewing should be her own property.

All which and much more of the kind Maurice Cumming could not hear; but he could see and imagine, which was worse. How innocent and inane are, after all, the flirtings of most young ladies, if all their words and doings in that line could be brought to paper! I do not know whether there be, as a rule, more vocal expression of the sentiment of love between a man and woman, than there is between two thrushes. They whistle and call to each other, guided by instinct rather than by reason.

"You are going home with the Leslies to-night, I believe?" said Maurice to Miss Jack, immediately after dinner. Miss Jack acknowledged that such was her destination for the night.

"Then my going back to Spanish Town at once won't hurt any one, for, to tell the truth, I have had enough of this work."

"Why, Maurice, you were in such a hurry to come."

"The more fool I; and so now I am in a hurry to go away. Don't notice it to anybody."

Miss Jack looked in his face and saw that he was really wretched; and she knew the cause of his wretchedness.

"Don't go yet, Maurice," she said, and then added, with a tenderness that was quite uncommon with her, "Go to her, Maurice, and speak to her openly and fairly, once for all. You will find that she will be altered then. Dear Maurice, do, for my sake."

He made her no answer, but walked away, roaming sadly by

18

himself among the tress. "Altered!" he exclaimed, to himself; "yes, she will alter a dozen times in as many hours. Who can care for a creature that can change as she changes?" And yet he could not help caring for her.

As he went on, climbing among rocks, he again came upon the sound of voices, and heard especially that of Captain Ewing. "Now, Miss Leslie, if you will take my hand you will soon be over all the difficulty." And then a party of seven or eight, scrambling over some stones, came nearly on the level on which he stood, in full view of him, and leading the others were Captain Ewing and Miss Leslie.

He turned on his heel to go away, when he caught the sound of a step following him, and a voice saying, "Oh, there is Mr. Cumming, and I want to speak to him," and in a minute a light hand was on his arm.

"Why are you running away from us?" said Marian.

"Because — oh, I don't know; I am not running away. You have your party made up, and I am not going to intrude on it."

"What nonsense! Do come, now. We are going to this wonderful grotto. I thought it so ill-natured of you not joining us at dinner. Indeed, you know you had promised."

He did not answer her, but he looked at her full in the face, with his sad eyes laden with love. She half understood his countenance, but only half understood it.

"What's the matter, Maurice?" she said. "Are you angry with me? Will you not come and join us?"

"No, Marian, I cannot do that; but if you can leave them and come with me for half an hour, I will not keep you longer."

She stood hesitating a moment, while her companions remained on the spot where she had left them. "Come, Miss Leslie," called Captain Ewing, "you will have it dark before we can get down."

"I will come with you," whispered she to Maurice, "but wait a moment." She tripped back, and in some five minutes returned, after an eager argument with her friends. "There," she said, "I don't care about the grotto one bit, and I will walk with you now; only they will think it so odd." And so they started off together.

Before the early tropical darkness had fallen upon them, Maurice had told the tale of his love, and had told it in a manner

19

differing much from that of Marian's usual admirers. He spoke with passion, and almost with violence. He declared that his heart was so full of her image, that he could not rid himself of it for one minute. "Nor would he wish to do so," he said, "if she would be his Marian, his own Marian, his very own. But if not," and then he explained to her, with all a lover's warmth, and with almost more than a lover's liberty, what was his idea of her being his own, his very own; and, in doing so, inveighed against her usual lightheartedness in terms which at any rate were strong enough.

But Marian bore it all well. Perhaps she knew that the lesson was somewhat deserved, and perhaps she appreciated at its value the love of such a man as Maurice Cumming, weighing in her judgment the difference between him and the Ewings and the Grahams.

And then she answered him well and prudently, with words which startled him by their prudent seriousness, as coming from her. She begged his pardon heartily, she said, for any grief which she had caused him; but yet how was she to be blamed, seeing that she had known nothing of his feelings? Her father and mother had said something to her of this proposed marriage — something, but very little; and she had answered by saying that she did not think Maurice had any warmer regard for her than that of a cousin. After this answer neither father nor mother had pressed the matter further. As to her own feelings, she could then say nothing, for she knew nothing — nothing but this, that she loved no one better than him — or rather, that she loved no one else. She would ask herself if she could love him, but he must give her some little time for that. In the meanwhile — and she smiled sweetly on him as she made the promise — she would endeavour to do nothing that would offend him; and then she added that on that evening she would dance with him any dances that he liked. Maurice, with a self-denial that was not very wise, contented himself with engaging her for the first quadrille.

They were to dance that night in the mess-room of the officers at Newcastle. This scheme had been added on as an adjunct to the picnic, and it therefore became necessary that the ladies should retire to their own or their friends' houses at Newcastle to adjust their dresses. Marian Leslie and Julia Davis were thus accommodated with the loan of a small room by the major's wife; and, as they were brushing their hair and putting on their danc-ing-shoes, something was said between them about Maurice Cumming.

"And so you are to be Mrs. C., of Mount Unpleasant?" said Julia. "Well, I didn't think it would come to that at last."

"But it has not come to that; and if it did, why should I not be Mrs. C., as you call it?"

"The 'Knight of the Rueful Countenance' I call him."

"I tell you what, then; he is an excellent young man, and the fact is, you don't know him."

"I don't like excellent young men with long faces. I suppose you won't be let to dance quick dances at all now?"

"I shall dance whatever dances I like, as I have always done," said Marian, with some little asperity in her tone.

"Not you; or, if you do, you'll lose your promotion. You'll never live to be my Lady Rue; and what will Graham say? You know you've given him half a promise."

"That's not true, Julia; I never gave him the tenth part of a promise."

"Well, he says so." And then words between the young ladies became a little more angry; but, nevertheless, in due time they came forth with faces smiling as usual, with their hair properly brushed, and without any signs of warfare.

But Marian had to stand another attack before the business of the evening commenced, and this was from no less doughty an antagonist than her aunt, Miss Jack. Miss Jack soon found that Maurice had not kept his threat of going home; and though she did not absolutely learn from him that he had gone so far towards perfecting her dearest hopes, as to make a formal offer to Marian, nevertheless she did gather that things were fast that way tend-ing. "If only this dancing were over!" she said to herself, dreading the unnumbered waltzes with Ewing, and the violent polkas with Graham. So Miss Jack resolved to say one word to Marian. "A wise word in good season," said Miss Jack to herself, "how sweet a thing it is!"

"Marian," said she, "step here a moment; I want to say a word to you."

"Yes, aunt Sarah," said Marian, following her aunt into a corner, not quite in the best humour in the world; for she had a dread of some further interference.

"Are you going to dance with Maurice to-night?"

"Yes, I believe so — the first quadrille."

"Well, what I was going to say is this — I don't want you to dance many quick dances to-night, for a reason I have — that is, not a great many."

"Why, aunt? What nonsense!"

"Now, my dearest, dearest girl, it is all for your own sake. Well, then, it must out. He does not like it, you know."

"What he?"

"Maurice."

"Well, aunt, I don't know that I'm bound to dance, or not to dance, just as Mr. Cumming may like. Papa does not mind my dancing. The people have come here to dance, and you can hardly want to make me ridiculous by sitting still." And so that wise word did not appear to be so very sweet.

And then the amusement of the evening commenced, and Marian stood up for a quadrille with her lover. She, however, was not in the very best humour. She had, as she thought, said and done enough for one day in Maurice's favour; and she had no idea, as she declared to herself, of being lectured by aunt Sarah.

"Dearest Marian," he said to her, as the quadrille came to a close, "it is in your power to make me so happy — so perfectly happy."

"But, then, people have such different ideas of happiness," she replied. "They can't all see with the same eyes, you know." And so they parted.

But during the early part of the evening she was sufficiently discreet; she did waltz with Lieutenant Graham and polka with Captain Ewing, but she did so in a tamer manner than was usual with her, and she made no emulous attempts to dance down other couples. When she had done she would sit down; and then she consented to stand up for two quadrilles with two very tame gentlemen, to whom no lover could object.

"And so, Marian, your wings are regularly clipped at last?" said Julia Davis, coming up to her.

"No more clipped than your own," said Marian.

"If Sir Rue won't let you waltz now, what will he require of you when you're married to him?"

"I am just as well able to waltz with whom I like as you are, Julia; and if you go on in that way, I shall think it's envy."

"Ha! ha! ha! Well, I may have envied you some of your beaux before now. I dare say I have. But I certainly do not envy you Sir Rue." And then she went off to her partner.

All this was too much for Marian's weak strength, and before long she was again whirling round with Captain Ewing.

"Come, Miss Leslie," said he, "let us see what we can do. Graham and Julia Davis have been saying that your waltzing days are over, but I think we can put them down."

Marian, as she got up, and raised her arm in order that Ewing might put his round her waist, caught Maurice's eye, as he leaned against a wall, and read in it a stern rebuke.

"This is too bad," she said to herself. "He shall not make a slave of me; at any rate, not as yet." And away she went as madly, more madly than ever; and for the rest of the evening she danced with Captain Ewing, and with him alone.

There is an intoxication quite distinct from that which comes from strong drink. When the judgment is altogether overcome by the spirits, this species of drunkenness comes on; and in this way Marian Leslie was drunk that night. For two hours she danced with Captain Ewing, and ever and anon she kept saying to herself, that she would teach the world to know — and of all the world, Mr. Cumming especially — that she might be led, but not driven.

Then, about four o'clock, she went home; and as she attempted to undress herself in her own room, she burst into violent hysteric tears, and opened her heart to her sister. "Oh, Fanny, I do love him; I do love him so dearly! And now he will never come to me again!"

Maurice stood still, with his back against the wall, for the full two hours of Marian's exhibition, and then he said to his aunt, before he left, "I hope you have now seen enough. You will hardly mention her name to me again." Miss Jack groaned from the bottom of her heart, but she said nothing. She said nothing that night to any one, but she lay awake in her bed thinking, till it was time to rise and dress herself. "Ask Miss Marian to come to me," she then said to the black girl who came to assist her. But

23

it was not till she had sent three times that Miss Marian obeyed the summons.

At three o'clock on the following day Miss Jack arrived at her own hall-door in Spanish Town. Long as the distance was, she ordinarily rode it all; but, on this occasion, she had procured a carriage to bring her over so much of the journey as it was practicable for her to perform on wheels. As soon as she reached her own hall-door she asked whether Mr. Cumming were at home. "Yes," the servant said, "he was in the small book-room, at the back of the house, up-stairs." Silently, as though afraid of being heard, she stepped up her own stairs, into her own drawing-room; and, very silently, she was followed by a pair of feet lighter and smaller than her own.

Miss Jack was usually somewhat of a despot in her own house; but there was nothing despotic about her now, as she peered into the book-room. This she did with her bonnet still on, looking round the half-opened door, as though she were afraid to disturb her nephew. He sat at the window, looking out into the verandah which ran behind the house, so intent were his thoughts that he did not hear her.

"Maurice," she said, "can I come in?"

"Come in! Oh, yes; of course!" And he turned round sharply at her. "I tell you what, aunt, I am not well here; and I cannot stay out this session. I shall go back to Mount Pleasant."

"Maurice!" — and she walked close up to him as she spoke — "Maurice, I have brought some one with me to ask your pardon!"

His face became red up to the roots of his hair, as he stood looking at her, without answering. "You would grant it, certainly," she continued, "if you knew how much it would be valued."

"Whom do you mean? who is it?" he asked, at last.

"One who loves you as well as you love her; and she cannot love you better. Come in, Marian!"

The poor girl crept in at the door, ashamed of what she was induced to do, but yet looking anxiously into her lover's face.

"You asked her yesterday to be your wife," said Miss Jack; "and she did not then know her own mind. Now she has had a lesson. You will ask her once again, will you not?"

What was he to say? How was he to refuse when that soft little hand was held out to him? when those eyes, laden with tears, just ventured to look into his face?

"I beg your pardon if I angered you last night," she said.

In half a minute Miss Jack had left the room, and in the space of another thirty seconds Maurice had forgiven her. "I am your own now, you know," she whispered to him, in the course of that long evening. "Yesterday, you know —" But the sentence was never finished.

It was in vain that Julia Davis was ill-natured and sarcastic — in vain that Ewing and Graham made joint attempts upon her constancy. From that night to the morning of her marriage — and the interval was only six months — Marian Leslie was never known to flirt.

"Miss Sarah Jack, of Spanish Town, Jamaica" appeared first in the November 3 and 10 issues of *Cassell's Illustrated Family Paper* for 1860.

The Man Who Kept
His Money in a Box

FIRST SAW THE MAN WHO KEPT his money in a box in the midst of the ravine of the Via Mala; I interchanged a few words with him or with his wife at the hospice at the top of the Splugen, and I became acquainted with him in the courtyard of Conradi's hotel at Chiavenna. It was, however, afterwards, at Bellaggio, on the Lake of Como, that that acquaintance ripened into an intimacy. A good many years have rolled by since then, and I believe this episode in his life may be told without pain to the feelings of anyone.

His name was —; let us for the present say that his name was Greene. How he learned that my name was Robinson I do not know; but I remember well that he addressed me by my name at Chiavenna. To go back, however, for a moment to the Via Mala. I had been staying for a few days at the Golden Eagle, at Tersis —which, by-the-bye, I hold to be the best small inn in all Switzerland, and its hostess to be, or to have been, certainly the prettiest landlady—and on the day of my departure southward, I had walked on into the Via Mala, so that the diligence might pick me up in the gorge. This pass I regard as one of the grandest spots to which my wandering steps have ever carried me, and though I had already lingered about it for many hours, I now walked thither again to take my last farewell of its dark towering rocks, its narrow causeway, and roaring river, trusting to my friend the landlady to see that my luggage was duly packed upon the diligence. I need hardly say that my friend did not betray her trust.

As one goes out from Switzerland towards Italy, the road through the Via Mala ascends somewhat steeply, and passengers by the diligence may walk from the inn at Tersis into the gorge, and make their way through the greater part of the ravine before the vehicle will overtake them. This, however, Mr. Greene, with his wife and daughter, had omitted to do. When the diligence passed me in the defile, the horses trotting for a few yards over some level portion of the road, I saw a man's nose pressed close against the glass of the *coupé* window. I saw more of his nose than of any other part of his face, but yet I could perceive that his neck was twisted and his eye upturned, and that he was making a painful effort to look upwards to the summit of the rocks from his position inside the carriage.

There was such a roar of wind and waters at the spot, that it was not practicable to speak to him, but I beckoned with my finger, and then pointed to the road, indicating that he should have walked. He understood me, though I did not at the moment understand his answering gesture. It was subsequently, when I knew somewhat of his habits, that he explained to me that in pointing to his open mouth he had intended to signify that he would be afraid of sore throat in exposing himself to the air of that damp and narrow passage.

I got up into the conductor's covered seat at the back of the diligence, and in this position encountered the drifting snow of the Splugen. I think it is coldest of all the passes. Near the top of the pass the diligence stops for a while, and it is here, if I remember, that the Austrian officials demand the travellers' passports — at least in those days they did so. These officials have now retreated behind the Quadrilatere — soon, as we hope, to make a further retreat — and the district belongs to the kingdom of United Italy. There is a place of refreshment, or hospice here, into which we all went for a few moments, and I then saw that my friend with the weak throat was accompanied by two ladies.

"You should not have missed the Via Mala," I said to him, as he stood warming his toes at the huge covered stove.

"We miss everything," said the elder of the two ladies, who, however, was very much younger than the gentleman, and not very much older than her companion.

"I saw it beautifully, mamma," said the younger one.

Whereupon mamma gave her head a tap, and made up her mind, as I thought, to take some little vengeance before long upon her step-daughter. I observed that Miss Greene always called her step-mother mamma on the first approach of any stranger, so that the nature of the connexion between them might be understood. And I observed also that the elder lady always gave her head a tap when she was so addressed.

"We don't mean to enjoy ourselves till we get down to the Lake of Como," said Mr. Greene.

As I looked at him cowering over the stove, and saw how oppressed he was with greatcoats and warm wrappings for his throat, I quite agreed with him that he had not begun to enjoy himself as yet. Then we all got into our places again, and I saw no more of the Greenes till we were all standing huddled together in the huge courtyard of Conradi's hotel at Chiavenna.

Chiavenna is the first Italian town which the tourist reaches by this route, and I know no town in the north of Italy which is so closely surrounded by beautiful scenery. The traveller, as he falls down to it from the Splugen road, is bewildered by the loneliness of the valleys — that is to say, if he so arranges that he can see them without pressing his nose against the glass of a coach window. And then, from the town itself, there are walks of two, three, or four hours which, I think, are unsurpassed for wild and sometimes startling beauties. One gets into little valleys, green as emeralds, and surrounded on all sides by grey broken rocks, in which Italian Rasselases must have lived in perfect bliss; and then again one comes upon distant views up the river courses, bounded far away by the spurs of the Alps, which are perfect, to which the fancy can add no additional charm. Conradi's hotel also is by no means bad, or was not in those days. For my part I am inclined to think that Italian hotels have received a worse name than they deserve; and I must profess, that, looking merely to creature comforts, I would much sooner stay a week at the Golden Key at Chiavenna, than with mine host of the King's Head in the thriving commercial town of Muddleboro', on the borders of Yorkshire and Lancashire.

I am always rather keen about my room in travelling, and having secured a chamber looking out upon the mountains, had re-

29

turned to the courtyard to collect my baggage, before Mr. Greene had succeeded in realizing his position or understanding that he had to take upon himself the duties of settling his family for the night in the hotel by which he was surrounded. When I descended he was stripping off the outermost of three greatcoats, and four waiters around him were beseeching him to tell them what accommodation he would require. Mrs. Greene was giving sundry very urgent instructions to the conductor respecting her boxes, but as these were given in English, I was not surprised to find that they were not accurately followed. The man, however, was much too courteous to say in any language that he did not understand every word that was said to him. Miss Greene was standing apart, doing nothing. As she was only eighteen years of age, it was of course her business to do nothing: and a very pretty girl she was, by no means ignorant of her own beauty, and possessed of quite sufficient art to enable her to make the most of it.

Mr. Greene was very leisurely in his proceedings, and the four waiters were almost reduced to despair.

"I want two bed-rooms, a dressing-room, and some dinner," he said at last, speaking very slowly, and in his own vernacular.

I could not in the least assist him by translating it into Italian, for I did not speak a word of the language myself; but I suggested that the men would understand French. The waiter, however, had understood English; waiters do understand all languages with a facility that is marvellous, and this one now suggested that Mrs. Greene should follow him upstairs. Mrs. Greene, however, would not move till she had seen that her boxes were all right, and as Mrs. Greene was also a pretty woman, I found myself bound to apply myself to her assistance.

"Oh, thank you," said she; "the people are so stupid that one can really do nothing with them. And as for Greene, he is of no use at all; for, see that box — the smaller one — I have four hundred pounds' worth of jewellery in that, and, therefore, I am obliged to look after it."

"Indeed!" said I, rather startled at this amount of confidence on rather a short acquaintance. "In that case I do not wonder at your being careful. But is it not rather rash? Perhaps —"

"I know what you are going to say. Well, perhaps it is rash; but when you are going to foreign courts, what are you to do? If you have got those sort of things you must wear them."

As I was not myself possessed of any things of that sort, and had no intention of going to any foreign court, I could not argue the matter with her; but I assisted her in getting together an enormous pile of luggage, among which there were seven large boxes covered with canvas, such as ladies not uncommonly carry with them when travelling. That one which she represented as being smaller than the others, and as holding her jewellery, might be about a yard long by a foot and a-half deep. Being ignorant in those matters, I should have thought it sufficient to carry all a lady's wardrobe for twelve months. When the boxes were collected together, she sat down upon the jewel-case and looked up into my face. She was a pretty woman, perhaps thirty years of age, with long light yellow hair, which she allowed to escape from her bonnet, knowing, perhaps, that it was not unbecoming to her when thus dishevelled. Her skin was very delicate, and her complexion good. Indeed, her face would have been altogether prepossessing had there not been a want of gentleness in her eyes. Her hands, too, were soft and small, and on the whole she may be said to have been possessed of a strong battery of feminine attractions. She also well knew how to use them.

"Whisper," she said to me, with a peculiar but very proper aspiration on the — "Wh-hisper," and both by the aspiration and the use of the word, I knew at once from what island she had come, "Mr. Greene keeps all his money in this box also, so I never let it go out of my sight for a moment. But, whatever you do, don't tell him that I told you so; he —"

I laid my hand on my heart and made a solemn asseveration that I would not divulge her secret. I need not, however, have troubled myself much on that head, for as I walked upstairs, keeping my eye upon the precious trunk, Mr. Greene addressed me.

"You are an Englishman, Mr. Robinson," said he.

I acknowledged that I was.

"I am another; my wife, however, is Irish. My daughter, by a former marriage, is English also. You see that box there."

"Oh, yes," said I; "I see it." I began to be so fascinated by the box that I could not keep my eyes off it.

"I don't know whether or not it is prudent, but I keep all my money there; my money for travelling, I mean."

"If I were you, then," I answered, "I would not say anything about it to anyone."

"Oh, no, of course not," said he. "I should not think of mentioning it; but those brigands in Italy always take away what you have about your person, but they don't meddle with the heavy luggage."

"Bills of exchange, or circular notes," I suggested.

"Ah, yes; and if you can't identify yourself, or happen to have a head-ache, you can't get them changed. I asked an old friend of mine, who has been connected with the Bank of England for the last fifty years, and he assured me that there was nothing like sovereigns."

"But you never get the value for them."

"Well, not quite. One loses a franc or a franc and a-half. But still, there's the certainty, and that's a great matter. An English sovereign will go anywhere;" and he spoke these words with considerable triumph.

"Undoubtedly, if you consent to lose a shilling on each sovereign."

"At any rate, I have got three hundred and fifty in that box," he said. "I have them done up in rolls of twenty-five pounds each."

I again recommended him to keep this arrangement of his as private as possible — a piece of counsel which I confess seemed to me to be much needed — and then I went away to my own room, having first accepted an invitation from Mrs. Greene to join their party at dinner.

"Do," said she; "we have been so dull, and it will be so pleasant."

I did not require to be much pressed to join myself to a party in which there was so pretty a girl as Miss Greene, and so attractive a woman as Mrs. Greene. I therefore accepted the invitation readily, and went away to make my toilet. As I did so, I passed the door of Mrs. Greene's room, and saw the long file of boxes being borne into the centre of it.

I spent a pleasant evening, with, however, one or two slight drawbacks. As to old Greene himself, he was all that was amiable, but then he was nervous, full of cares, and somewhat apt to be a bore. He wanted information on a thousand points, and did not seem to understand that a young man might prefer the conversation of his daughter to his own. Not that he showed any solicitude to prevent conversation on the part of his daughter. I should have been perfectly at liberty to talk to either of the ladies, had he not wished to engross all my attention to himself. He also had found it dull to be alone with his wife and daughter for the last six weeks.

He was a small, spare man, probably over fifty years of age, who gave me to understand that he had lived in London all his life, and had made his own fortune in the City. What he had done in the City to make his fortune he did not say. Had I come across him there I should no doubt have found him to be a sharp man of business, quite competent to teach me many a useful lesson of which I was as ignorant as an infant. Had he caught me on the Exchange, or at Lloyd's, or in the big rooms of the Bank of England, I should have been compelled to ask him everything. Now, in this little town under the Alps, he was as much lost as I should have been in Lombard-street, and was ready enough to look to me for information. I was by no means chary in giving him my counsel, and imparting to him my ideas on things in general in that part of the world; only I should have preferred to be allowed to make myself civil to his daughter.

In the course of conversation, it was mentioned by him that they intended to stay a few days at Bellaggio, which, as all the world knows, is a central spot on the Lake of Como, and a famous resting place for travellers. There are three lakes, which all meet here, and to all of which we give the name of Como. They are properly called the Lakes of Como, Colico, and Lecco; and Bellaggio is the spot at which their waters join each other. I had half made up my mind to sleep there one night on my road into Italy, and now, on hearing their purpose, I declared that such was my intention.

"How very pleasant!" said Mrs. Greene. "It will be quite delightful to have some one to show us how to settle ourselves, for really—"

"My dear, I'm sure you can't say that you ever have much trouble."

"And who does then, Mr. Greene? I'm sure Sophonisba does not do much to help me."

"You won't let me," said Sophonisba, whose name I had not before heard — her papa had called her Sophy, in the yard of the inn.

Sophonisba Greene! Sophonisba Robinson did not sound so badly in my ears, and I confess that I had tried the names together. Her papa had mentioned to me that he had no other child, and had mentioned also that he had made his fortune.

And then there was a little family contest as to the amount of travelling labour which fell to the lot of each of the party, during which I retired to one of the windows of the big front room in which we were sitting. And how much of this labour there is incidental to a tourist's pursuits! And how often these little contests do arise upon a journey! Who has ever travelled, and not known them? I had taken up such a position at the window as might, I thought, have removed me out of hearing; but nevertheless, from time to time, a word would catch my ears about that precious box.

"I have never taken my eyes off it since I left England," said Mrs. Greene, speaking quick, and with a considerable brogue superinduced by her energy. "Where would it have been at Basle if I had not been looking after it?"

"Quite safe," said Sophonisba; "those large things always are safe."

"Are they, miss? That's all you know about it. I suppose your bonnet-box was quite safe when I found it on the platform at — at — I forget the name of the place?"

"Freidrichshafen," said Sophonisba, with almost an unnecessary amount of Teutonic skill in her pronunciation. "Well, mamma, you've told me of that at least twenty times."

Soon after that the ladies took them to their own rooms, weary with the travelling of two days and a night, and Mr. Greene went fast asleep on the very comfortless chair on which he was seated.

At four o'clock the next morning, we started on our journey. "Early to bed and early to rise is the way to be healthy and wealthy and wise." We all know that lesson, and many of us believe in it. But if the lesson be true, the Italians ought to be the healthiest and wealthiest and wisest of all men and women. Three and four o'clock seems to them quite a natural hour for commencing the day's work. Why we should have started from

Chiavenna at four o'clock, in order that we might be kept waiting for the boat an hour and a-half on the little quay at Colico,
I don't know; but such was our destiny. There we remained for an
hour and a-half, Mrs. Greene sitting pertinaciously on the one
important box. She had designated it as being smaller than the
others, and as all the seven were now ranged in a row, I had an
opportunity of comparing them. It was something smaller, perhaps an inch less high, and an inch and a-half shorter. She was
a sharp woman, and observed my scrutiny.

"I always know it," she said in a loud whisper, "by this little
hole in the canvas;" and she put her finger on a slight rent on
one of the ends. "As for Greene, if one of those Italian brigands
were to walk off with it on his shoulders before his eyes,
he wouldn't be the wiser. How helpless you men are, Mr.
Robinson!"

"It is well for us that we have women to look after us."

"But you have got no woman to look after you; or, perhaps you
have left her behind?"

"No, indeed. I am all alone in the world as yet. But it's not my
own fault. I have asked half-a-dozen."

"Now — Mr. Robinson!"

And in this way the time passed on the quay at Colico, till the
boat came and took us away. I should have preferred to pass my
time in making myself agreeable to the younger lady; but the
younger lady stood aloof, turning up her nose, as I thought, at
her mamma.

I will not attempt to describe the scenery about Colico. The
little town itself is one of the vilest places under the sun, having
no accommodation for travellers, and being excessively unhealthy; but there is very little either north or south of the Alps —
and perhaps I may add very little elsewhere — to beat the beauty
of the mountains which cluster round the head of the lake. When
we had sat upon those boxes for that hour and a-half, we were
taken on board the steamer which had been lying off a little way
from the shore, and then we commenced our journey. Of course
there was a good deal of exertion and care necessary in getting
the packages off from the shore on to the boat; and I observed
that anyone with half an eye in his head might have seen that
the mental anxiety expended on that one box, which was marked

by the small hole in the canvas, far exceeded that which was extended to all the other six boxes.

"They deserve that it should be stolen," I said to myself, "for being such fools." And then we went down to breakfast in the cabin.

"I suppose it must be safe!" said Mrs. Greene to me—ignoring the fact that the cabin waiter understood English, although she had just ordered some veal cutlets in that language.

"As safe as a church!" I replied, not wishing to give much apparent importance to the subject.

"They can't carry it off here!" said Mr. Greene.

But he was innocent of any attempt at a joke, and was looking at me with all his eyes.

"They might throw it overboard," said Sophonisba.

I at once made up my mind that she could not be a good-natured girl.

The moment that breakfast was over Mrs. Greene returned again upstairs, and I found her seated on one of the benches near the funnel, on one of the benches, from which she could keep her eyes fixed upon the box.

"When one is obliged to carry about one's jewels with one, one must be careful, Mr. Robinson," she said to me, apologetically.

But I was becoming tired of the box, and the funnel was hot and unpleasant, therefore I left her.

I had made up my mind that Sophonisba was ill-natured; but, nevertheless, she was pretty, and I now went through some little manoeuvres, with the object of getting into conversation with her. This I soon did, and was surprised by her frankness.

"How tired you must be of mamma and her box!" she said to me.

To this I made some answer, declaring that I was rather interested than otherwise in the safety of the precious trunk.

"It makes me sick," said Sophonisba, "to hear her go on in that way to a perfect stranger. I heard what she said about her jewellery."

"It is natural she should be anxious;" I said, "seeing that it contains so much that is valuable."

"Why did she bring them?" said Sophonisba; "she managed to live very well without jewels till papa married her, about a year

36

since; and now she can't travel about a month without lugging them with her everywhere. I should be so glad if some one would steal them."

"But all Mr. Greene's money is there also."

"I don't want papa to be bothered; but I declare I wish the box might be lost for a day or so. She is such a fool. Don't you think so, Mr. Robinson?"

At this time it was just fourteen hours since first I had made their acquaintance in the yard of Conradi's hotel, and of those fourteen hours some half had been passed in bed. I must confess that I looked on Sophonisba as being almost more indiscreet than her mother-in-law; nevertheless, she was not stupid, and I continued my conversation with her the greatest part of the way down the lake towards Bellaggio.

These steamers, which run up and down the Lake of Como and the Lago Maggiore, put out their passengers at all the towns on the banks of the water by means of small rowing-boats, and the persons who are about to disembark generally have their own articles ready to their hands when their turn comes for leaving the steamer. As we came near to Bellaggio, I looked up my own portmanteau, and pointing to the beautiful wood-covered hill that stands at the fork of the waters, told my friend Greene that he was near his destination.

"I am very glad to hear it," said he, complacently.

But he did not at the moment busy himself about the boxes. Then the small boat ran up alongside the steamer, and the passengers for Como and Milan crowded up the side.

"We have to go in that boat," I said to Greene.

"Nonsense!" he exclaimed.

"Oh, but we have!"

"What! put our boxes into that boat?" said Mrs. Greene. "Oh, dear! Here, boatman; there are seven of these boxes, all in white, like this" — and she pointed to the one that had the hole in the canvas — "make haste; and there are three bags and my dressing-case, and Mr. Greene's portmanteau. Mr. Greene, where is your portmanteau?"

The boatman whom she addressed, no doubt, did not understand a word of English; but, nevertheless, he knew what she meant, and, being well accustomed to the work, got all the luggage together in an incredibly few number of moments.

"If you will get down into the boat," I said, "I will see that the luggage follows you before I leave the deck."

"I wish they would," Sophonisba whispered into my ear.

"I won't stir," she said, "till I see that box lifted down. Take care; you'll let it fall into the lake; I know you will!"

Mr. Greene said nothing; but I could see that his eyes were as anxiously fixed on what was going on as were those of his wife. At last, however, the three Greenes were in the boat, as also were all their packages. Then I followed them, my portmanteau having gone down before me, and we pushed off for Bellaggio. Up to this period most of the attendants around us had understood a word or two of English; but now it would be well if we could find some one to whose ears French would not be unfamiliar. As regarded Mr. Greene and his wife, they, I found, must give up all conversation, as they knew nothing of any language but their own. Sophonisba could make herself understood in French, and was quite at home, as she assured me, in German. And then the boat was beached on the shore at Bellaggio, and we all had to go again to work with the object of getting ourselves lodged at the hotel which overlooks the water.

I had learned before that the Greenes were quite free from any trouble in this respect, for their rooms had been taken for them before they left England. Trusting to this, Mrs. Greene gave herself no inconsiderable airs the moment her foot was on the shore, and ordered the people about as though she were the lady paramount of Bellaggio. Italians, however, are used to this from travellers of a certain description. They never resent such conduct; but simply put it down in the bill with the other articles. Mrs. Greene's words, on this occasion, were innocent enough, seeing that they were English; but had I been that headwaiter who came down to the beach, with his nice black shiny hair, and his napkin under his arm, I should have thought her manner very insolent.

Indeed, as it was, I did think so, and was inclined to be angry with her. She was to remain for some time at Bellaggio, and, therefore, it behoved her, as she thought, to assume the character of the grand lady at once. Hitherto she had been willing enough to do the work; but now she began to order about Mr.

Greene and Sophonisba; and — as it appeared to me — to order me about also! I did not quite enjoy this; so leaving her still among her luggage and satellites, I walked up to the hotel to see about my own bedroom. I had some seltzer-water, stood at the window for three or four minutes, and then walked up and down the room. But still the Greenes were not there. As I had put in at Bellaggio solely with the object of seeing something more of Sophonisba, it would not do for me to quarrel with them, or to allow them so to settle themselves in their private sitting-room that I should be excluded. So I returned again to the road by which they must come up, and met the procession near the house.

Mrs. Greene was leading it with great majesty, the waiter with the shiny hair walking by her side to point out to her the way. Then came all the luggage, each porter carrying a white canvas-covered box. That which was so valuable no doubt was carried next to Mrs. Greene, so that she might at a moment's notice put her eye upon the well-known valuable rent. I confess that I did not observe the hole as the train passed by me, nor did I count the number of boxes. Seven boxes, all alike, are very many; and then they were followed by three other men with the inferior articles — Mr. Greene's portmanteau, the carpet bags, &c. At the tail of the line I found Mr. Green, and behind him Sophonisba.

"All your fatigues will be over now," I said to the gentleman, thinking it well not to be too particular in my attentions to his daughter.

He was panting beneath a terrible great coat, having forgotten that the shores of an Italian lake are not so cold as the summits of the Alps, and did not answer me.

"I'm sure I hope so," said Sophonisba. "And I shall advise papa not to go any further, unless he can persuade Mrs. Greene to send her jewels home."

"Sophy, my dear," he said; "for heaven's sake let us have a little peace since we are here!"

From all which I gathered that Mr. Greene had not been fortunate in his second matrimonial adventure. We then made our way slowly up to the hotel, having been altogether distanced by the porters; and when we reached the house we found that the different packages were already being carried away through the house, some this way and some that. Mrs. Greene, the meanwhile, was talking loudly at the door of her own sitting-room.

"Mr. Greene," she said as soon as she saw her heavily-oppressed spouse — for the noon-day sun was now up — "Mr. Greene, where are you?"

"Here, my dear;" and Mr. Greene threw himself panting into the corner of a sofa.

"A little seltzer-water and brandy," I suggested.

Mr. Greene's inmost heart leapt at the hint, and nothing that his remonstrant wife could say would induce him to move, until he had enjoyed the delicious draught. In the meantime the box with the hole in the canvas had been lost.

Yes; when we came to look into matters, to count the packages, and to find out where we were, the box with the hole in the canvas was not there; or, at any rate, Mrs. Greene said it was not there. I worked hard to look it up, and even went into Sophonisba's bedroom in my search. In Sophonisba's bedroom there was but one canvas-covered box.

"That is my own," said she; "and it is all that I have except this bag."

"Where on earth can it be?" said I, sitting down on the trunk in question.

At the moment I almost thought that she had been instrumental in hiding it.

"How am I to know?" she answered; and I fancied that even she was dismayed. "What a fool that woman is!"

"The box must be in the house," I said.

"Do find it, for papa's sake, there's a good fellow. He will be so wretched without his money. I heard him say that he had only two pounds in his purse."

"Oh, I can let him have money to go on with," I answered, grandly.

And then I went off to prove that I was a good fellow, and searched throughout the house. Two white boxes had by order been left down-stairs, as they would not be needed; and these two were in a large cupboard off the hall, which was used expressly for stowing away luggage. And then there were three in Mrs. Greene's bedroom, which had been taken there as containing the wardrobe which she would require while remaining at Bellaggio.

I searched every one of these myself, to see if I could find the hole in the canvas. But the hole in the canvas was not there, and, let me count as I would, I could make out only six. Now there certainly had been seven on board the steamer, though I could not swear that I had seen the seven put into the small boat.

"Mr. Greene," said the lady, standing in the middle of her remaining treasures, all of which were now open, "you are worth nothing when travelling. Were you not behind?"

But Mr. Greene's mind was full, and he did not answer.

"It has been stolen before your very eyes," she continued.

"Nonsense, mamma," said Sophonisba. "If ever it came out of the steamboat, it certainly came into the house."

"I saw it out of the steamer," said Mrs. Greene, "and it certainly is not in the house. Mr. Robinson, may I trouble you to send for the police? — at once, if you please, sir."

I had been at Bellaggio twice before, but nevertheless I was ignorant of their system of police; and then, again, I did not know what was the Italian for the word.

"I will speak to the landlord," I said.

"If you will have the goodness to send for the police at once, I will be obliged to you." And as she thus reiterated her command, she stamped with her foot upon the floor.

"There are no police at Bellaggio," said Sophonisba.

"What on earth shall I do for money to go on with?" said Mr. Greene, looking piteously up to the ceiling, and shaking both his hands.

And now the whole house was in an uproar, including not only the landlord, his wife and daughters, and all the servants, but also every other visitor at the hotel. Mrs. Greene was not a lady who hid either her glories or griefs under a bushel, and though she spoke only in English she soon made her protestations sufficiently audible. She protested loudly that she had been robbed — and that she had been robbed since she left the steamer. The box had come on shore: of that she was quite certain. If the landlord had any regard either for his own character or for that of his house, he would ascertain, before an hour was over, where it was and who had been the thief. She would give him one hour. And then she sat herself down. But in two minutes she was up again, vociferating her wrongs as loudly as ever. All this was filtered through me and Sophonisba to the waiter in French, and from the waiter to the landlord. But the lady's gestures required no translations to make them intelligible, and the state of her mind was, I believe, perfectly well understood.

Mr. Greene I really did pity. His feeling of dismay seemed to be quite as deep, but his sorrow and solicitude was repressed with more decorum.

"What am I to do for money?" he said. "I have not a shilling to go on with!" And he still looked up at the ceiling.

"You must send to England," said Sophonisba.

"It will take a month," he replied.

"Mr. Robinson will let you have what you want at present," added Sophonisba.

Now I certainly had said so, and had meant it at the time; but my whole travelling store did not exceed forty or fifty pounds, with which I was going on to Venice and then back to England, through the Tyrol. Waiting a month for Mr. Greene's money from England might be more inconvenient to me than even to him. Then it occurred to me that the wants of Mr. Greene's family would be numerous and expensive, and that my small stock would go but a little way among so many. And what, also, if there had been no money and no jewels in that accursed box! I confess that at this moment such an idea did strike my mind. One hears of sharpers on every side committing depredations by means of most singular intrigues and contrivances. Might it not be possible that the whole batch of Greenes belonged to this order of society? It was a base idea, I own; but I confess that I entertained it for a moment.

I retired to my own room for a while, that I might think over all the circumstances. There certainly had been seven boxes, and one had had a hole in the canvas. All the seven had certainly been on board that steamer. To so much I felt that I might safely swear. I had not counted the seven into the small boat, but on leaving the larger vessel I had looked about the deck to see that none of Mr. Greene's trappings were forgotten. If left on the steamer, it had been so left through evil intent on the part of some one there employed. It was quite possible that the contents of the box had been ascertained through the imprudence of Mrs. Greene, and that it had been conveyed away so that it might be rifled at Como. As to Mrs. Greene's assertion that all the boxes had been put into the small boat, I thought nothing of it. The people at Bellaggio could not have known which box to steal, nor had there been time to concoct the plan in carrying the boxes up to the hotel. I came at last to this conclusion: that the missing trunk had either been purloined and carried on to Como — in which case it would be necessary to lose no time in going after it — or that it had been put out of sight in some uncommonly clever way, by the Greenes themselves, as an excuse for borrowing as much money as they could raise, and living without payment of their bills. With reference to the latter hypothesis, I declared to myself that Greene did not look like a swindler; but as to Mrs. Greene! — I confess that I did not feel so confident in regard to her.

Charity begins at home; so I proceeded to make myself comfortable in my room, feeling almost certain that I should not be able to leave Bellaggio on the following morning. I had opened my portmanteau when I first arrived, leaving it open on the floor, as is my wont. Some people are always being robbed, and are always locking up everything, while others wander safe over the world and never lock up anything. For myself I never have a key anywhere, and no one ever purloins from me even a handkerchief. *Cantabit vacuus* — and I am always sufficiently *vacuus*. Perhaps it is that I have not a handkerchief worth the stealing. It is green, heavy-laden, suspicious, mal-adroit persons that the thieves attack. I now found that the accommodating "Boots," who already knew my ways, had taken my portmanteau into a dark recess which was intended to do for a dressing-room, and had there spread my portmanteau open upon some table or stool in the corner. It was a convenient arrangement, and there I left it open during the whole period of my sojourn.

Mrs. Greene had given the landlord an hour to find the box; and during that time the landlord, the landlady, their three daughters, and all the servants in the house certainly did exert themselves to the utmost. Half-a-dozen times they came to my door, but I was luxuriating in a washing-tub, making up for that four-o'clock start from Chiavenna. I opened to them, however; but the box was not there, and so the search passed by. At the end of the hour I went back to the Greenes, according to promise, having resolved that some one must be sent on to Como to look after the missing article.

There was no necessity to knock at their sitting-room door, for it was wide open. I walked in and found Mrs. Greene still engaged in attacking the landlord, while all the porters who had carried the luggage up to the house were standing round. Her voice was loud above the others, but luckily for them all she was speaking English. The landlord, I saw, was becoming sulky. He spoke in Italian, and we none of us understood him. But I gathered that he was declining to do anything further. The box, he was certain, had never come out of the steamer. The "Boots" stood by interpreting into French, and, acting as second interpreter, I put it into English.

"Mr. Greene," said the lady, turning to her husband, "you must go at once to Como."

Mr. Greene, who was seated on the sofa, groaned audibly, but said nothing. Sophonisba, who was sitting by him, beat upon the floor with both her feet.

"Do you hear, Mr. Greene?" said she, turning to him. "Do you mean to allow that vast amount of property to be lost without any effort? Are you prepared to replace my jewels?"

"*Her* jewels!" said Sophonisba, looking up into my face. "Papa had to pay for every stitch she had when he married her."

These last words were so spoken as to be audible only by me; but her first exclamation was loud enough. Were they people for whom it would be worth my while to delay my journey, and put myself to serious inconvenience with reference to money?

A few minutes afterwards, I found myself with Greene on the terrace before the house.

"What ought I to do?" said he.

"Go to Como," said I, "and look after your box. I will remain here and go on board the return steamer. It may, perhaps, be there."

"But I can't speak a word of Italian," said he.

"Take the 'Boots,'" said I.

"But I can't speak a word of French."

And then it ended in my undertaking to go to Como. I swear that the thought struck me that I might as well take my portmanteau with me, and cut and run when I got there. The

Greenes were nothing to me.

I did not, however, do this. I made the poor man a promise, and I kept it. I took merely a dressing-bag, for I knew that I must sleep at Como; and thus resolving to disarrange my plans, I started. I was in the midst of beautiful scenery, but I found it quite impossible to draw any enjoyment from it, from that, or from anything around me. My whole mind was given up to anathemas against this odious box, as to which I had undoubtedly heavy cause of complaint. What was the box to me? I went to Como by the afternoon steamer, and spent a long dreary evening down on the steamboat quays searching everywhere, and searching in vain. The boat by which we had left Colico had gone back to Colico; but the people swore that nothing had been left on board it. It was just possible that such a box might have gone on to Milan with the luggage of other passengers.

I slept at Como, and on the following morning, I went on to Milan. There was no trace of the box to be found in that city. I went round to every hotel and travelling office, but could hear nothing of it. Parties had gone to Venice, and Florence, and Bologna, and any of them might have taken the box. No one, however, remembered it; and I returned back to Como, and thence to Bellaggio, reaching the latter place at nine in the evening, disappointed, weary and cross.

"Has Monsieur found the accursed trunk?" said the Bellaggio "Boots," meeting me on the quay.

"In the name of the —, no. Has it not turned up here?"

"Monsieur," said the "Boots," "we shall all be mad soon. The poor master — he is mad already." And then I went up to the house.

"My jewels!" shouted Mrs. Greene, rushing to me with her arms stretched out, as soon as she heard my step on the corridor.

I am sure that she would have embraced me had I found the box. I had not, however, earned any such reward.

"I can hear nothing of the box either at Como or Milan," I said.

"Then what on earth am I to do for my money?" said Mr. Greene.

I had had neither dinner nor supper, but the elder Greenes did not care for that. Mr. Greene sat silent in despair, and Mrs.

Greene stormed about the room in her anger.

"I am tired, and hungry, and thirsty," said I.

I was beginning to get angry, and to think myself ill used; and that idea as to a family of swindlers became strong again. Greene had borrowed ten napoleons from me before I started for Como, and I had spent above four in my fruitless journey to that place and Milan. I was beginning to fear that my whole purpose as to Venice and the Tyrol would be destroyed, and I had promised to meet friends at Innspruck, who—who were very much preferable to the Greenes. As events turned out, I did meet them. Had I failed in this, the present Mrs. Robinson would not now have been sitting opposite to me.

I went to my room and dressed myself, and then Sophonisba presided over the tea-table for me.

"What are we to do?" she asked me in a confidential whisper.

"Wait for money from England."

"But they will think we are all sharpers," she said; "and, upon my word, I do not wonder at it, from the way in which that woman goes on."

She then leaned forward, resting her elbows on the table, and her face in her hands, and told me a long history of all their family discomforts. Her papa was a very good sort of man, only he had been made a fool of by that intriguing woman who had been left without a sixpence with which to bless herself; and now they had nothing but quarrels and misery. Papa did not always get the worst of it; papa could rouse himself sometimes; only now he was beaten down and cowed by the loss of his money. This whispering confidence was very nice in its way, seeing that Sophonisba was a pretty girl; but the whole matter seemed to be full of suspicion.

"If they didn't want to take you in one way they did in another," said the present Mrs. Robinson, when I told the story to her at Innspruck.

I beg that it may be understood, that at the time of my meeting the Greenes, I was not engaged to the present Mrs. Robinson, and was open to any matrimonial engagement that might have been pleasing to me.

On the next morning after breakfast we held a council of war. I had been informed that Mr. Greene had made a fortune, and

46

was justified in presuming he was a rich man. It seemed to me, therefore, that his course was easy. Let him wait at Bellaggio for more money, and when he returned home let him buy Mrs. Greene more jewels. A poor man always presumes that a rich man is indifferent about his money. But in truth a rich man never is indifferent about his money, and poor Greene looked very blank at my proposition.

"Do you mean to say that it's gone forever?" he asked.

"I'll not leave the country without knowing more about it," said Mrs. Greene.

"It certainly is very odd," said Sophonisba. Even Sophonisba seemed to think that I was too off-hand.

"It will be a month before I can get money, and my bill here will be something tremendous," said Greene.

"I wouldn't pay them a farthing till I get my box," said Mrs. Greene.

"That's nonsense," said Sophonisba. And so it was.

"Hold your tongue, miss!" said the stepmother.

"Indeed, I shall not hold my tongue!" said the stepdaughter.

Poor Greene! He had lost more than his box within the last twelve months; for, as I had learned in that whispered communication over the tea-table with Sophonisba, this was in reality her papa's marriage trip.

Another day was now gone, and we all went to bed. Had I not been very foolish I should have had myself called at five in the morning, and have gone away by the early boat, leaving my ten napoleons behind me. But unfortunately, Sophonisba had exacted a promise from me that I would not do this, and thus all chance of spending a day or two in Venice was lost to me. Moreover, I was thoroughly fatigued, and almost glad of any excuse which would allow me to lie in bed on the following morning. I did lie in bed till nine o'clock, and then found the Greenes at breakfast.

"Let us go and look at the Serbelloni Gardens," said I, as soon as the silent meal was over, "or take a boat over to the Somma-riva Villa."

"I should like it so much," said Sophonisba.

"We will do nothing of the kind till I have found my property," said Mrs. Greene. "Mr. Robinson, what arrangement did you

47

make yesterday with the police at Como?"

"The police at Como!" I said; "I did not go to the police."

"Not go to the police? And do you mean to say that I am to be robbed of my jewels and no effort made for redress? Is there no such thing as a constable in this wretched country? Mr. Greene, I do insist upon it that you at once go to the nearest British consul."

"I suppose I had better write home for money," said he.

"And do you mean to say that you haven't written yet?" said I, probably with some acrimony in my voice.

"You need not scold papa," said Sophonisba.

"I don't know what I am to do," said Mr. Greene — and he began walking up and down the room. But still he did not call for pen and ink, and I began again to feel that he was a swindler. Was it possible that a man of business, who had made his fortune in London, should allow his wife to keep all her jewels in a box, and carry about his own money in the same?

"I don't see why you need be so very unhappy, papa," said Sophonisba. "Mr. Robinson, I'm sure, will let you have whatever money you may want at present." This was pleasant!

"And will Mr. Robinson return me my jewels, which were lost, I must say, in a great measure through his carelessness?" said Mrs. Greene. This was pleasanter.

"Upon my word, Mrs. Greene, I must deny that," said I, jumping up. "What on earth could I have done more than I did do? I have been to Milan, and nearly fagged myself to death."

"Why did not you bring a policeman back with you?"

"You would tell everybody on board the boat what there was in it," said I.

"I told nobody but you," she answered.

"I suppose you mean to imply that I've taken the box," I rejoined. So that on this, the third or fourth day of our acquaintance, we did not go on together quite pleasantly.

But what annoyed me perhaps the most was the confidence with which it seemed to be Mr. Greene's intention to lean upon my resources. He certainly had not written home yet, and had taken my ten napoleons, as one friend may take a few shillings from another when he finds that he has left his own silver on his dressing-table. What could he have wanted of ten napoleons? He had alleged the necessity of paying the porters, but the few francs he had had in his pocket would have been enough for that. And now Sophonisba was ever and again prompt in her assurances that he need not annoy himself about money, because I was at his right hand. I went up-stairs into my own room, and counting all my treasures found that thirty-six pounds and some odd silver was the extent of my wealth. With that I had to go, at any rate, as far as Innspruck, and from thence back to London. It was quite impossible that I should make myself responsible for Greene's bill at Bellaggio.

We dined early, and after dinner, according to a promise made in the morning, Sophonisba ascended with me into the Serbel-loni Gardens, and walked round the terraces on that beautiful hill which commands the view of the Nino Lakes. When we started I confess that I would sooner have gone alone, for I was sick of the Greenes in my very soul. We had had a terrible day. The landlord had been sent for so often, that he refused to show himself again. The landlady, though matrons of that class are al-ways courteous, had been so driven that she snapped her fingers in Mrs. Greene's face. The three girls would not show them-selves. The waiters kept out of the way as much as possible; and the "Boots" in confidence abused them to me behind their back.

"Monsieur," said the "Boots," "do you think there ever was such a box?"

"Perhaps not," said I. And yet I knew that I had seen it.

I would therefore have preferred to walk without Sophonisba, but that now was impossible. So I determined that I would utilise the occasion by telling her of my present purpose. I had resolved to start on the following day, and it was now necessary to make my friends understand that it was not in my power to extend to them any further pecuniary assistance.

Sophonisba, when we were on the hill, seemed to have for-gotten the box, and to be willing that I should forget it also. But that was impossible. When, therefore, she told me how sweet it was to escape from that terrible woman, and leaned on my arm with all the freedom of old acquaintance, I was obliged to cut short the pleasure of the moment.

"I hope your father has written that letter," said I.

"He means to write it from Milan. We know you want to get

on, so we propose to leave here the day after tomorrow."

"Oh!" said I, thinking of the bill immediately, and remembering that Mrs. Greene had insisted on having champagne for dinner.

"And if anything more is to be done about the nasty box, it will be done there," returned Sophonisba.

"But I must go to-morrow," said I, "at five, a.m."

"Nonsense," said Sophonisba. "Go to-morrow, when I — I mean we — are going on the next day?"

"And I might as well explain," said I, gently dropping the hand that was on my arm, "that I find — I find it will be impossible for me — to — to — "

"To what?"

"To advance Mr. Greene any more money just at present." Then Sophonisba's arm dropped all at once, and she exclaimed —

"Oh, Mr. Robinson!"

After all, there was a certain hard, good sense about Miss Greene, which would have protected her from any evil thoughts, had I known all the truth. I found out afterwards that she was a considerable heiress, and, in spite of the opinion expressed by the present Mrs. Robinson when Miss Walker, I do not for a moment think she would have accepted me had I offered to her.

"You are quite right not to embarrass yourself," she said, when I explained to her my immediate circumstances; "but why did you make papa an offer which you cannot perform? He must remain here now till he hears from England. Had you explained it all at first, the ten napoleons would have carried us to Milan." This was all true, and yet I thought it hard upon me.

It was evident to me that Sophonisba was prepared to join her stepmother in thinking that I had ill-treated them, and I had not much doubt that I should find Mr. Greene of the same opinion. There was very little more said between us during the walk, and when we reached the hotel at seven or half-past seven o'clock, I merely remarked that I would go in and wish her father and mother good-bye.

"I suppose you will drink tea with us?" said Sophonisba; and to this I assented.

I went into my own room and put all my things into a portmanteau; for, according to the custom which is invariable in Italy when an early start is premeditated, the "Boots" was imperative in his demand that the luggage should be ready over-night. I then went to the Greenes' sitting-room, and found that the whole party was now aware of my intention.

"So you are going to desert us," said Mr. Greene.

"I must go on upon my journey," I pleaded, in a weak, apologetic voice.

"Go on upon your journey, sir," said Mrs. Greene; "I would not for a moment have you put yourself to inconvenience on our account."

And yet I had already lost fourteen napoleons, and given up all prospect of going to Venice.

"Mr. Robinson is certainly right not to break the engagement with Miss Walker," said Sophonisba. Now I had said not a word about an engagement with Miss Walker, having only mentioned incidentally that she would be one of the party at Innspruck. "But," continued she, "I think he should not have misled us."

And in this way we enjoyed our evening meal.

I was just about to shake hands with them all, previous to my final departure from their presence, when the "Boots" came into the room.

"I'll leave the portmanteau till to-morrow morning," said he.

"All right," said I.

"*Buami*," said he, "there will be such a crowd of things in the hall. The big trunk I will take away now."

"Big trunk! — what big trunk?"

"The trunk with your rug over it, on which the portmanteau stood."

I looked around at Mr., Mrs., and Miss Greene, and saw that they were all looking at me. I looked round at them, and as their eyes met mine I felt that I turned as red as fire. I immediately jumped up and rushed away to my own room, hearing as I went that all their steps were following me. I rushed to the inner recess, pulled down the portmanteau, which still remained in its old place, tore away my own carpet rug which covered the support beneath it, and there saw a white canvas-covered box with a hole in the canvas on the side next to me."

"It is my box," said Mrs. Greene, pushing me away as she hurried up and put her fingers within the rent.

"It certainly does look like it," said Mr. Greene, peering over his wife's shoulder.

"There's no doubt about the box," said Sophonisba.

"Not the least in life," said I, trying to assume an indifferent look.

"*Mon Dieu!*" said the "Boots."

"*Corpo di Baccho!*" exclaimed the landlord, who had now joined the party.

"Oh-h-h-h!" screamed Mrs. Greene; and then she threw herself back on to my bed, and shrieked hysterically.

There was no doubt whatsoever about the facts. There was the lost box, and there it had been during all those tedious hours of unavailing search. While I was suffering all that fatigue in Milan, spending my precious zwanzigers in driving about from one hotel to another, the box had been standing safe in my own room at Bellaggio, hidden by my own rug. And now that it was found, everybody looked at me as though it were all my fault. Mrs. Greene's eyes, when she had done being hysterical, were terrible; and Sophonisba looked at me as though I were a convicted thief.

"Who put the box here?" I said, turning round fiercely upon the "Boots."

"I did," said the "Boots," "by Monsieur's express order."

"By my order?" I exclaimed.

"Certainly," said the "Boots."

"*Corpo di Baccho!*" said the landlord; and he looked at me as though I were a thief. In the meantime the landlady and the three daughters had clustered round Mrs. Greene, administering to her all manner of Italian consolation. The box, and the money, and the jewels, were, after all, a reality; and much incivility can be forgiven to a lady who has really lost her jewels, and has really got them again.

There and then there arose a hurly-burly among us as to the manner in which the odious trunk found its way into my room. Had anybody been just enough to consider the matter coolly, it must have been quite clear that I could not have ordered it there. When I entered the hotel the boxes were already being lugged about, and I had spoken a word to no one concerning them. That traitorous "Boots" had done it — no doubt without malice prepense; but he had done it; and, now that the Greenes were once more known as moneyed people, he turned upon me, and told me to my face that I had desired that box to be taken to my own room as part of my own luggage!

"My dear," said Mr. Greene, turning to his wife, "you should never mention the contents of your luggage to anyone."

"I never will again," said Mrs. Greene, with a meek, repentant air; "but I really thought—"

"One never can be sure of strangers," said Mr. Greene.

"That's true," said Mrs. Greene.

"After all, it may have been accidental," said Sophonisba — on hearing which good-natured surmise both Papa and Mamma Greene shook their suspicious heads.

I was resolved to say nothing then. It was all but impossible that they should really think that I had intended to steal their box; nor, if they did think so, would it have become me to vindicate myself there, before the landlord and all his servants. I stood by, therefore, in silence while two men raised the trunk, and joined the procession which followed it as it was carried out of my room into that of its legitimate owners. Everybody in the house was there by that time; and Mrs. Greene, enjoying her triumph, by no means grudged them the entrance into the sitting-room. She had felt that she was suspected, and now she was determined that the world of Bellaggio should know how much she was above suspicion. The box was put down upon two chairs, the supporters who had borne it retired a pace each, Mrs. Greene then advanced proudly with the selected key, and Mr. Greene stood by her right shoulder, ready to secure his portion of the hidden treasure. Sophonisba was now indifferent, and threw herself on the sofa; while I walked up and down the room thoughtfully, meditating what words I would say when I took my last farewell of the Greenes.

But as I walked I could see what occurred. Mrs. Greene opened the box and displayed to view the ample folds of a huge yellow woollen dressing gown. I could fancy that she would not willingly have exhibited this article of her toilet, had she not felt that its existence would speedily be merged in the presence of the glories which were to follow. This had merely been the padding at the top of the box. Under that lay a long papier maché case, and in that were all her treasures.

"Ah! they are safe," she said, opening the lid and looking upon her tawdry pearls and carbuncles.

Mr. Green, in the meantime, well knowing the passage for his hand, had dived down to the very bottom of the box, and seized hold of a small canvas bag. "It is here," said he, dragging it up; "and, as far as I can tell as yet, the knot has not been untied." Whereupon he sat himself down by Sophonisba, and, employing her to assist in holding them, began to count his rolls. "They are all right," said he, and he wiped the perspiration from his brow.

I had not yet made up my mind in what manner I might best utter my last words among them, so as to maintain the dignity of my character; and now I was standing over against Mr. Greene, with my arms folded on my breast. My arms were folded on my breast, and I had in my face a frown of displeasure, which I am able to assume upon occasions. But I had not yet determined what words I would use. After all, perhaps it might be as well that I should leave them without any last words.

"Greene, my dear," said the lady, "pay the gentleman his ten napoleons."

"Oh! yes, certainly." Whereupon Mr. Greene undid one of the rolls and extracted eight sovereigns. "I believe that will make it right, sir," said he, handing them to me.

I took the gold, slipped it with an indifferent air into my waistcoat pocket, and then refolded my arms across my breast.

"Papa," said Sophonisba, in a very audible whisper, "Mr. Robinson went for you to Como. Indeed, I believe he says he went to Milan."

"Do not let that be mentioned," said I.

"By all means pay him his expenses," said Mrs. Greene. "I would not owe him anything for worlds."

"He should be paid," said Sophonisba.

"Oh! certainly," said Mr. Greene; and he at once extracted another sovereign and tendered it to me in the face of the assembled multitude.

This was too much! "Mr. Greene," said I, "I intended to be of service to you when I went to Milan, and you are very welcome to the benefit of my intentions. The expense of that journey, whatever may be its amount, is my own affair." And I remained standing with my closed arms.

"We will be under no obligation to him," said Mrs. Greene, "and I shall insist on his taking the money."

"The servant will put it on his dressing-table," said Sophonisba; and she handed the sovereign to the "Boots," giving him instructions.

"Keep it to yourself, Antonio," I said; whereupon the man chucked it to the ceiling with his thumb, caught it as it fell, and with a well-satisfied air dropped it into the recesses of his pocket. The air of the Greenes was also well-satisfied, for they felt that they had paid me in full for all my service.

And now, with many obsequious bows and assurances of deep respect, the landlord and his family withdrew from the room. "Was there anything else they could do for Mrs. Greene?" Mrs. Greene was all affability. She had shewn her jewels to the girls, and allowed them to express their admiration in pretty Italian superlatives. There was nothing else she wanted to-night. She was very happy, and liked Bellaggio. She would stay yet a week, and would make herself quite happy. And though none of them understood a word that the other said, each understood that things were now rose-coloured, and so with scrapings, bows, and grinning smiles, the landlord and all his myrmidons withdrew. Mr. Greene was still counting his money, sovereign by sovereign, and I was still standing with my folded arms upon my bosom.

"I believe I may now go," said I.

"Good night," said Mrs. Greene.

"Adieu," said Sophonisba.

"I have the pleasure of wishing you good-bye," said Mr. Greene.

And then I walked out of the room. After all, what was the use of saying anything? And what could I say that would have done me any service? If they were capable of thinking me a thief — which they certainly did — nothing that I could say would remove the impression. Nor, as I thought, was it suitable that I should defend myself from such an imputation. What were the Greenes to me? So I walked slowly out of the room, and never again saw one of the family from that day to this.

As I stood upon the beach the next morning, while my portmanteau was being handed into the boat, I gave the "Boots" five

zwanzigers. I was determined to shew him that I did not conde-
scend to feel anger against him.

He took the money, looked into my face, and then whispered
to me. "Why did you not give me a word of notice beforehand?"
said he, and winked his eye. He was evidently a thief, and took
me to be another; but what did it matter?

I went thence to Milan, in which city I had no heart to look
at anything; thence to Verona, and so over the pass of the Bren-
ner to Innspruck. When I once found myself near to my dear
friends the Walkers, I was again a happy man; and I may safely
declare, that though a portion of my journey was so troublesome
and unfortunate, I look back upon that tour as the happiest and
the luckiest epoch of my life.

"The Man Who Kept His Money in a Box" appeared first in the
November 2 and 9 issues of *Public Opinion: Literary Supplement* for
1861.

An Unprotected Female
at the Pyramids

IN THE HAPPY DAYS WHEN WE were young, no description conveyed to us so complete an idea of mysterious reality as that of an Oriental city. We knew it was actually there, but had such vague notions of its ways and looks! Let any one remember his early impressions as to Bagdad or Grand Cairo, and then say if this was not so. It was probably taken from the "Arabian Nights," and the picture produced was one of strange, fantastic, luxurious houses; of women who were either very young and very beautiful, or else very old and very cunning, but in either state exercising much more influence on life than women in the East do now; of good-natured, capricious, though sometimes tyrannical monarchs; and of life full of quaint mysteries, quite unintelligible in every phasis, and on that account the more picturesque.

And perhaps Grand Cairo has thus filled us with more wonder even than Bagdad. We have been in a certain manner at home at Bagdad, but have only visited Grand Cairo occasionally. I know no place which was to me, in early years, so delightfully mysterious as Grand Cairo.

But the route to India and Australia has changed all this. Men from all countries, going to the East, now pass through Cairo, and its streets and costumes are no longer strange to us. It has become also a resort for invalids, or rather for those who fear that they may become invalids if they remain in a cold climate during the winter months. And thus at Cairo there is always to be found a considerable population of French, Americans, and English. Oriental life is brought home to us, dreadfully diluted by Western customs, and the delights of the "Arabian Nights" are shorn of half their value. When we have seen a thing, it is never so magnificent to us as when it was half unknown.

It is not much that we deign to learn from these Orientals — we who glory in our civilisation. We do not copy their silence or their abstemiousness, nor that invariable mindfulness of his own personal dignity which always adheres to a Turk or to an Arab. We chatter as much at Cairo as elsewhere, and eat as much, and drink as much, and dress ourselves generally in the same old ugly costume. But we do usually take upon ourselves to wear red caps, and we do ride on donkeys.

Nor are the visitors from the West to Cairo by any means confined to the male sex. Ladies are to be seen in the streets, quite regardless of the Mohammedan custom which presumes a veil to be necessary for an appearance in public; and, to tell the truth, the Mohammedans in general do not appear to be much shocked by their effrontery.

A quarter of the town has in this way become inhabited by men wearing coats and waistcoats, and by women who are without veils; but the English tongue in Egypt finds its centre at Shepherd's Hotel. It is here that people congregate who are looking out for parties to visit with them the Upper Nile, and who are generally all smiles and courtesy; and here also are to be found they who have just returned from this journey, and who are often in a frame of mind towards their companions that is much less amiable. From hence, during the winter, a *cortège* proceeds almost daily to the Pyramids, or to Memphis, or to the petrified forest, or to the City of the Sun. And then, again, four or five times a month the house is filled with young aspirants going out to India, male and female, full of valour and bloom; or with others coming home, no longer young, no longer aspiring, but laden with children and grievances.

The party with whom we are at present concerned is not about to proceed further than the Pyramids, and we shall be able to go with them and return in one and the same day.

It consisted chiefly of an English family, Mr. and Mrs. Damer, their daughter, and two young sons — of these chiefly, because they were the nucleus to which the others had attached them-selves as adherents; they had originated the journey, and in the whole management of it Mr. Damer regarded himself as the master.

The adherents were, firstly, M. de la Bordeau, a Frenchman, now resident in Cairo, who had given out that he was in some way concerned in the canal about to be made between the Med-iterranean and the Red Sea. In discussion on this subject he had become acquainted with Mr. Damer; and although the latter gentleman, true to English interests, perpetually declared that the canal would never be made, and thus irritated M. de la Bor-deau not a little — nevertheless, some measure of friendship had grown up between them.

There was also an American gentleman, Mr. Jefferson Ingram, who was comprising all countries and all nations in one grand tour, as American gentlemen so often do. He was young and good-looking, and had made himself especially agreeable to Mr. Damer, who had declared, more than once, that Mr. Ingram was by far the most rational American he had ever met. Mr. Ingram would listen to Mr. Damer by the half-hour as to the virtue of the British Constitution, and had even sat by almost with patience when Mr. Damer had expressed a doubt as to the good working of the United States scheme of policy—which, in an American, was most wonderful. But some of the sojourners at Shepherd's had observed that Mr. Ingram was in the habit of talking with Miss Damer almost as much as with her father, and had argued from that, that fond as the young man was of politics, he did sometimes turn his mind to other things also.

And then there was Miss Dawkins. Now, Miss Dawkins was an important person, both as to herself and as to her line of life, and she must be described. She was, in the first place, an unpro-tected female of about thirty years of age. As this is becoming an established profession, setting itself up as it were in opposition to the old-world idea that women, like green peas, cannot come to perfection without supporting sticks, it will be understood at once what were Miss Dawkins' sentiments. She considered — or at any rate so expressed herself — that peas could grow very well without sticks, and could not only grow thus unsupported, but could also make their way about the world without any incumbrance of sticks whatsoever. She did not intend, she said, to rival Ida Pfeiffer, seeing that she was attached in a moderate way to bed and board, and was attached to society in a manner almost more than moderate; but she had no idea of being prevented from seeing anything she wished to see because she had neither father, nor husband, nor brothers available for the purpose of escort. She was a human creature, with arms and legs, she said; and she intended to use them. And this was all very well; but nevertheless she had a strong inclination to use the arms and legs of other people when she could make them serviceable.

In person Miss Dawkins was not without attraction. I should exaggerate if I were to say that she was beautiful and elegant; but she was good-looking, and not usually ill-mannered. She was tall, and gifted with features rather sharp, and with eyes very bright. Her hair was of the darkest shade of brown, and was always worn in *bandeaux*, very neatly. She appeared generally in black, though other circumstances did not lead one to suppose that she was in mourning; but then, no other travelling costume is so convenient! She always wore a dark broad-brimmed straw hat, as to the ribbons on which she was rather particular. She was very neat about her gloves and boots; and though it cannot be said that her dress was got up without reference to expense, there can be no doubt that it was not effected without considerable outlay, and more than considerable thought.

Miss Dawkins — Sabrina Dawkins was her name, but she seldom had friends about her intimate enough to use the word Sabrina — was certainly a clever young woman. She could talk on most subjects, if not well, at least well enough to amuse. If she had not read much, she never showed any lamentable deficiency; she was good-humoured, as a rule, and could on occasions be very soft and winning. People who had known her long would sometimes say that she was selfish; but with new acquaintances she was forbearing and self-denying.

With what income Miss Dawkins was blessed no one seemed to know. She lived like a gentlewoman, as far as outward appearance went, and never seemed to be in want; but some people would say that she knew very well how many sides there were to

60

a shilling, and some enemy had once declared that she was an "old soldier." Such was Miss Dawkins.

She also, as well as Mr. Ingram and M. de la Bordeau, had laid herself out to find the weak side of Mr. Damer. Mr. Damer, with all his family, was going up the Nile, and it was known that he had room for two in his boat over and above his own family. Miss Dawkins had told him that she had not quite made up her mind to undergo so great a fatigue, but that, nevertheless, she had a longing of the soul to see something of Nubia. To this Mr. Damer had answered nothing but "Oh!" which Miss Dawkins had not found to be encouraging.

But she had not on that account despaired. To a married man there are always two sides, and in this instance there was Mrs. Damer as well as Mr. Damer. When Mr. Damer said "Oh!" Miss Dawkins sighed, and said, "Yes, indeed," then smiled, and betook herself to Mrs. Damer.

Now Mrs. Damer was soft-hearted, and also somewhat old-fashioned. She did not conceive any violent affection for Miss Dawkins, but she told her daughter that "the single lady by herself was a very nice young woman, and that it was a thousand pities she should have to go about so much alone like."

Miss Damer had turned up her pretty nose, thinking, perhaps, how small was the chance that it ever should be her own lot to be an unprotected female. But Miss Dawkins carried her point, at any rate as regarded the expedition to the Pyramids.

Miss Damer, I have said, had a pretty nose. I may also say that she had pretty eyes, mouth, and chin, with other necessary appendages, all pretty. As to the two Master Damers, who were respectively of the ages of fifteen and sixteen, it may be sufficient to say that they were conspicuous for red caps and for the constancy with which they raced their donkeys.

And now the donkeys, and the donkey-boys, and the dragomen were all standing at the steps of Shepherd's Hotel. To each donkey there was a donkey-boy, and to each gentleman there was a dragoman, so that a goodly *cortège* was assembled, and a goodly noise was made. It may here be remarked, perhaps with some little pride, that not half the noise is given in Egypt to persons speaking any other language as is bestowed on those whose vocabulary is English.

This lasted for half-an-hour. Had the party been French, the donkeys would have arrived only fifteen minutes before the appointed time. And then out came Damer *père* and Damer *mère*, Damer *fille* and Damer *fils*. Damer *mère* was leaning on her husband, as was her wont. She was not an unprotected female, and had no desire to make any attempts in that line. Damer *fille* was attended sedulously by Mr. Ingram, for whose demolishment, however, Mr. Damer still brought up, in a loud voice, the fag ends of certain political arguments, which he would fain have poured direct into the ears of his opponent, had not his wife been so persistent in claiming her privileges. M. de la Bordeau should have followed with Miss Dawkins, but his French politeness, or else his fear of the unprotected female, taught him to walk on the other side of the mistress of the party.

Miss Dawkins left the house with an eager young Damer yelling on each side of her; but nevertheless, though thus neglected by the gentlemen of the party, she was all smiles and prettiness, and looked so sweetly on Mr. Ingram when that gentleman stayed a moment to help her to her donkey, that his heart almost misgave him for leaving her as soon as she was in her seat.

And then they were off. In going from the hotel to the Pyramids, our party had not to pass through any of the queer old narrow streets of the true Cairo — Cairo the Oriental. They all lay behind them as they went down by the back of the hotel by the barracks of the Pasha and the College of Dervishes, to the village of old Cairo and the banks of the Nile.

Here they were kept half an hour, while their dragomans made a bargain with the ferryman, a stately *reis*, or captain of a boat, who declared with much dignity, that he could not carry them over for a sum less than six times the amount to which he was justly entitled; while the dragomans, with great energy on behalf of their masters, offered him only five times that sum. As far as the *reis* was concerned, the contest might soon have been at an end, for the man was not without a conscience, and would have been content with five times and a half; but then the three dragomans quarrelled among themselves as to which should have the paying of the money, and the affair became very tedious.

"What horrid, odious men!" said Miss Dawkins, appealing to Mr. Damer. "Do you think they will let us go over at all?"

"Well, I suppose they will; people do get over generally, I believe. Abdallah! Abdallah! why don't you pay the man? That fellow is always striving to save half a piastre for me."

"I wish he wasn't quite so particular," said Mrs. Damer, who was already becoming rather tired; "but I'm sure he's a very honest man in trying to protect us from being robbed."

"That he is," said Miss Dawkins; "what a delightful trait of national character it is, to see these men so faithful to their employers!" And then at last they got over the ferry, Mr. Ingram having descended among the combatants, and settled the matter in dispute by threats and shouts, and an uplifted stick.

They crossed the broad Nile exactly at the spot where the Nilometer, or river gauge, measures from day to day, and from year to year, the increasing or decreasing treasures of the stream, and landed at a village where thousands of eggs are made into chickens by the process of artificial incubation.

Mrs. Damer thought that it was very hard upon the maternal hens — the hens which should have been maternal — that they should be thus robbed of the delights of motherhood.

"So unnatural, you know," said Miss Dawkins; "so opposed to the fostering principles of creation. Don't you think so, Mr. Ingram?"

Mr. Ingram said he didn't know. He was again seating Miss Damer on her donkey, and it must be presumed that he performed this feat clumsily; for Fanny Damer could jump on and off the animal with hardly a finger to help her, when her brother or her father was her escort; but now, under the hands of Mr. Ingram, this work of mounting was one which required considerable time and care. All which Miss Dawkins observed with precision.

"It's all very well talking," said Mr. Damer, bringing up his donkey nearly alongside of that of Mr. Ingram, and ignoring his daughter's presence, just as he would have done that of his boys, or his dog; "but you must admit that political power is more equally distributed in England than it is in America."

"Perhaps it is," said Mr. Ingram, "equally distributed among, we will say, three dozen families," and he made a feint as though to hold in his impetuous donkey, using the spur, however, at the same time on the side that was unseen by Mr. Damer. As he did

so, Fanny's donkey became equally impetuous, and the two can-
tered on in advance of the whole party. It was quite in vain that
Mr. Damer, at the top of his voice, shouted out something about
"three dozen corruptible demagogues." Mr. Ingram found it quite
impossible to restrain his donkey so as to listen to the sarcasm.

"I do believe papa would talk politics," said Fanny, "if he were
at the top of Mont Blanc, or under the falls of Niagara. I do hate
politics, Mr. Ingram."

"I am sorry for that, very," said Mr. Ingram, almost sadly.

"Sorry, why! You don't want me to talk politics, do you!"

"In America, we are all politicians, more or less; and therefore,
I suppose, you would hate us all."

"Well, I rather think I should," said Fanny; "you would be such
bores." But there was something in her eye, as she spoke, which
atoned for the harshness of her words.

"A very nice young man is Mr. Ingram; don't you think so?"
said Miss Dawkins to Mrs. Damer. Mrs. Damer was going along
upon her donkey, not altogether comfortably. She much wished
to have her lord and legitimate protector by her side, but he had
left her to the care of a dragoman, whose English was not intelligible to her, and she was rather cross.

"Indeed, Miss Dawkins, I don't know who are nice and who
are not. This nasty donkey stumbles at every step. There! I know
I shall be down directly."

"You need not be at all afraid of that; they are perfectly safe,
I believe, always," said Miss Dawkins, rising in her stirrup and
handling her reins quite triumphantly. "A very little practice will
make you quite at home."

"I don't know what you mean by a very little practice. I have
been here six weeks. Why did you put me on such a bad donkey
as this?" and she turned to Abdallah, the dragoman.

"Him berry good donkey, my lady; berry good — best of all.
Call him Jack in Cairo. Him go to Pyramid and back, and mind
noting."

"What does he say, Miss Dawkins?"

"He says that that donkey is one called Jack. If so, I've had
him myself many times, and Jack is a very good donkey."

"I wish you had him now with all my heart," said Mrs. Damer.
Upon which Miss Dawkins offered to change, but those perils of

mounting and dismounting were to Mrs. Damer a great deal too severe to admit of this.

"Seven miles of canal to be carried out into the sea, at a minimum depth of twenty-three feet, and the stone to be fetched from Heaven knows where. All the money in France wouldn't do it." This was addressed by Mr. Damer to M. de la Bordeau, whom he had caught after the abrupt flight of Mr. Ingram.

"Den we will borrow a leetle from England," said M. de la Bordeau.

"Precious little, I can tell you. Such stock would not hold its price in our markets for twenty-four hours. If it were made, the freights would be too heavy to allow of merchandise passing through. The heavy goods would all go round; and as for passengers and mails, you don't expect to get them, I suppose, while there is a railroad ready made to their hand?"

"Ve vill carry all your ships through vidout any transportation. Think of that, my friend."

"Pshaw! You are worse than Ingram. Of all the plans I ever heard it is the most monstrous, the most impracticable, the most —" But here he was interrupted by the entreaties of his wife, who had, in absolute deed and fact, slipped from her donkey, and was now calling lustily for her husband's aid. Whereupon Miss Dawkins allied herself to the Frenchman, and listened with an air of strong conviction to those arguments which were so weak in the ears of Mr. Damer. M. de la Bordeau was about to ride across the Great Desert to Jerusalem; and it might perhaps be quite as well to do that with him, as to go up the Nile as far as the second cataract with the Damers.

"And so, M. de la Bordeau, you intend really to start for Mount Sinai?"

"Yes, mees; ve intend to make one start on Monday veek."

"And so on to Jerusalem. You are quite right. It would be a thousand pities to be in these countries, and to return without going over such ground as that. I shall certainly go to Jerusalem myself by that route."

"Vat, mees! you! Vould you not find it too much fatigante?"

"I care nothing for fatigue, if I like the party I am with—nothing at all, literally. You will hardly understand me, perhaps, M. de la Bordeau; but I do not see any reason why I, as a young woman, should not make any journey that is practicable for a young man."

"Ah! dat is great resolution for you, mees."

"I mean as far as fatigue is concerned. You are a Frenchman, and belong to the nation that is at the head of all human civilisation —"

M. de la Bordeau took off his hat, and bowed low, to the peek of his donkey saddle. He dearly loved to hear his country praised — as Miss Dawkins was aware.

"And I am sure you must agree with me," continued Miss Dawkins, "that the time is gone by for women to consider themselves helpless animals, or to be so considered by others."

"Mees Dawkins vould nevere be considered, not in any times at all, to be one helpless animal," said M. de la Bordeau, civilly.

"I do not, at any rate, intend to be so regarded," said she. "It suits me to travel alone; not that I am averse to society; quite the contrary; if I meet pleasant people, I am always ready to join them. But it suits me to travel without any permanent party, and I do not see why false shame should prevent my seeing the world as thoroughly as though I belonged to the other sex. Why should it, M. de la Bordeau?"

M. de la Bordeau declared that he did not see any reason why it should.

"I am passionately anxious to stand upon Mount Sinai," continued Miss Dawkins; "to press with my feet the earliest spot in sacred history, of the identity of which we are certain; to feel within me the awe-inspiring thrill of that thrice sacred hour."

The Frenchman looked as though he did not quite understand her, but he said that it would be *magnifique*.

"You have already made up your party, I suppose, M. de la Bordeau?"

M. de la Bordeau gave the names of two Frenchmen and one Englishman, who were going with him.

"Upon my word, it is a great temptation to join you," said Miss Dawkins, "only for that horrid Englishman."

"Vat, Mr. Stanley?"

"Oh, I don't mean any disrespect to Mr. Stanley. The horridness I speak of does not attach to him personally, but to his stiff, respectable, ungainly, well-behaved, irrational, and uncivilised country. You see I am not very patriotic."

"Not quite so much as my dear friend Mr. Damer."

"Ha! ha! ha! an excellent creature, isn't he? And so they all are, dear creatures. But then they are so backward. They are most anxious that I should join them up the Nile, but —" and then Miss Dawkins shrugged her shoulders gracefully, and, as she flattered herself, like a Frenchwoman. After that they rode on in silence for a few moments.

"Yes, I must see Mount Sinai," said Miss Dawkins, and then sighed deeply. M. de la Bordeau, notwithstanding that his country does stand at the head of all human civilisation, was not courteous enough to declare that if Miss Dawkins would join his party across the desert, nothing would be wanting to make his beatitude in this world perfect.

Their road from the village of the chicken-hatching ovens lay up along the left bank of the Nile, through an immense grove of lofty palm trees, looking out from among which our visitors could ever and anon see the heads of the two great Pyramids; that is, such of them could see it as felt any solicitude in the matter.

It is astonishing how much things lose their great interest as men find themselves in their close neighbourhood. To one living in New York or London, how ecstatic is the interest inspired by these huge structures. One feels that no price would be too high to pay for seeing them, as long as time and distance, and the world's inexorable task-work, forbid such a visit. How intense would be the delight of climbing over the wondrous handiwork of those wondrous architects so long since dead; how thrilling the awe with which one would penetrate down into their interior caves — those caves in which lay buried the bones of ancient kings, whose very names seem to have come to us almost from another world!

But all these feelings become strangely dim, their acute edges wonderfully worn, as the subjects which inspired them are brought near to us. "Ah! so those are the Pyramids, are they?" says the traveller, when the first glimpse of them is shown to him from the window of a railway carriage. "Dear Heaven's sake put the blind down, or we shall be destroyed by the sand." And then the ecstasy and keen delight of the Pyramids has vanished, and forever.

Our friends, therefore, who for weeks past had seen them from a distance, though they had not yet visited them, did not seem to have any strong feeling on the subject as they trotted through the grove of palm-trees. Mr. Damer had not yet escaped from his wife, who was still fretful from the result of her little accident.

"It was all the chattering of that Miss Dawkins," said Mrs. Damer. "She would not let me attend to what I was doing."

"Miss Dawkins is an ass," said her husband.

"It is a pity she has no one to look after her," said Mrs. Damer.

M. de la Bordeau was still listening to Miss Dawkins's raptures about Mount Sinai. "I wonder whether she has got any money," said M. de la Bordeau to himself. "It can't be much, " he went on thinking, " or she would not be left in this way by herself. " And the result of his thoughts was that Miss Dawkins, if undertaken, might probably become more plague than profit. As to Miss Dawkins herself, though she was ecstatic about Mount Sinai — which was not present — she seemed to have forgotten the poor Pyramids, which were then before her nose.

The two lads were riding races along the dusty path, much to the disgust of their donkey-boys. Their time for enjoyment was to come. There were hampers to be opened; and then the absolute climbing of the Pyramids would actually be a delight to them.

As for Miss Damer and Mr. Ingram, it was clear that they had forgotten palm-trees, Pyramids, the Nile, and all Egypt. They had escaped to a much fairer paradise.

"Could I bear to live among Republicans?" said Fanny, repeating the last words of her American lover, and looking down from her donkey to the ground as she did so. "I hardly know what Republicans are, Mr. Ingram."

"Let me teach you," said he.

"You do talk such nonsense. I declare there is that Miss Dawkins looking at us as though she had twenty eyes. Could you not teach her, Mr. Ingram?"

And so they emerged from the palm-tree grove, through a village crowded with dirty, straggling, Arab children, on to the cultivated plain, beyond which the Pyramids stood, now full before them; the two large Pyramids, a smaller one, and the huge sphynx's head all in a group together.

"Fanny," said Bob Damer, riding up to her, "mamma wants you; so toddle back."

"Mamma wants me! What can she want me for now?" said Fanny, with a look of anything but filial duty in her face.

"To protect her from Miss Dawkins, I think. She wants you to ride at her side, so that Dawkins mayn't get at her. Now, Mr. Ingram, I'll bet you half-a-crown I'm at the top of the big Pyramid before you."

Poor Fanny! She obeyed, however; doubtless feeling that it would not do as yet to show too plainly that she preferred Mr. Ingram to her mother. She arrested her donkey, therefore, till Mrs. Damer overtook her; and Mr. Ingram, as he paused for a moment with her while she did so, fell into the hands of Miss Dawkins.

"I cannot think, Fanny, how you get on so quick," said Mrs. Damer. "I'm always last; but then my donkey is such a very nasty one. Look there, now; he's always trying to get me off."

"We shall soon be at the Pyramids now, mamma."

"How on earth I am ever to get back again I cannot think. I am so tired now that I can hardly sit."

"You'll be better, mamma, when you get your luncheon and a glass of wine."

"How on earth we are to eat and drink with those nasty Arab people around us, I can't conceive. They tell me we shall be eaten up by them. But, Fanny, what has Mr. Ingram been saying to you all day?"

"What has he been saying, mamma? Oh! I don't know — a hundred things, I dare say. But he has not been talking to me all the time."

"I think he has, Fanny, nearly, since we crossed the river. Oh, dear! oh, dear! this animal does hurt me so! Every time he moves he flings his head about, and that gives me such a bump." And then Fanny commiserated her mother's sufferings, and in her commiseration contrived to elude any further questioning as to Mr. Ingram's conversation.

"Majestic piles, are they not?" said Miss Dawkins, who, having changed her companion, allowed her mind to revert from Mount Sinai to the Pyramids. They were now riding through cultivated grounds, with the vast extent of the sands of Lybia before them. The two Pyramids were standing on the margin of the sand, with the head of the recumbent sphynx plainly visible between them. But no idea can be formed of the size of this immense figure till it is visited much more closely. The body is covered with sand, and the head and neck alone stand above the surface of the ground. They were still two miles distant, and the sphynx as yet was but an obscure mound between the two vast Pyramids.

"Immense piles!" said Miss Dawkins, repeating her own words.

"Yes, they are large," said Mr. Ingram, who did not choose to indulge in enthusiasm in the presence of Miss Dawkins.

"Enormous! What a grand idea—eh, Mr. Ingram? The human race does not create such things as those now-a-days!"

"No, indeed," he answered; "but perhaps we create better things."

"Better! You do not mean to say, Mr. Ingram, that you are a utilitarian. I do, in truth, hope better things of you than that. Yes! steam mills are better, no doubt, and mechanics' institutes, and penny newspapers. But is nothing to be valued but what is useful?" and Miss Dawkins, in the height of her enthusiasm, switched her donkey severely over the shoulder.

"I might, perhaps, have said also that we create more beautiful things," said Mr. Ingram.

"But we cannot create older things."

"No, certainly; we cannot do that."

"Nor can we imbue what we do create with the grand associations which environ those piles with so intense an interest. Think of the mighty dead, Mr. Ingram, and of their great power when living. Think of the hands which it took to raise those huge blocks—"

"And of the lives which it cost."

"Doubtless. The tyranny and invincible power of the royal architects add to the grandeur of the idea. One would not perhaps wish to have back the kings of Egypt —"

"Well, no; they would be neither useful nor beautiful."

"Perhaps not; and I do not wish to be picturesque at the expense of my fellow-creatures."

"I doubt even whether the kings of Egypt would be picturesque."

"You know what I mean, Mr. Ingram. But the associations of such names, and the presence of the stupendous works with which they are connected, fill the soul with awe. Such, at least, is the effect with mine."

"I fear that my tendencies, Miss Dawkins, are more realistic than your own."

"You belong to a young country, Mr. Ingram, and are naturally prone to think of material life. The necessity of living looms large before you."

"Very large, indeed, Miss Dawkins."

"Whereas with us, with some of us at least, the material aspect has given place to one in which poetry and enthusiasm prevail. To such among us the associations of past times are very dear. Cheops, to me, is more than Napoleon Bonaparte."

"That is more than most of your countrymen can say — at any rate, just at present."

"I am a woman," continued Miss Dawkins.

Mr. Ingram took off his hat in acknowledgement both of the announcement and of the fact.

"And to us it is not given — not given as yet — to share in the great deeds of the present. The envy of your sex has driven us from the paths which lead to honour. But the deeds of the past are as much ours as yours."

"Oh, quite as much."

" 'Tis to your country that we look for enfranchisement from this thraldom. Yes, Mr. Ingram, the women of America have that strength of mind which has been wanting to those of Europe. In the United States woman will at last learn to exercise her proper mission."

Mr. Ingram expressed a sincere wish that such might be the case; and then wondering at the ingenuity with which Miss Dawkins had travelled round from Cheops and his Pyramid to the rights of women in America, he contrived to fall back, under the pretence of asking after the ailments of Mrs. Damer.

And now at last they were on the sand, in the absolute desert, making their way up to the very foot of the most northern of the two Pyramids. They were by this time surrounded by a crowd of Arab guides, or Arabs professing to be guides, who had already ascertained that Mr. Damer was the chief of the party, and were

71

accordingly driving him almost to madness by the offers of their services, and their assurance that he could not possibly see the outside or the inside of either structure, or even remain alive upon the ground, unless he at once accepted their offers made at their own prices.

"Get away, will you?" said he. "I don't want any of you, and I won't have you! If you take hold of me, I'll shoot you!" This was said to one specially energetic Arab, who, in his efforts to secure his prey, had caught hold of Mr. Damer by the leg.

"Yes, yes, I say! Englishman always take me; me — me — me, and than no break him leg. Yes — yes — yes — I go. Master say, yes. Only one leetle ten shilling!"

"Abdallah!" shouted Mr. Damer, "why don't you take this man away? Why don't you make him understand that if all the Pyramids depended on it, I would not give him sixpence!"

And then Abdallah, thus invoked, came up, and explained to the man in Arabic that he would gain his object more surely if he would behave himself a little more quietly: a hint which the man took for one minute, and for one minute only.

And then poor Mrs. Damer replied to an application for backsheish by the gift of a sixpence. Unfortunate woman! The word backsheish means, I believe, a gift; but it has come in Egypt to signify money, and is eternally dinned into the ears of strangers by Arab suppliants. Mrs. Damer ought to have known better, as, during the last six weeks, she had never shown her face out of Shepherd's Hotel without being pestered for backsheish; but she was tired and weak, and foolishly thought to rid herself of the man who was annoying her.

No sooner had the coin dropped from her hand into that of the Arab, than she was surrounded by a cluster of beggars, who loudly made their petitions, as though they would, each of them individually be injured if treated with less liberality than that first comer. They took hold of her donkey, her bridle, her saddle, her legs, and at last her arms and hands, screaming for backsheish in voices that were neither sweet nor mild.

In her dismay, she did give away sundry small coins — all, probably, that she had about her; but this only made the matter worse. Money was going, and each man, by sufficient energy, might hope to get some of it. They were very energetic, and so frightened the poor lady, that she would certainly have fallen, had she not been kept on her seat by their pressure around her.

"Oh, dear! oh, dear! get away," she cried. "I haven't got any more; indeed, I haven't. Go away, I tell you! Mr. Damer, oh, Mr. Damer!" and then, in the excess of her agony, she uttered one loud, long, and continuous shriek.

Up came Mr. Damer; up came Abdallah; up came M. de la Bordeau; up came Mr. Ingram; and at last she was rescued. "You shouldn't go away, and leave me to the mercy of these nasty people. As to that Abdallah, he is of no use to anybody."

"Why you bodder de good lady, you dam blackguard?" said Abdallah, raising his stick, as though he were going to lay them all low with a blow. "Now you get noting, you tief!"

The Arabs for a moment retired to a little distance, like flies driven from a sugar bowl; but it was easy to see that, like the flies, they would return at the first vacant moment.

Our party, whom we left on their road, had now reached the very foot of the Pyramids, and proceeded to dismount from their donkeys. Their intention was first to ascend to the top, then to come down to their banquet, and after that to penetrate into the interior. And all this would seem to be easy of performance. The Pyramid is undoubtedly high, but it is so constructed as to admit of climbing without difficulty. A lady mounting it would undoubtedly need some assistance, but any man possessed of moderate activity would require no aid at all.

But our friends were at once alarmed at the tremendous nature of the task before them. A sheikh of the Arabs came forth, who communicated with them through Abdallah. The work could be done, no doubt, he said; but a great many men would be wanted to assist. Each lady must have four Arabs, and each gentleman three; and then, seeing that the work would be peculiarly severe on this special day, each of these numerous Arabs must be remunerated by some very large number of piastres.

Mr. Damer, who was by no means a close man in his money dealings, opened his eyes with surprise, and mildly expostulated; M. de la Bordeau, who was rather a close man in his reckonings, immediately buttoned up his breeches pocket, and declared that he should decline to mount the Pyramid at all at that price; and then Mr. Ingram descended to the combat.

The protestations of the men were fearful. They declared with loud voices, eager actions, and manifold English oaths, that an attempt was being made to rob them. They had a right to demand the sums which they were charging, and it was a shame that English gentlemen should come and take the bread out of their mouths. And so they screeched, gesticulated, and swore, and frightened poor Mrs. Damer almost into fits.

But at last it was settled, and away they started, the sheikh declaring that the bargain had been made at so low a rate as to leave him not one piastre for himself. Each man had an Arab on each side of him, and Miss Dawkins and Miss Damer had each in addition one behind. Mrs. Damer was so frightened as altogether to have lost all ambition to ascend. She sat below on a fragment of stone, with the three dragomans standing around her as guards; but even with the three dragomans the attacks on her were frequent; and as she declared afterwards, she was so bewildered, that she never had time to remember that she had come there from England to see the Pyramids, and that she was now immediately under them.

The boys, utterly ignoring their guards, scrambled up quicker than the Arabs could follow them. Mr. Damer started off at a pace which soon brought him to the end of his tether, and from that point was dragged up by the sheer strength of his assistants; thereby accomplishing the wishes of the men, who induce their victims to start as rapidly as possible, in order that they may soon find themselves helpless from want of wind. Mr. Ingram endeavoured to attach himself to Fanny, and she would have been nothing loth to have had him at her right hand, instead of the hideous brown, shrieking, one-eyed Arab who took hold of her. But it was soon found that any such arrangement was impossible. Each guide felt that if he lost his own peculiar hold he would lose his prey, and held on, therefore, with invincible tenacity. Miss Dawkins looked, too, as though she ought to be attended by some Christian cavalier, but no Christian cavalier was forthcoming. M. de la Bordeau was the wisest, for he took the matter quietly, did as he was bid, and allowed the guides nearly to carry him to the top of the edifice.

"Ha! so this is the top of the Pyramid, is it?" said Mr. Damer, bringing out his words one by one, being terribly out of breath.

"Very wonderful, very wonderful indeed!"

"It is wonderful!" said Miss Dawkins, whose breath had not failed her in the least, "very wonderful indeed! Only think, Mr. Damer, you might travel on for days and days, till days became months, through those interminable sands, and yet you would never come to the end of them! Is it not quite stupendous?"

"Ah, yes, quite," — puff, puff — said Mr. Damer, striving to regain his breath.

Mr. Damer was now at her disposal — weak, and worn with toil and travel, out of breath, and with half his manhood gone; if ever she might prevail over him so as to procure from his mouth an assent to that Nile proposition, it would be now. And after all, that Nile proposition was the best one now before her. She did not quite like the idea of starting off across the Great Desert without any lady, and was not sure that she was prepared to be fallen in love with by M. de la Bordeau, even if there should ultimately be any readiness on the part of that gentleman to perform the *rôle* of lover. With Mr. Ingram the matter was different; nor was she so diffident of her own charms as to think it altogether impossible that she might succeed, in the teeth of that little chit, Fanny Damer. That Mr. Ingram would join the party up the Nile she had very little doubt; and then there would be one place left for her. She would thus, at any rate, become commingled with a most respectable family, who might be of material service to her.

Thus actuated, she commenced an earnest attack upon Mr. Damer.

"Stupendous!" she said again, for she was fond of repeating favourite words. "What a wondrous race must have been those Egyptian kings of old!"

"I dare say they were," said Mr. Damer, wiping his brow as he sat upon a large loose stone, a fragment lying on the flat top of the Pyramid, one of those stones with which the complete apex was once made, or was once about to be made.

"A magnificent race! so gigantic in their conceptions! Their ideas altogether overwhelm us, poor, insignificant, latter-day mortals. They built these vast Pyramids; but for us, it is task enough to climb to their top."

"Quite enough," ejaculated Mr. Damer.

But Mr. Damer would not always remain weak and out of breath, and it was absolutely necessary for Miss Dawkins to hurry away from Cheops and his tomb, to Thebes and Karnac.

"After seeing this it is impossible for any one, with a spark of imagination, to leave Egypt without going further a-field."

Mr. Damer merely wiped his brow and grunted. This Miss Dawkins took as a signal of weakness, and went on with her task perseveringly.

"For myself, I have resolved to go up, at any rate, as far as Asouan and the first cataract. I had thought of acceding to the wishes of a party who are going across the Great Desert by Mount Sinai to Jerusalem; but the kindness of yourself and Mrs. Damer is so great, and the prospect of joining in your boat is so pleasurable, that I have made up my mind to accept your very kind offer."

This, it will be acknowledged, was bold on the part of Miss Dawkins; but what will not audacity effect? To use the slang of modern language, cheek carries everything now-a-days. And whatever may have been Miss Dawkins' deficiencies, in this virtue she was not deficient.

"I have made up my mind to accept your very kind offer," she said, shining on Mr. Damer with her blandest smile.

What was a stout, breathless, perspiring, middle-aged gentleman to do under such circumstances? Mr. Damer was a man who, in most matters, had his own way. That his wife should have given such an invitation without consulting him, was, he knew, quite impossible. She would as soon have thought of asking all those Arab guides to accompany them. Nor was it to be thought of, that he should allow himself to be kidnapped into such an arrangement by the impudence of any Miss Dawkins. But there was, he felt, a difficulty in answering such a proposition from a young lady with a direct negative, especially while he was so scant of breath. So he wiped his brow again, and looked at her.

"But I can only agree to this on one understanding," continued Miss Dawkins, "and that is, that I am allowed to defray my own full share of the expense of the journey."

Upon hearing this Mr. Damer thought that he saw his way out of the wood. "Wherever I go, Miss Dawkins, I am always the pay-master myself," and this he contrived to say with some sternness, palpitating though he still was; and the sternness which was deficient in his voice he endeavoured to put into his countenance.

But he did not know Miss Dawkins. "Oh, Mr. Damer," she said — and as she spoke her smile became almost blander than it was before — "oh, Mr. Damer, I could not think of suffering you to be so liberal; I could not, indeed. But I shall be quite content that you should pay everything and let me settle with you in one sum afterwards."

Mr. Damer's breath was now rather more under his own command: "I am afraid, Miss Dawkins," he said, "that Mrs. Damer's weak state of health will not admit of such an arrangement."

"What, about the paying?"

"Not only as to that, but we are a family party, Miss Dawkins; and great as would be the benefit to all of us of your society, in Mrs. Damer's present state of health, I am afraid — in short, you would not find it agreeable. And therefore" — this he added, seeing that she was still about to persevere — "I fear that we must forego the advantage you offer."

And then, looking into his face, Miss Dawkins did perceive that even her audacity would not prevail.

"Oh, very well," she said, and moving from the stone on which she had been sitting, she walked off, carrying her head very high, to a corner of the Pyramid from which she could look forth alone towards the sands of Lybia.

In the meantime another little overture was being made at the top of the same Pyramid — an overture which was not received quite in the same spirit. While Mr. Damer was recovering his breath for the sake of answering Miss Dawkins, Miss Damer had walked to the further corner of the square platform on which they were placed, and there sat herself down with her face turned towards Cairo. Perhaps it was not singular that Mr. Ingram should have followed her.

This would have been very well if a dozen Arabs had not also followed them. But as this was the case, Mr. Ingram had to play his game under some difficulty. He had no sooner seated himself beside her than they came and stood directly in front of the seat, shutting out the view, and by no means improving the fragrance of the air around them.

"And this, then, Miss Damer, will be our last excursion," he said, in his tenderest, softest tone.

"De good Englishman will gib de poor Arab one little back-sheesh," said an Arab, putting out his hand and shaking Mr. In-gram's shoulder.

"Yes, yes, yes; him gib backsheesh," said another.

"Him berry good man," said a third, putting up a filthy hand, and touching Mr. Ingram's face.

"And young lady berry good, too; she gib backsheesh to poor Arab."

"Yes," said a fourth, preparing to take a similar liberty with Miss Damer.

This was too much for Mr. Ingram. He had already used very positive language in his endeavour to assure his tormentors that they would not get a piastre from him. But this only changed their soft persuasions into threats. Upon hearing which, and upon seeing what the man attempted to do in his endeavour to get money from Miss Damer, he raised his stick, and struck first one and then another as violently as he could upon their heads.

Any ordinary civilised men would have been stunned by such blows, for they fell on the bare foreheads of the Arabs; but the objects of the American's wrath merely skulked away; and the others, convinced by the only arguments which they understood, followed in pursuit of victims who might be less pugnacious.

It is hard for a man to be at once tender and pugnacious — to be sentimental, while he is putting forth his physical strength with all the violence in his power. It is difficult, also, for him to be gentle instantly after having been in a rage. So he changed his tactics at the moment, and came to the point at once in a man-ner befitting his present state of mind.

"Those vile wretches have put me in such a heat," he said, "that I hardly know what I am saying. But the fact is this, Miss Damer, I cannot leave Cairo without knowing—You understand what I mean, Miss Damer."

"Indeed I do not, Mr. Ingram; except that I am afraid you mean nonsense."

"Yes, you do; you know that I love you. I am sure you must know it. At any rate you know it now."

"Mr. Ingram, you should not talk in such a way."

"Why should I not? But the truth is, Fanny, I can talk in no other way. I do love you very dearly. Can you love me well enough to go and be my wife in a country far away from your own?"

Before she left the top of the Pyramid, Fanny Damer had said that she would try.

Mr. Ingram was now a proud and happy man, and seemed to think the steps of the Pyramid too small for his elastic energy. But Fanny feared that her troubles were to come. There was papa — that terrible bugbear on all such occasions! What would papa say? She was sure her papa would not allow her to marry and go so far away from her own family and country. For herself, she liked the Americans — always had liked them, so she said; would desire nothing better than to live among them. But papa! And Fanny sighed as she felt that all the recognised miseries of a young lady in love were about to fall upon her.

Nevertheless, at her lover's instance, she promised and declared, in twenty different loving phrases, that nothing on earth should ever make her false to her love or to her lover.

"Fanny, where are you? Why are you not ready to come down?" shouted Mr. Damer, not in the best of tempers. He felt that he had almost been unkind to an unprotected female, and his heart misgave him. And yet it would have misgiven him more had he allowed himself to be entrapped by Miss Dawkins.

"I am quite ready, papa," said Fanny running up to him — for it may be understood that there is quite room enough for a young lady to run on the top of the Pyramid.

"I am sure I don't know where you have been all the time," said Mr. Damer; "and where are those two boys?"

Fanny pointed to the top of the other Pyramid, and there they were, conspicuous with their red caps.

"And M. de la Bordeau?"

"Oh! he has gone down, I think — no, he is there with Miss Dawkins." And in truth Miss Dawkins was leaning on his arm most affectionately, as she stooped over and looked down upon the ruins below her.

"And where is that fellow, Ingram?" said Mr. Damer, looking about him. "He is always out of the way when he's wanted."

To this Fanny said nothing. Why should she? She was not Mr. Ingram's keeper.

And then they all descended, each again with his proper number of Arabs to hurry and embarrass him; and they found Mrs. Damer at the bottom, like a piece of sugar covered with flies. She was heard to declare afterwards that she would not go to the Pyramids again, not if they were to be given to her for herself, as ornaments for her garden.

The pic-nic lunch among the big stones at the foot of the Pyramids was not a very gay affair. Miss Dawkins talked more than any one else, being determined to show that she bore her defeat gallantly. Her conversation, however, was chiefly addressed to M. de la Bordeau, and he seemed to think more of his cold chicken and ham than he did of her wit and attention.

Fanny hardly spoke a word. There was her father before her, and she could not eat, much less talk, as she thought of all that she would have to go through. What would he say to the idea of having an American son-in-law?

Nor was Mr. Ingram very lively. A young man, when he has been just accepted, never is so. His happiness under the present circumstances was, no doubt, intense, but it was of a silent nature.

And then the interior of the building had to be visited. To tell the truth, none of the party would have cared to perform this feat, had it not been for the honour of the thing. To have come from Paris, New York, or London, to the Pyramids, and then not to have visited the very tomb of Cheops, would have shown on the part of all of them an indifference to subjects of interest which would have been altogether fatal to their character as travellers. And so a party for the interior was made up.

Miss Damer, when she saw the aperture through which it was expected that she should descend, at once declared for staying with her mother. Miss Dawkins, however, was enthusiastic for the journey. "Persons with so very little command over their nerves might really as well stay at home," she said to Mr. Ingram, who glowered at her dreadfully for expressing such an opinion about his Fanny.

This entrance into the Pyramids is a terrible task, which should be undertaken by no lady. Those who perform it have to creep down, and then to be dragged up through infinite dirt, foul smells, and bad air; and when they have done it, they see nothing. But they do earn the gratification of saying that they have been inside a Pyramid.

"Well, I've done that once," said Mr. Damer, coming out, "and I do not think that anyone will catch me doing it again. I never was in such a filthy place in my life."

"Oh, Fanny! I am so glad you did not go; I am sure it is not fit for ladies," said poor Mrs. Damer, forgetful of her friend Miss Dawkins.

"I should have been ashamed of myself," said Miss Dawkins, bristling up, and throwing back her head as she stood, "if I had allowed any consideration to have prevented my visiting such a spot. If it be not improper for men to go there, how can it be improper for women?"

"I did not say improper, my dear," said Mrs. Damer, apologetically.

"And as for the fatigue, what can a woman be worth who is afraid to encounter as much as I have now gone through for the sake of visiting the last resting-place of such a king as Cheops?" And Miss Dawkins, as she pronounced the last words, looked round her with disdain upon poor Fanny Damer.

"But I meant the dirt," said Mrs. Damer.

"Dirt!" ejaculated Miss Dawkins, and then walked away. Why should she now submit her high tone of feeling to the Damers, or why care longer for their good opinion? Therefore she scattered contempt around her as she ejaculated the last word, "dirt."

"And then the return home! I know I shall never get there," said Mrs. Damer, looking piteously up into her husband's face.

"Nonsense, my dear; nonsense; you must get there." Mrs. Damer groaned, and acknowledged in her heart that she must — either dead or alive.

"And, Jefferson," said Fanny, whispering — for there had been a moment since their descent in which she had been instructed to call him by his Christian name — "never mind talking to me going home. I will ride by mamma. Do you go with papa, and put him in a good humour; and if he says anything about the lords and the bishops, don't you contradict him, you know."

What will not a man do for love? Mr. Ingram promised. And in this way they started: the two boys led the van; then came Mr. Damer and Mr. Ingram, unusually and unpatriotically acquiescent as to England's aristocratic propensities; then Miss Dawkins, riding, alas! alone; after her, M. de la Bordeau, also alone—the ungallant Frenchman! And the rear was brought up by Mrs. Damer and her daughter, flanked on each side by a dragoman, with a third dragoman behind him.

And in this order they went back to Cairo, riding their donkeys and crossing the ferry solemnly, and, for the most part, silently. Mr. Ingram did talk, as he had an important object in view—that of putting Mr. Damer into a good humour.

In this he succeeded so well, that, by the time they had remounted, after crossing the Nile, Mr. Damer opened his heart to his companion on the subject that was troubling him, and told him all about Miss Dawkins.

"I don't see why we should have a companion that we don't like for eight or ten weeks, merely because it seems rude to refuse a lady."

"Indeed, I agree with you," said Mr. Ingram; "I should call it weak-minded to give way in such a case."

"My daughter does not like her at all," continued Mr. Damer.

"Nor would she be a nice companion for Miss Damer; not according to my way of thinking," said Mr. Ingram.

"And as to my having asked her, or Mrs. Damer having asked her — why, God bless my soul, it is pure invention on the woman's part!"

"Ha! ha! ha!" laughed Mr. Ingram; "I must say she plays her game well; but then she is an old soldier, and has the benefit of experience." What would Miss Dawkins have said had she known that Mr. Ingram called her an old soldier?

"I don't like the kind of thing at all," said Mr. Damer, who was very serious upon the subject. "You see the position in which I am placed. I am forced to be very rude, or —"

"I don't call it rude at all."

"Disobliging, then; or else I must have all my comfort invaded and pleasure destroyed by, by, by —" And Mr. Damer paused, being at a loss for an appropriate name for Miss Dawkins."

"By an unprotected female," suggested Mr. Ingram.

"Yes; just so. I am as fond of pleasant company as anybody; but then I like to choose it myself."

"So do I," said Mr. Ingram, thinking of his own choice.

"Now, Ingram, if you would join us, we should be delighted."

"Upon my word, sir, the offer is too flattering," said Ingram, hesitatingly; for he felt that he could not undertake such a journey until Mr. Damer knew on what terms he stood with Fanny.

"You are a terrible democrat," said Mr. Damer, laughing; "but then, on that matter, you know, we could agree to differ."

"Exactly so," said Mr. Ingram, who had not collected his thoughts or made up his mind as to what he had better say and do, on the spur of the moment.

"Well, what do you say to it?" said Mr. Damer, encouragingly. But Ingram paused before he answered.

"For Heaven's sake, my dear fellow, don't have the slightest hesitation in refusing, if you don't like the plan."

"The fact is, Mr. Damer, I should like it too well."

"Like it too well?"

"Yes, sir, and I may as well tell you now as later. I had intended this evening to have asked for your permission to address your daughter."

"God bless my soul!" said Mr. Damer, looking as though a totally new idea had now been opened to him.

"And under these circumstances, I will now wait and see whether or not you will renew your offer."

"God bless my soul!" said Mr. Damer again. It often does strike an old gentleman as very odd that any man should fall in love with his daughter, whom he has not ceased to look upon as a child. The case is generally quite different with mothers. They seem to think that every young man must fall in love with their girls.

"And have you said anything to Fanny about this?" asked Mr. Damer.

"Yes, sir; I have her permission to speak to you."

"God bless my soul!" said Mr. Damer; and by this time they had arrived at Shepherd's Hotel.

"Oh, mamma," said Fanny, as soon as she found herself alone with her mother that evening, "I have something that I must tell you."

"Oh, Fanny, don't tell me anything to-night, for I am a great deal too tired to listen."

"But oh, mamma, pray — you must listen to this; indeed you

must." And Fanny knelt down at her mother's knee, and looked beseechingly up into her face.

"What is it, Fanny? You know that all my bones are sore, and that I am so tired that I am almost dead."

"Mamma, Mr. Ingram has —"

"Has what, my dear? has he done anything wrong?"

"No, mamma; but he has — he has proposed to me." And Fanny, bursting into tears, hid her face in her mother's lap.

And thus the story was told on both sides of the house. On the next day, as a matter of course, all the difficulties and dangers of such a marriage as that which was now projected, were insisted on by both father and mother. It was improper; it would cause a severing of the family not to be thought of; it would be an alliance of a dangerous nature, and not at all calculated to insure happiness; and, in short, it was impossible. On that day, therefore, they all went to bed very unhappy. But on the next day, as was also a matter of course, seeing that there were no pecuniary difficulties, the mother and father were talked over, and Mr. Ingram was accepted as a son-in-law. It need hardly be said that the offer of a place in Mr. Damer's boat was again made, and that on this occasion it was accepted without hesitation.

There was an American Protestant clergyman resident in Cairo, with whom among other persons, Miss Dawkins had become acquainted. Upon this gentleman, or upon his wife, Miss Dawkins called a few days after the journey to the Pyramids, and finding him in his study, thus performed her duty to her neighbour:

"You know your countryman, Mr. Ingram, I think?" said she.

"Oh, yes; very intimately."

"If you have any regard for him, Mr. Burton," such was the gentleman's name, "I think you should put him on his guard."

"On his guard against what?" said Mr. Burton, with a serious air, for there was something solemn in the threat of impending misfortune as conveyed by Miss Dawkins.

"Why," said she, "those Damers, I fear, are dangerous people."

"Do you mean that they will borrow money of him?"

"Oh, no; not that exactly; but they are clearly setting their cap at him."

"Setting their cap at him?"

"Yes; there is a daughter, you know; a little chit of a thing; and I fear Mr. Ingram may be caught before he knows where he is. It would be such a pity, you know. He is going up the river with them, I hear. That, in his place, is very foolish. They asked me, but I positively refused."

Mr. Burton remarked that "in such a matter as that Mr. Ingram would be perfectly able to take care of himself."

"Well, perhaps so; but seeing what was going on, I thought it my duty to tell you." And so Miss Dawkins took her leave.

Mr. Ingram did go up the Nile with the Damers, as did an old friend of the Damers who arrived from England. And a very pleasant trip they had of it. And as far as the present historian knows, the two lovers were shortly afterwards married in England.

Poor Miss Dawkins was left in Cairo for some time on her beam ends. But she was one of those who are not easily vanquished. After an interval of ten days she made acquaintance with an Irish family — having utterly failed in moving the hard heart of M. de la Bordeau — and with them she proceeded to Constantinople. They consisted of two brothers and a sister, and were, therefore, very convenient for matrimonial purposes. But, nevertheless, when I last heard of Miss Dawkins, she was still an unprotected female.

"An Unprotected Female at the Pyramids" appeared first in the October 6 and 11 issues of *Cassell's Illustrated Family Paper* for 1860.

Relics of General Chassé:
A Tale of Antwerp

HAT BELGIUM IS NOW ONE OF the European kingdoms, living by its own laws, resting on its own bottom, with a King and Court, palaces and Parliament of its own, is known to all the world. And a very nice little kingdom it is; full of old towns, fine Flemish pictures, and interesting Gothic churches. But in the memory of very many of us, who do not think ourselves old men, Belgium, as it is now called — in those days it used to be Flanders and Brabant — was a part of Holland; and it obtained its own independence by a revolution. In that revolution the most important military step was the siege of Antwerp, which was defended, on the part of the Dutch, by General Chassé, with the utmost gallantry, but nevertheless ineffectually.

After the siege Antwerp became quite a show place; and among the visitors who flocked there to talk of the gallant general, and to see what remained of the great effort which he had made to defend the place, were two Englishmen. One was the hero of this little history; and the other was a young man of considerable less weight in the world. The less I say of the latter the better; but it is necessary that I should give some description of the former.

The Rev. Augustus Horne was, at the time of my narrative, a beneficed clergyman of the Church of England. The profession which he had graced sat easily on him. Its external marks and signs were as pleasing to his friends as were its internal comforts to himself. He was a man of much quiet mirth, full of polished wit, and on some rare occasions he could descend to the more noisy hilarity of a joke. Loved by his friends, he loved all the world. He had known no care and seen no sorrow. Always intended for holy orders, he had entered them without a scruple, and remained within their pale without a regret. At twenty-four he had been a deacon, at twenty-seven a priest, at thirty a rector, and at thirty-five a prebendary; and as his rectory was rich and his prebendal stall well paid, the Rev. Augustus Horne was called by all, and called himself, a happy man. His stature was about six feet two, and his corpulence exceeded those bounds which symmetry would have preferred as being most perfectly compatible even with such a height. But nevertheless Mr. Horne was a well-made man; his hands and feet were small; his face was handsome, frank, and full of expression; his bright eyes twinkled with humor; his finely-cut mouth disclosed two marvelous rows of well-preserved ivory; and his slightly aquiline nose was just such a projection as one would wish to see on the face of a well-fed, good-natured dignitary of the Church of England. When I add to all this that the reverend gentleman was as generous as he was rich — and the kind mother in whose arms he had been nurtured had taken care that he should never want — I need hardly say that I was blessed with a very pleasant travelling companion.

I must mention one more interesting particular. Mr. Horne was rather inclined to dandyism, in an innocent way. His clerical starched neckcloth was always of the whitest, his cambric handkerchief of the finest, his bands adorned with the broadest border; his sable suit never degenerated to a rusty brown; it not only gave, on all occasions, glossy evidence of freshness, but also of the talent which the artisan had displayed in turning out a well-dressed clergyman of the Church of England. His hair was ever brushed with scrupulous attention, and showed in its regular waves the guardian care of each separate bristle. And all this was done with that ease and grace which should be the characteristics of a dignitary of the established English Church.

I had accompanied Mr. Horne to the Rhine; and we had reached Brussels on our return, just at the close of that revolution which ended in affording a throne to the son-in-law of George the Fourth. At that moment General Chassé's name and fame were in every man's mouth, and, like other curious admirers of the brave, Mr. Horne determined to devote two days to the scene of the late events at Antwerp. Antwerp, moreover, possesses perhaps the finest spire, and certainly one of the three or four finest pictures, in the world. Of General Chassé, of the Cathedral, and of the Rubens, I had heard much, and was therefore well pleased that such should be his resolution. This accomplished, we were to return to Brussels; and thence, *via* Ghent, Ostend, and Dover, I to complete my legal studies in London, and Mr. Horne to enjoy once more the peaceful retirement of Ollerton rectory. As we were to be absent but one night we were enabled to indulge in the gratification of travelling without our luggage. A small *sac-de-nuit* was prepared; brushes, combs, razors, strops, a change of linen, etc., etc., were carefully put up; but our heavy baggage, our coats, waistcoats, and other wearing apparel, were unnecessary. It was delightful to feel one's self so light-handed. The reverend gentleman, with my humble self by his side, left the portal of the Hôtel de Belle Vue at 7 A.M., in good humor with all the world. There were no railroads in those days; but a cabriolet, big enough to hold six persons, with rope traces and corresponding appendages, deposited us at the Golden Fleece in something less than six hours. The inward man was duly fortified, and we started for the castle.

It boots not here to describe the effects which gunpowder and grape-shot had had on the walls of Antwerp. Let the curious in these matters read the horrors of the siege of Troy, or the history of Jerusalem taken by Titus. The one may be found in Homer, and the other in Josephus. Or if they prefer doings of a later date, there is the taking of Sebastopol, as narrated in the columns of the English *Times* newspaper. The accounts are equally true, instructive, and intelligible. In the mean time, allow the Rev. Augustus Horne and myself to enter the private chambers of the renowned though defeated general.

We rambled for a while through the covered way, over the glacis and along the counterscarp, and listened to the guide as he detailed to us, in already accustomed words, how the siege had gone. Then we got into the private apartments of the General, and having dexterously shaken off our attendant, wandered at large among the deserted rooms.

"It is clear that no one ever comes here," said I.

"No," said the Rev. Augustus; "it seems not: and, to tell the truth, I don't know why any one should come. The chambers in themselves are not attractive."

What he said was true. They were plain, ugly, square, unfurnished rooms, here a big one and there a little one, as is usual in most houses — unfurnished, that is, for the most part. In one place we did find a table and a few chairs, in another a bedstead, and so on. But to me it was pleasant to indulge in those ruminations which any traces of the great or unfortunate create in softly sympathizing minds. For a time we communicated our thoughts to each other as we roamed free as air through the apartments; and then I lingered for a few moments behind, while Mr. Horne moved on with a quicker step.

At last I entered the bedchamber of the General, and there I overtook my friend. He was inspecting, with much attention, an article of the great man's wardrobe which he held in his hand. It was precisely that virile habiliment to which a well-known gallant captain alludes, in his conversation with the posthumous appearance of Miss Bayley, as containing a Bank of England £5 note.

"The General must have been a large man, George, or he would hardly have filled these," said Mr. Horne, holding up to the light the respectable leathern articles in question. "He must have been a very large man — the largest man in Antwerp, I should think; or else his tailor has done him more than justice."

They were certainly large, and had about them a charming regimental military appearance. They were made of white leather, with bright metal buttons at the knees, and bright metal buttons at the top. They owned no pockets, and were, with the exception of the legitimate outlet, continuous in the circumference of the waistband. No dangling strings gave them an appearance of senile imbecility. Were it not for a certain rigidity, sternness, and mental inflexibility — we will call it military ardor with which they were imbued — they would have created envy in the bosom of a fox-hunter.

Mr. Horne was no fox-hunter, but still he seemed to be irresistibly taken with the lady-like propensity of wishing to wear them. "Surely, George," he said, "the General must have been a stouter man than I am"—and he contemplated his own proportions with complacency—"these what's-the-names are quite big enough for me."

I differed in opinion; and was obliged to explain that I thought he did the good living of Ollerton insufficient justice.

"I am sure they are large enough for me," he repeated, with considerable obstinacy. I smiled incredulously; and then, to settle the matter, he resolved that he would try them on. Nobody had been in these rooms for the last hour, and it appeared as though they were never visited. Even the guide had not come on with us, but was employed in showing other parties about the fortifications. It was clear that this portion of the building was left desolate, and that the experiment might be safely made. So the sportive rector declared that he would for a short time wear the regimentals which had once contained the valorous heart of General Chassé.

With all decorum the Rev. Mr. Horne divested himself of the work of the London artist's needle; and, carefully placing his own garments beyond the reach of dust, essayed to fit himself in military garb.

At that important moment — at the critical instant of the attempt — the clatter of female voices was heard approaching the chamber. They must have suddenly come round some passage corner; for it was evident by the sound that they were close upon us before we had any warning of their advent. At this very minute Mr. Horne was somewhat embarrassed in his attempts, and was not fully in possession of his usual active powers of movement, nor of his usual presence of mind. He only looked for escape; and seeing a door partly open he with difficulty retreated through it, and I followed him. We found that we were in a small dressing-room; and as, by good luck, the door was defended by an inner bolt, my friend was able to protect himself.

"There shall be another siege, at any rate as stout as the last, before I surrender," said he.

As the ladies seemed inclined to linger in the room, it became a matter of importance that the above-named articles should fit, not only for ornament but for use. It was very cold, and Mr. Horne was altogether unused to move in a Highland sphere of life. But alas, alas! General Chassé had not been nurtured in the classical retirement of Ollerton. The ungiving leather would stretch no point to accommodate the divine, though it had been willing to minister to the convenience of the soldier. Mr. Horne was vexed and chilled; and throwing the now hateful garments into a corner, and protecting himself from the cold as best he might, by standing with his knees together and his body some-what bent, so as to give the skirts of his coat an opportunity of doing extra duty, he begged me to see if those jabbering females were not going to leave him in peace to recover his own property. I accordingly went to the door, and opening it to a small extent I peeped through.

Who shall describe my horror at the sight which I then saw? The scene, which had hitherto been tinted with comic effect, was now becoming so decidedly tragic that I did not dare at once to acquaint my worthy pastor with that which was occurring — and, alas! had already occurred. Five country women of our own (it was easy to know them by their dress and general aspect) were standing in the middle of the room; and one of them, the centre of the group, the senior harpy of the lot, a maiden lady — I could have sworn to that — with a red nose, held in one hand a huge pair of scissors, and in the other — the already devoted goods of my most unfortunate companion! Down from the waist-band, through that goodly expanse, a fell gash had already gone through and through; and in useless, unbecoming disorder the broadcloth fell pendant from her arm on this side and on that. At that moment I confess that I had not the courage to speak to Mr. Horne — not even to look at him.

I must describe that group. Of the figure next to me I could only see the back. It was a broad back, done up in black silk not of the newest. The whole figure, one may say, was dumpy. The black silk was not long, as dresses now are worn, nor wide in its skirts. In every way it was skimpy, considering the breadth it had to cover; and below the silk I saw the heels of two thick shoes, and enough to swear by of two woolen stockings. Above the silk was a red-and-blue shawl; and above that a ponderous, elaborate brown bonnet, as to the materials of which I should not wish to undergo an examination. Over and beyond this I could only see the backs of her two hands. They were held up as though in won-der at that which the red-nosed holder of the scissors had dared to do.

Opposite to this lady, and with her face fully turned to me, was a kindly-looking, fat, motherly woman, with light-colored hair, not in the best order. She was hot and scarlet with exercise, being perhaps too stout for the steep steps of the fortress; and in one hand she held a handkerchief, with which from time to time she wiped her brow. In the other hand she held one of the extremities of my friend's property, feeling — good, careful soul! — what was the texture of that cloth. As she did so, I could see a glance of approbation pass across her warm features. I liked that lady's face, in spite of her untidy hair, and felt that had she been alone my friend would not have been injured.

On either side of her there stood a flaxen-haired maiden, with long curls, large blue eyes, fresh red cheeks, an undefined lumpy nose, and large good-humored mouth. They were as like as two peas, only that one was half an inch taller than the other; and there was no difficulty in discovering, at a moment's glance, that they were the children of that overheated matron who was feeling the web of my friend's cloth.

But the principal figure was she who held the centre place in the group. She was tall and thin, with fierce-looking eyes, rendered more fierce by the spectacles which she wore; with a red nose, as I have said before; and about her an undescribable something which quite convinced me that she had never known — could never know — aught of the comforts of married life. It was she who held the scissors and the black garments. It was she who had given that unkind cut. As I looked at her she whisked herself quickly round from one companion to the other, triumphing in what she had done, and ready to triumph further in what she was about to do. I immediately conceived a deep hatred for that Queen of the Harpies.

"Well, I suppose they can't be wanted again," said the mother, rubbing her forehead.

"Oh dear no!" said she of the red nose. "They are relics!"

I thought to leap forth; but for what purpose should I have leaped? The accursed scissors had already done their work; and the symmetry, nay, even the utility of the vestment was destroyed.

"General Chassé wore a very good article — I will say that for

93

him," continued the mother.

"Of course he did!" said the Queen Harpy. "Why should he not, seeing that the country paid for it for him? Well, ladies, who's for having a bit!"

"Oh my! you won't go for to cut them up," said the stout back.

"Won't I?" said the scissors; and she immediately made another incision. "Who's for having a bit? Don't all speak at once."

"I should like a morsel for a pin-cushion," said flaxen-haired Miss No. 1, a young lady about nineteen, actuated by a general affection for all sword-bearing, fire-eating heroes. "I should like to have something to make me think of the poor General!"

Snip, snip went the scissors with professional rapidity, and a round piece was extracted from the back of the calf of the left leg. I shuddered with horror; and so did the Rev. Augustus Horne with cold.

"I hardly think it's proper to cut them up," said Miss No. 2.

"Oh, isn't it?" said the harpy. "Then I'll do what's improper!" and she got her finger and thumb well through the holes in the scissors handles. As she spoke, resolution was plainly marked on her brow.

"Well, if they are to be cut up, I should certainly like a bit for a pen-wiper," said No. 2. No. 2 was a literary young lady with a periodical correspondence, a journal, and an album. Snip, snip went the scissors again, and the broad part of the upper right division afforded ample materials for a pen-wiper.

Then the lady with the back, seeing that the desecration of the article had been completed, plucked up heart of courage and put in her little request: "I think I might have a needle-case out of it," said she, "just as a *suvneer* of the poor General" — and a long fragment cut rapidly out of the waistband afforded her unqualified delight.

Mamma, with the hot face and untidy hair, came next. "Well girls," she said, "as you are all served, I don't see why I'm to be left out. Perhaps, Miss Grogram" — she was an old maid, you see — "perhaps, Miss Grogram, you could get me as much as would make a decent-sized reticule."

There was not the slightest difficulty in doing this. The harpy in the centre again went to work, snip, snip, and extracting from the portion of the affairs which usually sustained the greater portion of Mr. Horne's weight two large round pieces of cloth, presented them to the well-pleased matron. "The General knew well where to get a bit of good broadcloth, certainly," said she, again feeling the pieces.

"And now for No. 1," said she whom I so absolutely hated, "I think there is still enough for a pair of slippers. There's nothing so nice for the house as good black-cloth slippers that are warm to the feet and don't show the dirt." And so saying, she spread out on the floor the lacerated remainders.

"There's a nice bit there," said young lady No. 2, poking at one of the pockets with the end of her parasol.

"Yes," said the harpy, contemplating her plunder. But I'm thinking whether I couldn't get leggings as well. I always wear leggings in the thick of the winter." And so she concluded her operations, and there was nothing left but a melancholy skeleton of seams and buttons.

All this having been achieved, they pocketed their plunder and prepared to depart. There are people who have a wonderful appetite for relics. A stone with which Washington had broken a window when a boy — with which he had done so or had not, for there is little difference; a button that was on a coat of Napoleon's or on that of one of his lackeys; a bullet said to have been picked up at Waterloo or Bunker Hill; these, and such like things, are great treasures. And their most desirable characteristic is the ease with which they are attained. Any bullet or any button does the work. Faith alone is necessary. And now these ladies had made themselves happy and glorious with "Relics" of General Chassé cut from the ill-used habiliments of an elderly English gentleman!

They departed at last, and Mr. Horne, for once in an ill humor, followed me into the bedroom — here I must be excused if I draw a veil over his manly sorrow at discovering what fate had done for him. Remember what was his position! unclothed in the castle of Antwerp! The nearest suitable change for those which had been destroyed was locked up in his portmanteau at the Hôtel de Belle Vue in Brussels! He had nothing left to him — literally nothing, in that Antwerp world. There was no other wretched being wandering then in that Dutch town so utterly denuded of the goods of life. For what is a man fit — for what can he be fit — when left in such a position? There are some evils which seem utterly to crush a man; and if there be any misfortune to which a man may be allowed to succumb without imputation on his manliness, surely it is such as this. How was Mr. Horne to return to his hotel without incurring the displeasure of the municipality? That was my first thought.

He had a cloak, but it was at the inn; and I found that my friend was oppressed with a great horror at the idea of being left alone; so that I could not go in search of it. There was an old saying, that no man is a hero, to his *valet de chambre* — the reason doubtless being this: that it is customary for his valet to see the hero divested of those trappings in which so much of the heroic consists. Who reverences a clergyman without his gown, or a warrior without his sword and sabre-tasche? What would even Minerva be without her helmet?

I do not wish it to be understood that I no longer reverenced Mr. Horne because he was in an undress; but he himself certainly lost much of his composed, well-sustained dignity of demeanor. He was fearful and querulous, cold, and rather cross. When, forgetting his size, I offered him my own, he thought that I was laughing at him. He began to be afraid that the story would get abroad, and he then and there exacted a promise that I would never tell it during his lifetime. I have kept my word; but now my old friend has been gathered to his fathers, full of years.

At last I got him to the hotel. It was long before he would leave the castle, cloaked though he was; not, indeed, till the shades of evening had dimmed the outlines of men and things, and made indistinct the outward garniture of those who passed to and fro in the streets. Then, wrapped in his cloak, Mr. Horne followed me along the quays and through the narrowest of the streets; and at length, without venturing to return the gaze of any one in the hotel court, he made his way up to his own bedroom.

Dinnerless and supperless he went to his couch. But when there he did consent to receive some consolation in the shape of mutton cutlets and fried potatoes, a savory omelet, and a bottle of claret. The mutton cutlets and fried potatoes at the Golden Fleece at Antwerp are — or were then, for I am speaking now of well-nigh thirty years since — remarkably good; the claret, also, was of the best; and so, by degrees, the look of despairing dismay

passed from his face, and some scintillations of the old fire returned to his eyes.

"I wonder whether they find themselves much happier for
what they have got?" said he.

"A great deal happier," said I. "They'll boast of those things to
all their friends at home, and we shall doubtless see some account
of their success in the newspapers."

"It would be delightful to expose their blunder—to show them
up. Would it not, George? To turn the tables on them?"

"Yes," said I, "I should like to have the laugh against them."

"So would I, only that I should compromise myself by telling
the story. It wouldn't do at all to have the story told at Oxford
with my name attached to it."

To this also I assented. To what would I not have assented in
my anxiety to make him happy after his misery?

But all was not over yet. He was in bed now, but it was necessary that he should rise again on the morrow. At home, in England, what was required might, perhaps, have been made during
the night; but here, among the slow Flemings, any such exertion
would have been impossible. Mr. Horne, moreover, had no desire to be troubled in his retirement by a tailor.

Now the landlord of the Golden Fleece was a very stout man
—a very stout man indeed. Looking at him as he stood with his
hands in his pockets at the portal of his own establishment, I
could not but think that he was stouter even than Mr. Horne.
But then he was certainly much shorter, and the want of due proportion probably added to his unwieldy appearance. I walked
round him once or twice wishfully, measuring him in my eye, and
thinking of what texture might be the Sunday best of such a man.
The clothes which he then had on were certainly not exactly
suited to Mr. Horne's tastes.

He saw that I was observing him, and appeared uneasy and
offended. I had already ascertained that he spoke a little English.
Of Flemish I knew literally nothing, and in French, with which
probably he was also acquainted, I was by no means voluble. The
business which I had to transact was intricate, and I required the
use of my mother tongue.

It was intricate and delicate, and difficult withal. I began by
remarking on the weather, but he did not take my remarks kindly.

I am inclined to fancy that he thought I was desirous of borrowing money from him. At any rate he gave me no encouragement in my first advances.

"Vat misfortune?" as last he asked, when I had succeeded in making him understand that a gentleman up stairs required his assistance.

"He has lost these things," and I took hold of my own garments. "It's a long story, or I'd tell you how; but he has not a pair in the world till he get back to Brussels — unless you can lend him one."

"Lost hees br——?" and he opened his eyes wide, and looked at me with astonishment.

"Yes, yes, exactly so," said I, interrupting him. "Most astonishing thing, isn't it? But it's quite true."

"Vas hees money in de pocket?" asked my suspicious landlord.

"No, no, no. It's not so bad as that. His money is all right. I had the money luckily."

"Ah! dat is better. But he have lost hees b——?"

"Yes, yes." I was now getting rather impatient. "There is no mistake about it. He has lost them as sure as you stand there." And then I proceeded to explain that as the gentleman in question was very stout, and as he, the landlord, was stout also, he might assist us in this great calamity by a loan from his own wardrobe.

When he found that the money was not in the pocket, and that his bill therefore would be paid, he was not indisposed to be gracious. He would, he said, desire his servant to take up what was required to Mr. Horne's chamber. I endeavored to make him understand that a sombre color would be preferable; but he only answered that he would put the best that he had at the gentleman's disposal. He could not think of offering any thing less than his best on such an occasion. And then he turned his back and went his way, muttering as he went something in Flemish, which I believed to be an exclamation of astonishment that any man should, under any circumstances, lose such an article.

It was now getting late; so when I had taken a short stroll by myself, I went to bed without disturbing Mr. Horne again that night. On the following morning I thought it best not to go to him unless he sent for me; so I desired the boots to let him know that I had ordered breakfast in a private room, and that I would await him there unless he wished to see me. He sent me word back to say that he would be with me very shortly.

He did not keep me waiting above half an hour; but I confess that that half-hour was not pleasantly spent. I feared that his temper would be tried in dressing, and that he would not be able to eat his breakfast in a happy state of mind. So that when I heard his heavy footstep advancing along the passage my heart did misgive me, and I felt that I was trembling.

That step was certainly slower and more ponderous than usual. There was always a certain dignity in the very sound of his movements, but now this seemed to have been enhanced. To judge merely by the step, one would have said that a bishop was coming that way instead of a prebendary.

And then he entered. In the upper half of his august person no alteration was perceptible. The hair was as regular and as graceful as ever, the handkerchief as white, the coat as immaculate; but below his well-filled waistcoat a pair of red plush began to shine in unmitigated splendor, and continued from thence down to within an inch above his knee, nor, as it appeared, could any pulling induce them to descend lower. Mr. Horne always wore black silk stockings — at least so the world supposed — but it was now apparent that the world had been wrong in presuming him to be guilty of such extravagance. Those, at any rate, which he exhibited on the present occasion were more economical. They were silk to the calf, but thence upward they continued their career in white cotton. These then followed the plush; first two snowy, full-sized pillars of white, and then two jet columns of flossy silk. Such was the appearance, on that well-remembered morning, of the Reverend Augustus Horne, as he entered the room in which his breakfast was prepared.

I could see at a glance that a dark frown contracted his eyebrows, and that the compressed muscles of his upper lip gave a strange degree of austerity to his open face. He carried his head proudly on high, determined to be dignified in spite of his misfortunes, and advanced two steps into the room without a remark, as though to show that neither red plush nor black cloth could disarrange the equal poise of his mighty mind.

And after all what are a man's garments but the outward husks

in which the fruit is kept duly tempered from the wind?
<blockquote>
"The rank is but the guinea stamp,
The man's the gowd for a' that."
</blockquote>
And is not the tailor's art as little worthy, as insignificant as that of the king who makes
<blockquote>
"A marquis, duke, and a' that?"
</blockquote>
Who would be content to think that this manly dignity depended on his coat and waistcoat, or his hold on the world's esteem on any other garment of usual wear? That no such weakness soiled his mind Mr. Horne was determined to prove; and thus he entered the room with measured tread and stern, dignified demeanor.

Having advanced two steps his eye caught mine. I do not know whether he was moved by some unconscious smile on my part — for in truth I endeavored to seem as indifferent as himself to the nature of his dress — or whether he was invincibly tickled by some inward fancy of his own, but suddenly his advancing step ceased, a broad flash of comic humor spread itself over his features, he retreated with his back against the wall, and then burst out into an immoderate roar of loud laughter.

And I — what else could I do but laugh? He laughed, and I laughed. He roared, and I roared. He lifted up his vast legs to view till the rays of the morning sun shone through the window on the bright hues which he displayed; and he did not sit down to his breakfast till he had in every fantastic attitude shown off to the best advantage the red plush of which he had so recently become proud.

An Antwerp private cabriolet on that day reached the yard of the Hôtel de Belle Vue at about 4 P.M., and four waiters, in a frenzy of astonishment, saw the Reverend Augustus Horne descend from the vehicle and seek his chamber dressed in the garments which I have described; but I am inclined to think that he has never since favored any of his friends with such a sight.

It was on the next evening after this that I went out to drink tea with two maiden ladies, relatives of mine, who kept a seminary for English girls at Brussels. The Misses Macmanus were very worthy women, and earned their bread in an upright, painstaking manner. I would not for worlds have passed through Brussels without paying them this compliment. They were, however, perhaps a little dull, and I was aware that I should not probably meet in their drawing-room many of the fashionable inhabitants of the city. Mr. Horne had declined to accompany me; but in doing so he was good enough to express a warm admiration for the character of my worthy cousins.

The elder Miss Macmanus, in her little note, had informed me that she would have the pleasure of introducing me to a few of my "compatriots." I presumed she meant Englishmen; and as I was in the habit of meeting such every day of my life at home, I can not say that I was peculiarly elevated by the promise. When, however, I entered the room, there was no Englishman there — there was no man of any kind; there were twelve ladies collected together with the view of making the evening pass agreeably to me, the single virile being among them all. I felt as though I were a sort of Mohammad in Paradise; but I certainly felt also that the Paradise was none of my choosing.

In the center of the amphitheatre which the ladies formed sat the two Misses Macmanus — there, at least, they sat when they had completed the process of shaking hands with me. To the left of them, making one wing of the semicircle, were arranged the five pupils by attending to whom the Misses Macmanus earned their living; and the other wing consisted of the five ladies who had furnished themselves with the relics of General Chassé. They were my "compatriots."

I was introduced to them all, one after the other; but their names did not abide in my memory one moment. I was thinking too much of the singularity of the adventure, and could not attend to such minutiae. That the red-nosed harpy was Miss Grogram, that I remembered — that, I may say, I never shall forget. But whether the motherly lady with the somewhat blowsy hair was Mrs. Jones, or Mrs. Green, or Mrs. Walker, I can not now say, The dumpy female with the broad back was always called Aunt Sally by the young ladies.

Too much sugar spoils one's tea; I think I have heard that even prosperity will cloy when it comes in overdoses; and a school-boy has been known to be overdone with jam. I myself have always been peculiarly attached to ladies' society, and have avoided bachelor parties as things execrable in their very nature. But on this special occasion I felt myself to be that school-boy — I was literally overdone with jam. My tea was all sugar, so that I could not drink it. I was one among twelve — what could I do or say? The proportion of alloy was too small to have any effect in changing the nature of the virgin silver, and the conversation became absolutely feminine.

I must confess also that my previous experience as to these compatriots of mine had not prejudiced me in their favor. I regarded them with — I am ashamed to say so, seeing that they were ladies — but almost with loathing. When last I had seen them their occupation had reminded me of some obscene feast, of harpies, or almost of ghouls. They had brought down to the verge of desperation the man whom of all men I most venerated. On these accounts I was inclined to be taciturn with reference to them — and then what could I have to say to the Misses Macmanus's five pupils?

My cousins at first made an effort or two in my favor; but these efforts were fruitless. I soon died away into utter unrecognized insignificance; and the conversation, as I have before said, became feminine; and indeed that horrid Miss Grogram, who was, as it were, the princess of the ghouls, nearly monopolized the whole of it. Mamma Jones — we will call her Jones for the occasion — put in a word now and then, as did also the elder and more energetic Miss Macmanus. The dumpy lady with the broad back ate tea-cake incessantly; the two daughters looked scornful, as though they were above their company with reference to the five pupils; and the five pupils themselves sat in a row with the utmost propriety, each with her hands crossed on her lap before her.

Of what they were talking at last I became utterly oblivious. They had ignored me, going into realms of muslin, questions of maid servants, female rights, and cheap under-clothing; and I therefore had ignored them. My mind had gone back to Mr. Horne and his garments. While they spoke of their rights, I was thinking of his wrongs; when they mentioned the price of flannel, I thought of that broadcloth.

But of a sudden my attention was arrested. Miss Macmanus had said something of the black silks of Antwerp, when Miss Grogram replied that she had just returned from that city, and had there enjoyed a great success. My cousin had again asked something about the black silks, thinking, no doubt, that Miss

Grogram had achieved some bargain; but that lady had soon un-deceived her.

"Oh no," said Miss Grogram, "it was at the castle. We got such beautiful relics of General Chassé! Didn't we, Mrs. Jones?"

"Indeed we did," said Mrs. Jones, bringing out from beneath the skirts of her dress and ostensibly displaying a large black bag.

"And I've got such a beautiful needle-case," said the broad-back, displaying her prize. "I've been making it up all the morn-ing." And she handed over the article to Miss Macmanus.

"And only look at this duck of a pen-wiper," simpered flaxen-hair No. 2. "Only think of wiping one's pens with relics of General Chassé!" and she handed it over to the other Miss Macmanus.

"And mine's a pin-cushion," said No. 1, exhibiting the trophy.

"But that's nothing to what I've got," said Miss Grogram. "In the first place, there's a pair of slippers — a beautiful pair — they're not made up yet, of course; and then —"

The two Misses Macmanus and their five pupils were sitting open-eared, open-eyed, and open-mouthed. How all these sombre-looking articles could be relics of General Chassé did not at first appear clear to them.

"What are they, Miss Grogram?" said the elder Miss Mac-manus, holding the needle-case in one hand and Mrs. Jones's bag in the other. Miss Macmanus was a strong-minded female, and I reverenced my cousin when I saw the decided way in which she intended to put down the greedy annoyance of Miss Grogram.

"They are relics."

"But where do they come from, Miss Grogram?"

"Why, from the castle, to be sure — from General Chassé's own rooms."

"Did any body sell them to you?"

"No."

"Or give them to you?"

"Why, no — at least not exactly give."

"There they were, and she took 'em," said the broad-back.

Oh, what a look Miss Grogram gave her! "Took them! of course I took them. That is, you took them as much as I did. They were things that we found lying about."

"What things?" asked Miss Macmanus, in a peculiarly strong-minded tone.

Miss Grogram seemed to be for a moment silenced. I had been ignored, as I have said, and my existence forgotten; but now I observed that the eyes of the culprits were turned toward me — the eyes, that is, of four of them. Mrs. Jones looked at me from beneath her fan; the two girls glanced at me furtively, and then their eyes fell to the lowest flounces of their frocks; Miss Grogram turned her spectacles right upon me, and I fancied that she nodded her head at me as a sort of answer to Miss Macmanus; the five pupils opened their mouths and eyes wider; but she of the broad back was nothing abashed. It would have been nothing to her had there been a dozen gentlemen in the room. "We just found a pair of black ——." The whole truth was told in the plainest possible language.

"Oh, Aunt Sally!" "Aunt Sally, how can you?" "Hold your tongue, Aunt Sally!"

"And then Miss Grogram just cut them up with her scissors," continued Aunt Sally, not a whit abashed, "and gave us each a bit, only she took more than half for herself." It was clear to me that there had been some quarrel, some delicious quarrel, between Aunt Sally and Miss Grogram. Through the whole adventure I had rather respected Aunt Sally. "She took more than half for herself," continued Aunt Sally. "She kept all the ——."

"Jemima," said the elder Miss Macmanus, interrupting the speaker, and addressing her sister, "it is time, I think, for the young ladies to retire. Will you be kind enough to see them to their rooms?" The five pupils thereupon rose from their seats and courtesied. They then left the room in file, the younger Miss Macmanus showing them the way.

"But we haven't done any harm, have we?" asked Mrs. Jones, with some tremulousness in her voice.

"Well, I don't know," said Miss Macmanus. "What I'm thinking of now is this — to whom, I wonder, did the garments properly belong? Who had been the owner and wearer of them?"

"Why, General Chassé, of course," said Miss Grogram.

"They were the General's," repeated the two young ladies; blushing, however, as they alluded to the subject.

"Well, we thought they were the General's, certainly; and a very excellent article they were," said Mrs. Jones.

"Perhaps they were the butler's?" said Aunt Sally. I certainly had not given her credit for so much sarcasm.

"Butler's!" exclaimed Miss Grogram, with a toss of her head.

"Oh! Aunt Sally, Aunt Sally! how can you?" shrieked the two young ladies.

"Oh laws!" ejaculated Mrs. Jones.

"I don't think that they could have belonged to the butler," said Miss Macmanus, with much authority, "seeing that domestics in this country are never clad in garments of that description; so far my own observation enables me to speak with certainty. But it is equally sure that they were never the property of the General lately in command at Antwerp. Generals, when they are in full dress, wear ornamental lace upon their — their regimentals; and when—" So much she said, and something more, which it may be unnecessary that I should repeat; but such were her eloquence and logic that no doubt would have been left on the mind of any impartial hearer. If an argumentative speaker ever proved any thing, Miss Macmanus proved that General Chassé had never been the wearer of the article in question.

"But I know very well they were his!" said Miss Grogram, who was not an impartial hearer. "Of course they were; whose else's should they be?"

"I'm sure I hope they were his," said one of the young ladies, almost crying.

"I wish I'd never taken it," said the other.

"Dear, dear, dear!" said Mrs. Jones.

"I'll give you my needle-case, Miss Grogram," said Aunt Sally.

I had sat hitherto silent during the whole scene, meditating how best I might confound the red-nosed harpy. Now, I thought, was the time for me to strike in.

"I really think, ladies, that there has been some mistake," said I.

"There has been no mistake at all, Sir!" said Miss Grogram.

"Perhaps not," I answered, very mildly; "very likely not. But some affair of a similar nature was very much talked about in Antwerp yesterday."

"Oh laws!" again ejaculated Mrs. Jones.

"The affair I allude to has been talked about a good deal, certainly," I continued. "But perhaps it may be altogether a different circumstance."

"And what may be the circumstance to which you allude?" asked Miss Macmanus, in the same authoritative tone.

"I dare say it has nothing to do with these ladies," said I; "but a piece of cloth, of the nature they have described, was cut up in the Castle of Antwerp on the day before yesterday. It belonged to a gentleman who was visiting the place; and I was given to understand that he is determined to punish the people who have wronged him."

"It can't be the same," said Miss Grogram; but I could see that she was trembling.

"Oh laws! what will become of us?" said Mrs. Jones.

"You can all prove that I didn't touch them, and that I warned her not," said Aunt Sally. In the mean time the two young ladies had almost fainted behind their fans.

"But how had it come to pass," asked Miss Macmanus, "that the gentleman had—"

"I know nothing more about it, cousin," said I; "only it does seem that there is an odd coincidence."

Immediately after this I took my leave. I saw that I had avenged my friend, and spread dismay in the hearts of those who had injured him. I had learned in the course of the evening at what hotel the five ladies were staying; and in the course of the next morning I sauntered into the hall, and finding one of the porters alone, asked if they were still there. The man told me that they had started by the earliest diligence. "And," said he, "if you are a friend of theirs, perhaps you will take charge of these things, which they have left behind them?" So saying, he pointed to a table at the back of the hall, on which were lying the black bag, the black needle-case, the black pin-cushion, and the black pen-wiper. There was also a heap of fragments of cloth, which I well knew had been intended by Miss Grogram for the comfort of her feet and ankles.

I declined the commission, however. They were no special friends of mine, I said; and I left all the relics still lying on the little table in the back hall.

"Upon the whole, I am satisfied!" said the Rev. Augustus Horne, when I told him the finale of the story.

"The Relics of General Chassé" appeared first in the February issue of *Harper's New Monthly Magazine* for 1860.

The Banks of the Jordan

CIRCUMSTANCES TOOK ME TO the Holy Land without a companion, and compelled me to visit Bethany, the Mount of Olives, and the Church of the Sepulchre alone. I acknowledge myself to be a gregarious animal, or, perhaps, rather one of those which Nature has intended to go in pairs. At any rate I dislike solitude, and especially travelling solitude, and was, therefore, rather sad at heart as I sat one night at Z___'s hotel, in Jerusalem, thinking over my proposed wanderings for the next few days. Early on the following morning I intended to start, of course on horseback, for the Dead Sea, the banks of Jordan, Jericho, and those mountains of the wilderness through which it is supposed that Our Saviour wandered for the forty days when the devil tempted him. I would then return to the Holy City, and remaining only long enough to refresh my horse and wipe the dust from my hands and feet, I would start again for Jaffa, and there catch a certain Austrian steamer which would take me to Egypt. Such was my programme, and I confess that I was but ill contented with it, seeing that I was to be alone during the time.

I had already made all my arrangements, and though I had no reason for any doubt as to my personal security during the trip, I did not feel altogether satisfied with them. I intended to take a French guide, or dragoman, who had been with me for some days, and to put myself under the peculiar guardianship of two Bedouin Arabs, who were to accompany me as long as I should remain east of Jerusalem. This travelling through the desert under the protection of Bedouins was, in idea, pleasant enough; and I must here declare that I did not at all begrudge the forty shillings which I was told by our British consul that I must pay them for their trouble, in accordance with the established tariff. But I did begrudge the fact of the tariff. I would rather have fallen in with my friendly Arabs, as it were by chance, and have rewarded their fidelity at the end of our joint journeyings by a donation of piastres to be settled by myself, and which, under such circumstances, would certainly have been as agreeable to them as the stipulated sum. In the same way I dislike having waiters put down in my bill. I find that I pay them twice over, and thus lose money; and as they do not expect to be so treated, I never have the advantage of their civility. The world, I fear, is becoming too fond of tariffs.

"A tariff!" said I to the consul, feeling that the whole romance of my expedition would be dissipated by such an arrangement. "—Then I'll go alone; I'll take a revolver with me."

"You can't do it, sir," said the consul, in a dry and somewhat angry tone. "You have no more right to ride through that country without paying the regular price for protection than you have to stop in Z——'s hotel without settling the bill."

I could not contest the point, so I ordered my Bedouins for the appointed day, exactly as I would send for a ticket-porter at home, and determined to make the best of it. The wild unlimited sands, the desolation of the Dead Sea, the running water of Jordan, the outlines of the mountains of Moab — those things the consular tariff could not alter, nor deprive of the glories of their association.

I had submitted, and the arrangements had been made. Joseph, my dragoman, was to come to me with the horses and an Arab groom at five in the morning, and we were to encounter our Bedouins outside the gate of St. Stephen, down the hill, where the road turns, close to the tomb of the Virgin.

I was sitting alone in the public room at the hotel, filling my flask with brandy — for matters of primary importance I never leave to servant, dragoman, or guide — when the waiter entered and said that a gentleman wished to speak with me. The gentleman had not sent in his card or name; but any gentleman was

welcome to me in my solitude, and I requested that the gentleman might enter. In appearance the gentleman certainly was a
gentleman, for I thought that I had never before seen a young
man whose looks were more in his favour, or whose face and gait
and outward bearing seemed to betoken better breeding. He
might be some twenty or twenty-one years of age, was slight and
well made, with very black hair which he wore rather long, very
dark long bright eyes, a straight nose, and teeth that were perfectly white. He was dressed throughout in grey tweed clothing,
having coat, waistcoat, and trousers of the same; and in his hand
he carried a very broad-brimmed straw hat.

"Mr. Jones, I believe," he said, as he bowed to me. Jones is a
good travelling name, and if the reader will allow me, I will call
myself Jones on the present occasion.

"Yes," I said, pausing with the brandy-bottle in one hand and
the flask in the other. "That's my name, I'm Jones. Can I do anything for you, sir?"

"Why, yes, you can," said he. "My name is Smith — John
Smith."

"Pray sit down, Mr. Smith," I said, pointing to a chair. "Will
you do anything in this way?" and I proposed to hand the bottle
to him. "As far as I can judge from a short stay, you won't find
much like that in Jerusalem."

He declined the Cognac, however, and immediately began his
story. "I hear, Mr. Jones," said he, "that you are going to Moab
to-morrow."

"Well," I replied; "I don't know whether I shall cross the
water. It's not very easy, I take it, at all times; but I shall certainly
get as far as Jordan. Can I do anything for you in those parts?"

And then he explained to me what was the object of his visit.
He was quite alone in Jerusalem, as I was myself, and was staying
at H___'s hotel. He had heard that I was starting for the Dead
Sea, and had called to ask if I objected to his joining me. He had
found himself, he said, very lonely; and as he had heard that I
also was alone he had ventured to call and make his proposition.
He seemed to be very bashful, and half ashamed of what he was
doing; and when he had done speaking he declared himself conscious that he was intruding, and expressed a hope that I would
not hesitate to say so if his suggestion were from any cause dis-

agreeable to me.

As a rule I am rather shy of chance travelling English friends. It has so frequently happened to me that I have had to blush for the acquaintances whom I have selected, that I seldom indulge in any close intimacies of this kind. But, nevertheless, I was taken with John Smith, in spite of his name. There was so much about him that was pleasant, both to the eye and to the under-standing. One meets constantly with men from contact with whom one revolts without knowing the cause of such dislike. The cut of their beard is displeasing, or the mode in which they walk or speak. But, on the other hand, there are men who are attrac-tive, and I must confess that I was attracted by John Smith at first sight. I hesitated, however, for a minute; for there are sundry things of which it behoves a traveller to think before he can join a companion for such a journey as that which I was about to make. Could the young man rise early, and remain in the saddle for ten hours together? Could he live upon hard-boiled eggs and brandy-and-water? Could he take his chance of a tent under which to sleep, and make himself happy with the bare fact of being in the desert? He saw my hesitation, and attributed it to a cause which was not present in my mind at the moment, though the subject is one of the greatest importance when strangers con-sent to join themselves together for a time, and agree to become no strangers on the spur of the moment.

"Of course I will take half the expense," said he, absolutely blushing as he mentioned the matter.

"As to that there will be very little. You have your own horse, of course?"

"Oh, yes."

"My dragoman and groom-boy will do for both. But you'll have to pay forty shillings to the Arabs! There's no getting over that. The consul won't even look after your dead body, if you get mur-dered, without going through that ceremony."

Mr. Smith immediately produced his purse which he tendered to me. "If you will manage it all," said he, "it will make it so much the easier, and I shall be infinitely obliged to you." This of course I declined to do. I had no business with his purse, and explained to him that if we went together we could settle that on our return to Jerusalem. "But could he go through really hard work?" I asked. He answered me with an assurance that he would and could do anything in that way that it was possible for man to perform. As for eating and drinking he cared nothing about it, and would undertake to be astir at any hour of the morning that might be named. As for sleeping accommodation, he did not care if he kept his clothes on for a week together. He looked slight and weak; but he spoke so well, and that without boasting, that I ultimately agreed to his proposal, and in a few minutes he took his leave of me, promising to be at Z——'s door with his horse at five o'clock on the following morning.

"I wish you'd allow me to leave my purse with you," he said again.

"I cannot think of it. There is no possible occasion for it," I said again. "If there is anything to pay I'll ask you for it when the journey is over. That forty shillings you must fork out. It's a law of the Medes and Persians."

"I'd better give it to you at once," he said, again offering me money. But I would not have it. It would be quite time enough for that when the Arabs were leaving us.

"Because," he added, "strangers, I know, are sometimes suspicious about money; and I would not, for worlds, have you think that I would put you to expense." I assured him that I did not think so, and then the subject was dropped.

He was, at any rate, up to his time, for when I came down on the following morning I found him in the narrow street, the first on horseback. Joseph, the Frenchman, was strapping on to a rough pony our belongings, and was staring at Mr. Smith. My new friend, unfortunately, could not speak a word of French, and therefore I had to explain to the dragoman how it had come to pass that our party was to be enlarged.

"But the Bedouins will expect full pay for both," said he, alarmed. "Men in that class, and especially Orientals, always think that every arrangement of life, let it be made in what way it will, is made with the intention of saving some expense or cheating somebody out of some amount of money. They do not understand that men can have any other object, and are ever on their guard lest the saving should be made at their cost, or lest they should be the victims of the fraud."

"All right," said I.

"I shall be responsible, Monsieur," said the dragoman piteously.

"It shall be all right," said I again. "If that does not satisfy you,
you may remain behind."

"If Monsieur says it is all right, of course it is so;" and then he
completed his strapping. We took blankets with us, of which I
had to borrow two out of the hotel for my friend Smith, a small
hamper of provisions, a sack containing forage for the horses, and
a large empty jar so that we might supply ourselves with water
when leaving the neighbourhood of wells for any considerable
time.

"I ought to have brought these things for myself," said Smith,
quite unhappy at finding that he had thrown on me the necessity
of catering for him. But I laughed at him, saying that it was nothing; he should do as much for me another time. I am prepared to
own that I do not willingly rush upstairs and load myself with
blankets out of strange rooms for men whom I do not know; nor,
as a rule, do I make all the Smiths of the world free of my canteen.
But, with reference to this fellow I did feel more than ordinarily
goodnatured, and unselfish. There was something in the tone of
his voice which was satisfactory; and I should really have felt
vexed had anything occurred at the last moment to prevent his
going with me.

Let it be a rule with every man to carry an English saddle with
him when travelling in the East. Of what material is formed the
nether man of a Turk I have never been informed, but I am sure
that it is not flesh and blood. No flesh and blood — simply flesh
and blood — could withstand the wear and tear of a Turkish saddle. This being the case, and the consequences being well known
to me, I was grieved to find that Smith was not properly provided. He was seated in one of those hard, red, high-pointed
machines, to which the shovels intended to act as stirrups are
attached in such a manner, and hang at such an angle, as to be
absolutely destructive to the leg of a Christian. There is no part
of the Christian body with which the Turkish saddle comes in
contact that does not become more or less macerated. I have sat
in one for days, but I left it a flayed man; and therefore I was sorry
for Smith.

I explained this to him, taking hold of his leg by the calf to show how the leather would chafe him; but it seemed to me that he did not quite like my interference. "Never mind," said he, twitching his leg away, "I have ridden in this way before."

"Then you must have suffered the very mischief?"

"Only a little, and I shall be used to it now. You will not hear me complain."

"By heavens, you might have heard me complain a mile off when I came to the end of a journey I once took. I roared like a bull when I began to cool. Joseph, could you not get a European saddle for Mr. Smith?" But Joseph did not seem to like Mr. Smith, and declared such a thing to be impossible. No European in Jerusalem would think of lending so precious an article, except to a very dear friend. Joseph himself was on an English saddle, and I made up my mind that after the first stage we would bribe him to make an exchange. And then we started. The Bedouins were not with us, but we were to meet them, as I have said before, outside St. Stephen's gate; "And if they are not there," said Joseph, "we shall be sure to come across them on the road."

"Not there!" said I. "How about the Consul's tariff if they don't keep their part of the engagement?" But Joseph explained to me that their part of the engagement really amounted to this, — that we should ride into their country without molestation, provided that such and such payments were made.

It was the period of Easter and Jerusalem was full of pilgrims. Even at that early hour of the morning we could hardly make our way through the narrow streets. It must be understood that there is no accommodation in the town for the fourteen or fifteen thousand strangers who flock to the Holy Sepulchre at this period of the year. Many of them sleep out in the open air, lying on low benches which run along the outside walls of the houses, or even on the ground, wrapped in their thick hoods and cloaks. Slumberers such as these are easily disturbed, nor are they detained long at their toilets. They shake themselves like dogs, and growl and stretch themselves, and then they are ready for the day.

We rode out of the town in a long file. First went the groom-boy; I forget his proper Syrian appellation, but we used to call him Muckery, that sound being in some sort like the name. Then followed the horse with the forage and blankets, and next to him my friend Smith in the Turkish saddle. I was behind him and Jo-

seph brought up the rear. We moved slowly down the Via Do-
lorosa, noting the spot at which our Saviour is said to have fallen
while bearing his cross; we passed by Pilate's house, and paused
at the gate of the Temple — the gate which once was beautiful,
— looking down into the hole of the pool in which the maimed
and halt were healed whenever the waters moved. What names
they are! And yet there at Jerusalem they are bandied to and fro
with as little reverence as are the fanciful appellations given by
guides to rocks and stones and little lakes in all countries overrun
by tourists.

"For those who would still fain believe, — let them stay at
home," said my friend Smith.

"For those who cannot divide the wheat from the chaff, let
them stay at home," I answered. And then we rode out through
St. Stephen's gate, having the mountain of the men of Galilee
directly before us, and the Mount of Olives a little to our right,
and the Valley of Jehoshaphat lying between us and it. "Of
course you know all these places now," said Smith. I answered
that I did know them well. "And was it not better for you when
you knew them only in holy writ?" he asked.

"No, by Jove," said I. "The mountains stand where they ever
stood. The same valleys are still green with the morning dew, and
the water-courses are unchanged. The children of Mahomet may
build their tawdry temple on the threshing-floor which David
bought that there might stand the Lord's house. Man may undo
what man did, even though the doer was Solomon. But here we
have God's handywork and his own evidences."

At the bottom of the steep descent from the city gate we came
to the tomb of the Virgin; and by special agreement made with
Joseph we left our horses here for a few moments, in order that
we might descend into the subterranean chapel under the tomb,
in which mass was at this moment being said. There is something
awful in that chapel, when, as at the present moment, it is
crowded with Eastern worshippers from the very altar up to the
top of the dark steps by which the descent is made. It must be
remembered that Eastern worshippers are not like the church-
goers of London, or even of Rome or Cologne. They are wild men
of various nations and races — Maronites from Lebanon, Rou-
melians, Candiotes, Copts from Upper Egypt, Russians from the

114

Crimea, Armenians and Abyssinians. They savour strongly of Oriental life and of Oriental dirt. They are clad in skins or hairy cloaks with huge hoods. Their heads are shaved, and their faces covered with short, grisly, fierce beards. They are silent mostly, looking out of their eyes ferociously, as though murder were in their thoughts, and rapine. But they never slouch, or cringe in their bodies, or shuffle in their gait. Dirty, fierce-looking, uncouth, repellent as they are, there is always about them a something of personal dignity which is not compatible with an Englishman's ordinary hat and pantaloons.

As we were about to descend, preparing to make our way through the crowd, Smith took hold of my arm. "That will never do, my dear fellow," said I, "the job will be tough enough for a single file, but we should never cut our way two and two. I'm broad-shouldered and will go first." So I did, and gradually we worked our way into the body of the chapel. How is it that Englishmen can push themselves anywhere? These men were fierce-looking, and had murder and rapine, as I have said, almost in their eyes. One would have supposed that they were not lambs or doves, capable of being thrust here or there without anger on their part; and they, too, were all anxious to descend and approach the altar. Yet we did win our way through them, and apparently no man was angry with us. I doubt, after all, whether a ferocious eye and a strong smell and dirt are so efficacious in creating awe and obedience in others as an open brow and traces of soap and water. I know this, at least, — that a dirty Maronite would make very little progress if he attempted to shove his way unfairly through a crowd of Englishmen at the door of a London theatre. We did shove unfairly, and we did make progress, till we found ourselves in the centre of the dense crowd collected in the body of the chapel.

Having got so far our next object was to get out again. The place was dark, mysterious, and full of strange odours; but darkness, mystery, and strange odours soon lose their charms when men have much work before them. Joseph had made a point of being allowed to attend mass before the altar of the Virgin, but a very few minutes sufficed for his prayers. So we again turned round and pushed our way back again, Smith still following in my wake. The men who had let us pass once let us pass again without opposition or show of anger. To them the occasion was very holy. They were stretching out their hands in every direction, with long tapers, in order that they might obtain a spark of the sacred fire which was burning on one of the altars. As we made our way out we passed many who, with dumb motions, begged us to assist them in their object; and we did assist them, getting lights for their tapers, handing them to and fro, and using the authority with which we seemed to be invested. But Smith, I observed, was much more courteous in this way to the women than to the men, as I did not forget to remind him when we were afterwards on our road together.

Remounting our horses, we rode slowly up the winding ascent of the Mount of Olives, turning round at the brow of the hill to look back over Jerusalem. Sometimes, I think, that of all spots in the world this one should be the spot most cherished in the memory of Christians. It was there that He stood when He wept over the city. So much we do know, though we are ignorant, and ever shall be so, of the site of His cross and of the tomb. And then we descended on the eastern side of the hill, passing through Bethany, the town of Lazarus and his sisters, and turned our faces steadily towards the mountains of Moab.

Hitherto we had met no Bedouins, and I interrogated my dragoman about them more than once. But he always told me that it did not signify; we should meet them, he said, before any danger could arise. "As for danger," said I, "I think more of this than I do of the Arabs," and I put my hand on my revolver. "But as they agreed to be here, here they ought to be. Don't you carry a revolver, Smith?"

Smith said that he never had done so, but that he would take the charge of mine if I liked. To this, however, I demurred. "I never part with my pistol to any one," I said, rather drily. But he explained that he only intended to signify that if there were danger to be encountered, he would be glad to encounter it; and I fully believed him. "We shan't have much fighting," I replied; "but if there be any, the tool will come readiest to the hand of its master. But if you mean to remain here long I would advise you to get one. These Orientals are a people with whom appearances go a long way, and, as a rule, fear and respect mean the same thing with them. A pistol hanging over your loins is no great

116

trouble to you, and looks as though you could bite. Many a dog goes through the world well by merely showing his teeth."

And then my companion began to talk of himself. He did not, he said, mean to remain in Syria very long.

"Nor I either," said I. "I have done with this part of the world for the present, and shall take the next steamer from Jaffa for Alexandria. I shall only have one night in Jerusalem on my return."

After this he remained silent for a few moments, and then declared that that also had been his intention. He was almost ashamed to say so, however, because it looked as though he had resolved to hook himself on to me. So he answered, expressing almost regret at the circumstance.

"Don't let that trouble you," said I. "I shall be delighted to have your company. When you know me better, as I hope you will do, you will find that if such were not the case, I should tell you so as frankly. I shall remain in Cairo some little time; so that beyond our arrival in Egypt, I can answer for nothing."

He said that he expected letters at Alexandria which would govern his future movements. I thought he seemed sad as he said so, and imagined, from his manner, that he did not expect very happy tidings. Indeed, I had made up my mind that he was by no means free from care or sorrow. He had not the air of a man who could say of himself that he was "totus teres atque rotundus." But I had no wish to inquire, and the matter would have dropped had he not himself added— "I fear that I shall meet acquaintances in Egypt whom it will give me no pleasure to see."

"Then," said I, "if I were you, I would go to Constantinople instead — indeed, anywhere rather than fall among friends who are not friendly. And the nearer the friend is, the more one feels that sort of thing. To my way of thinking there is nothing on earth so pleasant as a pleasant wife; but then, what is there so damnable as one that is unpleasant?"

"Are you a married man?" he inquired. All his questions were put in a low tone of voice which seemed to give to them an air of special interest, and made one almost feel that they were asked with some special view to one's individual welfare. Now the fact is that I am a married man with a family; but I am not much given to talk to strangers about my domestic concerns, and therefore, though I had no particular object in view, I denied my obligations in this respect. "No," said I; "I have not come to that promotion yet. I am too frequently on the move to write myself down as Paterfamilias."

"Then you know nothing about that pleasantness of which you spoke just now?"

"Nor of the unpleasantness, thank God; my personal experiences are all to come, — as also are yours, I presume?"

It was possible that he had hampered himself with some woman, and that she was to meet him at Alexandria. Poor fellow! thought I. But his unhappiness was not of that kind. "No," said he; "I am not married; I am all alone in the world."

"Then I certainly would not allow myself to be troubled by unpleasant acquaintances."

It was now four hours since we had left Jerusalem, and we had arrived at the place at which it was proposed that we should breakfast. There was a large well there, and shade afforded by a rock under which the water sprang; and the Arabs had constructed a tank out of which the horses could drink, so that the place was ordinarily known as the first stage out of Jerusalem.

Smith had said not a word about his saddle, or complained in any way of discomfort, so that I had in truth forgotten the subject. Other matters had continually presented themselves, and I had never even asked him how he had fared. I now jumped from my horse, but I perceived at once that he was unable to do so. He smiled faintly, as his eye caught mine, but I knew that he wanted assistance. "Ah," said I, "that confounded Turkish saddle has already galled your skin. I see how it is: I shall have to doctor you with a little brandy — externally applied, my friend." But I lent him my shoulder, and with that assistance he got down, very gently and slowly.

We ate our breakfast with a good will: bread and cold fowl and brandy-and-water, with a hard boiled egg by way of a final delicacy; and then I began to bargain with Joseph for the loan of his English saddle. I saw that Smith could not get through the journey with that monstrous Turkish affair, and that he would go on without complaining till he fainted or came to some other signal grief. But the Frenchman, seeing the plight in which we were, was disposed to drive a very hard bargain. He wanted forty shil-

lings, the price of a pair of live Bedouins, for the accommodation, and declared that, even then, he should make the sacrifice
only out of consideration to me.

"Very well," said I. "I'm tolerably tough myself, and I'll change
with the gentleman. The chances are that I shall not be in a very
liberal humor when I reach Jaffa with stiff limbs and a sore skin.
I have a very good memory, Joseph."

"I'll take thirty shillings, Mr. Jones; though I shall have to
groan all the way like a condemned devil."

I struck a bargain with him at last for five-and-twenty, and set
him to work to make the necessary change on the horses. "It will
be just the same thing to him," I said to Smith. "I find that he is
as much used to one as to the other."

"But how much money are you to pay him?" he asked, "Oh,
nothing," I replied. "Give him a few piastres when you part with
him at Jaffa." I do not know why I should have felt thus inclined
to pay money out of my pocket for this Smith — a man whom I
had only seen for the first time on the preceding evening, and
whose temperament was so essentially different from my own; but
so I did. I would have done almost anything in reason for his
comfort; and yet he was a melancholy fellow, with good inward
pluck as I believed, but without that outward show of dash and
hardihood which I confess I love to see. "Pray tell him that I'll
pay him for it," said he. "We'll make that all right," I answered;
and then we remounted — not without some difficulty on his
part. "You should have let me rub in that brandy," I said. "You
can't conceive how efficaciously I would have done it." But he
made me no answer.

At noon we met a caravan of pilgrims coming up from Jordan.
There might be some three or four hundred, but the number
seemed to be treble that from the loose and straggling line in
which they journeyed. It was a very singular sight, as they moved
slowly along the narrow path through the sand, coming out of a
defile among the hills which was perhaps a quarter of a mile in
front of us, passing us as we stood still by the wayside, and then
winding again out of sight on the track over which we had come.
Some rode on camels, — a whole family, in many cases, being
perched on the same animal. I observed a very old man and a
very old woman slung in panniers over a camel's back—not such

panniers as might be befitting such a purpose, but square baskets, so that the heads and heels of each of the old couple hung out to the rear and front. "Surely the journey will be their death," I said to Joseph. "Yes, it will," he replied, quite coolly; "but what matters how soon they die now that they have bathed in Jordan?" Very many rode on donkeys; two, generally, on each donkey; others, who had command of money, on horses; but the greater number walked, toiling painfully from Jerusalem to Jericho on the first day, sleeping there in tents and going to bathe in Jordan on the second day, and then returning from Jericho to Jerusalem on the third. The pilgrimage is made throughout in accordance with fixed rules, and there is a tariff for the tent accommodation at Jericho—so much per head per night, including the use of hot water.

Standing there, close by the wayside, we could see not only the garments and faces of these strange people, but we could watch their gestures and form some opinion of what was going on within their thoughts. They were much quieter, — tamer, as it were, — than Englishmen would be under such circumstances. Those who were carried seemed to sit on their beasts in passive tranquility, neither enjoying anything nor suffering anything. Their object had been to wash in Jordan, — to do that once in their lives; — and they had washed in Jordan. The benefit expected was not to be immediately spiritual. No earnest prayerfulness was considered necessary after the ceremony. To these members of the Greek Christian Church it had been handed down from father to son that washing in Jordan once during life was efficacious towards salvation. And therefore the journey had been made at terrible cost and terrible risk; for these people had come from afar, and were from their habits but little capable of long journeys. Many die under the toil; but this matters not if they do not die before they have reached Jordan. Some few there are, undoubtedly, more ecstatic in this great deed of their religion. One man I especially noticed on this day. He had bound himself to make the pilgrimage from Jerusalem to the river with one foot bare. He was of a better class, and was even nobly dressed, as though it were a part of his vow to show to all men that he did this deed, wealthy and great though he was. He was a fine man, perhaps thirty years of age, with a well-grown beard descending on his breast, and at his girdle he carried a brace of pistols. But never in my life had I seen bodily pain so plainly written in a man's face. The sweat was falling from his brow, and his eyes were strained and bloodshot with agony. He had no stick, his vow, I presume, debarring him from such assistance, and he limped along, putting to the ground the heel of the unprotected foot. I could see it, and it was a mass of blood, and sores, and broken skin. An Irish girl would walk from Jerusalem to Jericho without shoes, and be not a penny the worse for it. This poor fellow clearly suffered so much that I was almost inclined to think that in the performance of his penance he had done something to aggravate his pain. Those around him paid no attention to him, and the dragoman seemed to think nothing of the affair whatever. "Those fools of Greeks do not understand the Christian religion," he said, being himself a Latin or Roman Catholic.

At the tail of the line we encountered two Bedouins, who were in charge of the caravan, and Joseph at once addressed them. The men were mounted, one on a very sorry-looking jade, but the other on a good stout Arab barb. They had guns slung behind their backs, coloured handkerchiefs on their heads, and they wore the striped bernouse. The parley went on for about ten minutes, during which the procession of pilgrims wound out of sight; and it ended in our being accompanied by the two Arabs, who thus left their greater charge to take care of itself back to the city. I understood afterwards that they had endeavoured to persuade Joseph that we might just as well go on alone, merely satisfying the demand of the tariff. But he had pointed out that I was a particular man, and that under such circumstances the final settlement might be doubtful. So they turned and accompanied us; but, as a matter of fact, we should have been as well without them.

The sun was beginning to fall in the heavens when we reached the actual margin of the Dead Sea. We had seen the glitter of its still waters for a long time previously, shining under the sun as though it were not real. We have often heard, and some of us have seen, how effects of light and shade together will produce so vivid an appearance of water where there is no water, as to deceive the most experienced. But the reverse was the case here. There was the lake, and there it had been before our eyes for the last two hours; and yet it looked, then and now, as though it were

121

an image of a lake and not real water. I had long since made up my mind to bathe in it, feeling well convinced that I could do so without harm to myself, and I had been endeavouring to persuade Smith to accompany me; but he positively refused. He would bathe, he said, neither in the Dead Sea nor in the river Jordan. He did not like bathing, and preferred to do his washing in his own room. Of course I had nothing further to say, and begged that, under these circumstances, he would take charge of my purse and pistols while I was in the water. This he agreed to do; but even in this he was strange and almost uncivil. I was to bathe from the furthest point of a little island, into which there was a rough causeway from the land made of stones and broken pieces of wood, and I exhorted him to go with me thither; but he insisted on remaining with his horse on the mainland, at some little distance from the island. He did not feel inclined to go down to the water's edge, he said.

I confess that at this I almost suspected that he was going to play me foul, and I hesitated. He saw in an instant what was passing through my mind. "You had better take your pistol and money with you. They will be quite safe on your clothes." But to have kept the things now would have shown suspicion too plainly, and as I could not bring myself to do that, I gave them up. I have sometimes thought that I was a fool to do so.

I went away by myself to the end of the island, and, then I did bathe. It is impossible to conceive anything more desolate than the appearance of the place. The land shelves very gradually away to the water, and the whole margin, to the breadth of some twenty or thirty feet, is strewn with a débris of rushes, bits of timber, and old white withered reeds. Whence these bits of timber have come it seems too difficult to say. The appearance is as though the water had receded and left them there. I have heard it said that there is no vegetation near the Dead Sea; but such is not the case, for these rushes do grow on the bank. I found it difficult enough to get into the water, for the ground shelves down very slowly, and is rough with stones and large pieces of half-rotten wood; moreover, when I was in nearly up to my hips, the water knocked me down. Indeed, it did so when I had gone as far as my knees, but I recovered myself, and by perseverance did proceed somewhat further. It must not be imagined that this knocking down was effected by the movement of the water. There is no such movement. Everything is perfectly still, and the fluid seems hardly to be displaced by the entrance of the body. But the effect is that one's feet are tripped up, and that one falls prostrate on to the surface. The water is so strong and buoyant, that, when above a foot in depth has to be encountered, the strength and weight of the bather are not sufficient to keep down his feet and legs. I then essayed to swim; but I could not do this in the ordinary way, as I was unable to keep enough of my body below the surface; so that my head and face seemed to be propelled down upon it. I turned round and floated, but the glare of the sun was so powerful that I could not remain long in that position. However, I had bathed in the Dead Sea, and was so far satisfied.

Anything more abominable to the palate than this water, if it be water, I never had inside my mouth. I expected it to be extremely salt, and no doubt, if it were analyzed, such would be the result; but there is a flavor in it which kills the salt. No attempt can be made at describing this taste. It may be imagined that I did not drink heartily, merely taking up a drop or two with my tongue from the palm of my hand; but it seemed to me as though I had been drenched with it. Even brandy would not relieve me from it. And then my whole body was in a mess, and I felt as though I had been rubbed with pitch. Looking at my limbs I saw no sign on them of the fluid. They seemed to dry from this as they usually do from any other water; but still the feeling remained. However, I was to ride from hence to a spot on the banks of Jordan, which I should reach in an hour, and at which I would wash; so I clothed myself, and prepared for my departure.

Seated in my position in the island, I was unable to see what was going on among the remainder of the party, and therefore could not tell whether my pistols and money were safe. I dressed, therefore, rather hurriedly, and on getting again to the shore, found that Mr. John Smith had not levanted. He was seated on his horse at some distance from Joseph and the Arabs, and had no appearance of being in league with those, no doubt, worthy guides. I certainly had suspected a ruse, and now was angry with myself that I had done so. And yet, in London, one would not trust one's money to a stranger whom one had met twenty-four hours since in a coffee-room! Why then do it with a stranger whom one chanced to meet in the desert?

"Thanks," I said, as he handed me my belongings. "I wish I could have induced you to come in also. The Dead Sea is now at your elbow, and therefore you think nothing of it; but in ten or fifteen years' time, you would be glad to be able to tell your children that you had bathed in it." "I shall never have any children to care for such tidings," he replied.

The river Jordan, for some miles above the point at which it joins the Red Sea, runs through very steep banks — banks which are almost precipitous — and is, as it were, guarded by thick trees and bushes which grow upon its sides. This is so much the case that one may ride, as we did, for a considerable distance along the margin, and not be able even to approach the water. I had a fancy for bathing in some spot of my own selection, instead of going to the open shore frequented by all the pilgrims; but I was baffled in this. When I did force my way down to the river side, I found that the water ran so rapidly and that the bushes and boughs of trees grew so far over and into the stream, as to make it impossible for me to do so. I could not have got in without my clothes, and having got in, I could not have got out again. I was, therefore, obliged to put up with the open muddy shore to which the pilgrims descend, and at which we may presume that Joshua passed when he came over as one of the twelve spies to spy out the land. And even here I could not go full into the stream as I would fain have done, lest I should be carried down, and so have assisted to whiten the shores of the Dead Sea with my bones. As to getting over to the Moabitish side of the river, that was plainly impossible; and, indeed, it seemed to be the prevailing opinion that the passage of the river was not practicable without going up as far as Samaria. And yet we know that here, or hereabouts, the Israelites did cross it.

I jumped from my horse the moment I got to the place, and once more gave my purse and pistols to my friend. "You are going to bathe again?" he said. "Certainly," said I; "you don't suppose that I would come to Jordan and not wash in it, even if I were not foul with the foulness of the Dead Sea!" "You'll kill yourself, in your present state of heat," he said remonstrating just as one's mother or wife might do. But even had it been my mother or wife

I could not have attended to such remonstrance then; and before he had done looking at me with those big eyes of his, my coat and waistcoat and cravat were on the ground, and I was at work at my braces; whereupon he turned from me slowly, and strolled away into the wood. On this occasion I had no base fears about my money.

And then I did bathe — very uncomfortably. The shore was muddy with the feet of the pilgrims, and the river so rapid that I hardly dared to get beyond the mud. I did manage to take a plunge in, head-foremost, but I was forced to wade out through the dirt and slush, so that I found it difficult to make my feet and legs clean enough for my shoes and stockings; and then, more-mover, the flies plagued me most unmercifully. I should have thought that the filthy flavour from the Dead Sea would have saved me from that nuisance; but the mosquitoes thereabouts are probably used to it. Finding this process of bathing to be so dif-ficult, I inquired as to the practice of the pilgrims. I found that with them, bathing in Jordan has come to be much the same as baptism has with us. It hardly means immersion. No doubt they do take off their shoes and stockings; but they do not strip and go bodily into the water.

As soon as I was dressed I found that Smith was again at my side with purse and pistols. We then went up a little above the wood and sat down together on the long sandy grass. It was now quite evening, so that the short Syrian twilight had commenced and the sun was no longer hot in the heavens. It would be night as we rode on to the tents at Jericho; but there was no difficulty as to the way, and therefore we did not hurry the horses who were feeding on the grass. We sat down together on a spot from which we could see the stream, close together, so that when I stretched myself out in my weariness, as I did before we started, my head rested on his legs. Ah, me! one does not take such liberties with new friends in England. It was a place which led one on to some special thoughts. The mountains of Moab were before us, very plain in their outline. "Moab is my wash-pot, and over Edom will I cast out my shoe!" There they were before us, very visible to the eye, and we began naturally to ask questions of each other. Why was Moab the wash-pot, and Edom thus cursed with in-dignity? Why had the right bank of the river been selected for such great purposes, whereas the left was thus condemned? Was there, at that time, any special fertility in this land or promise which has since departed from it? We are told of a bunch of grapes which took two men to carry it; but now there is not a vine in the whole country side. Now-a-days the sandy plain round Jericho is as dry and arid as are any of the valleys of Moab. The Jordan was running beneath our feet — the Jordan in which the leprous king had washed, though the bright rivers of his own Damascus were so much nearer to his land. It was but a humble stream to which he was sent; but the spot, probably, was higher up, above the Sea of Galilee, where the river is narrow. But another also had come down to this river, perhaps to this very spot on its shores, and submitted Himself to its waters — as to whom, perhaps, it will better that I should not speak much in this light story.

The Dead Sea was on our right, still glittering in the distance, and behind us lay the plains of Jericho and the wretched collection of huts which still bears the name of the ancient city. Beyond that, but still seemingly within easy distance of us, were the mountains of the wilderness. The wilderness! In truth the spot was one which did lead to many thoughts.

We talked of these things, as to many of which I found that my friend was much more free in his doubts and questionings than myself; and then our words came back to ourselves, the natural centre of all men's thoughts and words. "From what you say," I said, "I gather that you have had enough of this land?"

"Quite enough," he said. "Why seek such spots as these if they only dispel the associations and veneration of one's childhood?"

"But with me such associations and veneration are riveted the stronger by seeing the places and putting my hand upon the spots. I do not speak of that fictitious marble slab up there, but here, among the sandhills, by this river, at that Mount of Olives over which we passed, I do believe."

He paused a moment, and then replied: "To me it is all nothing — absolutely nothing. But then do we not know that our thoughts are formed, and our beliefs modelled, not on the outward signs or intrinsic evidence of things, — as would be the case were we always rational, — but by the inner workings of the mind itself? At the present turn of my life I can believe in nothing that is gracious."

"Ah; you mean that you are unhappy. You have come to grief in some of your doings or belongings, and therefore find that all things are bitter to the taste. I have had my palate out of order too, but the proper appreciation of flavours has come back to me. Bah—how noisome was that Dead Sea water!"

"The Dead Sea waters are noisome," he said; "and I have been drinking of them by long draughts."

"Long draughts?" I answered, thinking to console him. "Draughts have not been long which can have been swallowed in your years. Your disease may be acute, but it cannot yet have become chronic. A man always thinks at the moment of each misfortune that that special misery will last his lifetime; but God is too good for that. I do not know what ails you; but this day twelvemonth will see you again as sound as a roach."

We then sat silent for a while during which I was puffing at a cigar. Smith, among his accomplishments, did not reckon that of smoking—which was a grief to me; for a man enjoys his to-bacco doubly when another is enjoying it with him. "No, you do not know what ails me," he said at last.

"And therefore cannot judge. Perhaps not, my dear fellow. But my experience tells me that early wounds are generally ca-pable of cure, and therefore I surmise that yours may be so. The heart at your time of life is not worn out, and has strength and soundness left wherewith to throw off its maladies. I hope it may be so with you."

"God knows. I do not mean to say that there are none more to be pitied than I am; but, at the present moment, I am not— not light-hearted."

"I wish I could ease your burden, my dear fellow."

"It is most preposterous in me thus to force myself upon you, and then trouble you with my cares. But I had been alone so long, and I was weary of it!"

"By Jove, and so had I. Make no apology. And let me tell you this—though perhaps you will not credit me;—that I would sooner laugh with a comrade than cry with him, is true enough; but if occasion demand I can do the latter also." He then put out his hand to me, and I pressed it in token of my friendship. My own hand was hot and rough with the heat and sand; but his was

soft and cool almost as a woman's. I thoroughly hate an effemi-
nate man, but in spite of a certain womanly softness about this
fellow I could not hate him. "Yes," I continued, "though somewhat unused to the melting mood, I also can sometimes cry like
a very woman. I don't want to ask you any questions, and, as a
rule, I hate to be told secrets, but if I can be of any service to you
in any matter I will do my best. I don't say this with reference to
the present moment, but think of it before we part."

I looked round at him and saw that he was in tears. "I know
that you will think that I am a weak fool," he said, pressing his
handkerchief to his eyes.

"By no means. There are moments in a man's life when it becomes him to weep, but the older he grows the more seldom
those moments come to him. As far as I can see of men they
never cry at that which disgraces them."

"It is left for women to do that," he answered.

"Oh women! a woman cries for everything and for nothing. It
is the sharpest arrow she has in her quiver — the best card in her
hand. When a woman cries what can you do but give her all she
asks for?"

"Do you — dislike women?"

"No, by Jove! I am never really happy unless one is near me,
— or more than one. A man as a rule has an amount of energy
within him which he cannot turn to profit on himself alone. It
is good for him to have a woman by him that he may work for
her, and thus have exercise for his limbs and faculties. I am very
fond of women, but I always like those best who are the most
helpless."

We were silent again for a while, and it was during this time
that I found myself lying with my head on his lap. I had slept,
but it could have been but for a few minutes, and when I woke
I felt his hand upon my brow. As I started up he said that the flies
had been annoying me, and that he had not chosen to waken me
as I seemed weary. "It has been that double bathing," I said,
apologetically; for I always feel ashamed when I am detected
sleeping in the day. "In hot weather the water does make one
drowsy. By Jove, it's getting dark; we had better have the horses."

"Stay half a moment," he said, speaking very softly, and laying
his hand upon my arm, "I will not detain you a minute."

"There is no hurry in life," I said.

"You promised me just now that you would assist me."

"If it be in my power, I will."

"Before we part at Alexandria I will endeavour to tell you the story of my troubles, and then if you can aid me — " It struck me as he paused that I had made a rash promise, but nevertheless I must stand by it now — with one or two provisoes. The chances were that the young man was short of money, or else that he had got into a scrape about a girl. In either case I might give him some slight assistance; but, then, it behoved me to make him understand that I would not consent to become a participator in mischief. I was too old to get my head willingly into a scrape, and this I must endeavour to make him understand.

"I will if it be in my power," I said. "I will ask you no questions now; but if your trouble be about some lady — "

"It is not," said he.

"That is well. Of all troubles those are the most troublesome. If you are short of cash — "

"No, I am not short of cash."

"You are not. That's well too; for want of money is a sore trouble also." And then I paused before I came to the point. "I do not suspect anything bad of you, Smith. Had I done so I should not have spoken as I have done. And if there be nothing bad — "

"There is nothing disgraceful," he said.

"That is just what I mean; and in that case I will do anything for you that may be within my power. Now let us look for Joseph and the muckerry-boy, for it is time that we were at Jericho."

I cannot describe at length the whole of our journey from thence to our tents at Jericho, nor back to Jerusalem, nor even from Jerusalem to Jaffa. At Jericho we did sleep in tents, paying so much per night, according to the tariff. We wandered out at night, and drank coffee with a family of Arabs in the desert, sitting in a ring round their coffee-kettle. And we saw a Turkish soldier punished with the bastinado — a sight which did not do me any good, and which made Smith very sick. Indeed after the first blow he walked away. Jericho is a remarkable spot in that pilgrim week, and I wish I had space to describe it. But I have not, for I must hurry on, — back to Jerusalem and thence to Jaffa.

I had much to tell also of those Bedouins; how they were essentially true to us, but teased us almost to frenzy by their continual begging. They begged for our food and our drink, for our cigars and our gunpowder, for the clothes off our back and the handkerchiefs out of our pockets. As to gunpowder I had none to give them, for my charges were all made up in cartridges; and I learned that the guns behind their backs were a mere pretense, for they had not a grain of powder among them.

We slept one night in Jerusalem, and started early on the following morning. Smith came to my hotel, so that we might be ready together for the move. We still carried with us Joseph and the muckerry-boy; but for our Bedouins, who had duly received their forty shillings a piece, we had no further use. On our road down to Jerusalem we had much chat together, but only one adventure. Those pilgrims of whom I have spoken reach Jerusalem in the greatest number by the route which we were now taking in our departure from it, and they come in long droves, having reached Jaffa in crowds by the French and Austrian steamers from Smyrna, Damascus, and Constantinople. As their number confer security in that somewhat insecure country many travellers from the west of Europe make arrangements to travel with them. On our way down we met the last of these caravans for the year, and we were passing it for more than two hours. On this occasion I rode first and Smith was immediately behind me; but of a sudden I observed him to wheel his horse round and clamber downwards among bushes and stones towards a river that ran below us. "Hallo, Smith," I cried, "you will destroy your horse, and yourself too." But he would not answer me, and all I could do was to draw up in the path and wait. My confusion was made the worse, as at that moment a long string of pilgrims was passing by. "Good morning, sir," said an old man to me in good English. I looked up as I answered him, and saw a gray haired gentlemen, of very solemn and sad aspect. He might be seventy years of age, and I could see that he was attended by three or four servants. I shall never forget the severe and sorrowful expression of his eyes, over which his heavy eyebrows hung low. "Are there many English in Jerusalem?" he asked. "A good many," I replied: "there always are at Easter." "Can you tell me anything of any of them?" he asked. "Not a word," said I, for I knew no one; "but our consul can." And then we bowed to each other, and he passed on.

I got off my horse and scrambled down on foot after Smith. I found him gathering berries and bushes as though his very soul were mad with botany; but as I had seen nothing of this in him before, I asked what strange freak had taken him.

"You were talking to that old man," he said.

"Well, yes, I was."

"That is the relation of whom I have spoken to you."

"The d— he is!"

"And I would avoid him if it be possible."

I then learned that the old gentleman was his uncle. He had no living father or mother, and he now supposed that his relative was going to Jerusalem in quest of him. "If so," said I, "you will undoubtedly give him leg bail, unless the Austrian boat is more than ordinarily late. It is as much as we shall do to catch it, and you may be half over Africa, or far gone on your way to India, before he can be on your track again."

"I will tell you all about it at Alexandria," he replied; and then he scrambled up again with his horse, and we went on. That night we slept at the Armenian convent at Ramlath, or Ramath. This place is supposed to stand on the site of Arimathea, and is marked as such in many of the maps. The monks at this time of the year are very busy, as the pilgrims all stay here for one night on their routes backwards and forwards, and the place on such occasions is terribly crowded. On the night of our visit it was nearly empty, as a caravan had left it that morning; and thus we were indulged with separate cells, a point on which my companion seemed to lay considerable stress.

On the following day, at about noon, we entered Jaffa, and put up at an inn there which is kept by a Pole. The boat from Beyrout, which touches at Jaffa on its way to Alexandria, was not yet in, nor even sighted; we were therefore amply in time. "Shall we sail tonight?" I asked of the agent. "Yes, in all probability," he replied. "If the signal be seen before three we shall do so. If not, then not;" and so I returned to the hotel.

Smith had involuntarily shown signs of fatigue during the journey, but yet he had borne up well against it. I had never felt called on to grant any extra indulgence as to time because the work was too much for him. But now he was a good deal knocked up, and I was a little frightened, fearing that I had overdriven him under the heat of the sun. I was alarmed lest he should have fever, and proposed to send for the Jaffa doctor. But this he ut-terly refused. He would shut himself for an hour or two in his room, he said, and by that time he trusted the boat would be in sight. It was clear to me that he was very anxious on this subject, fearing that his uncle would be back upon his heels before he had started.

I ordered a serious breakfast for myself, for with me, on such occasions, my appetite demands more immediate attention than my limbs. I also acknowledge that I become fatigued, and can lay myself at length during such idle days and sleep from hour to hour; but the desire to do so never comes till I have well eaten and drunken. A bottle of French wine, three or four cutlets of goats' flesh, an omelet made not of the freshest eggs, and an enor-mous dish of oranges, was the banquet set before me; and though I might have found fault with it in Paris or London, I thought that it did well enough in Jaffa. My poor friend could not join me, but had a cup of coffee in his room. "At any rate take a little brandy in it," I said to him, as I stood over his bed. "I could not swallow it," said he, looking at me with almost beseeching eyes. "Beshrew the fellow," I said to myself, as I left him, carefully closing the door, so that the sound should not shake him; "He is little better than a woman, and yet I have become as fond of him as though he were my brother."

I went out at three, but up to that time the boat had not been signalled. "And we shall not get out to-night?" "No, not to-night," said the agent. "And at what time to-morrow?" "If she comes in this evening, you will start by daylight. But they so manage her departure from Beyrout, that she seldom is here in the evening." "It will be noon to-morrow, then." "Yes," the man said, "noon to-morrow." I calculated, however, that the old gentleman could not possibly be on our track by that time. He would not have reached Jerusalem till late in the day on which we saw him, and it would take him some time to obtain tidings of his nephew. But it might be possible that messengers sent by him should reach Jaffa by four or five on the day after his arrival. That would be this very day which we were now wasting at Jaffa. Having thus made my calculations, I returned to Smith, to give him such consolation as it might be in my power to afford.

He seemed to be dreadfully afflicted by all this. "He will have traced me to Jerusalem, and then again away; and will follow me immediately."

"That is all very well," I said; "but let even a young man do the best he can, and he will not get from Jerusalem to Jaffa in less than twelve hours. Your uncle is not a young man, and could not possibly do the journey under two days."

"But he will send. He will not mind what money he spends."

"And if he does send, take off your hat to his messengers, and bid them carry your compliments back. You are not a felon whom he can arrest."

"No, he cannot arrest me; but, ah! you do not understand;" and then he sat up on the bed, and seemed as though he were going to wring his hands in despair.

I waited for some half hour in his room, thinking that he would tell me this story of his. If he required that I should give him any aid in the presence either of his uncle or of his uncle's myrmidons, I must at any rate know what was likely to be the dispute between them. But as he said nothing, I suggested that he should stroll out with me among the orange-groves by which the town is surrounded. In answer to this he looked up piteously into my face as though begging me to be merciful to him. "You are strong," said he, "and cannot understand what it is to feel fatigue as I do." And yet he had declared on commencing his journey that he would not be found to complain! Nor had he complained by a single word till after that encounter with his uncle. Nay he had borne up well till this news had reached us of the boat being late. I felt convinced that if the boat were at this moment lying in the harbour all that appearance of excessive weakness would soon vanish. What it was that he feared I could not guess; but it was manifest to me that some great terror almost overwhelmed him.

"My idea is," said I, — and I suppose that I spoke with something less of good-nature in my tone than I had assumed for the last day or two, "that no man should, under any circumstances, be so afraid of another man as to tremble at his presence — either at his presence or his expected presence."

"Ah, now you are angry with me, now you despise me!" he

said.

"Neither the one or the other. But if I may take the liberty of a friend with you, I would advise you to combat this feeling of horror. If you do not, it will unman you. After all, what can your uncle do to you? He cannot rob you of your heart or soul. He cannot touch your inner self."

"You do not know," he said.

"Ah but, Smith, I do know that. Whatever may be this quarrel between you and him, you should not tremble at the thought of him, unless indeed — "

"Unless what?"

"Unless you had done aught that should make you tremble before every honest man." I own I had begun to have my doubts of him, and to fear that he had absolutely disgraced himself. Even in such case I — I individually — did not wish to be severe on him; but I should be annoyed to find that I had opened my heart to a swindler or a practised knave.

"I will tell you all to-morrow," said he, "but I have been guilty of nothing of that sort."

In the evening he did come out, and sat with me as I smoked my cigar. The boat, he was told, would almost undoubtedly come in by daybreak on the following morning, and be off at nine; whereas it was very improbable that any arrival from Jerusalem would be so early as that. "Besides," I reminded him, "your uncle will hardly hurry down to Jaffa, because he will have no reason to think but what you have already started. There are no telegraphs here you know."

In the evening he was still very sad, though the paroxysm of his terror seemed to have passed away. I would not bother him, as he had himself chosen the following morning for the telling of his story. So I sat and smoked, and talked to him about our past journey, and by degrees the power of speech came back to him, and I again felt that I loved him. Yes, loved him! I have not taken many such fancies into my head at so short a notice, but I did love him as though he were a younger brother. I felt a delight in serving him, and though I was almost old enough to be his father I ministered to him, as though he had been an old man, or a woman.

On the following morning we were stirring at daybreak, and

found that the vessel was in sight. She would be in the roads off the town in two hours' time, they said, and would start at eleven or twelve. And then we walked round by the gate of the town, and sauntered a quarter of a mile or so along the way that leads towards Jerusalem. I could see that his eye was anxiously turned down the road, but he said nothing. We saw no cloud of dust, and then we returned to breakfast.

"The steamer has come to anchor," said our dirty Polish host to us in execrable English. "And we may be off on board," said Smith. "Not yet," he said; "they must put their cargo out first." I saw, however, that Smith was uneasy, and I made up my mind to go off to the vessel at once. When they should see an English portmanteau making an offer to come up the gangway, the Austrian sailors would not stop it. So I called for the bill, and ordered that the things should be taken down to the wretched broken heap of rotten timber, which they called a quay. Smith had not told me his story, but no doubt he would as soon as he was on board.

I was in the very act of squabbling with the Pole over the last demand for piastres, when we heard a noise in the gateway of the inn, and I saw Smith's countenance become pale. It was an Englishman's voice asking if there were any strangers there; so I went into the courtyard, closing the door behind me, and turning the key upon the landlord and Smith. "Smith," said I to myself, "will keep the Pole quiet if he have any wit left."

The man who had asked the question had the air of an upper English servant, and I thought that I recognized one of those whom I had seen with the old gentleman on the road; but the matter was soon put at rest by the appearance of that gentleman himself. He walked up into the courtyard, looked hard at me from under those bushy eyebrows, just raised his hat, and then said, — "I believe I am speaking to Mr. Jones."

"Yes," said I, "I am Mr. Jones. Can I have the honour of serving you?"

There was something peculiarly unpleasant about this man's face. At the present moment I examined it closely, and could understand the great aversion which his nephew felt towards him. He looked like a gentleman and like a man of talent, nor was there anything of meanness in his face; neither was he ill-

135

looking, in the usual acceptation of the word. But one could see that he was solemn, austere, and overbearing; that he would be incapable of any light enjoyment, and unforgiving towards all offences. I took him to be a man who, being old himself, could never remember that he had been young, and who therefore hated the levities of youth. To me such a character is specially odious; for I would fain, if it be possible, be young even to my grave. Smith, if he were clever, might escape from the window of the room, which opened out upon a terrace, and still get down to the steamer. I would keep the old man in play for some time; and, even though I lost my passage, would be true to my friend. There lay our joint luggage at my feet in the yard. If Smith would venture away without his portion of it, all might yet be right.

"My name, sir, is Sir William Weston," he began. I had heard of the name before, and knew him to be a man of wealth, and family, and note. I took off my hat, and said that I had much honour in meeting Sir William Weston.

"And I presume you know the object with which I am now here," he continued.

"Not exactly," said I. "Nor do I understand how I possibly should know it, seeing that, up to this moment, I did not even know your name, and have heard nothing concerning either your movements or your affairs."

"Sir," said he, "I have hitherto believed that I might at any rate expect from you the truth."

"Sir," said I, "I am bold to think that you will not dare to tell me, that either now, or at any other time, you have received, or expect to receive, from me anything that is not true."

He then stood still, looking at me for a moment or two, and I beg to assert that I looked as fully at him. There was, at any rate, no cause why I should tremble before him. I was not his nephew, nor was I responsible for his nephew's doings toward him. Two of his servants were behind him, and on my side there stood a boy and girl belonging to the inn. They, however, could not understand a word of English. I saw that he was hesitating, but at last he spoke out. I confess, now, that his words, when they were spoken, did, at the first moment, make me tremble.

"I have to charge you," said he, "with eloping with my niece, and I demand of you to inform me where she is. You are perfectly

136

aware that I am her guardian by law."

I did tremble — not that I cared much for Sir William's guardianship, but I saw before me so terrible an embarrassment! And then I felt so thoroughly abashed in that I had allowed myself to be so deceived! It all came back upon me in a moment, and covered me with a shame that even made me blush. I had travelled through the desert with a woman for days, and had not discovered her though she had given me a thousand signs. All those signs I remembered now, and I blushed painfully. When her hand was on my forehead I still thought that she was a man! I declare that at this moment I felt a stronger disinclination to face my late companion than I did to encounter her angry uncle.

"Your niece!" I said, speaking with a sheepish bewilderment which should have convinced him at once of my innocence. She had asked me, too, whether I was a married man, and I had denied it. How was I to escape from such a mess of misfortunes? I declare that I began to forget her troubles in my own.

"Yes, my niece, Miss Julia Weston. The disgrace which you have brought upon me must be wiped out; but my first duty is to save that unfortunate young woman from further misery."

"If it be as you say," I exclaimed, "by the honour of a gentleman — "

"I care nothing for the honour of a gentleman till I see it proved. Be good enough to inform me, sir, whether Miss Weston is in this house."

For a moment I hesitated; but I saw at once that I should make myself responsible for certain mischief, of which I was at any rate hitherto in truth innocent, if I allowed myself to become a party to concealing a young lady. Up to this period I could at any rate defend myself, whether my defence were believed or not believed. I still had a hope that the charming Julia might have escaped through the window, and a feeling that if she had done so I was not responsible. When I turned the lock I turned it on Smith.

For a moment I hesitated, and then walked slowly across the yard and opened the door. "Sir William," I said, as I did so, "I travelled here with a companion dressed as a man; and I believed him to be what he seemed till this minute."

"Sir!" said Sir William, with a look of scorn in his face,

which gave me the lie in my teeth as plainly as any words could do. And then he entered the room. The Pole was standing in one corner, apparently amazed at what was going on, and Smith — I may as well call her Miss Weston at once, for the baronet's statement was true — was sitting on a sort of divan in the corner of the chamber, hiding her face in her hands. She had made no attempt at an escape, and a full explanation was therefore indispensable. For myself I own that I felt ashamed of my part in the play, ashamed even of my own innocency. Had I been less innocent I should certainly have contrived to appear much less guilty. Had it occurred to me on the banks of Jordan that Smith was a lady, I should not have travelled with her in her gentleman's habiliments from Jerusalem to Jaffa. Had she condescended to remain under my protection, she must have done so without a masquerade.

The uncle stood still and looked at his niece. He probably understood how thoroughly stern and disagreeable was his own face, and considered that he could punish the crime of his relative in no severer way than by looking at her. In this I think he was right. But at last there was a necessity for speaking. "Unfortunate young woman!" he said, and then paused.

"We had better get rid of the landlord," I said, "before we come to any explanation." And I motioned to the man to leave the room. This he did very unwillingly, but at last he was gone.

"I fear that it is needless to care on her account who may hear the story of her shame," said Sir William. I looked at Miss Weston, but she still sat hiding her face. However, if she did not defend herself, it was necessary that I should defend both her and me.

"I do not know how far I may be at liberty to speak with reference to the private matters of yourself or of your — your niece, Sir William Weston. I would not willingly interfere — "

"Sir," said he, "your interference has already taken place. Will you have the goodness to explain to me what are your intentions with regard to that lady?"

My intentions! Heaven help me! My intentions, of course, were to leave her in her uncle's hands. Indeed, I could hardly be said to have formed any intention since I had learned that I had been honoured by a lady's presence. At this moment I deeply re-

gretted that I had thoughtlessly stated to her that I was an unmarried man. In doing so I had had no object. But at that time
"Smith" had been quite a stranger to me, and I had not thought
it necessary to declare my own private concerns. Since that I had
talked so little of myself that the fact of my family at home had
not been mentioned. "Will you have the goodness to explain
what are your intentions with regard to that lady?" said the baronet.

"Oh, Uncle William!" exclaimed Miss Weston, now at length
raising her head from her hands.

"Hold your peace, madam," said he. "When called upon to
speak you will find your words with difficulty enough. Sir, I am
waiting for an answer from you."

"But, uncle, he is nothing to me; — the gentleman is nothing
to me!"

"By the heavens above us he shall be something; or I will know
the reason why! What! he has gone off with you; he has travelled
through the country with you, hiding you from your only natural
friend; he has been your companion for weeks — "

"Six days, sir," said I.

"Sir!" said the baronet, again giving me the lie. "And now,"
he continued, addressing his niece, "you tell me that he is nothing to you! He shall give me his promise that he will make you
his wife at the consulate at Alexandria, or I will destroy him. I
know who he is."

"If you know who I am," said I, "you must know — "

But he would not listen to me. "And as for you, madam, unless
he makes me that promise — ." And then he paused in his threat,
and, turning round, looked me in the face. I saw that she also
was looking at me, though not openly as he did; and some flattering devil that was at work round my heart would have persuaded me that she also would have heard a certain answer given
without dismay — would even have received comfort in her agony from such answer. But the reader knows how completely that
answer was out of my power.

"I have not the slightest ground for supposing," said I, "that
the lady would accede to such an arrangement — if it were possible. My acquaintance with her has been altogether confined to
— . To tell the truth, I have not been in Miss Weston's confi-

dence, and have taken her to be only that which she has seemed to be."

"Sir!" said the Baronet, again looking at me as though he would wither me on the spot for my falsehood.

"It is true!" said Julia, getting up from her seat, and appealing with clasped hands to her uncle — "as true as heaven."

"Madam!" said he, "do you both take me for a fool?"

"That you should take me for one," said I, "would be very natural. The facts are as we state to you. Miss Weston — as I now learn that she is — did me the honour of calling at my hotel, having heard — ." And then it seemed to me as though I were attempting to screen myself by telling the story against her, so I was again silent. Never in my life had I been in a position of such extra-ordinary difficulty. The duty which I owed to Julia as a woman, and to Sir William as a guardian and to myself as the father of a family, all clashed with each other. I was anxious to be generous, honest, and prudent; but it was impossible, so I made up my mind to say nothing further.

"Mr. Jones," said the baronet, "I have explained to you the only arrangement which under the present circumstances I can permit to pass without open exposure and condign punishment. That you are a gentleman by birth, education, and position I am aware," — whereupon I raised my hat, and then he continued. "That lady has three hundred a year of her own — "

"And attractions, personal and mental, which are worth ten times the money," said I; and I bowed to my fair friend, who looked at me the while with sad beseeching eyes. I confess that the mistress of my bosom, had she known my thoughts at that one moment, might have had room for anger.

"Very well," continued he. "Then the proposal which I named cannot, I imagine, but be satisfactory. If you will make to her and to me the only amends which it is in your power as a gentleman to afford, I will forgive all. Tell me that you will make her your wife on your arrival in Egypt."

I would have given anything not to have looked at Miss Weston at this moment, but I could not help it. I did turn my face half round to her before I answered, and then felt that I had been cruel in doing so. "Sir William," said I, "I have at home already a wife and family of my own."

"It is not true!" said he, retreating a step, and staring at me with amazement.

"There is something, sir," I replied, "in the unprecedented circumstances of this meeting, and in your position with regard to that lady, which, joined to your advanced age, will enable me to regard that useless insult as unspoken. I am a married man. There is the signature of my wife's last letter," and I handed him one which I had received as I was leaving Jerusalem.

But the coarse violent contradiction which Sir William had given me was as nothing compared with the reproach conveyed in Miss Weston's countenance. She looked at me as though all her anger were now turned against me. And yet, methought, there was more of sorrow than of resentment in her countenance. But what cause was there for either? Why should I be reproached, even by her look? She did not remember at the moment that when I answered her chance question as to my domestic affairs, I had answered it as to a man who was a stranger to me, and not as to a beautiful woman with whom I was about to pass certain days in close and intimate society. To her, at the moment, it seemed as though I had cruelly deceived her. In truth the one person really deceived had been myself.

And here I must explain, on behalf of the lady, that when she first joined me she had no other view than that of seeing the banks of the Jordan in that guise which she had chosen to assume in order to escape from the solemnity and austerity of a disagreeable relative. She had been very foolish, and that was all. I take it that she had first left her uncle at Constantinople, but on this point I never got certain information. Afterwards, while we were travelling together, the idea had come upon her, that she might go on as far as Alexandria with me. And then —. I know nothing further of the lady's intentions, but I am certain that her wishes were good and pure. Her uncle had been intolerable to her, and she had fled from him. Such had been her offence and no more.

"Then, sir," said the baronet, giving me back my letter, "you must be a double-dyed villain."

"And you, sir," said I "—" But here Julia Weston interrupted me.

"Uncle, you altogether wrong this gentleman," she said. "He has been kind to me beyond my power of words to express; but, till told by you, he knew nothing of my secret. Nor would he have known it," she added, looking down upon the ground. As to that latter assertion I was at liberty to believe as much as I pleased.

The Pole now came to the door, informing us that any who wished to start by the packet must go on board, and therefore, as the unreasonable old gentleman perceived, it was necessary that we should all make our arrangements. I cannot say that they were such as enable me to look back on them with satisfaction. He did seem, now at last, to believe that I had been an unconscious agent in his niece's strategem, but he hardly on that account became civil to me. "It was absolutely necessary," he said, "that he, and that unfortunate young woman," as he would continue to call her, "should depart at once, — by this ship now going." To this proposition of course I made no opposition. "And you, Mr. Jones," he continued, "will at once perceive that you, as a gentleman, should allow us to proceed on our journey without the honour of your company."

This was very dreadful, but what could I say; or, indeed, what could I do? My most earnest desire in the matter was to save Miss Weston from annoyance; and under existing circumstances my presence on board could not but be a burden to her. And then, if I went, — if I did go, in opposition to the wishes of the baronet, could I trust my own prudence? It was better for all parties that I should remain.

"Sir William," said I, after a minute's consideration, "if you will apologize to me for the gross insults you have offered me, it shall be as you say."

"Mr. Jones," said Sir William, "I do apologize for the words which I used to you while I was labouring under a very natural misconception of the circumstances." I do not know that I was much the better for the apology, but at the moment I regarded it as sufficient.

Their things were then hurried down to the strand, and I accompanied them to the ruined quay. I took off my hat to Sir William as he was first let down into the boat. He descended first, so that he might receive his niece — for all Jaffa now knew that it was a lady—and then I gave her my hand for the last time. "God bless you, Miss Weston," I said, pressing it closely. "God bless you, Mr. Jones," she replied. And from that day to this I have neither spoken to her nor seen her.

I waited a fortnight at Jaffa for the French boat, eating cutlets of goats' flesh, and wandering among the orange groves. I certainly look back on that fortnight as the most miserable period of my life. I had been deceived, and had failed to discover the deceit, even though the deceiver had perhaps wished that I should do so. For that blindness I have never forgiven myself.

"The Banks of the Jordan" appeared first in the January 5, 12, and 19 issues of *The London Review* for 1861.

John Bull on the Guadalquivir

I AM AN ENGLISHMAN, LIVING, as all Englishmen should do, in England, and my wife would not, I think, be well pleased were any one to insinuate that she were other than an Englishwoman; but in the circumstances of my marriage I became connected with the south of Spain, and the narrative which I am about to tell requires that I should refer to some of those details.

The Pomfrets and Daguilars have long been in trade together in this country, and one of the partners has usually resided at Seville for the sake of the works which the firm there possesses. My father, James Pomfret, lived there for ten years before his marriage; and since that, and up to the present period, old Mr. Daguilar has been always on the spot. He was, I believe, born in Spain, but he came very early to England; he married an English wife, and his sons have been educated exclusively in England. His only daughter, Maria Daguilar, did not pass so large a proportion of her early life in this country, but she came to us for a visit at the age of seventeen, and when she returned I made up my mind that I most assuredly would go after her. So I did, and she is now sitting on the other side of the fireplace with a legion of small linen habiliments in a huge basket by her side.

I felt, at the first, that there was something lacking to make my cup of love perfectly delightful. It was very sweet, but there was wanting that flavour of romance which is generally added to the heavenly draught by a slight admixture of opposition. I feared that the path of my true love would run too smooth. When Maria came to our house, my mother and elder sister seemed to be quite willing that I should be continually alone with her; and she had not been there ten days before my father, by chance, remarked that there was nothing old Mr. Daguilar valued so highly as a thorough feeling of intimate alliance between the two families which had been so long connected in trade. I was never told that Maria was to be my wife, but I felt that the same thing was done without words; and when, after six weeks of somewhat elaborate attendance upon her, I asked her to be Mrs. John Pomfret, I had no more fear of a refusal, or even of hesitation on her part, than I now have when I suggest to my partner some commercial trans- action of undoubted advantage.

But Maria, even at that age, had about her a quiet, sustained decision of character quite unlike anything I had seen in English girls. I used to hear, and do still hear, how much more flippant is the education of girls in France and Spain than in England; and I know that this is shown to be the result of many causes; but, nevertheless, I rarely see in one of our own young women the same power of self-sustained demeanour as I meet on the conti- nent. It goes no deeper than the demeanour, people say. I can only answer that I have not found that shallowness in my own wife.

Miss Daguilar replied to me that she was not prepared with an answer; she had only known me six weeks, and wanted more time to think about it; besides, there was one in her own country with whom she would wish to consult. I knew she had no mother; and as for consulting old Mr. Daguilar on such a subject, that idea, I knew, could not have troubled her. Besides, as I afterwards learned, Mr. Daguilar had already proposed the marriage to his partner, exactly as he would have proposed a division of assets. My mother declared that Maria was a foolish chit — in which, by-the-bye, she showed her entire ignorance of Miss Daguilar's character; my eldest sister begged that no constraint might be put on the young lady's inclinations — which provoked me to assert that the young lady's inclinations were by no means opposed to my own; and my father, in the coolest manner, suggested that the matter might stand over for twelve months! — and that I might then go to Seville, and see about it. Stand over for twelve months! Would not Maria, long before that time, have been snapped up and carried off by one of those inordinately rich Spanish grandees who are still to be met with occasionally in Andalusia?

My father's dictum, however, had gone forth; and Maria, in the calmest voice, protested that she thought it very wise. I should be less of a boy by that time, she said, smiling at me, but driving wedges between every fibre of my body as she spoke. "Be it so," I said, proudly; "at any rate, I am not so much of a boy that I shall forget you." "And, John, you still have the trade to learn," she added, with her deliciously foreign intonation — speaking very slowly, but with perfect pronunciation. The trade to learn! However, I said not a word, but stalked out of the room, meaning to see her no more before she went. But I could not resist attending on her in the hall as she started; and, when she took leave of us, she put her face up to be kissed by me, as she did by my father, and seemed to receive as much emotion from one embrace as from the other. "He'll go out by the packet of the 1st of April," said my father, speaking of me as though I were a bale of goods. "Ah! that will be so nice," said Maria, settling her dress in the carriage; "the oranges will be ripe for him then!"

On the 17th of April I did sail, and felt still very like a bale of goods. I had received one letter from her, in which she merely stated that her papa would have a room ready for me on my arrival; and in answer to that, I had sent an epistle somewhat longer, and, as I then thought, a little more to the purpose. Her turn of mind was more practical than romantic, and I must confess my belief that she did not appreciate my poetry.

I landed at Cadiz, and was there joined by an old family friend, one of the very best fellows that ever lived. He was to accompany me up as far as Seville; and, as he had lived for a year or two at Xeres, was supposed to be more Spanish almost than a Spaniard. His name was Johnson, and he was in the wine trade; and whether for travelling, or whether for staying at home—whether for paying you a visit in your own house, or whether for entertaining you in his—there never was (and I am prepared to maintain there never will be) a stancher friend, a choicer companion, or a safer guide than Thomas Johnson. Words cannot produce an eulogium sufficient for his merits. But, as I have since learned, he was not quite so Spanish as I had imagined. Three years among the *bodegas* of Xeres had taught him, no doubt, to appreciate the exact twang of a good, dry sherry; but not, as I now conceive, the exactest flavour of the true Spanish character. I was very lucky, however, in meeting such a friend, and now reckon him as one of the stanchest allies of the house of Pomfret Daguilar and Pomfret.

He met me at Cadiz, and took me about the town, which appeared to me to be of no very great interest. The young ladies were all very well; but, in this respect, I was then a stoic, till such time as I might be able to throw myself at the feet of her whom I was ready to proclaim the most lovely of all the dulcineas of Andalusia. He carried me up by boat and railway to Xeres; gave me a most terrific headache, by dragging me out into the glare of the sun, after I had tasted some half-a-dozen different wines, and went through all the ordinary hospitalities. On the next day we returned to Puerto, and from thence, getting across to St. Lucar and Bonanza, found ourselves on the banks of the Guadalquivir, and took our places in the boat for Seville. I need say but little to my readers respecting that far-famed river. Thirty years ago we in England generally believed that on its banks was to be found a pure elysium of pastoral beauty; that picturesque shepherds and lovely maidens here fed their flocks in fields of asphodel; that the limpid stream ran cool and crystal over bright stones and beneath perennial shade; and that everything on the Guadalquivir was as lovely and poetical as its name. Now, it is pretty widely known that no uglier river oozes down to its bourn in the sea, through unwholesome banks of low mud. It is brown and dirty; ungifted by any scenic advantage; margined for miles upon miles of huge, flat, expansive fields, in which cattle are reared — the bulls wanted for the bull-fights among the other uses — and birds of prey sit constant on the shore, watching for the carcasses of such as die. Such are the charms of the golden Guadalquivir.

At first, we were very dull on board that steamer. I never found myself in a position in which there was less to do. There was a nasty smell about the little boat which made me almost ill; every turn in the river was so exactly like the last, that we might have been standing still; there was no amusement except eating, and that, when once done, was not of a kind to make an early repe-

tition desirable. Even Johnson was becoming dull, and I began
to doubt whether I was so desirous as I once had been to travel
the length and breadth of all Spain. But about noon a little in-
cident occurred which did for a time remove some of our tedium.
The boat had stopped to take in passengers on the river; and,
among others, a man had come on board dressed in a fashion
that, to my eyes, was equally strange and picturesque. Indeed his
appearance was so singular, that I could not but regard him with
care, though I felt, at first, averse to stare at a fellow-passenger
on account of his clothes. He was a man of about fifty, but as
active, apparently, as though not much more than twenty-five;
he was of low stature, but of admirable make; his hair was just
becoming grizzled, but was short and crisp, and well cared-for; his
face was prepossessing, having a look of good humour added to
courtesy, and there was a pleasant, soft smile round his mouth
which ingratiated one at the first sight. But it was his dress rather
than his person which attracted attention. He wore the ordinary
Andalusian cap — of which such hideous parodies are now making themselves common in England — but was not contented
with the usual ornament of the double tuft. The cap was small
and jaunty; trimmed with silk velvet — as is common here with
men careful to adorn their persons; but this man's cap was finished off with a jewelled button and golden filigree work. He was
dressed in a short jacket with a stand-up collar; and that also was
covered with golden buttons and with golden buttonholes. It was
all gilt down the front, and all lace down the back. The row of
buttons was double; and those of the more backward row hung
down in heavy pundules. His waistcoat was of coloured silk —
very pretty to look at; and ornamented with a small sash, through
which gold threads were worked. The bindings of his breeches
also were of gold; and there were gold tags to all the buttonholes.
His stockings were of the finest silk, and clocked with gold from
the knee to the ankle.

Dress any Englishman in such a garb as this and he will at once
give you the idea of a hog in armour. In the first place, he will
lack the proper spirit to carry it off; and in the next place, the
motion of his limbs will disgrace the ornaments they bear. "And
so best," most Englishmen will say. Very likely; and, therefore,
let no Englishman try it. But my Spaniard did not look at all like

a hog in armour. He walked slowly down the plank into the boat, whistling lowly, but very clearly, a few bars from an opera tune. It was plain to see that he was master of himself, of his ornaments, and of his limbs. He had no appearance of thinking that men were looking at him, or of feeling that he was beauteous in his attire — nothing could be more natural than his foot-fall, or the quiet glance of his cheery grey eye. He walked up to the captain, who held the helm, and lightly raised his hand to his cap. The captain, taking one hand from the wheel, did the same, and then the stranger, turning his back to the stern of the vessel, and fronting down the river with his face, continued to whistle slowly, clearly, and in excellent time. Grand as were his clothes, they were no burthen on his mind.

"What is he?" said I, going up to my friend Johnson, with a whisper.

"Well, I've been looking at him," said Johnson — which was true enough; "he's a—an uncommonly good-looking fellow, isn't he?"

"Particularly so," said I; "and got up quite irrespective of expense. Is he a — a — a gentleman, now, do you think?"

"Well, those things are so different in Spain that it's almost impossible to make an Englishman understand them; one learns to know all these sort of people by being with them in the country, but one can't explain."

"No; exactly. Are they real gold?"

"Yes, yes; I dare say they are. They sometimes have them silver gilt."

"It is quite a common thing, then, isn't it?" asked I.

"Well, not exactly that — Ah! yes; I see! of course. He is a torero."

"A what?"

"A mayo. I will explain it all to you. You will see them about in all places, and will get used to them."

"But I haven't seen one other as yet."

"No, and they are not all so gay as this, nor so new in their finery, you know."

"And what is a torero?"

"Well, a torero is a man engaged in bull-fighting."

"Oh! he is a matador, is he?" said I, looking at him with more than all my eyes.

"No, not exactly that — not of necessity. He is probably a mayo — a fellow that dresses himself smart for fairs, and will be seen hanging about with the bull-fighters. What would be a sporting fellow in England — only he won't drink and curse like a low man on the turf there. Come, shall we go and speak to him?"

"I can't talk to him," said I, diffident of my Spanish. I had received lessons in England from Maria Daguilar; but six weeks is little enough for making love, let alone the learning of a foreign language.

"Oh! I'll do the talking. You'll find the language easy enough, before long. It soon becomes the same as English to you, when you live among them." And then Johnson, walking up to the stranger, accosted him with that good-natured familiarity with which a thoroughly nice fellow always opens a conversation with his inferiors. Of course I could not understand the words which were exchanged; but it was clear enough that the "mayo" took the address in good part, and was inclined to be communicative and social.

"They are all of pure gold," said Johnson, turning to me after a minute, making as he spoke a motion with his head to show the importance of the information.

"Are they indeed!" said I. "Where on earth did a fellow like that get them!" Whereupon Johnson again returned to his conversation with the man. After another minute he raised his hand, and began to finger the button on the shoulder; and to aid him in doing so, the man of the bull-ring turned a little on one side.

"They are wonderfully well made," said Johnson, talking to me, and still fingering the button. "They are manufactured, he says, at Osuna, and he tells me that they make them better than anywhere else."

"I wonder what the whole set would cost?" said I. "An enormous deal of money for a fellow like him, I should think!"

"Over twelve ounces," said Johnson, having asked the question; "and that will be more than forty pounds."

"What an uncommon ass he must be!" said I.

As Johnson, by this time, was very closely scrutinising the

whole set of ornaments, I thought I might do so also, and going up close to our friend, I too began to handle the buttons and tags on the other side. Nothing could have been more good-humoured than he was — so much so, that I was emboldened to hold up his arm that I might see the cut of his coat, to take off his cap and examine the make, to stuff my finger beneath his sash, and at last to kneel down while I persuaded him to hold up his legs that I might look to the clocking of the stocking. The fellow was thoroughly good-natured, and why should I not indulge my curiosity?

"You'll upset him if you don't take care," said Johnson; for I had got fast hold of him by one ankle, and was determined to finish the survey completely.

"Oh, no, I sha'n't," said I; "a bull-fighting chap can surely stand on one leg. But what I wonder at is, how on earth he can afford it!" Whereupon Johnson again began to interrogate him in Spanish.

"He says he has got no children," said Johnson, having received a reply, "and that, as he has nobody but himself to look after, he is able to allow himself such little luxuries."

"Tell him that I say he would be better with a wife and couple of babies," said I — and Johnson interpreted.

"He says that he'll think of it some of these days, when he finds that the supply of fools in the world is becoming short," said Johnson.

We had nearly done with him now; but after regaining my feet, I addressed myself once more to the heavy pendules, which hung down almost under his arm. I lifted one of these, meaning to feel its weight between my fingers; but unfortunately I gave a lurch, probably through the motion of the boat, and still holding by the button, tore it almost off from our friend's coat.

"Oh, I am so sorry!" I said, in broad English.

"It do not matter at all," he said, bowing, and speaking with equal plainness. And then, taking a knife from his pocket, he cut the pendule off, leaving a bit of torn cloth on the side of his jacket.

"Upon my word, I am quite unhappy," said I; "but I always am so awkward." Whereupon he bowed low.

"Couldn't I make it right?" said I, bringing out my purse.

He lifted his hand, and I saw that it was small and white; he lifted it, and gently put it upon my purse, smiling sweetly as he did so. "Thank you, no, *señor*; thank you, no." And then, bowing to us both, he walked away down into the cabin.

"Upon my word, he is a deuced well-mannered fellow," said I.

"You shouldn't have offered him money," said Johnson; "a Spaniard does not like it."

"Why, I thought you could do nothing without money in this country. Doesn't every one take bribes?"

"Ah! yes; that is a different thing; but not the price of a button. By Jove! he understood English, too. Did you see that?"

"Yes; and I called him an ass! I hope he doesn't mind it."

"Oh! no; he won't think anything about it," said Johnson. "Those sort of fellows don't. I daresay we shall see him in the bull-ring next Sunday, and then we"ll make it all right with a glass of lemonade."

And so our adventure ended with the man of the gold ornaments. I was sorry that I had spoken English before him so heedlessly, and resolved that I would never be guilty of such a *gaucherie* again. But, then, who would think that a Spanish bullfighter would talk a foreign language? I was sorry, also, that I had torn his coat — it had looked so awkward; and sorry, again, that I had offered the man money. Altogether I was a little ashamed of myself; but I had too much to look forward to at Seville to allow any heaviness to remain long at my heart; and, before I had arrived at the marvellous city, I had forgotten both him and his buttons.

Nothing could be nicer than the way in which I was welcomed at Mr. Daguilar's house, or more kind — I may almost say affectionate — than Maria's manner to me. But it was too affectionate; and I am not sure that I should not have liked my reception better had she been more diffident in her tone, and less inclined to greet me with open warmth. As it was, she again gave me her cheek to kiss, in her father's presence, and called me "dear John," and asked me specially after some rabbits, which I had kept at home merely for a younger sister; and then it seemed as though she were in no way embarrassed by the peculiar circumstances of our position. Twelve months since I had asked her to be my wife, and now she was to give me an answer; and yet she was as assured in

153

her gait, and as serenely joyous in her tone, as though I were a brother just returned from college. It could not be that she meant to refuse me, or she would not smile on me and be so loving; but I could almost have found it in my heart to wish that she would. "It is quite possible," said I to myself, "that I may not be found so ready for this family bargain. A love that is to be had like a bale of goods is not exactly the love to suit my taste." But then, when I met her again in the morning, I could no more have quarrelled with her than I could have flown.

I was inexpressibly charmed with the whole city, and especially with the house in which Mr. Daguilar lived. It opened from the corner of a narrow, unfrequented street — a corner like an elbow — and, as seen from the exterior, there was nothing prepossessing to recommend it; but the outer door led by a short hall or passage to an inner door, or *grille*, made of open ornamental iron-work, and through that we entered a court, or *patio*, as they called it. Nothing could be more lovely or deliciously cool than was this small court. The building on each side was covered by trellis work; and beautiful creepers, vines, and parasite flowers, now in the full mangificence of the early summer, grew up and clustered round the window. Every inch of wall was covered, so that none of the glaring whitewash wounded the eye. In the four corners of the *patio* were four large orange trees, covered with fruit. I would not say a word in special praise of these, remembering the childish promise she had made on my behalf. In the middle of the court there was a fountain, and round about on the marble floor there were chairs, and here and there a small table, as though the space were really a portion of the house. It was here that we used to take our cup of coffee and smoke our cigarrettas, I and old Mr. Daguilar, while Maria sat by, not only approving, but occasionally rolling for me the thin paper round the fragrant weed with her taper fingers. Beyond the *patio* was an open passage or gallery, filled also with flowers in pots; and then beyond this, one entered the drawing-room of the house. It was by no means a princely place or mansion, fit for the owner of untold wealth. The rooms were not over large, nor very numerous; but the most had been made of a small space, and everything had been done to relieve the heat of an almost tropical sun.

"It is pretty, is it not?" she said, as she took me through it.

"Very pretty," I said. "I wish we could live in such houses."

"Oh, they would not do at all for dear old fat, cold, cozy England. You are quite different, you know, in everything from us of the south; more phlegmatic, but then so much steadier. The men and the houses are all the same."

I can hardly tell why, but even this wounded me. It seemed to me as though she were inclined to put into one and the same category things English, dull, useful, and solid, and that she was disposed in talking to me to show an appreciation for such necessaries of life; but that she had another and inner sense — a sense keenly alive to the poetry of her own southern clime, and that I, as being English, was to have no participation in that. An English husband might do very well, the interests of the firm might make such an arrangement desirable, such a *mariage de convenance* — so I argued to myself — might be quite compatible with — with Heaven only knows what delights of super-terrestrial romance, from which I, as being an English thick-headed lump of useful, coarse morality, was to be altogether debarred. She had spoken to me of oranges, and having finished the survey of the house, she offered me some sweet little cakes. It could not be that of such things were the thoughts which lay undivulged beneath the clear waters of those deep black eyes — undivulged to me, though no one else could have so good a right to read them — it could not be that that noble brow gave index of a mind intent on the trade of which she spoke so often! Words of other sort than any that had been vouchsafed to me must fall, at times, from the rich curves of that perfect mouth.

So felt I then, pining for something to make me unhappy. Ah, me! I know all about it now, and am content. But I wish that some learned pundit would give us a good definition of romance, would describe in words that feeling with which our hearts are so pestered when we are young, which makes us sigh for we know not what, and forbids us to be contented with what God sends us. We invest female beauty with impossible attributes, and are angry because our women have not the spiritualised souls of angels, anxious, as we are, that they should also have human affections. A man looks at her he would love as he does at a distant landscape in a mountainous land. The peaks are glorious with more than the beauty of earth, and rock, and vegetation. He

155

dreams of some mysterious grandeur of design which tempts him on under the hot sun, and over the sharp stones, till he has reached the mountain goal which he had set before him. But when there, he finds that the beauty is well nigh gone, and as for that delicious mystery on which his soul had fed, it has vanished for ever!

I know all about it now, and am, as I said, content. Beneath those deep black eyes there lay wells of love — good, honest, homely love — love of father, and husband, and children that were to come — of that love which loves to see the loved ones prospering in honesty. That noble brow — for it is noble, I am unchanged in that opinion, and will go unchanged to my grave — covers thoughts as to the welfare of many, and an intellect fit-ted to the management of a household; of servants, namely, and children, and, perchance, a husband. That mouth can speak words of wisdom, of very useful wisdom — though of poetry it has latterly uttered little that was original. Poetry and romance! They are splendid mountain views seen in the distance. So let men be content to see them, and not attempt to tread upon the fallacious heather of the mystic hills.

In the first week of my sojourn in Seville I spoke no word of overt love to Maria, thinking, as I confess, to induce her thereby to alter her mode of conduct to myself. "She knows that I have come here to make love to her — repeat my offer; and she will, at any rate, be chagrined if I am slow to do so." But it had no effect. At home, my mother was rather particular about her ta-ble, and Maria's greatest efforts seemed to be used in giving me as nice dinners as we gave her. In those days I did not care a straw about my dinner, and so I took an opportunity of telling her. "Dear me," said she, looking at me almost with grief, "do you not? What a pity! And do you not like music either?" "Oh, yes, I adore it," I replied. I felt sure at the time that had I been born in her own sunny clime, she would never have talked to me about eating. But that was my mistake.

I used to walk out with her about the city, seeing all that is there of beauty and magnificence. And in what city is there more that is worth the seeing? At first, this was very delightful to me, for I felt that I was blessed with a privilege that would not be granted to any other man. But its value soon fell in my eyes, for others would accost her, and walk on the other side, talking to her in Spanish, as though I hardly existed, or were a servant there for her protection. And I was not allowed to take her arm, and thus to appropriate her, as I should have done in England. "No, John," she said, with the sweetest, prettiest smile, "we don't do that here; only when people are married." And she made this allusion to married life, out, openly, and with not the slightest tremor on her tongue.

"Oh, I beg pardon," said I, drawing back my hand, and feeling angry with myself for not being fully acquainted with all the customs of a foreign country.

"You need not beg pardon," said she; "when we were in England we always walked so. It is just a custom, you know." And then I saw her drop her large eyes to the ground, and bow gracefully in answer to some salute.

I looked around, and saw that we had been joined by a young cavalier, a Spanish nobleman, as I saw at once; a man with jet-black hair, and a straight nose, and a black moustache, and patent leather boots, very slim and very tall, and — though I would not confess it then — uncommonly handsome. I myself am inclined to be stout, my hair is light, my nose broad, I have no hair on my upper lip, and my whiskers are rough and uneven. "I could punch your head though, my fine fellow," said I to myself, when I saw that he placed himself at Maria's side, "and think very little of the achievement."

The wretch went on with us round the Plaza for some quarter of an hour, talking Spanish with the greatest fluency, and she was every whit as fluent. Of course, I could not understand a word that they said. Of all positions that a man can occupy, I think that that is about the most uncomfortable; and I cannot say that, even up to this day, I have quite forgiven her for that quarter of an hour.

"I shall go in," said I, unable to bear my feelings, and preparing to leave her; "the heat is unendurable."

"Oh, dear John, why did you not speak before?" she answered. "You cannot leave me here, you know, as I am in your charge; but I will go with you almost directly." And then she finished her conversation with the Spaniard, speaking with an animation she had never displayed in her conversations with me.

It had been agreed between us, for two or three days before this, that we were to rise early on the following morning for the sake of ascending the tower of the Cathedral, and visiting the Giralda, as the iron figure is called, which turns upon a pivot on the extreme summit. We had often wandered together up and down the long, dark, gloomy aisle of the stupendous building, and had, together, seen its treasury of art; but as yet we had not performed the task which has to be achieved by all visitors to Seville; and in order that we might have a clear view over the surrounding country, and not be tormented by the heat of an advanced sun, we had settled that we would ascend the Giralda before breakfast.

And now, as I walked away from the Plaza towards Mr. Daguilar's house, with Maria by my side, I made up my mind that I would settle my business during this visit to the Cathedral. Yes; and I would so manage the settlement that there should be no doubt left as to my intentions and my own ideas. I would not be guilty of shilly-shally conduct; I would tell her frankly what I felt and what I thought, and would make her understand that I did not desire her hand if I could not have her heart. I did not value the kindness of her manner, seeing that that kindness sprang from indifference rather than passion; and so I would declare to her. And I would ask her also who was this young man with whom she was so intimate — for whom all her energy and volubility of tone seemed to be employed? She had told me once that it behoved her to consult a friend in Seville as to the expediency of her marriage with me. Was this the friend whom she had wished to consult? If so, she need not trouble herself. Under such circumstances, I should decline the connection. And I resolved that I would find out how this might be. A man who proposes to take a woman to his bosom as his wife, has a right to ask for information — ay, and to receive it too. It flashed upon my mind at this moment that Donna Maria was well enough inclined to come to me as my wife, but —. I could hardly define the "buts" to myself, for there were three or four of them. Why did she always speak to me in a tone of childish affection, as though I were a schoolboy home for the holidays? I would have all this out with her on the tower on the following morning, standing under the Giralda.

On that morning we met together in the *patio*, soon after five o'clock, and started for the Cathedral. She looked beautiful, with her black mantilla over her head, and with black gloves on, and her black morning silk dress — beautiful, composed, and at her ease, as though she were well satisfied to undertake this early morning walk from feelings of good nature — sustained, probably, by some under-current of a deeper sentiment. Well; I would know all about it before I returned to her father's house.

There hardly stands, as I think, on the earth a building more remarkable than the Cathedral of Seville, and hardly one more grand. Its enormous size; its gloom and darkness; the richness of ornamentation in the details, contrasted with the severe simplicity of the larger outlines; the variety of its architecture; the glory of its paintings; and the wondrous splendours of its metallic decorations, its altar-pieces, screens, rails, gates, and the like, render it, to my mind, the first in interest among churches. It has not the coloured glass of Chartres, or the marble glory of Milan, or such a forest of aisles as Antwerp, or so perfect a hue in stone as Westminster; nor in mixed beauty of form and colour does it possess anything equal to the choir of Cologne; but, for combined magnificence and awe-compelling grandeur, I regard it as superior to all other ecclesiastical edifices.

It is its deep gloom with which the stranger is so greatly struck on his first entrance. In a region so hot as the south of Spain a cool interior is a main object with the architect, and this it has been necessary to effect by the exclusion of light; consequently, the church is dark, mysterious, and almost cold. On the morning in question, as we entered, it seemed to be filled with gloom, and the distant sound of a slow footstep here and there beyond the transept inspired one almost with dread. Maria, when she first met me, had begun to talk with her usual smile, offering me coffee and a biscuit before I started. "I never eat biscuits," I said, with almost a severe tone, as I turned from her. That dark-haired man of the Plaza — would she have offered him a cake had she been going to walk with him in the gloom of the morning? After that, little had been spoken between us. She walked by my side with her accustomed smile; but she had, as I flattered myself, begun to learn that I was not to be won by a meaningless good nature. "We are lucky in our morning for the view;" that was all she said, speaking with that peculiarly clear, but slow, pronunciation which she had assumed in learning our language.

We entered the Cathedral, and walking the whole length of the aisle, left it again at the porter's porch at the further end. Here we passed through a low door on to the stone flight of steps, and at once began to ascend. "There are a party of your countrymen up before us," said Maria; "the porter says that they went through the lodge half an hour since." "I hope they will return before we are on the top," said I, bethinking myself of the task that was before me. And indeed my heart was hardly at ease within me, for that which I had to say would require all the spirit of which I was master.

The ascent to the Giralda is very long and very fatiguing; and we had to pause on the various landings and in the singular belfry in order that Miss Daguilar might recruit her strength and breath. As we rested on one of these occasions, in a gallery which runs round the tower below the belfry, we heard a great noise of shouting, and a clattering of sticks among the bells. "It is the party of your countrymen who went up before us," said she. "What a pity that Englishmen should always make so much noise!" And then she spoke in Spanish to the custodian of the bells, who is usually to be found in a little cabin up there within the tower. "He says that they went up shouting like demons," continued Maria; and it seemed to me that she looked as though I ought to be ashamed of the name of an Englishman. "They may not be so solemn in their demeanour as Spaniards," I answered; "but, for all that, there may be quite as much in them."

We then again began to mount, and before we had ascended much further we passed my three countrymen. They were young men, with grey coats and grey trousers, with slouched hats, and without gloves. They had fair faces and fair hair, and swung big sticks in their hands, with crooked handles. They laughed and talked loud, and, when we met them, seemed to be racing with each other; but, nevertheless, they were gentlemen. No one who knows by sight what an English gentleman is could have doubted that; but I did acknowledge to myself that they should have remembered that the edifice they were treading was a church, and that the silence they were invading was the cherished property of a courteous people.

"They are all just the same as big boys," said Maria. The colour instantly flew into my face, and I felt that it was my duty to speak up for my own countrymen. The word "boys" especially wounded my ears. It was as a boy that she treated me; but, on looking at that befringed young Spanish Don — who was not, apparently, my elder in age — she had recognised a man. However, I said nothing further till I reached the summit. One cannot speak with manly dignity while one is out of breath on a staircase.

"There, John," she said, stretching her hands away over the fair plain of the Guadalquivir, as soon as we stood against the parapet; "is not that lovely?"

I would not deign to notice this. "Maria," I said, "I think that you are too hard upon my countrymen!"

"Too hard! No; for I love them. They are so good and industrious; and they come home to their wives, and take care of their children. But why do they make themselves so — so — what the French call, *gauches?*"

"Good, and industrious, and come home to their wives!" thought I. "I believe you hardly understand us as yet," I answered. "Our domestic virtues are not always so very prominent; but I believe we know how to conduct ourselves as gentlemen — at any rate, as well as Spaniards." I was very angry — not at the faults, but at the good qualities imputed to us.

"In the affairs of business, yes," said Maria, with a look of firm confidence in her own opinion — that look of confidence she has never lost, and I pray that she may never lose it while I remain with her — "but in the little intercourses of the world, no! A Spaniard never forgets what is personally due either to himself or to his neighbours. If he is eating an onion, he eats it as an onion should be eaten."

"In such matters as that he is very grand, no doubt," said I, angrily.

"And why should you not eat an onion properly, John? Now, I heard a story yesterday from Don — about two Englishmen, which annoyed me very much." I did not exactly catch the name of the Don in question, but I felt, through every nerve in my body, that it was the man who had been talking to her on the Plaza.

"And what have they done?" said I. "But it is the same every-

where. We are always abused; but, nevertheless, no people are so
welcome. At any rate, we pay for the mischief we do." I was angry
with myself the moment the words were out of my mouth; for,
after all, there is no feeling more mean than that pocket-
confidence with which an Englishman sometimes swaggers.

"There was no mischief done in this case," she answered; "it
was simply that two men have made themselves ridiculous for
ever. The story is all about Seville, and, of course, it annoys me
that they should be Englishmen."

"And what did they do?"

"The Marquis D'Almavivas was coming up to Seville in the
boat, and they behaved to him in the most outrageous manner.
He is here now, and is going to give a series of *fêtes*. Of course he
will not ask a single Englishman."

"We shall manage to live, even though the Marquis
D'Almavivas may frown upon us," said I, proudly.

"He is the richest and also the best of our noblemen," continued Maria; "and I never heard of anything so absurd as what they
did to him. It made me blush when Don—told me." Don Tomás,
I thought she said.

"If he be the best of your noblemen, how comes it that he is
angry because he has met two vulgar men? It is not to be supposed
that every Englishman is a gentleman."

"Angry! Oh no! he was not angry; he enjoyed the joke too
much for that. He got completely the best of them, though they
did not know it, poor fools! How would your Lord John Russell
behave if two Spaniards in an English railway carriage were to
pull him about and tear his clothes?"

"He would give them in charge to a policeman, of course," said
I, speaking of such a matter with the contempt it deserved.

"If that were done here, your ambassador would be demanding
national explanations. But Almavivas did much better — he
laughed at them without letting them know it."

"But do you mean that they took hold of him violently, without any provocation? They must have been drunk."

"Oh, no; they were sober enough. I did not see it, so I do not
quite know exactly how it was, but I understand that they com-
mitted themselves most absurdly; absolutely took hold of his coat
and tore it, and—; but they did such ridiculous things that I can-

not tell you." And yet Don Tomás, if that was the man's name, had been able to tell her, and she had been well able to listen to him.

"What made them take hold of the marquis?" said I.

"Curiosity, I suppose," she answered. "He dresses somewhat fancifully, and they could not understand that any one should wear garments different from their own." But even then the blow did not strike home upon me.

"Is it not pretty to look down upon the quiet town?" she said, coming close up to me, so that the skirt of her dress pressed me, and her elbow touched my arm. Now was the moment in which I should have asked her how her heart stood towards me; but I was sore and uncomfortable, and my destiny was before me. She was willing enough to let these English faults pass by without further notice, but I would not allow the subject to drop.

"I will find out who these men are," said I, "and learn the truth of it. When did it occur?"

"Last Thursday, I think he said."

"Why, that was the day we came up in the boat, Johnson and myself. There was no marquis there then, and we were the only Englishmen on board."

"It was on Thursday, certainly, because it was well known in Seville that he arrived on that day. You must have remarked him, because he talks English perfectly, though, by-the-bye, these men would go on chattering before him about himself as though it were impossible that a Spaniard should know their language. They are ignorant of Spanish, and they cannot bring themselves to believe that any one should be better educated than themselves."

Now the blow had fallen, and I straightway appreciated the necessity of returning immediately to Clapham, where my family resided, and giving up forever all idea of Spanish connections. I had resolved to assert the full strength of my manhood on that tower, and now words had been spoken which left me weak as a child. I felt that I was shivering, and did not dare pronounce the truth which must be made known. As to speaking of love, and signifying my pleasure that Don Tomás should for the future be kept at a distance, any such effort was quite beyond me. Had Don Tomás been there, he might have walked off with her from before my face without a struggle on my part. "Now I remember about it," she continued, "I think he must have been in the boat on Thursday."

"And now that I remember," I replied, turning away from her to hide my embarrassment, "he was there. Your friend down below in the Plaza seems to have made out a grand story. No doubt he is not fond of the English. There was such a man there, and I did take hold — "

"Oh, John, was it you?"

"Yes, Donna Maria, it was I; and if Lord John Russell were to dress himself in the same way — " But I had no time to complete my description of what might occur under so extravagantly impossible a concatenation of circumstances, for, as I was yet speaking, the little door leading out on the leads of the tower was opened, and my friend, the "mayo" of the boat, still bearing all his gewgaws on his back, stepped up on to the platform. My eye instantly perceived that the one pendule was still missing from his jacket. He did not come alone, but three other gentlemen followed him, who, however, had no peculiarities in their dress. He saw me at once, and bowed and smiled; and then observing Donna Maria, he lifted his cap from his head, and addressing himself to her in Spanish, began to converse with her as though she were an old friend.

"Señor," said Maria, after the first words of greeting had been spoken between them, "you must permit me to present to you my father's most particular friend—and my own, Mr. Pomfret; John, this is the Marquis D'Almavivas."

I cannot now describe the grace with which this introduction was effected, or the beauty of her face as she uttered the words. There was a boldness about her as though she had said out loud, "I know it all — the whole story. But, in spite of that, you must take him on my representation, and be gracious to him in spite of what he has done. You must be content to do that; or in quarrelling with him you must quarrel with me also." And it was done at the spur of the moment — without delay. She, who not five minutes since had been loudly condemning the unknown Englishman for his rudeness, had already pardoned him, now that he was known to be her friend, and had determined that he should be pardoned by others also, or that she would share his disgrace. I recognised the nobleness of this at the moment; but, nevertheless, I was so sore that I would almost have preferred that she should have disowned me.

The marquis immediately lifted his cap with his left hand while he gave me his right. "I have already had the pleasure of meeting this gentleman," he said; "we had some conversation in the boat together."

"Yes," said I, pointing to his coat, "and you still bear the marks of our encounter."

"Was it not delightful, Donna Maria," he continued, turning to her; "your friend's friend took me for a torero?"

"And it served you properly, señor," said Donna Maria, laughing; "you have no right to go about with all those rich ornaments upon you."

"Oh! quite properly; indeed, I make no complaint; and I must beg your friend to understand, and his friend also, how grateful I am for their solicitude as to my pecuniary welfare. They were inclined to be severe on me for being so extravagant in such trifles. I was obliged to explain that I had no wife at home kept without her proper allowance of dresses, in order that I might be gay."

"They are foreigners, and you should forgive their error," said she.

"And in token that I do so," said the marquis, "I shall beg your friend to accept the little ornament which attracted his attention." And, so saying, he pulled the identical button out of his pocket, and gracefully proffered it to me.

"I shall carry it about with me always," said I, accepting it, "as a memento of humiliation. When I look at it, I shall ever remember the folly of an Englishman and the courtesy of a Spaniard;" and as I made the speech I could not but reflect whether it might, under any circumstances, be possible that Lord John Russell should be induced to give a button off his coat to a foreigner.

There were other civil speeches made, and before we left the tower the marquis had asked me to his parties, and exacted from me an unwilling promise that I would attend them. "The señora," he said, bowing again to Maria, "would, he was sure, grace them. She had done so the previous year; and as I had accepted his little

165

present I was bound to acknowledge him as my friend." All this was very pretty, and of course I said that I would go, but I had not at that time the slightest intention of doing so. Maria had behaved admirably; she had covered my confusion, and shown herself not ashamed to own me, delinquent as I was; but not the less had she expressed her opinion, in language terribly strong, of the awkwardness of which I had been guilty, and had shown almost an aversion to my English character. I should leave Seville as quickly as I could, and should certainly not again put myself in the way of the Marquis D'Almavivas. Indeed, I dreaded the moment that I should be first alone with her, and should find myself forced to say something indicative of my feelings—to hear something also indicative of her feelings. I had come out this morning resolved to demand my rights and to exercise them — and now my only wish was to run away. I hated the marquis, and longed to be alone, that I might cast his button from me. To think that a man should be so ruined by such a trifle!

We descended that prodigious flight without a word upon the subject, and almost without a word at all. She had carried herself well in the presence of Almavivas, and had been too proud to seem ashamed of her companion; but now, as I could well see, her feeling of disgust and contempt had returned. When I begged her not to hurry herself, she would hardly answer me; and when she did speak, her voice was constrained and unlike herself. And yet, how beautiful she was! Well, my dream of Spanish love must be over. But I was sure of this: that having known her, and given her my heart, I could never afterwards share it with another.

We came out at last on to the dark, gloomy aisle of the Cathedral, and walked together without a word up along the side of the choir, till we came to the transept. There was not a soul near us, and not a sound was to be heard but the distant, low pattering of a mass, then in course of celebration at some far-off chapel in the Cathedral. When we got to the transept, Maria turned a little, as though she was going to the transept door, and then stopped herself. She stood still; and when I stood also, she made two steps towards me, and put her hand on my arm. "Oh, John!" she said.

"Well," said I, "after all, it does not much signify. You can make a joke of it when my back is turned."

"Dearest John!" — she had never spoken to me in that way before — "you must not be angry with me. It is better that we should explain to each other, is it not?"

"Oh, much better. I am very glad you heard of it at once. I do not look at it quite in the same light that you do; but nevertheless —"

"What do you mean? But I know you are angry with me. And yet you cannot think that I intended those words for you. Of course I know now that there was nothing rude in what passed."

"Oh, but there was."

"No, I am sure there was not. You could not be rude, though you are so free-hearted. I see it all now, and so does the marquis. You will like him so much when you come to know him. Tell me that you won't be cross with me for what I have said. Sometimes I think that I have displeased you, and yet my whole wish has been to welcome you to Seville, and to make you comfortable as an old friend. Promise me that you will not be cross with me."

Cross with her! I certainly had no intention of being cross; but I had begun to think that she would not care what my humour might be. "Maria," I said, taking hold of her hand.

"No, John, do not do that. It is in the church, you know."

"Maria, will you answer me a question?"

"Yes," she said, very slowly, looking down upon the stone slabs beneath our feet.

"Do you love me?"

"Love you!"

"Yes, do you love me? You were to give me an answer here, in Seville, and now I ask for it. I have almost taught myself to think that it is needless to ask; and now this horrid mischance —"

"What do you mean?" said she, speaking very quickly.

"Why, this miserable blunder about the marquis's button! After that, I suppose —"

"The marquis! Oh, John, is that to make a difference between you and me? — a little joke like that?"

"But does it not?"

"Make a change between us! — such a thing as that! Oh, John, John!"

"But tell me, Maria, what am I to hope? If you will say that you can love me, I shall care nothing for the marquis. In that case, I can bear to be laughed at."

"Who will dare to laugh at you? Not the marquis, whom I am sure you will like."

"Your friend in the Plaza, who told you of all this."

"What, poor Tomás?"

"I do not know about his being poor — I mean the gentleman who was with you last night."

"Yes, Tomás. You do not know who he is?"

"Not in the least."

"How droll. He is your own clerk — partly your own, now that you are one of the firm. And, John, I mean to make you do something for him; he is such a good fellow; and last year he married a young girl whom I love — oh, almost like a sister."

Do something for him! Of course I would. I promised, then and there, that I would raise his salary to any conceivable amount that a Spanish clerk could desire; which promise I have since kept, if not absolutely to the letter, at any rate, to an extent which has been considered satisfactory by the gentleman's wife.

"But, Maria — dearest Maria — "

"Remember, John, we are in the church; and poor papa will be waiting breakfast."

I need hardly continue the story further. It will be known to all that my love-suit throve in spite of my unfortunate raid on the button of Marquis D'Almavivas, at whose series of *fêtes* through that month I was, I may boast, an honoured guest. I have since that had the pleasure of entertaining him in my own poor house in England, and one of our boys bears his Christian name.

From that day in which I ascended the Giralda to this present day in which I write, I have never once had occasion to complain of a deficiency of romance either in Maria Daguilar or in Maria Pomfret.

"John Bull on the Guadalquivir" appeared first in the November 17 and 21 issues of *Cassell's Illustrated Family Paper* for 1860.

The Chateau of
Prince Polignac

F EW ENGLISHMEN OR ENGLISHWOMEN are inti-
mately acquainted with the little town of Le Puy. It is the capital
of the old province of Le Velay, which also is now but little
known, even to French ears, for it is in these days called by the
imperial name of the Department of the Haute Loire. It is to the
southeast of Auvergne, and is nearly in the centre of the southern
half of France.

But few towns, merely as towns, can be better worth visiting.
In the first place, the volcanic formation of the ground on which
it stands is not only singular in the extreme, so as to be interesting to the geologist; but it is so picturesque as to be equally gratifying to the general tourist. Within a narrow valley there stand
several rocks, rising up from the ground with absolute abruptness.
Round two of these the town clusters, and a third stands but a
mile distant, forming the centre of a faubourg, or suburb. These
rocks appear to be, and I believe are, the harder particles of volcanic matter, which have not been carried away through succes-
sive ages by the joint agency of water and air. When the tide of
lava ran down between the hills, the surface left was no doubt on
a level with the heads of these rocks; but here and there the de-
posit became harder than elsewhere, and these harder points
have remained, lifting up their steep heads in a line through the
valley.

The highest of these is called the Rocher de Corneille. Round this and up its steep sides the town stands. On its highest summit there was an old castle; and there now is, or will be before these pages are printed, a colossal figure in bronze of the Virgin Mary, made from the cannon taken at Sebastopol. Half way down the hill the cathedral is built, a singularly gloomy edifice, Roman-esque, as it is called, in its style, but extremely similar in its mode of architecture to what we know of Byzantine structures. But there has been no surface on the rock side large enough to form a resting-place for the church, which has therefore been built out on huge supporting piles, which form a porch below the west front; so that the approach is by numerous steps laid along the side of the wall below the church, forming a wondrous flight of stairs. Let all men who may find themselves stopping at Le Puy, visit the top of these stairs at the time of the setting sun, and look down from thence through the framework of the porch on the town beneath, and at the hill-side beyond.

Behind the church is the seminary of the priests, with its beau-tiful walks stretching round the Rocher de Corneille, and over-looking the town and valley below.

Next to this rock, and within a quarter of a mile of it, is the second peak, called the Rock of the Needle. It rises narrow, sharp, and abrupt from the valley, allowing of no buildings on its sides. But on its very point has been erected a church sacred to St. Michael, that lover of rock summits, accessible by stairs cut from the stone. This, perhaps — this rock, I mean — is the most wonderful of the wonders which Nature has formed at Le Puy.

Above this, at a mile's distance, is the rock of Espailly, formed in the same way and almost equally precipitous. On its summit is a castle, having its own legend, and professing to have been the residence of Charles VII., when little of France belonged to its kings but the provinces of Berry, Auvergne, and Le Velay. Some three miles further up there is another volcanic rock, larger, indeed, but equally sudden in its spring, — equally re-markable as rising abruptly from the valley, — on which stands the castle and old family residence of the house of Polignac. It was lost by them at the time of the revolution, but was repur-chased by the minister of Charles X., and is still the property of the head of the race.

Le Puy itself is a small moderate pleasant French town, in

which the language of the people has not the pure Parisian aroma, nor is the glory of the boulevards of the capital emulated in its streets. These are crooked, narrow, steep, and intricate, forming here and there excellent sketches for a lover of street picturesque beauty; but hurtful to the feet with their small round-topped paving stones, and not always as clean as pedestrian ladies might desire.

And now I would ask my readers to join me at the morning table d'hôte at the Hotel des Ambassadeurs. It will of course be understood that this does not mean a breakfast in the ordinary fashion of England, consisting of tea or coffee, bread and butter, and perhaps a boiled egg. It comprises all the requisites for a composite dinner, excepting soup; and as one gets further south in France, this meal is called dinner. It is, however, eaten without any prejudice to another similar and somewhat longer meal at six or seven o'clock, which, when the above name is taken up by the earlier enterprise, is styled supper.

The *déjeuner*, or dinner, at the Hotel des Ambassadeurs, on the morning in question, though very elaborate, was not a very gay affair. There were some fourteen persons present, of whom half were residents in the town, men employed in some official capacity, who found this to be the cheapest, the most luxurious, and to them the most comfortable mode of living. They clustered together at the head of the table, and as they were customary guests at the house, they talked their little talk together — it was very little — and made the most of the good things before them. Then there were two or three *commis-voyageurs*, a chance traveller or two, and an English lady with a young daughter. The English lady sat next to one of the accustomed guests; but he, unlike the others, held converse with her rather than with them. Our story, at present, has reference only to that lady and to that gentleman.

Place aux dames. We will speak first of the lady, whose name was Mrs. Thompson. She was, shall I say, a young woman, of about thirty-six. In so saying, I am perhaps creating a prejudice against her in the minds of some readers, as they will, not unnaturally, suppose her, after such an announcement, to be in truth over forty. Any such prejudice will be unjust. I would have it believed that thirty-six was the outside, not the inside of her age. She was good-looking, lady-like, and considering that she was an Englishwoman, fairly well-dressed. She was inclined to be rather full in her person, but perhaps not more so than is becoming to ladies at her time of life. She had rings on her fingers and a brooch on her bosom which were of some value, and on the back of her head she wore a jaunty small lace cap, which seemed to tell, in conjunction with her other appointments, that her circumstances were comfortable.

The little girl who sat next to her was the youngest of her two daughters, and might be about thirteen years of age. Her name was Matilda, but infantine circumstances had invested her with the nick-name of Mimmy, by which her mother always called her. A nice, pretty, playful little girl was Mimmy Thompson, wearing two long tails of plaited hair behind her head, and inclined occasionally to be rather loud in her sport.

Mrs. Thompson had another and an elder daughter, now some fifteen years old, who was at school in Le Puy; and it was with reference to her tuition that Mrs. Thompson had taken up a temporary residence at the Hotel des Ambassadeurs in that town. Lilian Thompson was occasionally invited down to dine or breakfast at the inn, and was visited daily at her school by her mother.

"When I'm sure that she'll do, I shall leave her there and go back to England," Mrs. Thompson had said, not in the purest French, to the neighbour who always sat next to her at the table d'hôte, the gentleman, namely, to whom we have above alluded. But still she had remained at Le Puy a month, and did not go; a circumstance which was considered singular, but by no means unpleasant, both by the innkeeper and by the gentleman in question.

The facts, as regards Mrs. Thompson, were as follows: — She was the widow of a gentleman who had served for many years in the civil service of the East Indies, and who, on dying, had left her a comfortable income of — it matters not how many pounds, but constituting quite a sufficiency to enable her to live at her ease and educate her daughters.

Her children had been sent home to England before her husband's death, and after that event she had followed them; but there, though she was possessed of moderate wealth, she had no friends and few acquaintances, and after a little while she had found life to be rather dull. Her customs were not those of England, nor were her propensities English; therefore she had gone abroad, and having received some recommendation of this school at Le Puy, had made her way thither. As it appeared to her that she really enjoyed more consideration at Le Puy than had been accorded to her either at Torquay or Leamington, there she remained from day to day. The total payment required at the Hotel des Ambassadeurs was but six francs daily for herself and three and a half for her little girl; and where else could she live with a better junction of economy and comfort? And then the gentleman who always sat next to her was so exceedingly civil!

The gentleman's name was M. Lacordaire. So much she knew, and had learned to call him by his name very frequently. Mimmy, too, was quite intimate with M. Lacordaire; but nothing more than his name was absolutely known of him. But M. Lacordaire carried a general letter of recommendation in his face, manner, gait, dress, and tone of voice. In all these respects there was nothing left to be desired; and, in addition to this, he was decorated, and wore the little ribbon of the Legion of Honour, ingeniously twisted into the shape of a small flower.

M. Lacordaire might be senior in age to Mrs. Thompson by about ten years, nor had he about him any of the airs and graces of a would-be young man. His hair, which he wore very short, was grizzled, as was also the small pretence of a whisker, which came down about as far as the middle of his ear; but the tuft on his chin was still brown, without a grey hair. His eyes were bright and tender, his voice was low and soft, his hands were very white, his clothes were always new and well-fitting, and a better-brushed hat could not be seen out of Paris, nor perhaps in it.

Now, during the weeks which Mrs. Thompson had passed at Le Puy, the acquaintance which she had formed with M. Lacordaire had progressed beyond the prolonged meals in the *salle à manger*. He had occasionally sat beside her evening table as she took her English cup of tea in her own room, her bed being duly screened off in its distinct niche by becoming curtains; and then he had occasionally walked beside her, as he civilly escorted her to the lions of the place; and he had once accompanied her, sitting on the back seat of a French *voiture*, when she had gone forth to see something of the surrounding country.

On all such occasions she had been accompanied by one of her daughters, and the world of Le Puy had had nothing material to say against her. But still the world of Le Puy had whispered a little, suggesting that M. Lacordaire knew very well what he was about. But might not Mrs. Thompson also know as well what she was about? At any rate, everything had gone very pleasantly since the acquaintance had been made; and now, so much having been explained, we will go back to the elaborate breakfast at the Hotel des Ambassadeurs.

Mrs. Thompson, holding Mimmy by the hand, walked into the room some few minutes after the last bell had been rung, and took the place which was now hers by custom. The gentlemen who constantly frequented the house all bowed to her, but M. Lacordaire rose from his seat and offered her his hand.

"And how is Mees Meemy this morning?" said he; for 'twas thus he always pronounced her name.

Miss Mimmy, answering for herself, declared that she was very well, and suggested that M. Lacordaire should give her a fig from off a dish that was placed immediately before him on the table. This M. Lacordaire did, presenting it very elegantly between his two fingers, and making a little bow to the little lady as he did so.

"Fie, Mimmy!" said her mother; "why do you ask for the things before the waiter brings them round?"

"But, Mamma," said Mimmy, speaking English, "M. Lacordaire always gives me a fig every morning."

"M. Lacordaire always spoils you, I think," answered Mrs. Thompson, in French. And then they went thoroughly to work at their breakfast. During the whole meal M. Lacordaire attended assiduously to his neighbour; and did so without any evil result, except that one Frenchman with a black moustache, at the head of the table, trod on the toe of another Frenchman with another black moustache — winking as he made the sign — just as M. Lacordaire having selected a bunch of grapes put it on Mrs. Thompson's plate with infinite grace. But who among us all is free from such impertinences as these?

"But madame really must see the château of Prince Polignac before she leaves Le Puy," said M. Lacordaire.

"The château of who?" asked Mimmy, to whose young ears the French words were already becoming familiar.

"Prince Polignac, my dear. Well, I really don't know, M. Lacordaire—I have seen a great deal of the place already, and I shall be going now very soon; probably in a day or two," said Mrs. Thompson.

"But madame must positively see the château," said M. Lacordaire, very impressively; and then after a pause, he added, "If madame will have the complaisance to commission me to procure a carriage for this afternoon, and will allow me the honour to be her guide, I shall consider myself one of the most fortunate of men."

"Oh, yes, mamma, do go," said Mimmy, clapping her hands. "And it is Thursday, and Lilian can go with us."

"Be quiet, Mimmy, do. Thank you, no, M. Lacordaire. I could not go to-day; but I am extremely obliged by your politeness."

M. Lacordaire still pressed the matter, and Mrs. Thompson still declined, till it was time to rise from the table. She then declared that she did not think it possible that she should visit the château before she left Le Puy; but that she would give him an answer at dinner.

The most tedious time in the day to Mrs. Thompson was the two hours after breakfast. At one o'clock she daily went to the school, taking Mimmy, who for an hour or two shared her sister's lessons. This, and her little excursions about the place and her shopping, managed to make away with her afternoon. Then, in the evening, she generally saw something of M. Lacordaire. But these two hours after breakfast were hard of killing.

On this occasion, when she gained her own room, she, as usual, placed Mimmy on the sofa with a needle. Her custom then was to take up a novel; but on this morning she sat herself down in her armchair, and resting her head upon her hand and elbow, began to turn over certain circumstances in her mind.

"Mamma," said Mimmy, "why won't you go with M. Lacordaire to that place belonging to the prince? Prince — *Polly* something, wasn't it?"

"Mind your work, my dear," said Mrs. Thompson.

"But I do so wish you'd go, mamma. What was the prince's name?"

"Polignac."

"Mamma, ain't princes very great people?"

"Yes, my dear; sometimes."

"Is Prince Polly-nac like our Prince Alfred?"

"No, my dear; not at all. At least, I suppose not."

"Is his mother a queen?"

"No, my dear."

"Then his father must be a king?"

"No, my dear. It is quite a different thing here. Here, in France, they have a great many princes."

"Well, at any rate, I should like to see a prince's château; so I do hope you'll go." And then there was a pause. "Mamma, could it come to pass, here in France, that M. Lacordaire should ever be a prince?"

"M. Lacordaire, a prince! No; don't talk such nonsense, but mind your work."

"Isn't M. Lacordaire a very nice man? ain't you very fond of him?"

To this question Mrs. Thompson made no answer.

"Mamma," continued Mimmy, after a moment's pause, "won't you tell me whether you are fond of M. Lacordaire? I'm quite sure of this — that he's very fond of you."

"What makes you think that?" asked Mrs. Thompson, who could not bring herself to refrain from the question.

"Because he looks at you in that way, mamma, and squeezes your hand."

"Nonsense, child," said Mrs. Thompson; "hold your tongue. I don't know what can have put such stuff into your head."

"But he does, mamma," said Mimmy, who rarely allowed her mother to put her down.

Mrs. Thompson made no further answer, but again sat with her head resting on her hand. She also, if the truth must be told, was thinking of M. Lacordaire and his fondness for herself. He had squeezed her hand and he had looked into her face. However much it may have been nonsense on Mimmy's part to talk of such things, they had not the less absolutely occurred. Was it really the fact that M. Lacordaire was in love with her?

And if so, what return should she, or could she make to such a passion? He had looked at her yesterday, and squeezed her hand to-day. Might it not be probable that he would advance a step further to-morrow? If so, what answer would she be prepared to

176

make to him?

She did not think — so she said to herself — that she had any particular objection to marrying again. Thompson had been dead now for four years, and neither his friends, nor her friends, nor the world could say she was wrong on that score. And as to marrying a Frenchman, she could not say that she felt within herself any absolute repugnance to doing that. Of her own country, speaking of England as such, she, in truth, knew but little — and, perhaps, cared less. She had gone to India almost as a child, and England had not been specially kind to her on her return. She had found it dull and cold, stiff, and almost ill-natured. People there had not smiled on her and been civil as M. Lacordaire had done. As far as England and Englishmen were considered, she saw no reason why she should not marry M. Lacordaire.

And then, as regarded the man; could she in her heart say that she was prepared to love, honour, and obey M. Lacordaire? She certainly knew no reason why she should not do so. She did not know much of him, she said to herself at first; but she knew as much, she said afterwards, as she had known personally of Mr. Thompson before their marriage. She had known, to be sure, what was Mr. Thompson's profession, and what his income; or, if not, some one else had known for her. As to both these points she was quite in the dark, as regarded M. Lacordaire.

Personally, she certainly did like him, as she said to herself more than once. There was a courtesy and softness about him which were very gratifying to her; and then, his appearance was so much in his favour. He was not very young, she acknowledged; but neither was she young herself. It was quite evident that he was fond of her children, and that he would be a kind and affectionate father to them. Indeed, there was kindness in all that he did.

Should she marry again — and she put it to herself quite hypothetically — she would look for no romance in such a second marriage. She would be content to sit down in a quiet home to the tame, dull realities of life, satisfied with the companionship of a man who would be kind and gentle to her, and whom she could respect and esteem. Where could she find a companion with whom this could be more safely anticipated than with M. Lacordaire?

And so she argued the question within her own breast in a manner not unfriendly to that gentleman. That there was as yet one great hindrance she at once saw; but then that might be remedied by a word. She did not know what was his income or his profession. The chambermaid, whom she had interrogated, told her that he was a "*marchand*." To merchants, generally, she felt that she had no objection. The Barings and the Rothschilds were merchants, as was also that wonderful man at Bombay, Sir Hommajee Bommajee, who was worth she did not know how many thousand lacs of rupees.

That it would behove her, on her own account and that of her daughters, to take care of her own little fortune in contracting any such connection, that she felt strongly. She would never so commit herself as to put security in that respect out of her power. But then she did not think that M. Lacordaire would ever ask her to do so; at any rate, she was determined on this, that there should never be any doubt on that matter; and as she firmly resolved on this, she again took up her book, and for a minute or two made an attempt to read.

"Mamma," said Mimmy, "will M. Lacordaire go up to the school to see Lilian when you go away from this?"

"Indeed, I cannot say, my dear. If Lilian is a good girl, perhaps he may do so now and then."

"And will he write to you and tell you how she is?"

"Lilian can write for herself; can she not?"

"Oh! yes; I suppose she can; but I hope M. Lacordaire will write too. We shall come back here some day; sha'n't we, mamma?"

"I cannot say, my dear."

"I do so hope we shall see M. Lacordaire again. Do you know what I was thinking, mamma?"

"Little girls like you ought not to think," said Mrs. Thompson, walking slowly out of the room to the top of the stairs and back again; for she had felt the necessity of preventing Mimmy from disclosing any more of her thoughts. "And now, my dear, get yourself ready, and we will go up to the school."

Mrs. Thompson always dressed herself with care, though not in especially fine clothes, before she went down to dinner at the table-d'hôte; but on this occasion she was more than usually particular. She hardly explained to herself why she did this; but, nevertheless, as she stood before the glass, she did in a certain manner feel that the circumstances of her future life might perhaps depend on what might be said and done that evening. She had not absolutely decided whether or no she would go to the Prince's château; but if she did go— Well, if she did; what then? She had sense enough, as she assured herself more than once, to regulate her own conduct with propriety in any such emergency.

During the dinner, M. Lacordaire conversed in his usual manner, but said nothing whatever about the visit to Polignac. He was very kind to Mimmy, and very courteous to her mother, but did not appear to be at all more particular than usual. Indeed, it might be a question whether he was not less so. As she had entered the room Mrs. Thompson had said to herself that, perhaps, after all, it would be better that there should be nothing more about it; but before the four or five courses were over, she was beginning to feel a little disappointed.

And now the fruit was on the table, after the consumption of which it was her practice to retire. It was, certainly, open to her to ask M. Lacordaire to take tea with her that evening, as she had done on former occasions; but she felt that she must not do this now, considering the immediate circumstances of the case. If any further steps were to be taken, they must be taken by him, and not by her;—or else by Mimmy, who just as her mother was slowly consuming her last grapes, ran round to the back of M. Lacordaire's chair, and whispered something into his ear. It may be presumed that Mrs. Thompson did not see the intention of the movement in time to arrest it, for she did nothing till the whispering had been whispered; and then she rebuked the child, bade her not to be troublesome, and, with more than usual austerity in her voice, desired her to get herself ready to go up stairs to their chamber.

As she spoke, she herself rose from her chair, and made her final little bow to the table, and her other final little bow and smile to M. Lacordaire; but this was certain to all who saw it, that the smile was not as gracious as usual.

As she walked forth, M. Lacordaire rose from his chair—such being his constant practice when she left the table; but on this occasion he accompanied her to the door.

"And has madame decided," he asked, "whether she will per-mit me to accompany her to the château?"

"Well, I really don't know," said Mrs. Thompson.

"Mees Meemy," continued M. Lacordaire, "is very anxious to see the rock, and I may perhaps hope that Mees Leelian would be pleased with such a little excursion. As for myself—" and then M. Lacordaire put his hand upon his heart in a manner that seemed to speak more plainly than he had ever spoken.

"Well, if the chilren would really like it, and as you are so very kind,"—said Mrs. Thompson; and so the matter was conceded.

"To-morrow afternoon?" suggested M. Lacordaire. But Mrs. Thompson fixed on Saturday, thereby showing that she herself was in no hurry for the expedition.

"Oh, I am so glad!" said Mimmy, when they had re-entered their own room. "Mamma, do let me tell Lilian myself when I go up to the school to-morrow!"

But Mamma was in no humour to say much to her child on this subject at the present moment. She threw herself back on her sofa in perfect silence, and began to reflect whether she would like to sign her name in future as Fanny Lacordaire, in-stead of Fanny Thompson. It certainly seemed as though things were verging towards such a necessity. A *marchand!* But a *marchand* of what? She had an instinctive feeling that the people here were talking about her and M. Lacordaire, and was therefore more than ever averse to asking any one a question.

As she went up to the school the next afternoon, she walked through more of the streets of Le Puy than was necessary, and in every street she looked at the names which she saw over the doors of the more respectable houses of business. But she looked in vain. It might be that M. Lacordaire was a *marchand* of so spe-cially high a quality as to be under no necessity to put up his name at all. Sir Hommajee Bommajee's name did not appear over any door in Bombay—at least, she thought not.

And then came the Saturday morning. "We shall be ready at two," she said as she left the breakfast-table; "and perhaps you would not mind calling for Lilian on the way."

M. Lacordaire would be delighted to call anywhere for anybody on behalf of Mrs. Thompson; and then, as he got to the door of the *salon,* he offered her his hand. He did so with so much French courtesy, that she could not refuse it; and then she felt that his purpose was more tender than ever it had been. And why not, if this was the destiny which Fate had prepared for her?

Mrs. Thompson would rather have got into the carriage at any other spot in Le Puy than at that at which she was forced to do so — the chief entrance, namely, of the Hotel des Ambassadeurs. And what made it worse was this, that an appearance of a special *fête* was given to the occasion. M. Lacordaire was dressed in more than his Sunday best. He had on new yellow kid gloves. His coat, if not new, was newer than any Mrs. Thompson had yet observed, and was lined with silk up to the very collar. He had on patent leather boots, which glittered, as Mrs. Thompson thought, much too conspicuously. And as for his hat, it was quite evident that it was fresh that morning from the maker's block.

In the costume we described in our last, with his hat in his hand, he stood under the great gateway of the hotel, ready to hand Mrs. Thompson into the carriage. This would have been nothing if the landlord and landlady had not been there also, as well as the man cook, and the four waiters, and the fille de chambre. Two or three other pair of eyes Mrs. Thompson also saw, as she glanced round, and then Mimmy walked across the yard in her best clothes with a *fête* day air about her for which her mother would have liked to have whipped her.

But what did it matter? If it was written in the book that she should become Madame Lacordaire, of course the world would know that there must have been some preparatory love-making. Let them have their laugh; a good husband would not be dearly purchased at so trifling an expense. And so they sallied forth with already half the ceremony of a wedding.

Mimmy seated herself opposite to her mother, and M. Lacordaire also sat with his back to the horses, leaving the second place of honour for Lilian. "Pray make yourself comfortable, M. Lacordaire, and don't mind her," said Mrs. Thompson. But he was firm in his purpose of civility, perhaps making up his mind that when he should in truth stand in the place of papa to the young lady, then would be his time for having the front seat of the carriage.

Lilian, also in her best frock, came down the school steps, and three of the school teachers came with her. It would have added to Mrs. Thompson's happiness at that moment if M. Lacordaire would have kept his polished boots out of sight, and put his yellow gloves into his pocket.

And then they started. The road from Le Puy to Polignac is nearly all up hill; and a very steep hill it is, so that there was plenty of time for conversation. But the girls had it nearly all to themselves. Mimmy thought that she had never found M. Lacordaire so stupid; and Lilian told her sister on the first safe opportunity that occurred, that it seemed very much as though they were all going to church.

"And do any of the Polignac people ever live at this place?" asked Mrs. Thompson, by way of making conversation; in answer to which M. Lacordaire informed madame that the place was at present only a ruin; and then there was again silence till they found themselves under the rock, and were informed by the driver that the rest of the ascent must be made on foot.

The rock now stood abrupt and precipitous above their heads. It was larger in its circumference and with much larger space on its summit than those other volcanic rocks in and close to the town; but then at the same time it was higher from the ground, and quite as inaccessible except by the single path which led up to the château.

M. Lacordaire, with conspicuous gallantry, first assisted Mrs. Thompson from the carriage, and then handed down the two young ladies. No lady could have been so difficult to please as to complain of him, and yet Mrs. Thompson thought that he was not as agreeable as usual. Those horrid boots and those horrid gloves gave him such an air of holiday finery that neither could he be at his ease wearing them, nor could she, in seeing them worn.

They were soon taken in hand by the poor woman whose privilege it is to show the ruins. For a little distance they walked up the path in single file; not that it was too narrow to accommodate two, but M. Lacordaire's courage had not yet been screwed to a point which admitted of his offering his arm to the widow. For in France, it must be remembered, this means more than it does in some other countries.

Mrs. Thompson felt that all this was silly and useless. If they were not to be dear friends, this coming out *fêteing* together, those boots and gloves and new hat were all very foolish; and if they were, the sooner that they understood each other the better. So Mrs. Thompson, finding that the path was steep and the weather warm, stood still for a while leaning against the wall, with a look of considerable fatigue in her face.

"Will madame permit me the honour of offering her my arm?" said M. Lacordaire. "The road is so extraordinarily steep for madame to climb."

Mrs. Thompson did permit him the honour, and so they went on till they reached the top.

The view from the summit was both extensive and grand; but neither Lilian nor Mimmy were much pleased with the place. The elder sister, who had talked over the matter with her school companions, expected a fine castle with turrets, battlements, and romance; and the other expected a pretty smiling house, such as princes, in her mind, ought to inhabit.

Instead of this, they found an old turret, with steps so broken that M. Lacordaire did not care to ascend them, and the ruined walls of a mansion, in which nothing was to be seen but the remains of an enormous kitchen chimney.

"It was the kitchen of the family," said the guide.

"Oh," said Mrs. Thompson.

"And this," said the woman, taking them into the next ruined compartment, "was the kitchen of *monsieur et madame*."

"What! two kitchens?" exclaimed Lilian, upon which M. Lacordaire explained that the ancestors of the Prince de Polignac had been very great people, and had therefore required culinary performances on a great scale.

And then the woman began to chatter something about an oracle of Apollo. There was, she said, a hole in the rock, from which in past times, perhaps more than a hundred years ago, the oracle used to speak forth mysterious words.

"There," she said, pointing to a part of the rock at some distance, "was the hole. And if the ladies would follow her to a little outhouse which was just beyond, she would show them the huge stone mouth out of which the oracle used to speak."

Lilian and Mimmy both declared at once for seeing the oracle, but Mrs. Thompson expressed her determination to remain sitting where she was upon the turf. So the guide started off with

the young ladies; and will it be thought surprising that M. Lacordaire should have remained alone by the side of Mrs.
Thompson?

It must be now or never, Mrs. Thompson felt; and as regarded
M. Lacordaire, he probably entertained some idea of the same
kind. Mrs. Thompson's inclinations, though they had never been
very strong in the matter, were certainly in favour of the "now."
M. Lacordaire's inclinations were stronger. He had fully and
firmly made up his mind in favour of matrimony; but then he was
not so absolutely in favour of the "now." Mrs. Thompson's mind,
if one could have read it, would have shown a great objection to
shilly-shallying, as she was accustomed to call it. But M. Lacordaire, were it not for the danger which might thence arise, would
have seen no objection to some slight further procrastination.
His courage was beginning, perhaps, to ooze out from his fingers'
ends.

"I declare that those girls have scampered away ever so far,"
said Mrs. Thompson.

"Would madame wish that I should call them back?" said M.
Lacordaire, innocently.

"Oh, no, dear children! Let them enjoy themselves. It will be
a pleasure to them to run about the rock, and I suppose they will
be safe with that woman?"

"Oh, yes, quite safe," said M. Lacordaire, and then there was
another little pause.

Mrs. Thompson was sitting on a broken fragment of a stone
just outside the entrance to the old family kitchen, and M. Lacordaire was standing immediately before her. He had in his hand
a little cane with which he sometimes slapped his boots and
sometimes poked about among the rubbish. His hat was not quite
straight on his head, having a little jaunty twist to one side, with
reference to which, by-the-bye, Mrs. Thompson then resolved
that she would make a change, should ever the gentleman become her own property. He still wore his gloves and was very
smart; but it was clear to see that he was not at his ease.

"I hope the heat does not incommode you," he said, after a few
moments' silence. Mrs. Thompson declared that it did not, that
she liked a good deal of heat, and that, on the whole, she was
very well where she was. She was afraid, however, that she was

detaining M. Lacordaire, who might probably wish to be moving about upon the rock. In answer to which, M. Lacordaire declared that he never could be so happy anywhere as in her close vicinity.

"You are too good to me," said Mrs. Thompson, almost sighing. "I don't know what my stay here would have been without your great kindness."

"It is madame that has been kind to me," said M. Lacordaire, pressing the handle of his cane against his heart.

There was then another pause, after which Mrs. Thompson said that that was all his French politeness; that she knew that she had been very troublesome to him, but that she would now soon be gone; and that then, in her own country, she would never forget his great goodness.

"Ah, madame!" said M. Lacordaire; and, as he said it, much more was expressed in his face than in his words. But, then, you can neither accept nor reject a gentleman by what he says in his face. He blushed, too, up to his grizzled hair, and, turning round, walked a step or two away from the widow's seat, and back again.

Mrs. Thompson the while sat quite still. The displaced fragment, lying, as it did, near a corner of the building, made not an uncomfortable chair. She had only to be careful that she did not injure her hat or crush her clothes, and throw in a word here and there to assist the gentleman, should occasion permit it.

"Madame!" said M. Lacordaire, on his return from a second little walk.

"Monsieur!" replied Mrs. Thompson, perceiving that M. Lacordaire paused in his speech.

"Madame," he began again, and then, as he again paused, Mrs. Thompson looked up to him very sweetly; "madame, what I am going to say will, I am afraid, seem to evince by far too great audacity on my part."

Mrs. Thompson may, perhaps, have thought that, at the present moment, audacity was not his fault. She replied, however, that she was quite sure that monsieur would say nothing that was in any way unbecoming either for him to speak or for her to hear.

"Madame, may I have ground to hope that such may be your sentiments after I have spoken! Madame" — and now he went down, absolutely on his knees, on the hard stones; and Mrs. Thompson, looking about into the distance almost thought that

she saw the top of the guide's cap — "Madame, I have looked forward to this opportunity as one in which I may declare for you
the greatest passion that I have ever yet felt. Madame, with all
my heart and soul I love you. Madame, I offer to you the homage
of my heart, my hand, the happiness of my life, and all that I
possess in this world;" and then, taking her hand gracefully between his gloves, he pressed his lips against the tips of her fingers.

If the thing was to be done, this way of doing it was, perhaps,
as good as any other. It was one, at any rate, which left no doubt
whatever as to the gentleman's intentions. Mrs. Thompson,
could she have had her own way, would not have allowed her
lover of fifty to go down upon his knees, and would have spared
him much of the romance of his declaration. So also would she
have spared him his yellow gloves and his polished boots. But
these were a part of the necessity of the situation, and therefore
she wisely took them as matters to be passed over with indifference. Seeing, however, that M. Lacordaire still remained on his
knees, it was necessary that she should take some step toward
raising him, especially as her two children and the guide would
infallibly be upon them before long.

"M. Lacordaire," she said, "you surprise me greatly; but pray
get up."

"But will madame vouchsafe to give me some small ground for
hope?"

"The girls will be here directly, M. Lacordaire; pray get up. I
can talk to you much better if you will stand up, or sit down on
one of these stones."

M. Lacordaire did as he was bid; he got up, wiped the knees of
his trousers with his handkerchief, sat down beside her, and then
pressed the handle of his cane to his heart.

"You really have so surprised me that I hardly know how to
answer you," said Mrs. Thompson. "Indeed, I cannot bring myself to imagine that you are in earnest."

"Ah, madame, do not be so cruel! How can I have lived with
you so long, sat beside you for so many days, without having received your image into my heart? I am in earnest! Alas! I fear too
much in earnest!" And then he looked at her with all his eyes,
and sighed with all his strength.

Mrs. Thompson's prudence told her that it would be well to

settle the matter, in one way or the other, as soon as possible. Long periods of love-making were fit for younger people than herself and her future possible husband. Her object would be to make him comfortable if she could, and that he should do the same for her, if that also were possible. As for lookings and sighings, and pressings of the hand, she had gone through all that some twenty years ago in India, when Thompson had been young, and she was still in her teens.

"But, M. Lacordaire, there are so many things to be considered. There! I hear the children coming! Let us walk this way for a minute." And they turned behind a wall, which placed them out of sight, and walked on a few paces till they reached a parapet, which stood on the uttermost edge of the high rock. Leaning upon this they continued their conversation.

"There are so many things to be considered," said Mrs. Thompson again.

"Yes, of course, " said M. Lacordaire. "But my one great consideration is this — that I love madame to distraction."

"I am very much flattered; of course, any lady would so feel. But, M. Lacordaire — "

"Madame, I am all attention. But, if you would deign to make me happy, say that one word, 'I love you!'" M. Lacordaire, as he uttered these words, did not look, as the saying is, at his best. But Mrs. Thompson forgave him. She knew that elderly gentlemen under such circumstances do not look at their best.

"But if I consented to — to — to such an arrangement, I could only do so on seeing that it would be beneficial — or, at any rate, not injurious — to my children; and that it would offer to ourselves a fair promise of future happiness."

"Ah, madame! it would be the dearest wish of my heart to be a second father to those two young ladies; except, indeed — " And then M. Lacordaire stopped the flow of his speech.

"In such matters it is so much the best to be explicit at once," said Mrs. Thompson.

"Oh, yes; certainly! Nothing can be more wise than madame."

"And the happiness of a household depends so much on money."

"Madame!"

"Let me say a word or two, Monsieur Lacordaire. I have

enough for myself and my children; and, should I ever marry again, I should not, I hope, be felt as a burden by my husband; but it would, of course, be my duty to know what were his circumstances before I accepted him. Of yourself, personally, I have seen nothing that I do not like."

"Oh, madame!"

"But, as yet I know nothing of your circumstances."

M. Lacordaire, perhaps, did feel that Mrs. Thompson's prudence was of a strong, masculine description; but he hardly liked her the less on this account. To give him his due, he was not desirous of marrying her solely for her money's sake. He also wished for a comfortable home, and proposed to give as much as he got; only he had been anxious to wrap up the solid cake of this business in a casing of sugar of romance. Mrs. Thompson would not have the sugar; but the cake might not be the worse on that account.

"No, madame; not as yet: but they shall all be made open and at your disposal," said M. Lacordaire; and Mrs. Thompson bowed approvingly.

"I am in business," continued M. Lacordaire; "and my business gives me over eight thousand francs a year."

"Four times eight are thirty-two," said Mrs. Thompson to herself; putting the francs into pounds sterling, in the manner that she had always found to be the readiest. Well, so far the statement was satisfactory. An income of three hundred and twenty pounds a year from business, joined to her own, might do very well. She did not in the least suspect M. Lacordaire of being false, and so far the matter sounded well.

"And what is the business?" she asked, in a tone of voice intended to be indifferent, but which nevertheless showed that she listened anxiously for an answer to her question.

They were both standing with their arms upon the wall, looking down upon the town of Le Puy; but they had so stood that each could see the other's countenance as they talked. Mrs. Thompson could now perceive that M. Lacordaire became red in the face, as he paused before answering her. She was near to him and seeing his emotion, gently touched his arm with her hand. This she did to reassure him, for she saw that he was ashamed of having to declare that he was a tradesman. As for herself, she had made up her mind to bear with this, if she found, as she felt sure she would find, that the trade was one which would not degrade either him or her. Hitherto, indeed, in her early days, she had looked down on trade; but of what benefit had her grand ideas been to her when she had returned to England? She had tried her hand at English genteel society, and no one had seemed to care for her. Therefore, she touched his arm lightly with her fingers that she might encourage him.

He paused for a moment, as I have said, and became red; and then feeling that he had shown some symptoms of shame — and feeling also, probably, that it was unmanly in him to do so, he shook himself slightly, raised his head up somewhat more proudly than was his wont, looked her full in the face with more strength of character than she had yet seen him assume; and then declared his prospects.

"Madame," he said, in a very audible, but not in a loud voice; "madame — *je suis tailleur*." And having so spoken, he turned slightly from her and looked down over the valley towards Le Puy.

There was nothing more said upon the subject as they drove down from the rock of Polignac back to the town. Immediately on receiving the announcement, Mrs. Thompson found that she had no answer to make. She withdrew her hand — and felt at once that she had received a blow. It was not that she was angry with M. Lacordaire for being a tailor; nor was she angry with him in that, being a tailor, he had so addressed her. But she was surprised, disappointed, and altogether put beyond her ease. She had, at any rate, not expected this. She had dreamed of his being a banker; thought that, perhaps, he might have been a wine merchant; but her idea had never gone below a jeweller or watchmaker. When those words broke upon her ear, "Madame, *je suis tailleur*," she had felt herself to be speechless.

But the words had not been a minute spoken, when Lilian and Mimmy marched up to their mother. "Oh, mamma," said Lilian, "we thought you were lost; we have searched for you all over the château."

"We have been sitting very quietly here, my dear, looking at the view," said Mrs. Thompson.

"But, mamma, I do wish you'd see the·mouth of the oracle. It is so large, and so round, and so ugly. I put my arm into it all the way," said Mimmy.

But at the present moment, her mamma felt no interest in the mouth of the oracle; and so they all walked down together to the carriage. And, though the way was steep, Mrs. Thompson managed to pick her steps without the assistance of an arm; nor did M. Lacordaire presume to offer it.

The drive back to town was very silent. Mrs. Thompson did make one or two attempts at conversation, but they were not effectual. M. Lacordaire could not speak at his ease till this matter was settled, and he already had begun to perceive that his business was against him. Why is it that the trade of a tailor should be less honourable than that of an haberdasher, or even a grocer?

They sat next to each other at dinner, as usual; and here, as all eyes were upon them, they both made a great struggle to behave in their accustomed way. But even in this they failed. All the world of the Hotel des Ambassadeurs knew that M. Lacordaire had gone forth to make an offer to Mrs. Thompson, and all the world, therefore, was full of speculation. But all the world could make nothing of it. M. Lacordaire did look like a rejected man, but Mrs. Thompson did not look like the woman who had rejected him. That the offer had been made — in that everybody agreed, from the senior *habitué* of the house who always sat at the head of the table, down to the junior assistant garçon; but as to the reading the riddle, there was no accord among them.

When the dessert was done, Mrs. Thompson, as usual, withdrew, and M. Lacordaire, as usual, bowed as he stood behind his own chair. He did not, however, attempt to follow her.

But she, when she reached the door, called him. He was at her side in a moment, and then she whispered in his ear —

"And I, also — I will be of the same business!"

When M. Lacordaire regained the table the senior *habitué*, the junior garçon, and all the intermediate ranks of men at the Hotel des Ambassadeurs, knew that they might congratulate him.

Mrs. Thompson had made a great struggle; but, speaking for myself, I am inclined to think that she arrived at last at a wise decision.

"The Chateau of Prince Polignac" appeared first in the October 20 and 27 issues of *Cassell's Illustrated Family Paper* for 1860.

George Walker at Suez

O F ALL THE SPOTS ON THE WORLD'S surface
that I, George Walker, of Friday-street, London, have ever visited, Suez, in Egypt, at the head of the Red Sea, is by far the
vilest, the most unpleasant, and the least interesting. There are
no women there, no water, and no vegetation. It is surrounded,
and, indeed, often filled, by a world of sand. A scorching sun is
always overhead, and one is domiciled in a huge, cavernous hotel, which seems to have been made purposely destitute of all the
comforts of civilised life. Nevertheless, in looking back upon the
week of my life which I spent there, I always enjoy a certain sort
of triumph — or, rather, upon one day of that week, which lends
a sort of halo, not only to my sojourn at Suez, but to the whole
period of my residence in Egypt.

I am free to confess that I am not a great man, and that, at any
rate in the earlier part of my career, I had a hankering after the
homage which is paid to greatness. I would fain have been a popular orator, feeding myself on the incense tendered to me by
thousands, or, failing that, a man born to power, whom those
around him were compelled to respect, and perhaps to fear. I am
not ashamed to acknowledge this, and I believe that most of my
neighbours in Friday-street would own as much were they as can-
did and open-hearted as myself.

It is now nearly ten years since I was recommended to pass the
four first months of the year in Cairo, because I had a sore throat.

The doctor may have been right, but I shall never divest myself of the idea that my partners wished to be rid of me while they made certain changes in the management of the firm. They would not otherwise have shown such interest every time I blew my nose or relieved my huskiness by a slight cough; they would not have been so intimate with that surgeon from St. Bartholomew's, who dined with them thrice at the Albion; nor would they have gone to work directly that my back was turned, and have done those very things which they could not have done had I remained at home. Be that as it may, I was frightened and went to Cairo, and while there I made a trip to Suez for a week.

I was not happy at Cairo, for I knew nobody there, and the people at the hotel were, as I thought, uncivil. It seemed to me as though I were allowed to go in and out merely by sufferance; and yet I paid my bill regularly every week. The house was full of company, but the company was made up of parties of two and threes, and they all seemed to have their own friends. I did make attempts to overcome that terrible British exclusiveness — that *noli me tangere* with which an Englishman arms himself, and in which he thinks it necessary to envelop his wife; but it was in vain; and I found myself sitting down to breakfast and dinner, day after day, as much alone as I should do if I called for a chop at a separate table in the Cathedral Coffee-house. And yet, at breakfast and at dinner, I made one of an assemblage of thirty or forty people. That I thought dull.

But as I stood one morning on the steps before the hotel, bethinking myself that my throat was as well as ever I remembered it to be, I was suddenly slapped on the back. Never in my life did I feel a more pleasant sensation, or turn round with more unaffected delight to return a friend's greeting. It was as though a cup of water had been handed to me in the desert. I knew that a cargo of passengers for Australia had reached Cairo that morning, and were to be passed on to Suez as soon as the railway would take them, and did not, therefore, expect that the greeting had come from any sojourner in Egypt. I should, perhaps, have explained that the even tenour of our life at the hotel was disturbed, some four times a month, by a flight through Cairo of a flock of travellers, who, like locusts, eat up all that there was eatable at the inn for the day. They sat down at the same tables with us, never mixing with us, having their own separate interests and hopes, and being often, as I thought, somewhat loud and almost selfish in their expression of them. These flocks consisted of passengers passing and repassing by the overland route to and from India and Australia; and had I nothing else to tell, I should delight to describe all that I watched of their habits and manners — the outwardbound being so different in their traits from their brethren on their return. But I have to tell of my own triumph at Suez, and must, therefore, hasten on to say, that on turning round quickly with my outstretched hand, I found it clasped by John Robinson.

"Well, Robinson, is this you?"

"Halloo, Walker, what are you doing here?"

That, of course, was the style of greeting. Elsewhere I should not have cared much to meet John Robinson, for he was a man who had never done well in the world; he had been in business, and connected with a fairly good house in Size-lane; but he had married early, and things had not exactly gone well with him. I don't think the house broke — but he did; and so he was driven to take himself and five children off to Australia. Elsewhere I should not have cared to come across him; but I was positively glad to be slapped on the back by anybody on that landing-place in front of Shepheard's hotel at Cairo.

I soon learned that Robinson, with his wife and children, and, indeed, with all the rest of the Australian cargo, was to be passed on to Suez that afternoon; and after a while I agreed to accompany the party. I had made up my mind, on coming out from England, that I would see all the wonders of Egypt, and hitherto I had seen nothing. I did ride, on one day, some fifteen miles on a donkey to see the petrified forest; but the guide, who called himself a dragoman, took me wrong or cheated me in some way. We rode on, half the day, over a stony, sandy plain, seeing nothing, with a terrible wind that filled my mouth with hot grit; and at last the dragoman got off. "Dere," said he, picking up a small bit of stone, "dis is de forest made of stone. Carry dat home." Then we turned around and rode back to Cairo. My chief observation, as to the country, was this — that whichever way we went, the wind blew right into our teeth. The day's work cost me five-and-twenty shillings; and since that, I had not as yet made any other expedition. I was, therefore, glad of an opportunity of going to Suez, and of making the journey in company with an acquaintance.

At that time the railway was open, as far as I remember, nearly half the way from Cairo to Suez. It did not run four or five times a day as railways do in other countries, but four or five times a month. In fact it only carried passengers, on the arrival of these flocks camping between England and her Eastern possessions. There were trains passing backwards and forwards constantly, as I perceived in walking to and from the station, but, as I learned, they carried nothing but the labourers working on the line, and the water sent into the desert for their use. It struck me forcibly at the time that I should not have liked to have money in that investment.

Well, I went with Robinson to Suez. The journey, like everything else in Egypt, was sandy, hot, and unpleasant. The railway carriages were pretty fair, and we had room enough, but even in them the dust was a great nuisance. We travelled about ten miles an hour, and stopped about half an hour at every ten miles. This was tedious, but we had cigars with us and a trifle of brandy-and-water, and in this manner the railway journey wore itself away. In the middle of the night, however, we were moved from the railway carriages into omnibuses, as they were called, and then I was not comfortable. These omnibuses were wooden boxes, placed each upon a pair of wheels, and supposed to be capable of carrying six passengers. I was thrust into one with Robinson, his wife, and five children, and immediately began to repent of my good nature in accompanying them. To each vehicle were attached four horses or mules, and I must acknowledge, that as on the railway they went as slow as possible, so now in these conveyances dragged through the sand, they went as fast as the beasts could be made to gallop. I remember the Fox Tally-ho coach on the Birmingham road, when Boyce drove it, but, as regards pace, the Fox Tally-ho was nothing to these machines in Egypt. On the first going off I was jolted right on to Mrs. R. and her infant; and for a long time that lady thought that the child had been squeezed out of its proper shape; but at last we arrived at Suez and the baby seemed to me to be all right when it was handed down into the boat at the quay.

194

The Robinsons were allowed time to breakfast at that cavern-ous hotel — which looked to me like a scheme to save the ex-pense of the passengers' meal on board the ship — and then they were off. I shook hands with him heartily as I parted with him at the quay, and wished him well through all his troubles. A man who takes a wife and five young children out into a colony, and that with his pockets but indifferently lined, certainly has his troubles before him. So he has at home, no doubt, but, judging for myself, I should always prefer sticking to the old ship as long as there is a bag of biscuits in the locker. Poor Robinson! I have never heard a word of him or his since that day, and sincerely trust that the baby was none the worse for the little accident in the box.

And now I had the prospect of a week before me at Suez, and the Robinsons had not been gone half an hour, before I began to feel that I should have been better off even at Cairo. I secured a bedroom at the hotel — I might have secured sixty bedrooms had I wanted them — and then went out and stood at the front door, or gate. It is a huge house, built round a quadrangle, looking with one front towards the head of the Red Sea, and with the other into an arid, or a sandy, dead-looking open square. There I stood for ten minutes, and, finding that it was too hot to go forth, re-turned to the long cavernous room in which we had all break-fasted. In that long cavernous room I was destined to eat all my meals alone for the next six days. Now, at Cairo, I could at any rate see my fellow creatures at their food. So I lit a cigar, and began to wonder whether I could survive the week. It was now clear to me that I had done a very rash thing in coming to Suez with the Robinsons.

Somebody about the place had asked me my name, and I had told it plainly — George Walker. I never was ashamed of my name yet, and never had cause to be. I believe at this day it will go as far in Friday-street as any other. A man may be popular, or he may not. That depends mostly on circumstances, which are in themselves trifling. But the value of his name depends on the way in which he is known at his bank. I have never dealt in tea-spoons or gravy-spoons, but my name will go, I believe, as far as another man's. "George Walker," I answered, therefore, in a tone of some little authority, to the man who asked me, and who sat inside the gate of the hotel in an old dressing-gown and slippers.

That was a melancholy day with me, and twenty times before dinner did I wish myself back at Cairo. I had been travelling all night, and therefore hoped that I might get through some time in sleeping, but the mosquitoes attacked me the moment I had laid myself down. In other places mosquitoes torment you only at night, but at Suez they buzz around you without ceasing at all hours. A scorching sun was blazing overhead, and absolutely for-bade me to leave the house. I stood for a while in the verandah, looking down at the few small vessels which were moored to the quay, but there was no life in them; not a sail was set, not a boat-man or sailor was to be seen, and the very water looked as though it were hot. I could fancy that the glare of the sun was cracking the paint on the gunwales of the boats. I was the only visitor in the house, and during all the long hours of the morning it seemed as though the servants had deserted it.

I dined at four; not that I chose that hour, but because no choice was given to me. At the hotels in Egypt, one has to dine at an hour fixed by the landlord, and no entreaties will suffice to obtain a meal at any other. So at four I dined, and after dinner was again reduced to despair.

I was sitting in the cavernous chamber, almost mad at the prospect of the week before me, when I heard a noise as of various feet in the passage leading from the quadrangle. Was it possible that other human beings were coming into the hotel—Christian human beings at whom I could look, whose voices I could hear, whose words I could understand, and with whom I might possibly associate? I did not move, however, for I was still hot, and I knew that my chances might be better if I did not show myself over eager for companionship at the first moment. The door, how-ever, was soon opened, and I saw that at least in one respect, I was destined to be disappointed. The strangers who were enter-ing the room were not Christians, if I might judge by the nature of the garments in which they were clothed.

The door had been opened by the man in an old dressing-gown and slippers, whom I had seen sitting inside the gate. He was the Arab porter of the hotel, and as he marshalled the new visitors into the room, I heard him pronounce some sound similar to my own name, and perceived that he pointed me out to the most prominent person of those who then entered the apartment. This was a stout portly man, dressed from head to foot in Eastern costume of the brightest colours. He wore, not only the red fez cap which everybody wears — even I myself had accustomed myself to a fez cap — but a turban round it, of which the voluminous folds were snowy white. His face was fat, but not the less grave, and the lower part of it was enveloped in a magnificent beard which projected round it on all sides, and touched his breast as he walked. It was a grand grizzled beard, and I acknowledged at a moment that it added a singular dignity to the appearance of the stranger. His flowing robe was of bright colours, and the under garment, which fitted close round his breast and then descended, becoming beneath his sash a pair of the loosest pantaloons — I might perhaps better describe them as bags — of a rich tawny silk. These loose pantaloons were tied close round his leg above the ankle, and over a pair of scrupulously white stockings, and on his feet he wore a pair of yellow slippers. It was manifest to me at a glance that the Arab gentleman was got up in his best raiment, and that no expense had been spared on the suit.

And here I cannot but make a remark on the personal bearing of these Arabs. Whether they be Arabs, or Turks, or Copts, it is always the same. They are a mean, false, cowardly race, I believe. They will bear blows, and respect the man who gives them. Fear goes farther with them than love, and between man and man they understand nothing of forebearance. He who does not exact from them all that he can exact is simply a fool in their estimation, to the extent of that which he looses. In all this they are immeasurably inferior to us, who have Christian teaching. But in one thing they beat us — they always know how to maintain their personal dignity.

Look at my friend and partner Judkins, as he stands with his hands in his trousers pockets at the door of our house in Friday-street. What can be meaner than his appearance? He is a stumpy, short, podgy man; but then so also was my Arab friend at Suez. Judkins is always dressed from head to foot in a decent black cloth suit; his coat is ever a dress coat, and is neither old nor shabby. On his head he carries a shining new silk hat, such as fashion in our metropolis demands. Judkins is rather a dandy than otherwise, piquing himself somewhat on his apparel. And yet how mean is his appearance as compared with the appearance of that Arab! how mean also is his gait, how ignoble his step! Judkins could buy that Arab out five times over and hardly feel the loss; and yet, were they to enter a room together, Judkins would know and acknowledge by his look that he was the inferior personage. Not the less, should a personal quarrel arise between them, would Judkins punch the Arab's head; ay, and reduce him to utter ignominy at his feet. Judkins would break his heart in despair rather than not return a blow, whereas the Arab would put up with any indignity of that sort. Nevertheless, Judkins is altogether deficient in personal dignity. I often thought, as the hours hung heavy on my hands in Egypt, whether it might not be practicable to introduce an Oriental costume into Friday-street.

At this moment, as the Arab gentleman entered the cavernous coffee-room, I felt that I was greatly the inferior personage. He was followed by four or five others dressed somewhat as himself — though by no means in such magnificent colours — and by one gentleman in a coat and trousers. The gentleman in the coat and trousers came last, and I could see that he was one of the least of the number. As for myself I felt almost overawed by the dignity of the stout party in the turban, and seeing that he came directly across the room to the place where I was seated, I got up on my legs, and made to him some sign of Christian obeisance. I am a little man, and not podgy as is Judkins, and I flatter myself that I showed more deportment at any rate than he would have exhibited.

I made, as I have said, some Christian obeisance — I bobbed my head, that is, rubbing my hands together the while, and expressed an opinion that it was a fine day. But if I was civil, as I hope I was, the Arab was much more so. He advanced till he was about six paces from me, then placed his right hand open upon his silken breast, and, inclining forward with his whole body, made to me a bow which Judkins never could accomplish. The turban and flowing robe might be passable in Friday-street, but of what avail would be the outer garments and mere symbols, if the inner sentiment of personal dignity were wanting? I have often since tried it when alone, but I could never accomplish anything like that bow. The Arab with the flowing robe bowed,

and then the other Arabs all bowed also; and after that the Christian gentleman with the coat and trousers made a leg. I made a
leg also, rubbed my hands again, and added to my former remarks
that it was rather hot.

"Dat berry true," said the porter in the dirty dressing-gown,
who stood by. I could see at a glance that the manner of that porter towards me was greatly altered, and I began to feel comforted
in my wretchedness. Perhaps a Christian from Friday-street, with
plenty of money in his pockets, would stand in higher esteem at
Suez than at Cairo. If so, that alone would go far to atone for the
apparent wretchedness of the place. At Cairo I had not received
that attention which had certainly been due to me as the second
partner in the flourishing Manchester house of Grimes, Walker,
and Judkins.

But now, as my friend with the beard again bowed to me, I felt
that this deficiency was to be made up. It was clear, however, that
this new acquaintance, though I liked the manner of it, would be
attended with considerable inconvenience, for the Arab gentleman commenced an address to me in French. It has always been
to me a source of sorrow that my parents did not teach me the
French language; and the deficiency on my part has given rise to
an incredible amount of supercilious overbearing pretension on
the part of Judkins, who, after all, can hardly do more than trans-
late a correspondent's letter. I do not believe that he could have
understood a word of that Arab's oration; but, at any rate, I did
not. He went on to the end, however, speaking for some three or
four minutes, and then again he bowed. If I could only have
learned that bow, I might still have been greater than Judkins,
with all his French.

"I am very sorry," said I, "but I don't exactly follow the French
language — when it is spoken."

"Ah! no French!" said the Arab, in very broken English; "dat
is one sorrow." How is it that these fellows learn all languages
under the sun? I afterwards found that this man could talk Italian, and Turkish, and Armenian fluently, and say a few words in
German, as he could also in English. I could not ask for my dinner in any other language than English, if it were to save me from
starvation. Then he called to the Christian gentleman in the
pantaloons, and, as far as I could understand, made over to him

the duty of interpreting between us. There seemed, however, one difficulty in the way of this being carried on with efficiency—the Christian gentleman could not speak English himself. He knew of it, perhaps, something more than did the Arab, but by no means enough to enable us to have a fluent conversation. And, indeed, had the interpreter — who turned out to be an Italian from Trieste, attached to the Austrian Consulate at Alexandria — had the interpreter spoken English with the greatest ease, I should have had considerable difficulty in understanding and digesting, in all its bearings, the splendid proposition that was made to me. But before I proceed to the proposition, I must describe a ceremony which took place previous to its discussion. I had hardly observed, when first the procession entered the room, that one of my friend's followers—my friend's name, as I learned afterwards, was Mahmoud al Ackbar, and I will therefore call him Mahmoud — that one of Mahmoud's followers bore in his arms a bundle of long sticks, and that another carried an iron pot and a tray. Such was the case; and now these followers came forward to perform their services, while I, having been literally pressed down on to the sofa by Mahmoud, watched them in their progress. Mahmoud also sat down, and not a word was spoken while the ceremony went on. The man with the sticks first placed on the ground two little pans, one at my feet, and then one at the feet of his master. After that he loosed an ornamental bag which he carried round his neck, and producing from it tobacco, proceeded to fill two pipes. This he did with the utmost gravity, and apparently with very peculiar ease. The pipes had been already fixed to one end of the sticks, and to the other end the man had fastened two large yellow balls. These, as I afterwards perceived, were mouthpieces made of amber. Then he lit the pipes, drawing up the difficult smoke by long painful suckings at the mouthpieces; and then, when the work had become apparently easy, he handed one pipe to me and the other to his master. The bowls he had first placed in the little pans on the ground.

During all this time no word was spoken, and I was left altogether in the dark as to the cause which had produced this extraordinary courtesy. There was a stationary sofa—they called it there a divan—which was fixed into the corner of the room; and on one side of the angle sat Mahmoud al Ackbar, with his feet

turned in under him, while I sat on the other. The remainder of
the party stood around, and I felt so little master of the occasion
that I did not know whether it would become me to bid them be
seated. I was not the master of the entertainment — they were
not my pipes; nor was it my coffee which I saw one of the followers preparing in a distant part of the room. And, indeed, I was
much confused as to the management of the stick and amber
mouthpiece with which I had been presented. With a cigar I am
as much at home as any man in the City; I can nibble off the end
of it, and smoke it to the last ash, when I am three parts asleep.
But I had never before been invited to regale myself with such an
instrument as this. What was I to do with that huge yellow ball?
So I watched my friend closely.

It had manifestly been a part of his urbanity not to commence
till I had done so, but seeing my difficulty, he at last raised the
ball to his mouth and sucked it. I looked at him, and envied the
gravity of his countenance and the dignity of his demeanour. I
sucked also, but I made a sputtering noise, and must confess that
I did not enjoy it. The smoke curled gracefully from his mouth
and nostrils as he sat there in mute composure. I was mute also,
as regarded speech, but I coughed as the smoke came from me in
convulsive puffs. And then the attendant brought us coffee in
little tin cups — black coffee, without sugar and full of grit, of
which the berries had been only bruised and not ground. I took
the cup and swallowed the mixture, for I could not refuse; but I
wished that I might have asked for some milk and sugar. Nevertheless, there was something very pleasing in the whole ceremony, and at last I began to find myself more at home with my
pipe.

When Mahmoud had exhausted his tobacco, and perceived
that I also had ceased to puff forth smoke, he spoke in Italian to
the interpreter, and the interpreter forthwith proceeded to explain to me the purport of their visit. This was done with much
difficulty, for the interpreter's stock of English was very scanty;
but after a while I understood, or thought that I understood, as
follows: — At some previous period of my existence, I had done
some deed which had given infinite satisfaction to Mahmoud al
Ackbar. Whether, however, I had done it myself or whether my
father had done it, was not quite clear to me. My father, then

some time deceased, had been a wharfinger at Liverpool, and it was quite possible that Mahmoud might have found himself at the port. Mahmoud had heard of my arrival in Egypt, and had been given to understand that I was coming to Suez, to carry myself away in the ship, as the interpreter phrased. This I could not understand, but I let it pass. Having heard these agreeable tidings — and Mahmoud, sitting in the corner, bowed low to me as this was said — he had prepared for my acceptance a slight re-fection for the morrow, hoping that I would not carry myself away in the ship till this had been eaten. On this subject I soon made him quite at ease, and he then proceeded to explain that as there was no point of interest at Suez, Mahmoud was anxious that I should partake of the refection, somewhat in the guise of a pic-nic, at the well of Moses, over in Asia, on the other side of the head of the Red Sea. Mahmoud would provide a boat to take across the party in the morning, and camels on which we would return after sunset; or else we would go and return on camels, or go on camels and return in the boat. Indeed, any arrangement could be made that I preferred. If I was afraid of the heat, and disliked the open boat, I could be carried round in a litter. The provisions had already been sent over to the well of Moses, in the anticipation that I would not refuse this little request.

I did not refuse it. Nothing could have been more agreeable to me than this plan of seeing something of the sights and wonders of this land, and of thus seeing them in good company. I had not heard of the well of Moses before; but now that I learned that it was in Asia, in another quarter of the globe — to be reached by a transit of the Red Sea — and be returned from by a journey on camels' backs, I burned with anxiety to visit its waters. What a story would this be for Judkins! This was, no doubt, the point at which the Israelites had passed; of these waters had they drunk. I almost felt that I had already found one of Pharaoh's chariot wheels. I readily gave my assent, and then with much ceremony and many low salaams Mahmoud and his attendants left me. "I am very glad that I came to Suez," said I to myself.

I did not sleep much that night, for the mosquitoes of Suez are very persevering; but I was saved from the agonising despair which these animals so frequently produce by my agreeable thoughts as to Mahmoud al Ackbar. I will put it to any of my readers who have travelled whether it is not a painful thing to find oneself regarded among strangers without any kindness or ceremonious courtesy. I had on this account been wretched at Cairo, but all this was to be made up to me at Suez. Nothing could be more pleasant than the whole conduct of Mahmoud al Ackbar, and I determined to take full advantage of it, not caring overmuch what might be the nature of those previous favours to which he had alluded. That was his affair, and if he was satisfied, why should not I be also?

On the following morning I was dressed at six, and looking out of my bed-room, I saw the boat in which we were to be wafted over into Asia, being brought up to the quay close under my window. It had been arranged that we should start early, so as to avoid the mid-day sun, breakfast in the boat—Mahmoud having in this way engaged to provide me with two refections—take our rest at noon in a pavilion which had been built close upon the well of the patriarch, then eat our dinner, and return, riding upon camels, in the cool of the evening. Nothing could sound more pleasant than such a plan, and knowing, as I did, that the hampers of provisions had already been sent over, I did not doubt that the table arrangements would be excellent. Even now, standing at my window, I could see a basket laden with long-necked bottles, going into the boat, and became aware that we should not depend altogether for our morning repasts on that gritty coffee which my friend Mahmoud's follower prepared.

I had promised to be ready at six, and having carefully completed my toilet, and put a clean collar and comb into my pocket, ready for dinner, I descended to the great gateway and walked slowly round to the quay. As I passed out the porter greeted me with a low obeisance, and walking on, I felt that I stepped the ground with a sort of dignity of which I had before been ignorant. It is not, as a rule, the man who gives grace and honour to the position, but the position which confers the grace and honour upon the man. I have often envied the solemn gravity and grand demeanour of the Lord Chancellor, as I have seen him on the bench, but I doubt whether even Judkins would not look grave and dignified under such a wig. Mahmoud al Ackbar had called upon me and done me honour, and I felt myself personally capable of sustaining, before the people of Suez, the honour which he had done me.

As I walked forth with a proud step from beneath the portal, I perceived, looking down from the square along the street, that there was already some commotion in the town. I saw the flowing robes of many Arabs, with their backs turned towards me, and I thought that I observed the identical gown and turban of my friend Mahmoud on the back and head of a stout, short man, who was hurrying round a corner in the distance. I felt sure that it was Mahmoud. Some of his servants must have failed in their preparations, I said to myself, as I made my way round to the water's edge. This was only another testimony how anxious he was to do me honour.

I stood for a while on the edge of the quay, looking into the boat, and admiring the comfortable cushions which were luxuriously arranged round the seats. The men who were at work did not know me, and I was unnoticed, but I should soon take my place upon the softest of those cushions. I walked slowly backwards and forwards on the quay, listening to a hum of voices that came to me from a distance. There was clearly something stirring in the town, and I felt certain that all the movement and all those distant voices were connected in some way with my expedition to the well of Moses. At last there came a lad upon the walk, dressed in Frank costume, and I asked what was in the wind. He was a clerk, attached to an English warehouse, and he told me that there had been an arrival from Cairo. He knew no more than that, but he had heard that the omnibuses had just come in. Could it be possible that Mahmoud al Ackbar had heard of another old acquaintance, and had gone to welcome him also?

At first my ideas on the subject were altogether pleasant. I by no means wished to monopolise the delights of all those cushions, nor would it be to me a cause of sorrow that there should be someone to share with me the conversational powers of that interpreter. Should another guest be found, he might also be an Englishman, and I might thus form an acquaintance, which would be desirable. Thinking of these things, I walked on the quay for some minutes in a happy frame of mind; but by degrees I became impatient, and by degrees also disturbed in my spirit. I observed that one of the Arab boatmen walked round from the vessel to the front of the hotel, and that on his return he looked at me, as I thought, not with courteous eyes. Then also I saw, or rather heard someone in the verandah of the hotel above me, and was conscious that I was being viewed from thence. I walked and walked, and nobody came to me, and I perceived by my watch that it was seven o'clock. The noise, too, had come nearer and nearer, and I was now aware that wheels had been drawn up be-fore the front door of the hotel, and that many voices were speak-ing there. It might be well that Mahmoud should wait for some other friend, but why did he not send someone to inform me? And then, as I made a sudden turn at the end of the quay, I caught sight of the retreating legs of the Austrian interpreter, and I became aware that he had been sent down, and had gone away, afraid to speak to me. "What can I do?" said I to myself; "I can but keep my ground." I own that I feared to go round to the front of the hotel; so I still walked slowly up and down the length of the quay, and began to whistle to show that I was not uneasy. The Arab sailors looked at me uncomfortably, and from time to time someone peered at me round the corner. It was now fully half-past seven, and the sun was becoming hot in the heavens. Why did we not hasten to place ourselves beneath the awning in the boat?

I had just made up my mind that I would go round to the front, and penetrate this mystery, when, on turning, I saw approaching to me a man dressed at any rate like an English gentleman. As he came near to me, he raised his hat, and accosted me in my own language.

"Mr. George Walker, I believe?" said he.

"Yes," said I, with some little attempt at a high demeanour; "of the firm of Grimes, Walker, and Judkins, Friday-street, London."

"A most respectable house, I am sure," said he; "I'm afraid there has been a little mistake here."

"No mistake as to the respectability of that house," said I. I felt that I was again alone in the world, and that it was necessary that I should support myself. Mahmoud al Ackbar had separated him-self from me forever. Of that I had no longer a doubt.

"Oh, none at all," said he. "But about this little expedition over the water" — and he pointed contemptuously to the boat — "there has been a mistake about that. Mr. Walker, I happen to be the English Vice-Consul here."

I took off my hat and bowed. It was the first time I had ever been addressed civilly by any British Consular authority.

"And they have made me get out of bed to come down and explain all this to you."

"All what?" said I.

"You are a man of the world, I know, and I'll just tell it you plainly. My old friend Mahmoud al Ackbar has mistaken you for Sir George Walker, the new Lieutenant-Governor of Pegu. Sir George Walker is now here; he has come this morning, and Mahmoud does not know how to get him into the boat, because he is ashamed to face you after what has occurred. If you won't object to withdraw with me into the hotel, I'll explain it all."

I felt as though a thunderbolt had fallen, and I must say that even up to this day I think that the Consul might have been a little less abrupt.

"We can get in here," said he, evidently in a hurry, and pointing to a small door which opened out from one corner of the house to the quay. What could I do but follow him? I did follow him, and in a few words learned the remainder of the story. When he had once withdrawn me from the public walk, he seemed but little anxious about the rest, and soon left me again alone. The facts, as far as I could learn them, were simply these:

Sir George Walker, who was now going out to Pegu as governor, had been in India in former years, commanding an army there. I had never heard of him, and had made no attempt to pass myself off as his relative. Nobody could have been more innocent than I was, or have received worse usage. I have as much right to the name as he has. Well; when he was in India before, he had taken the city of Begum after a terrible siege, — Begum, I think the Consul called it; and Mahmoud had been there, having been, as it seemed, a great man at Begum, and Sir George had spared him and his money. In this way the whole thing had come to pass. There was no further explanation than that. The rest of it was all transparent. Mahmoud, having heard my name from the porter, had hurried down to invite me to his party. So far, so good. But why had he been afraid to face me in the morning? And, seeing that the fault had all been his, why had he not asked me to join his expedition? Sir George and I may, after all, be cousins. But, coward as he was, he had been afraid of me. When they found that I was on the quay, they had not dared to face me. I wish that I had kept the quay all day, and faced them one by one as they entered the boat. But I was down in the mouth, and when the Consul left me I crept wearily back to my bed-room.

And the Consul did leave me almost immediately. A faint hope had at one time come upon me that he would have asked me to breakfast. Had he done so, I should have felt it as some compensation for what I had suffered. I am not an exacting man; but I own that I like civility. In Friday-street I can command it, and in Friday-street for the rest of my life will I remain. From this Consul I received no civility. As soon as he had got me out of the way, and spoken the few words which he had to say, he again raised his hat and left me; I also again raised mine, and then crept up to my bed-room.

From my window, standing a little behind the white curtain, I could see the whole embarcation. There was Mahmoud al Ack-bar, looking, indeed, a little hot, but still going through his work with all that excellence of deportment which had graced him on the preceding evening. Had his foot slipped, and had he fallen backwards into that shallow water, my spirit would, I confess, have been relieved; but, on the contrary, everything went well with him. There was the real Sir George, my namesake, and, perhaps, my cousin, as fresh as paint, cool from the bath which he had been taking while I had been walking on that terrace. How is it that these governors and commanders-in-chief go through such heavy work without fagging? It was not yet two hours since he was jolting about in that omnibus-box; and there he had been all night! I could not have gone off to the well of Moses immediately on my arrival. It's the dignity of the position that does it. I have long known that the head of a firm must never count on a mere clerk to get through as much work as he can do himself. It's the interest in the matter that supports the man.

There they went; and Sir George, as I was well assured, had never heard a word about me. Had he done so, is it not probable that he would have requested my attendance? But Mahmoud and his followers, no doubt, kept their own counsel as to that little mistake. There they went; and the gentle, rippling breeze filled their sail pleasantly as the boat moved away into the bay. I felt no spite against any of them but Mahmoud. Why had he avoided me with such cowardice? I could still see them when the morning tchibouk was handed to Sir George; and though I wished him no harm, I did envy him, as he lay there reclining luxuriously upon the cushions.

A more wretched day than that I never spent in my life. As I went in and out the porter at the gate absolutely scoffed at me. Once I made up my mind to complain within the house; but what could I have said of the dirty Arab? They would have told me that it was his religion, or a national observance, or meant for a courtesy. What can a man do in a strange country, when he is told that a native spits in his face by way of civility? I bore it. I bore it — like a man; and sighed for the comforts of Friday-street.

As to one matter I made up my mind on that day, and I fully carried out my purpose on the next. I would go across to the well of Moses in a boat. I would visit the coasts of Asia, and I would ride back into Africa on a camel. Though I did it alone, I would have my day's pleasuring. I had money in my pocket, and though it might cost me twenty pounds, I would see all that my namesake had seen. It did cost me the best part of twenty pounds, and as for the pleasuring I can't say much for it.

I went to bed early that night, having concluded my bargain for the morrow with a rapacious Arab who spoke English. I went to bed early in order to escape the returning party, and was again on the quay at six the next morning. On this occasion I stept boldly into the boat the very moment that I came along the shore. It was my boat. There is nothing in the world like paying for what you use. I served myself to the bottle of brandy, and the cold meat, and acknowledged that a cigar out of my case would suit me better than that long stick. The long stick might do very well for a Governor of Pegu, but would be highly inconvenient in Friday-street. Well, I am not going to give an account of my day's journey here, though, perhaps, I may do so some day. I did go to the well of Moses, if a small dirty pool of salt water, lying high above the sands, can be called a well. I did eat my dinner in the miserable ruined cottage which they graced by the name of a pavilion; and, alas, for my poor bones, I did ride home upon a camel. If Sir George did so also, and started for Pegu early the next morning — and I was informed that such was the fact — he must indeed have been made of iron. I lay in bed the whole day, suffering grievously; but I was told that on such a journey I should have slackened my thirst with oranges, and not with brandy.

I survived those four terrible days which remained to me at Suez, and after another month was once again in Friday-street. I suffered greatly on the occasion; but it is some consolation to me to reflect that I did smoke a pipe with Mahmoud al Ackbar; that I saw the hero of Begum, while journeying out to new triumphs at Pegu; that I sailed into Asia in my own yacht—hired for the occasion; and that I rode back into Africa on a camel. Nor can Judkins, with all his ill-nature, rob me of those remembrances.

"George Walker at Suez" appeared first in the December 28 issue of *Public Opinion: Literary Supplement* for 1861.

Aaron Trow

I WOULD WISH TO DECLARE, at the beginning of this story, that I shall never regard that cluster of islets which we call Bermuda as the fortunate islands of the ancients. Do not let professional geographers take me up, and say that no one has so accounted them, and that the ancients have never been supposed to have gotten themselves so far westward. What I mean to assert is this: — that had any ancient been carried thither by enterprise or stress of weather, he would not have given those islands so good a name. That the Neapolitan sailors of King Alonzo should have been wrecked here, I consider to be more likely. The word Bermoothes is a good name for them. There is no getting in or out of them without the greatest difficulty, and a patient, slow navigation, which is very heartrending. That Caliban should have lived here I can imagine; that Ariel would have been sick of the place is certain; and that Governor Prospero should have been willing to abandon his governorship, I conceive to be only natural. When one regards the present state of the place, one is tempted to doubt whether any of the governors have been conjurors since his days.

Bermuda, as all the world know, is a British colony at which we maintain a convict establishment. Most of our outlying convict estabishments have been sent back upon our hands from our colonies; but here one is still maintained. There is also in the islands a strong military fortress, though not a fortress looking magnificent to the eyes of civilians as do Malta and Gibraltar. There are also here some six thousand white people and some six thousand black people, eating, drinking, sleeping, and dying.

The convict establishment is the most notable feature of Bermuda to a stranger, but it does not seem to attract much attention from the regular inhabitants of the place. There is no intercourse between the prisoners and the Bermudians; the convicts are rarely seen by them, and the convict islands are rarely visited. As to the prisoners themselves, of course it is not open to them — or should not be open to them — to have intercourse with any but the prison authorities.

There have, however, been instances in which convicts have escaped from their confinement, and made their way out among the islands. Poor wretches! As a rule there is but little chance for any that can so escape. The whole length of the cluster is but twenty miles, and the breadth is under four. The prisoners are of course white men, and the lower orders of Bermuda, among whom alone could a runagate have any chance of hiding himself, are all negroes; so that such a one would be known at once. Their clothes are all marked. Their only chance of a permanent escape would be in the hold of an American ship. But what captain of an American or other ship would willingly encumber himself with an escaped convict? But, nevertheless, men have escaped, and in one instance, I believe, a convict got away so that of him no further tidings were ever heard.

For the truth of the following tale I will by no means vouch. If one were to inquire on the spot one might probably find that the ladies all believed it, and the old men; that all the young men knew exactly how much of it was false and how much true; and that the steady, middle-aged, well-to-do islanders were quite convinced that it is romance from beginning to end. My readers may range themselves with the ladies, the young men, or the steady, well-do-do, middle-aged islanders, as they please.

Some years ago, soon after the prison was first established on its present footing, three men did escape from it, and among them a certain notorious prisoner named Aaron Trow. Trow's antecedents in England had not been so villainously bad as those of many of his fellow convicts, though the one offence for which he was punished had been of a deep dye. He had shed man's blood. At a period of great distress in a manufacturing town he had led men on to riot, and with his own hand had slain the first constable who had endeavoured to do his duty against him. There had been courage in the doing of the deed, and probably no malice; but the deed, let its moral blackness have been what it might, had sent Trow to Bermuda, with a sentence against him of penal servitude for life. Had he been then amenable to prison discipline — even then, with such a sentence against him as that — he might have won his way back, after the lapse of the years, to the children, and perhaps, to the wife that he had left behind him. But he was amenable to no laws — to no discipline. His heart was sore to death with an idea of injury; and he lashed himself against the bars of his cage with a feeling that it would be well if he could so lash himself till he might perish in his fury.

And then a day came in which an attempt was made by a large body of convicts, under his leadership, to get the better of the officers of the prison. It is hardly necessary to say that the attempt failed. Such attempts always fail. It failed on this occasion signally, and Trow, with two other men, were condemned to be scourged terribly, and then kept in solitary confinement for some lengthened term of months. Before, however, the day of scourging came, Trow and his two associates had escaped.

I have not the space to tell how this was effected, nor the power to describe the manner. They did escape from the establishment into the islands, and though two of them were taken after a single day's run at liberty, Aaron Trow had not been yet retaken even when a week was over. When a month was over he had not been retaken, and the officers of the prison began to say that he had got away from them in a vessel to the States. It was impossible, they said, that he should have remained in the islands and not been discovered. It was not impossible that he might have destroyed himself, leaving his body where it had not yet been found. But he could not have lived on in Bermuda during that month's search.

So, at least, said the officers of the prison. There was, however, a report through the island that he had been seen from time to time; that he had gotten bread from the negroes at night, threatening them with death if they told of his whereabouts; and that all the clothes of the mate of a vessel had been stolen while

213

the man was bathing, including a suit of dark blue cloth, in which suit of clothes, or in one of such nature, a stranger had been seen skulking about the rocks near St. George. All this the governor of the prison affected to disbelieve, but the opinion was becoming very rife in the islands that Aaron Trow was still there.

A vigilant search, however, is a task of great labour, and cannot be kept up for ever. By degrees it was relaxed; the warders and gaolers ceased to patrol the island roads by night, and it was agreed that Aaron Trow was gone, or that he would be starved to death, or that he would, in time, be driven to leave such traces of his whereabouts as must lead to his discovery. And this, at last, did turn out to be the fact.

There is a sort of prettiness about these islands which, though it never rises to the loveliness of romantic scenery, is, nevertheless, attractive in its way. The land breaks itself into little knolls, and the sea runs up, hither and thither, in a thousand creeks and inlets. And, then, too, when the oleanders are in bloom, they give a wonderfully bright colour to the landscape. Oleanders seem to be the roses of Bermuda, and are cultivated round all the cottages of the better class through the islands. There are two towns, St. George and Hamilton, and one main high-road which connects them. But even this high-road is broken by a ferry, over which every vehicle going from St. George to Hamilton must be conveyed. Most of the locomotion in these parts is done by boats, and the residents look to the sea, with its narrow creeks, as their best highway, their best farm, and their best market. In those days — and those days were not very long since — the building of small ships was their chief trade, and they valued their land mostly for the small scrubby cedar-trees with which this trade was carried on.

As one goes from St. George to Hamilton, the road runs between two seas. That to the right is the ocean; that on the left is an island creek, which runs up through a large portion of the island, so that the land on the other side of it is near to the traveller. In a considerable portion of the way there are no houses lying near the road, and there is one residence some way from the road, so situated that no other house lies within a mile of it by land. By water it might probably be reached within half-a-mile. This place was called Crump Island, and here lived, and had lived for many years, an old gentleman, a native of Bermuda, whose business it had been to buy up cedar-wood, and sell it to the ship-builders at Hamilton. In our story we shall not have very much to do with old Mr. Bergen, but it will be necessary to say a word or two about his house.

It stood on what would have been an island in the creek, had not a narrow causeway, barely broad enough for a road, joined it to that larger island on which stands the town of St. George. As the main road approaches the ferry, it runs through some rough, hilly, open ground, which, on the right side, towards the ocean, has never been cultivated. The distance from the ocean here may perhaps be a quarter of a mile, and the ground is for the most part covered with low furze. On the left of the road the land is cultivated in patches, and here, some half-mile or more from the ferry, a path turns away to Crump Island. The house cannot be seen from the road, and, indeed, can hardly be seen at all except from the sea. It is, perhaps, three furlongs from the high-road, and the path to it is but little used, as the passage to and from it is chiefly made by water.

Here, at the time of our story, lived Mr. Bergen, and here lived Mr. Bergen's daughter. Anastasia Bergen was well known at St. George as a steady, good girl, who spent her time in looking after her father's household matters, in managing his two black maid-servants and the black gardener, and who did her duty in that sphere of life to which she had been called. She was a comely, well-shaped young woman, with a sweet countenance, rather large in size, and very quiet in demeanour. In her earlier years, when, as a rule, girls first bud forth into womanly beauty, the neighbours had not thought much of Anastasia Bergen, nor had the young men of St. George been wont to stay their boats under the windows of Crump Cottage, in order that they might listen to her voice or feel the light of her eye. But slowly, as years went by, Anastasia Bergen became a woman that a man might well love, and a man learned to love her who was well worthy of a woman's heart. This was Caleb Morton, the Presbyterian minister of St. George; and Caleb Morton had been engaged to marry Miss Bergen for the last two years past, at the period of Aaron Trow's escape from prison.

Caleb Morton was not a native of Bermuda, but had been sent

thither by the synod of his church from Nova Scotia. He was a tall, handsome man, at this time, of some thirty years of age — of a presence which might almost have been called commanding. He was very strong, but of a temperament which did not often give him opportunity to put forth his strength; and his life had been such that neither he nor others knew of what nature might be his courage. The greater part of his life was spent in preaching to some few of the white people around him, and in teaching as many of the blacks as he could get to hear him. His days were very quiet, and had been altogether without excitement until he had met with Anastasia Bergen. It will suffice for us to say that he did meet her, and that now for two years past they had been engaged as man and wife.

Old Mr. Bergen, when he heard of the engagement, was not well pleased at the information. In the first place his daughter was very necessary to him, and the idea of her marrying and going away had hardly as yet occurred to him. And then he was by no means inclined to part with any of his money. It must not be presumed that he had amassed a fortune by his trade in cedar-wood. Few tradesmen in Bermuda do, as I imagine, amass fortunes. Of some few hundred pounds he was possessed, and these, in the course of nature, would go to his daughter when he died; but he had no inclination to hand any portion of them over to his daughter before they did go to her in the course of nature. Now the income which Caleb Morton earned as a Presbyterian clergyman was not large, and therefore had no day been fixed as yet for his marriage with Anastasia.

But though the old man had been from the first averse to the match, his hostility had not been active. He had not forbidden Mr. Morton his house, or affected to be in any degree angry because his daugher had a lover. He had merely grumbled forth an intimation that those who marry in haste repent at leisure — that love kept nobody warm if the pot didn't boil, and that, as for him, it was as much as he could do to keep their own pot boiling at Crump Cottage. In answer to this, Anastasia said nothing. She asked him for no money, but still kept his accounts, managed his household, and looked patiently forward for better days.

Old Mr. Bergen himself spent much of his time at Hamilton, where he had a wood-yard with a couple of rooms attached to it.

It was his custom to remain here three nights of the week, during which Anastasia was left alone at the cottage. And it happened by no means seldom that she was altogether alone; for the negro whom they called the gardener would go to her father's place at Hamilton, and the two black girls would crawl away up to the road, tired with the monotony of the sea and the cottage. Caleb had more than once told her that she was too much alone; but she had laughed at him, saying that solitude in Bermuda was not dangerous. Nor, indeed, was it; for the people are quiet and well-mannered, lacking much energy, but being in the same degree free from any propensity to violence.

"So you are going?" she said to her lover one evening, as he rose from the chair on which he had been surveying himself at the door of the cottage, which looks down over the creek of the sea. He had sat there for an hour talking to her as she worked, or watching her as she moved about the place. It was a beautiful evening, and the sun had been falling to rest with almost tropical glory before his feet. The bright oleanders were red with their blossom all around him, and he had thoroughly enjoyed his hour of easy rest. "So you are going?" she said to him, not putting her work out of her hand as he rose to depart.

"Yes; and it is time for me to go. I have still work to do before I can get to bed. Ah! well; I suppose the day will come at last when I need not leave you as soon as my hour of rest is over."

"Come! of course it will come — that is, if your reverence chooses to wait for it another ten years or so."

"I believe you would not mind waiting twenty years."

"Not if a certain friend of mine would come down to see me of evenings, and when I'm alone after the day. It seems to me, that I shouldn't mind waiting, as long as I have that to look for."

"You are right not to be impatient," he said to her after a pause, as he held her hand before he went — "quite right. I only wish I could school myself to be as easy about it."

"I did not say I was easy," said Anastasia. "People are seldom easy in this world, I take it. I said I could be patient. Do not look in that way, as though you pretended that you were dissatisfied with me. You know that I am true to you, and you ought to be very proud of me."

"I am proud of you, Anastasia;" on hearing which she got up

217

and curtseyed to him — "I am proud of you; so proud of you that I feel you should not be left here all alone, with no one to help you if you were in trouble."

"Women don't get into trouble as men do, and do not want any one to help them. If you were alone in the house you would have to go to bed without your supper, because you could not make a basin of boiled milk ready for your own meal. Now, when your reverence has gone, I shall go to work and have my tea comfortably," and then he did go, bidding God bless her as he left her. Three hours after that he was disturbed in his own lodgings by one of the negro girls from the cottage rushing to the door and begging him, in Heaven's name, to come down to the assistance of her mistress.

When Morton left her, Anastasia did not proceed to do as she had said, and seemed to have forgotten her evening meal. She had been working sedulously with her needle during all that last conversation; but when her lover was gone, she allowed the work to fall from her hands, and sat motionless for a while, gazing at the last streak of colour left by the setting sun, till there was no longer a ray of its glory to be traced in the heavens around her. The twilight in Bermuda is not long and enduring as it is with us, though the daylight does not depart suddenly, leaving the darkness of night behind it without any intermediate time of warning, as is the case further south, down among the islands of the tropics. But the soft, sweet light of the evening had waned and gone, and night had absolutely come upon her, while Anastasia was still seated before the cottage, with her eyes fixed upon the white streak of motionless sea which was still visible through the gloom. She was thinking of him, of his ways of life, of his happiness, and of her duty towards him. She had told him, with her pretty feminine falseness, that she could wait without impatience; but now she said to herself that it would not be good for her to wait longer. He lived alone, and without comfort, working very hard for his poor pittance, and she could see and feel and understand that a companion in his life was to him almost a necessity. She would tell her father that all this must be brought to an end. She would not ask him for money; but she would make him understand that her services must, at any rate in part, be transferred. Why should not she and Morton still live at the cottage when they were married? And so thinking, and at last resolving, she sat there till the dark night fell upon her.

She was at last disturbed by feeling a man's hand upon her shoulder. She jumped from her chair and faced him — not screaming, for it was especially within her power to control herself, and to make no utterance except with forethought. Perhaps it might have been better for her had she screamed, and sent a sharp shriek down the shore of that inland sea. She was silent, however, and with awe-struck face and outstretched hands gazed into the face of him who still held her by the shoulder. The night was dark, but her eyes were now accustomed to the darkness, and she could see indistinctly something of his features. He was a low-sized man, dressed in a suit of sailor's blue clothing, with a rough cap of hair on his head, and a beard that had not been clipped for many weeks. His eyes were large and hollow, and frightfully bright, so that she seemed to see nothing else of him; but she felt the strength of his fingers as he grasped her tighter and more tightly by the arm.

"Who are you?" she said, after a moment's pause.

"Do you know me?" he asked

"Know you! — no." But the words were hardly out of her mouth before it struck her that the man was Aaron Trow, of whom everyone in Bermuda had been talking.

"Come into the house," he said, "and give me food;" and he still held her with his hand as though he would compel her to follow him.

She stood for a moment thinking what she would say to him, for even then, with that terrible man standing close to her in the darkness, her presence of mind did not desert her. "Surely," she said; "I will give you food if you are hungry. But take your hand from me; no man would lay his hand upon a woman."

"A woman!" said the stranger. "What does the starved wolf care for that? A woman's blood is as sweet to him as that of a man. Come into the house, I tell you;" and then she preceded him through the open door into the narrow passage, and thence to the kitchen. Then she saw that the back-door, leading out on the other side of the house, was open; and she knew that he had come down from the road, and entered on that side. She threw her eyes round, looking for the negro girls, but they were away;

and she remembered that there was no human being within sound of her voice but this man, who had told her that he was as a wolf thirsting after her blood.

"Give me food at once," he said.

"And will you go if I give it you?" she asked.

"I will knock out your brains if you do not," he replied, lifting up from the grate a short, thick poker which lay there. "Do as I bid you this moment. You also would be like a tiger if you had fasted for two days, as I have done."

She could see, as she moved across the kitchen, that he had already searched there for something that he might eat, but that he had searched in vain. With the close economy common among his class in the island, all comestibles were kept under close lock and key in the house of Mr. Bergen. Their daily allowance was given day by day to the negro servants, and even the fragments were then gathered up and locked away in safety. She moved across the kitchen to the accustomed cupboard, taking the keys from her pocket, and he followed close upon her. There was a small oil lamp hanging from the low ceiling, which just gave them light to see each other. She lifted her hand to this to take it from its hook, but he prevented her. "No, by Heaven," he said; "you don't touch that till I've done with it. There is light enough for you to drag out your scraps."

She did drag out her scraps, and a bowl of milk, which might hold perhaps a quart. There was a fragment of bread, a morsel of cold potato-cake, and the bone of a leg of kid.

"And is that all?" said he; but as he spoke he fleshed his teeth against the bone, as a dog would have done.

"It is the best I have," she said. "I wish it were better, and you should have had it without violence, as you have suffered so long from hunger."

"Bah! Better—yes. You would give the best, no doubt, and set the hell-hounds on my track the moment I am gone! — I know how much I might expect from your charity."

"I would have fed you for pity's sake," she answered.

"Pity! Who are you, that you should dare to pity me? By —, my young woman, it is I that pity you. I must cut your throat unless you give me money. Do you know that?"

"Money! I have got no money."

"I'll make you have some before I go. Come; don't move till I have done," and as he spoke to her he went on tugging at the bone, and swallowing the lumps of stale bread. He had already finished the bowl of milk. "And now," said he, "tell me who I am."

"I suppose you are Aaron Trow," she answered very slowly.

He said nothing on hearing this, but continued his meal, standing close to her, so that she might not possibly escape from him out into the darkness. Twice or thrice in those few minutes she made up her mind to make such an attempt, feeling that it would be better to leave him in possession of the house and make sure, if possible, of her own life. There was no money there — not a dollar. What money her father kept in his possession was locked up in his safe at Hamilton. And might he not keep to his threat, and murder her, when he found that she could give him nothing? She did not tremble outwardly as she stood there watching him as he eat, but she thought how probable it might be that her last moments were very near. And yet she could scrutinise his features, form, and garments, so as to carry away in her mind a perfect picture of them. Aaron Trow — for, of course, it was the escaped convict — was not a man of frightful, hideous aspect. Had the world used him well — giving him when he was young ample wages, and separating him from turbulent spirits — he also might have used the world well; and then women would have praised the brightness of his eye, and the manly vigour of his brow. But things had not gone well with him. He had been separated from the wife he had loved, and the children who had been raised at his knee — separated by his own violence; and now, as he had said of himself, he was a wolf rather than a man. Now, as he stood there satisfying the craving of his appetite, breaking up the large morsels of food, he was an object very sad to be seen. Hunger had made him gaunt and yellow; he was squalid with the dirt of his hidden lair, and he had the look of a beast — that look to which men fall when they live like the beasts of prey, as outcasts from their brethren. But still there was that about his brow which might have redeemed him — which might have turned her horror into pity, had he been willing that it should be so.

"And now, give me some brandy," he said.

There was brandy in the house — in the sitting-room, which was close at their hand; and the key of the little press which held it was in her pocket. It was useless, she thought, to refuse him; and so she told him that there was a bottle partly full, but that she must go to the next room to fetch it him.

"We'll go together, my darling," he said. "There's nothing like good company." And he again put his hand upon her arm as they passed into the family sitting-room.

"I must take the light," she said. But he unhooked it himself, and carried it in his own hand.

Again she went to work without trembling. She found the key of the side cupboard, and, unlocking the door, handed him a bottle which might contain about half a pint of spirits.

"And is that all?" he said.

"There is a full bottle here," she answered, handing him another; "but if you drink it you will be drunk, and they will catch you."

"By heavens, yes; and you would be the first to help them — would you not?"

"Look here," she answered. "If you will go now, I will not say a word to any one of your coming, nor set them on your track to follow you. There, take the full bottle with you. If you will go you shall be safe from me."

"What! and go without money?"

"I have none to give you; you may believe me when I say so. I have not a dollar in the house."

Before he spoke again he raised the half-empty bottle to his mouth, and drank as long as there was a drop to drink.

"There," said he, putting the bottle down, "I am better after that. As for the other, you are right, and I will take it with me. And now, young woman — about the money?"

"I tell you that I have not a dollar."

"Look here," said he, and he spoke now in a softer voice, as though he would wish to be on friendly terms with her, "give me ten sovereigns, and I will go. I know you have it, and with ten sovereigns it is possible that I may save my life. You are good, and would not wish that a man should die so horrid a death. I know you are good; come, give me the money." And he put his hands up beseeching her, and looked into her face with imploring eyes.

"On the word of a Christian woman, I have not got money to give you!" she replied.

"Nonsense!" And as he spoke he took her by the arm and shook her. He shook her violently, so that he hurt her, and her breath, for a moment, was all but gone from her. "I tell you, you must make dollars before I leave you, or I will so handle you that it would have been better for you to coin your very blood."

"May God help me at my need," she said, "as I have not above a few penny pieces in the house!"

"And you expect me to believe that! Look here; I will shake the teeth out of your head but I will have it from you!" And he did shake her again, using both his hands, and striking her against the wall.

"Would you — murder me?" she said, hardly able now to utter the words.

"Murder you? Yes. Why not? I cannot be worse than I am, were I to murder you ten times over. But, with money, I may possibly be better."

"I have it not."

"Then I will do worse than murder you. I will make you such an object that all the world shall loathe to look at you." And, so saying, he took her by the arm and dragged her forth from the wall against which she had stood.

Then there came from her a shriek that was heard far down the shore of that silent sea, and away across to the solitary houses of those living on the other side — a shriek very sad, sharp, and prolonged, which told plainly to those who heard it of woman's woe when in her extremest peril. That sound was spoken of in Bermuda for many a day after that as something which had been terrible to hear. But then, at that moment, as it came wailing through the dark, it sounded as though it were not human. Of those who heard it not one guessed from whence it came, nor was the hand of any brother put forward to help that woman at her need.

"Did you hear that," said the young wife to her husband, "from the far side of the arm of the sea?"

"Hear it! Oh, Heaven! yes. Whence did it come?"

The young wife could not say from whence it came, but clung close to her husband's breast, comforting herself with the knowledge that the terrible sorrow was not hers.

But aid did come at last, or rather that which served as aid. Long and terrible was the fight between the human beast of prey and the poor victim which had fallen into his talons. Anastasia Bergen was a strong, well-built woman, and now that the time had come to her when a struggle was necessary — a struggle for life, for honour, for the happiness of him who was more to her than herself — she fought like a tigress attacked in her own lair. At such a moment as this she also could become wild and savage as the beast of the forest. When he pinioned her arms with one of his, as he pressed her down upon the floor, she caught the first joint of the forefinger of his other hand between her teeth, till he yelled in agony, and another sound was heard across the silent water. And then, when one hand was loosed in the struggle, she twisted it through his long hair, and dragged back his head till his eyes were nearly starting from their sockets. Anastasia Bergen had hitherto been sheer woman — all feminine in her nature. But now the foam came to her mouth, and fire sprang from her eyes, and the muscles of her body worked as though she had been trained to deeds of violence. Of violence Aaron Trow had known much in his rough life; but never had he combated with harder antagonist than her whom he now held beneath his breast.

"By — I will put an end to you!" he exclaimed in his wrath, as he struck her violently across the face with his elbow. His hand was occupied, and he could not use it for a blow, but, nevertheless, the violence was so great that the blood gushed from her nostrils, while the back of her head was driven with violence against the floor. But yet she did not lose her hold of him. Her hand still twined closely through his thick hair, and in every move he made she clung to him with all her weight.

"Leave go my hair!" he shouted at her; but she still kept her hold, though he again dashed her head against the floor.

There was still light in the room, for when he first grasped her with both his hands, he had put the lamp down on a small table. Now they were rolling on the floor together, and twice he had essayed to kneel on her, that he might thus crush the breath from her body, and deprive her altogether of her strength. But she had been too active for him, moving herself along the ground, though in doing so she dragged him along with her. But, by degrees, he got one hand at liberty, and with that he pulled a clasp-knife out of his pocket, and opened it.

"I will cut your hand off if you do not let go my hair!" he said.

But still she held fast by him. He then stabbed at her arm, using his left hand, and making short, ineffectual blows. Her dress partly saved her, and partly also the continual movements of all her limbs; but, nevertheless, the knife wounded her. It wounded her in several places about the arm, covering them both with blood; but still she hung on. So close was her grasp in her agony, that, as she afterwards found, she cut the skin of her own hand with her own nails. Had the man's hair been less thick or strong, or her own tenacity less steadfast, he must have murdered her before any interruption could have saved her.

And yet he had not been purposed to murder her, or even, in the first instance, to inflict on her any bodily harm. But he had determined to get money. With such a sum of money as he had named it might he thought be possible for him to win his way across to America. He might bribe men to hide him in the hold of a ship, and thus there might be for him, at any rate, a possibility of escape. That there must be money in the house he had still thought when first he laid hands on the poor woman; and then, when the struggle had once begun, when he had felt her muscles contending with his, the passion of the beast was aroused within him, and he strove against her as he would have striven against a dog. But yet, when the knife was in his hand, he had not driven it against her heart.

Then, suddenly, while they were yet rolling on the floor, there was a sound of footsteps in the passage. Aaron Trow instantly leaped to his feet, leaving his victim on the ground, and leaving with her huge lumps of his thick, clotted hair. Thus, and thus only, could he have liberated himself from her grasp. He rushed at the door, with the open knife still in his hand, and there he came against the two negro servant girls, who had returned down to their kitchen from the road on which they had been straying. Trow, as he half saw them in the dusk, not knowing how many there might be, or whether there was a man among them, rushed through them, upsetting one scared girl in his passage. With the instinct and with the timidity of a beast, his impulse now was to escape, and he hurried away back to the road and to his lair, leaving the three women together in the cottage. Poor wretch! As he crossed the road, not skulking in his impotent haste, but running at his best, another pair of eyes saw him, and when the search became hot after him, it was known that his hiding-place was not distant.

It was some time before any of the women were able to act, and when some step was taken, Anastasia was the first to take it. She had not absolutely swooned, but the reaction, after the violence of her efforts, was so great that for some minutes she had been unable to speak. She had risen from the floor when Trow left her, and had even followed him to the door; but since that, she had fallen back into her father's old arm-chair, and there she sat gasping, not only for words, but for breath also. At last she bade one of the girls run into St. George, and beg Mr. Morton to come to her aid. The girl would not stir without her companion, and even then Anastasia, covered as she was with blood, with dishevelled hair, and her clothes half torn from her body, accompanied them as far as the road. There they found a negro lad still hanging about the place, and he told them that he had seen the man cross the road, and run down over the open ground, towards the rocks of the sea coast.

"He must be there," said the lad, pointing in the direction of a corner of the rocks, "unless he swims across the mouth of the ferry."

Now, the mouth of that ferry is an arm of the sea, and it was not probable that a man would do that, when he might have taken the narrow water by keeping on the other side of the road.

At about one that night Caleb Morton reached the cottage, breathless with running, and before a word was spoken between them, Anastasia had fallen on his shoulder and had fainted. As soon as she was in the arms of her lover, all her power had gone from her; the spirit and passion of the tiger had gone, and she was again a weak woman, shuddering at the thought of what she had suffered. She remembered that she had had the man's hand between her teeth, and by degrees she found his hair still clinging to her fingers; but even then she could hardly call to mind the nature of the struggle she had undergone. His hot breath close to her own cheek she did remember, and his glaring eyes, and even the roughness of his beard as he pressed his face against her own;

but she could not say whence had come the blood, nor till her arm became stiff and motionless did she know that she had been wounded.

It was all joy with her now, as she sat motionless, without speaking, while he ministered to her wants and spoke words of love into her ears. She remembered the man's horrid threat, and knew that by God's mercy she had been saved. And he was there — caressing her, loving her, comforting her! As she thought of the fate that had threatened her — of the evil that had been so imminent, she fell forward on her knees, and with incoherent sobs, uttered her thanksgivings on her knees, while her head was still supported in his arms.

It was almost morning before she could endure herself to leave him and lie down. With him she seemed to be so perfectly safe, but the moment he was away she could see Aaron Trow's eyes gleaming at her across the room. At last, however, she slept; and when he saw that she was at rest he told himself that his work must then begin. Hitherto, Caleb Morton had lived in all respects the life of a man of peace; but now, asking himself no questions as to the propriety of what he would do, using no inward arguments as to this or that line of conduct, he girded the sword on his loins and prepared himself for war. The wretch who had thus treated the woman whom he loved should be hunted down like a wild beast, as long as he had arms and legs with which to carry on the hunt. He would pursue the miscreant with any weapons that might come to his hands — and might Heaven help him at his need, as he dealt forth punishment to that man, if he caught him within his grasp! Those who had hitherto known Morton in the island could not recognise the man as he came forth on that day, thirsty after blood, and desirous to thrust himself into personal conflict with the wild ruffian who had injured him. The meek Presbyterian minister had been a preacher preaching ways of peace, and living in accordance with his own doctrines. The world had been very quiet for him, and he had walked quietly in his appointed path. But now the world was quiet no longer, nor was there any preaching of peace. His cry was for blood — for the blood of the untamed, savage brute who had come upon his young doe in her solitude, and striven with such brutal violence to tear her heart from her bosom.

He got to his assistance, early in the morning, some of the con-stables from St. George, and before the day was over he was joined by two or three of the warders from the convict establish-ment. There were with him also a friend or two, and thus a party was formed, numbering together ten or twelve persons. They were of course all armed, and therefore it might be thought that there would be but small chance for the wretched man if they should come upon his track. At first they all searched together, thinking from the tidings which had reached them that he must be near to them, but gradually they spread themselves along the rocks between St. George and the ferry, keeping watchmen on the road so that he should not escape unnoticed into the island.

Ten times during the day did Anastasia send from the cottage up to Morton, begging him to leave the search to others and come down to her. But not for a moment would he lose the scent of his prey. What! should it be said that she had been so treated, and that others had avenged her? He sent back to say that her father was with her now, and that he would come when his work was over. And in that job of work the life-blood of Aaron Trow was counted up.

Towards evening they were all congregated on the road near to the spot at which the path turns off towards the cottage, when a voice was heard hallooing to them from the summit of a little hill which lies between the road and the sea on the side towards the ferry, and presently a boy came running down to them, full of news.

"Danny Land has seen him," said the boy; "he has seen him plainly, in among the rocks." And then came Danny Land him-self, a small negro lad, about fourteen years of age, who was known in those parts as the idlest, most dishonest, and most use-less of his race. On this occasion, however, Danny Land became important, and everyone listened to him. He had seen, he said, a pair of eyes moving, down in a cave of the rocks which he well knew. He had been in the cave often, he said, and could get there again; but not now — not while that pair of eyes was mov-ing at the bottom of it. And so they all went up over the hill, Morton leading the way with hot haste. In his waistband he held a pistol, and his hand grasped a short iron bar with which he had armed himself. They ascended the top of the hill, and, when there, the open sea was before them on two sides, and on a third was the narrow creek over which the ferry passed. Immediately beneath their feet were the broken rocks; for on that side, towards the sea, the earth and grass of the hill descended but a little way towards the water. Down among the rocks they all went, silently, Caleb Morton leading the way, and Danny Land directing him from behind.

"Mr. Morton," said an elderly man from St. George, "had you not better let the warders of the gaol go first? He is a desperate man, and they will best understand his ways."

In answer to this Morton said nothing, but he would let no one put a foot before him. He still pressed forward among the rocks, and at last came to a spot from whence he might have sprung, at one leap, into the ocean. It was a broken cranny on the sea shore, into which the sea beat, and was surrounded on every side but the one by huge, broken fragments of stone, which at first sight seemed as though they would have admitted of a path down among them to the water's edge, but which, when scanned more closely, were seen to be so large in size, that no man could climb from one to another. It was a singularly romantic spot, but now known to them all there, for they had visited it over and over again that morning.

"In there!" said Danny Land, keeping well behind Morton's body, and pointing at the same time to a cavern high up among the rocks, but quite on the opposite side of the little inlet of the sea. The mouth of the cavern was not twenty yards from them, where they stood; but at the first sight it seemed as though it must be impossible to reach it. The precipice on the brink of which they all now stood ran down sheer into the sea, and the fall from the mouth of the cavern on the other side was as steep; but Danny solved the mystery by pointing upwards, and showing them how he had been used to climb to a projecting rock over their heads, and from thence creep round by certain vantages of the stone till he was able to let himself down into the aperture. But now, at the present moment, he was unwilling to make essay of his prowess as a cragsman. He had, he said, been up on that projecting rock thrice, and there had seen the eyes moving in the cavern. He was quite sure of that fact of the pair of eyes, and declined to ascend up on the rock again.

Traces soon became visible to them by which they knew that some one had passed in and out of the cavern recently. The stone, when examined, bore those marks of friction which passage and re-passage over it will always give. At the spot from whence the climber left the platform and commenced his ascent the side of the stone had been rubbed by the close friction of a man's body. A light boy like Danny Land might find his way in and out without leaving such marks behind him, but no heavy man could do so. Thus, before long, they all were satisfied that Aaron Trow was in the cavern before them.

Then there was a long consultation as to what they would do, to carry on the hunt, and how they would drive the tiger from his lair. That he should not again come out except to fall into their hands was to all of them a matter of course. They would keep watch and ward there, though it might be for days and nights. But that was a process which did not satisfy Morton, and did not, indeed, well satisfy any of them. It was not only that they desired to inflict punishment on the miscreant in accordance with the law, but also that they did not desire that the miserable man should die in a hole like a starved dog, and that then they should go after him to take out his wretched skeleton. There was something in that idea so horrid in every way that all agreed that active steps must be taken. The warders of the prison felt that they would all be disgraced if they could not take their prisoner alive; yet who would get round that perilous ledge in the face of such an adversary? A touch to any man while climbing there would send him headlong down among the waves! And then his fancy told to each what might be the nature of an embrace with such an animal as that, driven to despair, hopeless of life, armed, as they knew, at any rate, with a knife! If the first adventurous spirit should succeed in crawling round that ledge, what would be the reception which he might expect in the terrible depth of that cavern?

They called to their prisoner, bidding him come out, and telling him that they would fire in upon him if he did not show himself; but not a sound was heard. It was, indeed, possible that they should send their bullets to, perhaps, every corner of the cavern, and, if so, in that way they might slaughter him; but even of this they were not sure. Who could tell that there might not be some protected nook in which he could live secure? and who could tell when the man was struck, or whether he were wounded?

"I will get across to him," said Morton, after a while; and, so saying, he clambered up to the rock to which Danny Land had pointed. Many voices at once attempted to restrain him, and one or two put their hands upon him to keep him back; but he was too quick for them, and now stood upon the ledge of rock.

"Can you see him?" they asked below.

"I can see nothing within the cavern," said Morton.

"Look down bery hard, massa," said Danny, — "bery hard indeed, down in de deep dark hole, and then see him big eyes rolling."

Morton now crept along the ledge, or, rather he was beginning to do so, having put forward his shoulders and arms to make a first step in advance from the spot on which he was resting, when a hand was put forth from one corner of the cavern's mouth — a hand armed with a pistol — and a shot was fired. There could be no doubt now but that Danny Land was right, and no doubt now as to the whereabouts of Aaron Trow.

A hand was put forth, a pistol was fired, and Caleb Morton, still clinging to a corner of the rock with both his arms, was seen to falter.

"He is wounded," said one of the voices from below; and then they all expected to see him fall into the sea. But he did not fall, and after a moment or two he proceeded carefully to pick his steps along the ledge. The ball had touched him, grazing his cheek and cutting through the light whiskers that he wore; but he had not felt it, though the blow had nearly knocked him from his perch. And then four or five shots were fired from the rocks into the mouth of the cavern. The man's arm had been seen, and, indeed, one or two declared that they had traced the dim outline of his figure. But no sound was heard to come from the cavern, except the sharp crack of the bullets against the rock, and the echo of the gunpowder. There had been no groans as of a man wounded, no sound of a body falling, no voice wailing in despair. In a few seconds all was dark with the smoke of the gunpowder, and then the empty mouth of the cave was again yawning before their eyes. Morton was now near it, still cautiously creeping. The first dan-ger to which he was exposed was this — that his enemy within his recess might push him down from the rocks with a touch. But, on the other hand, there were three or four men ready to fire the moment that a hand should be put forth; and then Morton could swim — was known to be a strong swimmer, whereas, of Aaron Trow, it was already declared by the prison gaolers that he could not swim. Two of the warders had now followed Morton on the rocks, so that, in the event of his making good his entrance into the cavern, and holding his enemy at bay for a minute, he could be joined by aid.

It was strange to see how those different men conducted themselves, as they stood on the opposite platform watching the attack. The officers from the prison had no other thought but of their prisoner, and were intent on taking him alive or dead. To them it was little or nothing what became of Morton. It was their business to encounter peril, and they were ready to do so, feeling, however, by no means sorry to have such a man as Morton in advance of them. Very little was said by them. They had their wits about them, and remembered that every word spoken for the guidance of their ally, would be heard also by the escaped convict. Their prey was sure, sooner or later, and had not Morton been so eager in his pursuit, they would have waited till some plan had been devised of trapping him without danger. But the townsmen from St. George, of whom some dozen were now standing there, were quick and eager, and loud in their counsels. "Stay where you are, Mr. Morton — stay awhile, for the love of God, or he'll have you down!" "Now's your time, Caleb; in on him now, and you'll have him." "Close with him, Morton; close with him at once; it's your only chance!" "There's four of us here will fire on him if he as much as shows a limb!" all of which words, as they were heard by that poor wretch within, must have sounded to him as the barking of a pack of hounds thirsting for his blood. For him, at any rate, there was no longer any home in this world.

My readers, when chance has taken you into the hunting-field, has it ever been your lot to sit by on horseback and watch the digging out of a fox? The operation is not a common one, but in some countries it is held to be in accordance with the rules of fair sport. For myself, I think that when the brute has so far saved himself, he should be entitled to the benefit of his cunning. But

I will not now discuss the propriety or impropriety of that practice in venery. I can never, however, watch the doing of that work, without thinking much of the agonising struggles of the poor beast whose last refuge is being torn from over his head. There he lies, within a few yards of his arch-enemy the huntsman. The thick breath of the hounds makes hot the air within his hole. The sound of their voices is close upon his ears. His heart is nearly bursting with the violence of that effort which at last has brought him to his retreat. And then pickaxe and mattock is plied above his head, and nearer and more near to him press his foes and his double foes, human and canine, till at last a huge hand grasps him, and he is dragged forth among his enemies. Before his eyes have seen the light, the eager noses of a dozen hounds have moistened themselves in his entrails. Ah, me! I know that he is vermin—the vermin after whom I have been breaking my neck with the ambitious hope that I might ultimately witness his death struggles; but, nevertheless, I could fain have saved him that last half-hour of gradually diminished hope.

And Aaron Trow was now like a hunted fox, doomed to be dug out from his last refuge, with this addition to his misery, that those hounds, when they caught their prey, would not put him at once out of his misery. When first he saw that throng of men coming down from the hill-top and resting on the platform, he knew that his fate was come. When they called to him to surrender himself he was silent, but he knew that his silence was of no avail. To them who were so eager to be his captors the matter seemed to be still one of considerable difficulty, but to his thinking there was no difficulty. There were there some score of men, fully armed, within twenty yards of him. If he but showed a trace of his limbs he would become a mark for their bullets. And then if he were wounded, and no one would come to him! If they allowed him to lie there without food till he perished! Would it not be well for him to yield himself? Then they called again, and he was still silent. That idea of yielding is very terrible to the heart of a man, and, when the worst had come to the worst, did not the ocean run deep beneath his cavern mouth?

But as they yelled at him, and hallooed, making their preparation for his death, his presence of mind deserted the poor wretch. He had stolen an old pistol on one of his marauding expeditions, of which one barrel had been loaded. That in his mad despair he had fired; and now, as he lay near the mouth of the cavern, under the cover of the projecting stone, he had no weapon with him but his hands. He had had a knife, but that had dropped from him during the struggle on the floor of the cottage. He had now nothing but his hands, and was considering how he might best use them in ridding himself of the first of his pursuers. The man was near him, armed with all the power and majesty of right and might on his side; whereas, on his side, Aaron Trow had nothing—not a hope. He raised his head that he might look forth, and a dozen voices shouted as his face appeared above the aperture. A dozen weapons were levelled at him, and he could see the gleaming of the muzzles of the guns. And then the foot of his pursuer was already on the corner stone at the cavern's mouth.

"Now, Caleb, on him at once!" shouted a voice. Ah, me, it was a moment in which to pity even such a man as Aaron Trow!

"Now, Caleb, on him at once!" shouted the voice. "No, by heavens! not so, even yet." The sound of triumph in those words roused the last burst of energy in the breast of that wretched man, and he sprang forth, head foremost, from his prison-house. Forth he came, manifest enough before the eyes of them all, and with head well down, and hands outstretched, but with his wide glaring eyes still turned towards his pursuers as he fell, he plunged down into the waves beneath them. Two of those who stood by, almost unconscious of what they did, fired at his body as it made its rapid way to the water, but, as they afterwards found, neither of the bullets struck him. Morton, when his prey thus leaped forth, escaping him for a while, was already on the verge of the cavern, had even then prepared his foot for that onward spring, which should bring him to the throat of his foe. But he arrested himself, and for a moment stood there watching the body as it struck the water, and hid itself at once beneath the ripple. He stood there for a moment watching the deed and its effect, and then, leaving his hold upon the rock, he once again followed his quarry. Down he went, head foremost, right on to the track in the water which the other had made, and when the two rose to the surface together each was struggling in the grasp of the other.

It was a foolish, nay, a mad deed to do. The poor wretch who had first fallen could not have escaped. He could not even swim, and had, therefore, flung himself to certain destruction, when he took that leap from out of the cavern's mouth. It would have been sad to see him perish beneath the waves — to watch him as he rose gasping for breath, and then to see him sinking again, to rise again, and then to go for ever. But his life had been fairly forfeit; and why should one so much more precious have been flung after it? It was surely with no view of saving that forfeit life that Caleb Morton had leaped after his enemy. But the hound, hot with the chase, will follow the stag over the precipice, and dash himself to pieces against the rocks. The beast thirsting for blood will rush in even among the weapons of men. Morton in his fury had felt but one desire — burned with but one passion. If the fates would but grant him to fix his clutches in the throat of the man who had illused his love, for the rest it might all go as it would.

In the earlier part of the morning, while they were all searching for their victim, they had brought a boat up into this very inlet among the rocks, and the same boat had been at hand during the whole day. Unluckily, before they had come hither, it had been taken round the headland to a place among the rocks, at which a government skiff is always moored. The sea was still so quiet that there was hardly a ripple on it, and the boat had been again sent for when first it was supposed that they had at last traced Aaron Trow to his hiding-place. Anxiously now were all eyes turned to the headland, but as yet no boat was there.

The two men rose to the surface, each struggling in the arms of the other. Trow, though he was in an element to which he was not used — though he had sprung thither as another suicide might spring to certain death beneath a railway engine — did not altogether lose his presence of mind. Prompted by a double instinct, he had clutched hold of Morton's body when he encountered it beneath the waters. He held on to it as to his only protection, and he held on to him also as to his only enemy. If there was a chance for a life struggle they would share that chance together, and if not, then together would they meet that other fate.

Caleb Morton was a very strong man, and though one of his arms was altogether encumbered by his antagonist, his other arm

235

and his legs were free. With these he seemed to succeed in keeping his head above the water, weighted as he was with the body
of the other man. But Trow's efforts were also used with the view
of keeping himself above the water. Though he had purposed to
destroy himself in taking that leap, and now hoped for nothing
better than that they might both perish together, he yet struggled
to keep his head above the waves. Bodily power he had none left
to him, except that of holding on to Morton's arm and plunging
with his legs; but he did hold on, and thus both their heads remained above the water.

But this could not last long. It was easy to see that Trow's
strength was nearly spent, and that when he went down Morton
must go with him. If, indeed, they could be separated — if Morton could once make himself free from that embrace into which
he had been so anxious to leap — then, indeed, there might be
a hope. All round that little inlet the rock fell sheer down into
the deep sea, so that there was no resting-place for a foot; but
round the headlands on either side, even within forty or fifty
yards of that spot, Morton might rest on their rocks, till a boat
should come to his assistance. To him that distance would have
been nothing, if only his limbs had been at liberty.

Up on the platform of rock they were all at their wit's-end.
Many were anxious to fire at Trow, but even if they hit him,
would Morton's position have been better? Would not the
wounded man have still clung to the other? And then there could
be no certainty that any one of them would hit the right man.
The ripple of the waves, though it was very slight, nevertheless
sufficed to keep the bodies in motion; and then, too, there was
not among them any marksman peculiar for his skill.

Morton's efforts in the water were too severe to admit of his
speaking, but he could hear and understand the words which
were addressed to him. "Shake him off, Caleb!" "Strike him from
you with your foot!" "Swim to the right shore; swim for it even
if you take him with you!" Yes; he could hear them all; but hearing and obeying were very different. It was not easy to shake off
that dying man; and as for swimming with him, that was clearly
impossible; it was as much as he could do to keep his head above
water, let alone any attempt to move in one settled direction.

For some four or five minutes they lay thus battling in the

waves, before the head of either of them went down. Trow had been twice below the surface, but it was before he had succeeded in supporting himself by Morton's arm. Now it seemed as though he must sink again — as though both must sink. His mouth was barely kept above the water, and even as Morton shook him with his arm, the tide would pass over him. It was horrid to watch from the shore the glaring up-turned eyes of the dying wretch, as his long streaming hair lay back upon the wave. "Now, Caleb, hold him down! Hold him under!" shouted the voice of some eager friend. Rising up on the water, Morton made a last effort to do as he was bid. He did press the man's head down — well down below the surface, but still the hand clung to him, and as he struck out against the water he was powerless against that grasp.

Then there came a loud shout along the shore, and all those on the platform, whose eyes had been fixed so closely on that terrible struggle beneath them, rushed towards the rocks on the outer coast. The sound of oars was heard close to them — an eager, pressing stroke, as of men who knew well that they were rowing for the salvation of a life. On they came close under the rocks, obeying with every muscle of their bodies the behests of those who called to them from the shore. The boat came with such rapidity — was so recklessly urged — that it was driven somewhat beyond the inlet; but in passing a blow was struck which made Caleb Morton once more the master of his own life. The two men had been carried out in their struggle towards the open sea; and as the boat curved in, so as to be as close as the rocks would allow, the bodies of the men were brought within the sweep of the oars. He in the bow — for there were four pulling in the boat — had raised his oar as he neared the rocks — had raised it high above the water; and now, as they passed close by the struggling men, he let it fall with all its force on the upturned face of the wretched convict. It was a terrible, frightful thing to do, thus striking one who was so stricken; but who shall say that the blow was not good and just? Methinks, however, that the eyes and face of that dying man will haunt forever the dreams of him who carried that oar!

Trow never rose again to the surface. Three days afterwards his body was found at the ferry, and then they carried him to the convict island and buried him. Morton was picked up and taken into the boat. His life was saved; but it may be a question how the battle might have gone had not that friendly oar been raised in his behalf. As it was, he lay at the cottage for days before he was able to be moved or to receive the congratulations of those who had watched that terrible conflict from the shore. Nor did he feel that there had been anything in that day's work of which he could be proud — much, rather, of which it behoved him to be thoroughly ashamed. Some six months after that he obtained the hand of Anastasia Bergen, but they did not remain long in Bermuda. "He went away, back to his own country," my informant told me, "because he could not endure to meet the ghost of Aaron Trow at that point of the road which passes near the cottage." That the ghost of Aaron Trow may be seen there, and round the little rocky inlet of the sea, is part of the creed of every young woman in Bermuda.

"Aaron Trow" appeared first in the December 14 and 21 issues of *Public Opinion: Literary Supplement* for 1861.

Returning Home

IT IS GENERALLY SUPPOSED THAT people who live at home — good domestic people who love tea and their arm-chairs, and who keep the parlour hearthrug ever warm — it is generally supposed that these are the people who value home the most, and best appreciate all the comforts of that cherished in-stitution. I am inclined to doubt this. It is, I think, to those who live farthest away from home, to those who find the greatest dif-ficulty in visiting home, that the word conveys the sweetest idea. In some distant parts of the world it may be that an Englishman acknowledges his permanent restingplace, but there are many others in which he will not call his daily house his home. He would, in his own idea, desecrate the word by doing so. His home is across the blue waters, in the little northern island, which, per-haps, he may visit no more; which he has left at any rate for half his life; from which circumstances, and the necessity of living, have banished him. His home is still in England; and when he speaks of home his thoughts are there.

No one can understand the intensity of this feeling, who has not seen or felt the absence of interest in life, which falls to the lot of many who have to eat their bread on distant soils. We are all apt to think that a life in strange countries will be a life of excitement, of stirring enterprise and varied scenes; that, in abandoning the comforts of home, we shall receive in exchange more of movement and of adventure than would come in our way in our own tame country; and this feeling has, I am sure, sent many a young man roaming. Take any spirited fellow of twenty, and ask him whether he would like to go to Mexico for the next ten years. Prudence and his father may ultimately save him from such banishment, but he will not refuse without a pang of regret.

Alas! it is a mistake. Bread may be earned, and fortunes, perhaps, made in such countries; and as it is the destiny of our race to spread itself over the wide face of the globe, it is well that there should be something to gild and paint the outward face of that lot which so many are called upon to choose. But for a life of daily excitement, there is no life like life in England; and the farther that one goes from England, the more stagnant, I think, do the waters of existence become.

But if it be so for men, it is ten times more so for women. An Englishman, if he be at Guatemala or at Belise, must work for his bread, and that work will find him in thought and excitement. But what of his wife? where will she find excitement? by what pursuit will she repay herself for all that she has left behind her at her mother's fireside? She will love her husband, yes, that at least. If there be not that, there will be a hell indeed. Then she will nurse her children, and talk of her home. When the time shall come that her promised return thither is within a year or two of its accomplishment, her thoughts will all be fixed on that coming pleasure, as are the thoughts of a young girl on her first ball for the fortnight before that event comes off.

On the central plain of that portion of Central America which is called Costa Rica, stands the city of San José. It is the capital of the Republic — for Costa Rica is a Republic, and, for Central America, is a town of some importance. It is in the middle of the coffee district, surrounded by rich soil, on which the sugar-cane is produced; is blessed with a climate only moderately hot, and the native inhabitants are neither cut-throats nor cannibals. It may be said, therefore, that by comparison with some other spots to which Englishmen and others are congregated for the gathering together of money, San José may be considered as a happy region; but, nevertheless, a life there is not in every way desirable. It is a dull place, with little to interest either the eye or the ear. Although the heat of the tropics is but little felt there, on account of its altitude, men and women become too listless for much enterprise. There is no society. There are a few Germans and a few Englishmen in the place, who see each other on matters of business during the day, but, sombre as life generally is, they seem to care little for each other's company on any other footing. I know not to what point the aspirations of the Germans may stretch themselves, but to the English the one idea that gives salt to life is the idea of home. On some day, however distant it may be, they will once more turn their faces towards the little northern island, and then all will be well with them.

To a certain Englishman then, and to his dear little wife, this prospect came some few years since somewhat suddenly. Events and tidings, it matters not which or what, brought it about that they resolved between themselves that they would start immediately—almost immediately. They would pack up and leave San José within four months of the day on which their purpose was first formed. At San José, a period of only four months for such a purpose was immediately. It created a feeling of instant excitement, a necessity for instant doing, a consciousness that there was in those few weeks ample work both for the hands and thoughts, work almost more than ample. The dear little wife who, for the last two years, had been so listless, felt herself flurried.

"Harry," she said to her husband, "how shall we ever be ready?" and her pretty face was lighted up with unusual brightness, at the happy thought of so much haste with such an object. "And baby's things, too?" she said, as she thought of all the various little articles of dress that would be needed.

A journey from San José to Southampton cannot in truth be made as easily as one from London to Liverpool. Let us think of a month to be passed without any aïd from the washerwoman, and the greatest part of that month amidst the sweltering heats of the West Indian tropics!

For the first month of her hurry and flurry Mrs. Arkwright was a happy woman. She would see her mother again, and her sisters. It was now four years since she had left them on the quays at Southampton, while all their hearts were broken at the parting. She was a young bride then going forth with her new lord, to meet the stern world. He had then been home to look for a wife, and he had found what he looked for in the youngest sister of his

241

partner. For he, Henry Arkwright, and his wife's brother, Abel Ring, had established themselves together in San José. And now she thought how there should be another meeting on those quays, at which there should be no broken hearts — at which there should be love without sorrow, and kisses sweet with the sweetness of welcome, not bitter with the bitterness of parting. And people told her — the few neighbours around her — how happy, how fortunate she was to get home thus early in her life. They had been out some ten, some twenty years, and still the day of their return was distant. And then she pressed her living baby to her breast, and wiped away a tear as she thought of the other darling, whom she would leave beneath that distant sod.

And then came the question as to the route home. San José stands in the middle of the high plain of Costa Rica, half-way between the Pacific and the Atlantic. The journey thence down to the Pacific is by comparison easy. There is a road, and the mules on which the travellers must ride go steadily and easily down to Puntas Arenas, the port in that ocean. There are inns, too, on the way — places of public entertainment, at which refreshment may be obtained, and beds, or fair substitutes for beds. But then, by this route, the traveller must take a long additional sea voyage. He must convey himself and his baggage down to that wretched place on the Pacific, there wait for a steamer to take him to Panama, cross the isthmus, and reship himself in the other waters for his long journey home. That terrible unshipping and reshipping is a sore burden to the unaccustomed traveller. When it is absolutely necessary, then, indeed, it is done without much thought; but in the case of the Arkwrights it was not absolutely necessary. And there was another reason which turned Mrs. Arkwright's heart against that journey by Puntas Arenas. The place is unhealthy, having at certain seasons a very bad name; and here, on their outward journey, her husband had been taken ill. She had never ceased to think of the fortnight she had spent there among uncouth strangers, during a portion of which his life had trembled in the balance. Early, therefore, in those four months she begged that she might not be taken round by Puntas Arenas. There was another route.

"Harry, if you love me, let us go by the Serapiqui."

As to Harry's loving her, there was no doubt about that, as she well knew.

There was this other route by the Serapiqui river, and by Grey-town. Greytown, it is true, is quite as unhealthy as Puntas Are-nas, and by that route one's baggage must be shipped and un-shipped into small boats. There are all manner of difficulties attached to it; perhaps no direct road to or from any city on the world's surface is subject to sharper fatigue while it lasts. Jour-neying by this route also, the traveller leaves San José mounted on his mule, and so mounted he makes his way through the vast primeval forests down to the banks of the Serapiqui river. That there is a track for him is of course true, but it is simply a track, and during nine months out of the twelve is so deep in mud that the mules sink in it to their bellies. Then, when the river has been reached, the traveller seats him in his canoe, and for two days is paddled down — down along the Serapiqui, into the San Juan river, and down along the San Juan till he reaches Grey-town, passing one night at some hut on the river side. At Grey-town he waits for the steamer, which will carry him his first stage on his road towards Southampton. He must be a connoisseur in disagreeables of every kind who can say with any precision whether Greytown or Puntas Arenas is the better place for a week's sojourn.

For a full month Mr. Arkwright would not give way to his wife. At first he all but conquered her by declaring that the Serapiqui journey would be dangerous for the baby; but she heard from someone that it could be made less fatiguing for the baby than the other route. A baby had been carried down in a litter, strapped on to a mule's back. A guide at the mule's head would be necessary, and that was all. When once in her boat the baby would be as well as in her cradle. What purpose cannot a woman gain by perseverance? Her purpose in this instance Mrs. Ark-wright did at last gain by persevering.

And then their preparations for the journey went on with much flurrying and hot haste. To us at home, who live and feel our life every day, the manufacture of endless baby-linen, and the packing of mountains of clothes, does not give an idea of much pleasurable excitement; but at San José, when there was scarcely motion enough in existence to prevent its water from becoming foul with stagnation, this packing of baby-linen was delightful,

243

and for a month or so the days went by with happy wings.

But by degrees reports began to reach both Arkwright and his wife as to this new route, which made them uneasy. The wet season had been prolonged, and even though they might not be deluged by rain themselves, the path would be in such a state of mud as to render the labour incessant. One or two people declared that the road was unfit, at any time, for a woman; and then the river would be much swollen. These tidings did not reach Arkwright and his wife together, or at any rate not till late amidst their preparations, or a change might still have been made. As it was, after all her entreaties, Mrs. Arkwright did not like to ask him now again to alter his plans, and he, having altered them once, was averse to change them again. So things went on till the mules and the boats had been hired, and things had gone so far that no change could then be made without much cost and trouble.

During the last ten days of their sojourn in San José, Mrs. Arkwright had lost all that appearance of joy which had cheered up her sweet face during the last few months. Terror at that terrible journey obliterated in her mind all the happiness which had arisen from the hope of being soon at home. She was thoroughly cowed by the dangers to be encountered, and would gladly have gone down to Puntas Arenas, had it been now possible that she could so arrange it. It rained and rained, and still rained when there was now only a week's further time before they started. Oh! if they could only wait for another month! But this she said to no one. After what had passed between her and her husband, she had not the heart to say such words to him. Arkwright himself was a man not given to much talking—a silent, thoughtful man, stern withal in his outward bearing, but tender-hearted and loving in his nature. The sweet young wife, who had left all and come with him out to that dull, distant place, was very dear to him, dearer than she herself was aware; and in these days he was thinking much of her coming troubles. Why had he given way to her foolish prayers? Ah, why indeed?

And thus the last few days of their sojourn in San José passed away from them. Once or twice during these days she did speak out, expressing her fears. Her feelings were too much for her, and she could not restrain herself. "Poor mama," she said, "I shall never see her!" And then again — "Harry, I know I shall never reach home alive!"

"Fanny, my darling, that is nonsense." But in order that his spoken word might not sound stern to her, he took her in his arms and kissed her.

"You must behave well, Fanny," he said to her the day before they started. Though her heart was then very low within her, she promised him that she would do her best, and then she made a great resolution. Though she should be dying on the road, she would not complain beyond the absolute necessity of her nature. She fully recognised his thoughtful, tender kindness; for though he thus cautioned her, he never told her that the dangers which she feared were the result of her own choice. He never threw in her teeth those prayers which she had made, in yielding to which he knew that he had been weak.

Then came the morning of their departure. The party of travellers consisted of four, besides the baby. There was Mr. Arkwright, his wife, and an English nurse who was going home to England with them, and her brother, Abel Ring, who was to accompany them as far as the Serapiqui river. When they had reached that, the real labour of the journey would be over. They had eight mules — four for the four travellers, one for the baby, a spare mule, laden simply with blankets, so that Mrs. Arkwright might change, in order that she should not be fatigued by the fatigue of her beast, and two for their luggage. The heavier portion of the baggage had already been sent off by Puntas Arenas, and would meet them at the other side of the isthmus of Panama.

For the last four days the rain had ceased — had ceased, at any rate, at San José. Those who knew the country well would know that it might still be raining over those vast forests; but now, as the matter was settled, they would all hope for the best. On that morning on which they started, the sun shone fairly, and they accepted this as an omen of good. Baby seemed to lie comfortably on her pile of blankets on the mule's back, and the face of the tall Indian guide who took his place at that mule's head pleased the anxious mother. "Not leave him ever," he said, in Spanish, laying his hand on the cord which was fastened to the beast's head; and not for one moment did he leave his charge, though the labour of sticking close to him was very great.

245

They had four attendants, or guides, all of whom made the journey on foot. That they were all men of mixed race was probable; but three of them would have been called Spaniards — Spaniards, that is, of Costa Rica—and the other would be called an Indian. One of the Spaniards was the leader, or chief man of the party; but the others seemed to stand on an equal footing with each other, and, indeed, the place of greatest care had been given to the Indian.

In the first four or five miles their route lay along the high road which leads from San José to Puntas Arenas, and so far a group of acquaintances followed them, all mounted on mules. Here, where the ways forked, their road leading away through the great forests to the Atlantic, they all separated, and many tears were shed on each side. What might be the future life of the Arkwrights had not been absolutely fixed, but there was a strong hope on their part that they might never be forced to return to Costa Rica. Those from whom they now parted had not seemed to be dear to them in any especial degree, while they all lived together in the same small town, seeing each other day by day; but now — now that they might never meet again, a certain love sprang up for the old familiar faces, and women kissed each other who hitherto had hardly cared to enter each other's houses.

And then the party of the Arkwrights again started, and its steady work began. For the whole of the first day the way beneath their feet was tolerably good, and the weather continued fine. It was one long gradual ascent from the place where the roads parted, but there was no real labour in travelling. Mrs. Arkwright rode beside her baby's mule, at the head of which the Indian always walked, and the two men went together in front. The husband had found that his wife would prefer this, as long as the road allowed of such an arrangement. Her heart was too full to admit of much speaking, and so they went on in silence.

The first night was passed in a hut by the road-side, which seemed to have been deserted—a hut or "rancho," as it is called in that country. Their food they had of course brought with them; and here, by common consent, they endeavoured in some sort to make themselves merry.

"Fanny," Arkwright said to her, "it is not so bad, after all; eh, my darling?"

"No," she answered; "only that the mule tires one so. Will all the days be as long as that?"

He had not the heart to tell her that, as regarded hours of work, that first day must of necessity be the shortest. They had risen to a considerable altitude, and the night was very cold; but baby was enveloped among a pile of coloured blankets, and things did not go very badly with them; only this — that when Fanny Arkwright rose from her hard bed, her limbs were more weary and much more stiff than they had been when Arkwright had lifted her from her mule.

On the second morning they mounted before the day had quite broken, in order that they might breakfast on the summit of the ridge which separates the two oceans. At this spot the good road comes to an end, and the forest track begins; and here also they would in truth enter the forest, though their path had for some time been among straggling trees and bushes. And now again they rode two and two up to this place of halting, Arkwright and Ring well knowing that from hence their labours would in truth commence.

Poor Mrs. Arkwright, when she reached this resting-place, would fain have remained there for the rest of the day. One word in her low plaintive voice she said, asking whether they might not sleep in the large shed which stands there. But this was manifestly impossible; at such a pace they would never reach Greytown; and she spoke no further word when he told her that they must go on.

At about noon that day the file of travellers formed itself into the line which it afterwards kept during the whole of the journey, and then started by the narrow path into the forest. First walked the leader of the guides; then another man following him; Abel Ring came next, and behind him the maid-servant; then the baby's mule, with the Indian ever at its head; close at his heels followed Mrs. Arkwright, so that the mother's eye might be always on her child; and after her her husband. Then another guide on foot completed the number of the travellers. In this way they went on and on, day after day, till they reached the banks of the Serapiqui, never once varying their places in the procession. As they started in the morning so they went on till their noon-day's rest; and so again they made their evening march. In that journey there was no idea of variety, no searching after the pleasures of scenery, no attempts at conversation with any object of interest or amusement. What words were spoken were those simply needful, or produced by sympathy for suffering. So they journeyed, always in the same places, with one exception—they began their work with two guides leading them; but before the first day was over, one of them had fallen back to the side of Mrs. Arkwright, for she was unable to sit on her mule without support.

Their daily work was divided into two stages, so as to give some time for rest in the middle of the day. It had been arranged that the distance for each day should not be long — should be very short, as was thought by them all when they talked it over up at San José; but now the hours which they passed in the saddle seemed to be endless. Their descent began from that ridge of which I have spoken; and they had no sooner turned their faces down upon the mountain slopes looking towards the Atlantic, than that passage of mud began to which there was no cessation till they found themselves on the banks of the Serapiqui river. I doubt whether it be possible to convey in words an adequate idea of the labour of riding over such a path. It is not that any active exertion is necessary — that there is anything which requires doing. The traveller has before him the simple task of sitting on his mule from hour to hour, and of seeing that his knees do not get themselves jammed against the trees. But at every step the beast he rides has to drag his legs out from the deep clinging mud, and the body of the rider never knows one moment of ease. Why the mules do not die on the road, I cannot say; they live through it, and do not appear to suffer. They have their own way in everything, for no exertion on the rider's part will make them walk either faster or slower than is their wont.

On the day on which they entered the forest, that being the second of their journey, Mrs. Arkwright had asked for mercy — for permission to escape that second stage. On the next she allowed herself to be lifted into her saddle, after her midday rest, without a word. She had tried to sleep, but in vain, and had sat within a little hut, looking out upon the desolate scene before her, with her baby in her lap. She had this one comfort, that of all the travellers she and the baby suffered the least. They had now left the high grounds, and the heat was becoming great, though not as yet intense. And then the Indian guide, looking out slowly over the forest, saw that the rain was not yet over. He spoke a word or two to one of his companions in a low voice, and in a *patois* which Mrs. Arkwright did not understand; and then, going after her husband, told him that the heavens were threatening.

"We have only two leagues," said Arkwright, "and it may perhaps hold up."

"It will begin in an hour," said the Indian, "and the two leagues are four hours."

"And to-morrow?" asked Arkwright.

"To-morrow, and to-morrow, and to-morrow it will still rain," said the guide, looking , as he spoke, up over the huge primeval forest.

"Then we had better start at once," said Arkwright, "before the first falling drops frighten the woman."

So the mules were brought out, and he lifted his uncomplaining wife on to the blankets which formed her pillow. The file again formed itself, and slowly they wound their way out upon the small enclosure by which the hut was surrounded — out from the enclosure on to a rough scrap of undrained pasture ground, from which the trees had been cleared. In a few minutes they were once more struggling through the mud.

The name of the spot which our travellers had just left is Careblanco. There they had found a woman living, all alone. Her husband was away, she told them, at San José, but would be back to her when the dry weather came, to look up the young cattle which were straying in the forest. What a life for a woman! Nevertheless, in talking with Mrs. Arkwright she made no complaint of her own lot, but had done what little she could to comfort the poor lady who was so little able to bear the fatigues of her journey.

"Is the road very bad?" Mrs. Arkwright asked her in a whisper.

"Ah, yes, it is a bad road."

"And when shall we be at the river?"

"It took me four days," said the woman.

"Then I shall never see my mother again;" and as she spoke Mrs. Arkwright pressed her baby to her bosom. Immediately after that her husband came in, and then they started.

Their path now led away across the slope of a mountain, which seemed to fall from the very top of that central ridge in an unbroken descent, down to the valley at its foot. Hitherto, since they had entered the forest, they had had nothing before their eyes but the trees and bushes which grew close around them. But now a prospect of unrivalled grandeur was opened before them, if only they had been able to enjoy it. At the bottom of the valley ran a river which, so great was the depth, looked like a moving silver cord; and on the other side of this there arose another mountain, steep, but unbroken, like that which they were passing — unbroken, so that the eye could stretch from the river up to the very summit. Not a spot on that mountain side, or on their side either, was left uncovered by thick forest, which had stood there, untouched by man, since nature first produced it.

But all this was nothing to our travellers; nor was the clang of the macaws anything, or the roaring of the little congo ape. Nothing was gained by them from beautiful scenery, nor was there any fear from beasts of prey. The immediate pain of each step of the journey drove all other feelings from them, and their thoughts were bounded by an intense longing for the evening halt.

And then, as the guide had prophesied, the rain began. At first it came in such small soft drops that it was found to be refreshing, but the clouds soon gathered, and poured forth their collected waters as though it had not rained for months among those mountains. Not that they came in big drops, or with the violence which wind can give them, beating hither and thither, breaking branches from the trees, and rising up again as they pattered against the ground. There was no violence in the rain. It fell softly in a long continuous noiseless stream, sinking into everything that it touched, converting the deep rich earth on all sides into mud.

Not a word was said by any of them as it came on. The Indian covered the baby with her blanket, closer than she was covered before, and the guide who walked by Mrs. Arkwright's side drew her cloak around her knees. But such efforts were in vain. There is a rain that will penetrate everything, and such was the rain which fell upon them now. Nevertheless, as I have said, hardly a word was spoken. The poor woman, finding that the heat of her cloak increased her sufferings, threw it open again.

"Fanny," said her husband, "you had better let him protect you as well as he can."

She answered him merely by an impatient wave of the hand, intending to signify that she could not speak, but that in this matter she must have her way.

After that her husband made no further attempt to control her. He could see, however, that ever and again she would have slipped forward from her mule and fallen, had not the man by her side steadied her with his hand. At every tree he protected her knees and feet, though there was hardly room for him to move between the beast and the bank against which he was thrust.

And then, at last, that day's work was also over, and Fanny Arkwright slipped from her pillow down into her husband's arms, at the door of another rancho in the forest. Here there lived a large family, adding from year to year to the patch of ground which they had rescued from the wood, and valiantly doing their part in the extension of civilisation.

Our party was but a few steps from the door when they left their mules, but Mrs. Arkwright did not now as heretofore hasten to receive her baby in her arms. When placed upon the ground she still leaned against the mule, and her husband saw that he must carry her into the hut. This he did, and then, wet, mud-laden, dishevelled as she was, she laid herself down upon the planks that were to form her bed, and then stretched out her arms for her infant. On that evening they undressed and tended her like a child, and then, when she was alone with her husband, she repeated to him her sad foreboding.

"Harry," she said, "I shall never see my mother again."

"Oh, yes, Fanny. You will see her and talk over all these troubles with pleasure. It is very bad, I know; but we shall win through it yet."

"You will, of course; and you will take baby home to her."

"And face her without you! No, my darling. Three more days' riding, or rather two-and-a-half, will bring us to the river, and then your trouble will be over. All will be easy after that."

"Ah! Harry, you do not know."

"I do know that it is very bad, my girl, but you must cheer up. We shall be laughing at all this in a month's time."

On the following morning she allowed herself again to be lifted up, speaking no word of remonstrance. Indeed, she was like a child in their hands, having dropped all the dignity and authority of a woman's demeanour. It rained again during the whole of this day, and the heat was becoming oppressive, as every hour they were descending nearer and nearer to the sea-level. During this first stage hardly a word was spoken by anyone, but when she was again taken from her mule she was in tears. The poor servant-girl, too, was almost prostrate with fatigue, and absolutely unable to wait upon her mistress, or even to do anything for herself. Nevertheless they did make the second stage, seeing that their midday resting-place had been under the trees of the forest. Had there been any but these, they would have remained for the night.

On the following day they rested altogether, though the place at which they remained had but few attractions. It was another forest hut, inhabited by an old Spanish couple, who were by no means willing to give them room, although they paid for their accommodation at exorbitant rates. It is one singularity of places, strange and out of the way like such forest tracks as these, that money in small sums is hardly valued. Dollars there were not appreciated as sixpences are in this rich country. But there they stayed for a day, and the guides employed themselves in making a litter with long poles, so that they might carry Mrs. Arkwright over a portion of the ground. Poor fellows! When once she had thus changed her mode of conveyance, she never again was lifted on to the mule.

There was strong reason against this day's delay. They were to go down the Serapiqui, along with the post, which would overtake them on its banks; but if the post should pass them before they got there, it could not wait, and then they would be deprived of the best canoe on the water. Then also it was possible, if they encountered further delay, that the steamer might sail from Greytown without them, and a month's residence at that frightening place be thus made necessary. That would indeed be a finish to their misfortunes!

The day's rest apparently did little to relieve Mrs. Arkwright's sufferings. On the following day she allowed herself to be put upon the mule, but after the first hour the beasts were stopped, and she was taken off it. During that hour they had travelled hardly over half a league. At that time she so sobbed and moaned that Arkwright absolutely feared that she would perish in the forest, and he implored the guides to use the poles which they had prepared. She had declared to him over and over again that she felt sure that she should die, and, half delirious with weariness and suffering had begged him to leave her at the last hut. They had not yet come to the flat ground, over which a litter might be carried with comparative ease; but nevertheless, the men yielded, and she was placed in a recumbent position upon blankets supported by boughs of trees. In this way she went through that day, with somewhat less of suffering than before, and without that necessity for self-exertion, which had been worse to her than any suffering.

There were places between that and the river at which one could have said it was impossible that a litter should be carried, or even impossible that a mule should work with a load on his back. But still they went on, and the men carried their burdens without complaining. Not a word was said about extra pay — not a word, at least by them; and when Arkwright was profuse in his offer, their leader told him that they would not have done it for money. But for the poor suffering Senora they would make exertions which no money would have bought from them.

On the next day, about noon, the post did pass them, consisting of three strong men, carrying great weights on their backs, suspended by bands from their foreheads. They travelled much quicker than our friends, and would reach the banks of the river that evening. In their ordinary course they would start down the river close after daybreak the following day; but after some consultation with the guides they agreed to wait till noon. Poor Mrs. Arkwright knew nothing of hours, or of any such arrangements now, but her husband greatly doubted their power of catching this mail dispatch. However, it did not much depend on their exertions that afternoon. Their resting-place was marked out for them, and they would not go beyond it, unless, indeed, they could make the whole journey, which was impossible.

But towards evening matters seemed to improve with them. They had now got on to ground which was more open, and the men who carried the litter could walk with greater ease. Mrs.

Arkwright also complained less, and when they reached their resting-place on that night, said nothing of a wish to be left there to her fate. This was a place called Padregal, a cacao plantation, which had been cleared in the forest with much labour. There was a house here, containing three rooms, and some forty or fifty acres around it had been stripped of the forest trees. But, nevertheless, the adventure had not been a prosperous one, for the place was at that time deserted. There were the cacao plants, but there was no one to pick the cocoa. There was a certain melancholy beauty about the place. A few grand trees had been left standing near the house, and the grass around was rich and park-like. But it was deserted, and nothing was to be heard but the roaring of the congos. Ah me! Indeed, it was a melancholy place as it was seen by some of them afterwards.

On the following morning they were astir very early, and Mrs. Arkwright was so much better that she offered to ride again upon her mule. The men, however, declared that they would finish their task, and she was placed again upon the litter, and thus, with slow and weary steps, they did make their way to the river bank. It was not yet noon when they saw the mud fort which stands there, and as they drew into the enclosure, round a small house which stands close by the river side, they saw the three postmen still busy about their packages.

"Thank God!" said Arkwright.

"Thank God, indeed," said his brother. "All will be right with you now."

"Well, Fanny," said her husband, as he took her gently from the litter and seated her on a bench which stood outside the door, "it is all over now, is it not?"

She answered by a shower of tears, but they were tears which brought her relief. He was aware of this, and therefore stood by her, still holding her by both her hands, while her head rested against his side.

"You will find the motion of the boat very gentle," he said; "indeed, there will be no motion, and you and baby will sleep all the way down to Greytown."

She did not answer him in words, but she looked up into his face, and he could see that her spirit was recovering itself.

There was almost a crowd of people collected on the spot,

preparatory to the departure of the canoes. In the first place there
was the commandant of the fort, to whom the small house belonged. He was looking to the passports of our friends, and with
due diligence endeavouring to make something of the occasion
by discovering fatal legal impediments to the further prosecution
of their voyage, which impediments would disappear on the payment of certain dollars. And then there were half-a-dozen Costa
Rica soldiers, men with coloured caps and old muskets, ready to
support the dignity and authority of the commandant. There
were the guides taking payment from Abel Ring for their past
work, and the postmen preparing their boats for the further journey. And then there was a certain German there, with a German
servant, to whom the boats belonged; he also was very busy preparing for the river voyage. He was not going down with them,
but it was his business to see them well started. A singular-
looking man was he, with a huge shaggy beard and shaggy un-
combed hair, but with bright blue eyes, which gave to his face a
remarkable look of sweetness. He was an uncouth man to the
eye, and yet a child would have trusted herself with him in a forest.

At this place they remained some two hours. Coffee was prepared here, and Mrs. Arkwright refreshed herself and her child.
They washed and arranged their clothes, and when she stepped
down the steep bank, clinging to her husband's arm as she made
her way towards the boat, she smiled upon him as he looked at
her.

It is all over now — is it not, my girl?" he said, encouraging
her.

"Oh, Harry, do not talk about it!" she answered, shuddering.

"But I want you to say a word to me to let me know that you
are better."

"I am better — much better."

"And you will see your mother again, will you not; and give
baby to her yourself?"

To this she made no immediate answer, for she was on a level
with the river, and the canoe was close at her feet. And then she
had to bid farewell to her brother. He now was the unfortunate
one of the party, for his destiny required that he should go back
to San José alone, — go back and remain there, perhaps, some

255

ten years longer before he might look for the happiness of home.

"God bless you, dearest Abel!" she said, kissing him and sob-bing as she spoke.

"Good-bye, Fanny!" he said, "and do not let them forget me in England. It is a great comfort to think that the worst of your troubles are over."

"Oh, she's all right now," said Arkwright. "Good-bye, old boy," and the two brothers-in-law grasped each other's hands heartily; "keep up your spirits, and we'll have you home before long."

"Oh, I am all right," said the other. But from the tone of their voices it was clear that poor Ring was despondent at the thoughts of his coming solitude, and that Arkwright was already triumph-ing at his emancipation.

And then, with much care, Fanny Arkwright was stowed away in her boat. There was a great contest about the baby, but at last it was arranged, that at any rate, for the first few hours she should be placed in the same boat with the servant. The mother was told that by this plan she would feel herself at liberty to sleep during the heat of the day, and then she might hope to have strength to look to the child when they should be on shore during the night. In this way, therefore, they prepared to start, while Abel Ring stood on the bank looking at them with wishful eyes. In the first boat were two Indians paddling, and a third man steering with another paddle. In the middle there was much luggage, and near the luggage, so as to be under shade, was the baby's soft bed. If nothing evil happened to the boat, the child could not be more safe in the best cradle that was ever rocked. With her was the maid servant and some stranger who was also going down to Greytown.

In the second boat there was the same number of men to pad-dle, the Indian guide being one of them, and there were the mails placed. Then there was a seat arranged with blankets, cloaks, and cushions, for Mrs. Arkwright, so that she might lean back and sleep without fatigue, and immediately opposite to her her hus-band placed himself.

"You all look very comfortable," said poor Abel from the bank.

"We shall do very well now," said Arkwright.

"And I do think I shall see mama again," said his wife.

"That's right, old girl; of course you will see her. Now then, we are all ready!" and with some little assitance from the German on the bank, the first boat was pushed off into the stream.

The river in this place is rapid, because the full course of the water is somewhat impeded by a bank of earth jutting out from the opposite side of the river into the stream; but it is not so rapid as to make any recognized danger in the embarcation. Below this bank, which is opposite to the spot at which the boats were entered, there were four or five broken trees in the water, some of the shattered boughs of which showed themselves above the surface. These are called snags, and are very dangerous if met with in the course of the stream; but in this instance no danger was apprehended from them, as they lay considerably to the left of the passage which the boats would take. The first canoe was pushed off by the German, and went rapidly away. The waters were strong with the rain, and it was pretty to see with what velocity the boat was carried on some hundred of yards in advance of the other, by the force of the first efforts of the paddles. The German, however, from the bank, hallooed to the first men in Spanish, bidding them relax their efforts for a while; and then he said a word or two of caution to those who were now on the point of starting.

The boat then was pushed steadily forward, the man at the stern keeping it with his paddle a little further away from the bank at which they had embarked. It was close under the land that the stream ran the fastest, and in obedience to the directions given to him, he made his course somewhat nearer the sunken trees. It was but one turn of his hand that gave the light boat its direction, but that turn of the hand was too strong. Had the anxious master of the canoes been but a thought less anxious all might have been well; but, as it was, the prow of the boat was caught by some slight hidden branch which impeded its course, and turned it round in the rapid river. The whole length of the canoe was thus brought against the sunken tree, and in half a minute the five occupants of the boat were struggling in the stream.

Abel Ring and the German were both standing on the bank close to the water when this happened, and each for a moment looked into the other's face.

"Stand where you are," shouted the German, "so that you may assist them from the shore. I will go in." And then, throwing from him his boots and coat, he plunged into the river.

The canoe had been swept round so as to be brought by the force of the waters absolutely in among the upturned roots and broken stumps of the trees which impeded the river, and thus when the party was upset they were, at first, to be seen scrambling among the branches. But, unfortunately, there was much more wood below the water than above it, and the force of the stream was so great that those who caught hold of the timber were not able to support themselves above the surface. Arkwright was soon to be seen some fifty yards down, having been carried clear of the trees, and here he got out of the river on the further bank. The distance to him was not above forty yards, but, from the nature of the ground, he could not get up towards his wife unless he could have forced his way against the stream.

The Indian who had had charge of the baby rose quickly to the surface, was carried once round in the eddy with his head high above the water, and then was seen to throw himself among the broken wood. He had seen the dress of the poor woman, and made his efforts to save her. The other two men were so caught by the fragments of the boughs, that they could not extricate themselves, so as to make any exertions; ultimately, however, they also got out on the further bank.

Mrs. Arkwright had sunk at once on being precipitated into the water, but the buoyancy of her clothes had brought her for a moment again to the surface. She had risen for a moment, and then had again gone down, immediately below the forked trunk of a huge tree — had gone down, alas, alas! never to rise again with life within her bosom. The poor Indian made two attempts to save her, and then came up himself, incapable of further effort.

It was then that the German, the owner of the canoes, who had fought his way with great efforts across the violence of the waters, and, indeed, up against the stream, for some few yards, made his effort to save the life of that poor frail creature. He had watched the spot at which she had gone down, and, even while struggling across the river, had seen how the Indian had followed her and had failed. It was now his turn. His life was in his hand,

and he was prepared to throw it away in that attempt. Having succeeded in placing himself a little above the large tree, he turned his face towards the bottom of the river, and dived down among the branches. And he also, after that, was never again seen with the life blood flowing round his heart.

When the sun set that night the two swollen corpses were lying in the commandant's hut, and Abel Ring and Arkwright were sitting beside them. Arkwright had his baby sleeping in his arms, but he sat there for hours — into the middle of the long night — without speaking a word to anyone.

"Harry," said his brother at last, "come away and lie down; it will be good for you to sleep."

"Nothing ever will be good for me again," said he.

"You must bear up against your sorrow as other men do," said Ring.

"Why am I not sleeping with her as the poor German sleeps? Why did I let another man take my place in dying for her?" And then he walked away that the other might not see the tears on his face.

It was a sad night — that at the commandant's hut, and a sad morning followed upon it. It must be remembered that they had there none of those appurtenances which are so necessary to make woe decent and misfortune comfortable. They sat through the night in the small hut, and in the morning they came forth with their clothes still wet and dirty, with their haggard faces and weary, stiff limbs, encumbered with the horrid task of burying that loved body among the forest trees. And then, to keep life in them till it was done, the brandy flask passed from hand to hand; and after that, with slow but resolute efforts, they re-formed the litter on which the living woman had been carried thither, and took her body back to the wild plantation at Padregal. There they dug for her her grave, and repeating over her some portions of the service for the dead, left her to sleep the sleep of death. But before they left her they erected a palisade of timber round the grave, so that the beasts of the forest should not tear the body from its resting-place.

When that was done Arkwright and his brother made their slow journey back to San José. The widowed husband could not face his darling's mother with such a tale upon his tongue as that!

"Returning Home" appeared first in the November 30 and December 7 issues of *Public Opinion: Literary Supplement* for 1861.

THIS BOOK WAS DESIGNED BY
JUDITH OELFKE SMITH
SET IN ELEVEN POINT GOUDY OLDSTYLE
BY FORT WORTH LINOTYPING COMPANY
PRINTED ON WARREN'S OLDSTYLE WOVE
BY MOTHERAL PRINTING COMPANY
AND BOUND BY JOHN D. ELLIS BINDERY